THE GIRL AND THE Gargoyle

PAULINE GRUBER

DRAGONFLY INK, LTD.

The Girl and the Gargoyle
Copyright © 2015 by Pauline Gruber

Excerpt from The Girl and the Demon © 2020 by Pauline Gruber

Dragonfly Ink, Ltd.
P.O. Box 2042
Palatine, IL 60078

The characters and events portrayed in this book are fictitious. Any similarity to real persons, living or dead, is coincidental and not intended by the author.

ISBN-13: 978-0-9910774-6-5

Cover Art by Fay Lane Graphic Design and Illustration
Formatting by Author E.M.S.
Author Photo by Sopho Studio

Published in the United States of America

In loving memory of my sister,

Susan Gruber,

my very own protector.

OTHER BOOKS BY PAULINE GRUBER

The Girl and the Raven
The Girl and the Demon

CHAPTER ONE

– Lucy Walker –

The clatter of my cell phone bouncing against the nightstand startles me awake. My heavy lids refuse to open. Another late night on the roof with Marcus and that was after spending two grueling hours creating a killer CD mix for him. Did he struggle this much when he made my CDs last year? It's a good thing he has a stereo in his car to play them.

I snuggle into my pillow, sleep beckoning. My phone vibrates again. I reach for it with a groan. Marcus is probably the only person I would forgive for bugging me this early. Maybe my gargoyle boyfriend wants to meet me for an early morning kiss? Nothing could top that.

Seriously??? Are you kidding me??? You're the luckiest girl alive!

I reread Katie's text, but it makes no sense.

Suddenly, I bolt upright. Is it possible she saw us last night? *Crap*. I fell asleep on the roof with Marcus. He and his wings, in all their glorious beauty, delivered me safely to the ground.

He doesn't need his wings for that small of a jump. He did it for me. He knows I love them.

I swallow a shriek as I spot the figure leaning against my dresser.

"What are you doing in my bedroom?" I snap, my heart hammering against my rib cage.

Jude crosses his arms over his chest. In the year that I've known him, my father has learned to mimic human gestures well. Then it hits me. That's one of my most common gestures.

"I would like to meet your great-uncles," Jude announces.

As I tamp down the adrenaline surge and glare at my intruder—Daddy Demon and not Seamus the Demon here to kill me—I swallow a different kind of fear. "I told you it would happen when the time's right."

"I'm done waiting." His voice is cold. I know that tone well. He isn't going to budge.

"Let me ease them into it," I plead.

My phone vibrates in my hand. That's when I remember Katie's message.

Well????

What do I say to my best friend and neighbor if she saw Marcus deliver me to my bedroom window? Play dumb?

My uncles putter around the kitchen, clanging pans and chopping vegetables. The smell of freshly brewed coffee drifts into my bedroom, followed by the heavy, smoky smell of bacon.

"Perfect. We can have breakfast together," Jude says.

I return my cell to the bedside table.

"Please," I whisper. "Not today."

The front door creaks open. Sheldon grabbing the Sunday

paper from the sidewalk? How do I get rid of Jude? I throw off my sheet and blanket, thinking through a safe response to Katie.

"Bernard? Can you come here, please?"

Something about Sheldon's tone, muffled through my closed bedroom door, causes the back of my neck to prickle. Do they know Jude's here? How did he get in, anyway? Did he pick the lock on the front door?

"Lucy?" Bernard calls out.

Jude pushes himself off the dresser. "I'll be out front. Come and invite me in." In one smooth motion, he climbs out the window. So that's how he got in.

I change out of pajamas and into shorts and a T-shirt, my stomach churning.

How do I introduce Jude?

Sheldon despises him for what he did to Momma. Never mind that he's been absent my entire life. How do I explain that Gram played a role in keeping my father and me apart? That she used magic to do it? My uncles are in the dark about everything. They don't know Gram was a witch. They don't know about all the supernaturals living in our three-flat apartment building. And they don't know I'm half-witch, half-demon. If they did, I think their heads would explode.

"Lucy?" Sheldon's voice is much louder this time.

"Hey, Sheldon. Bernard. What's up?" I ask as I enter the living room. Travel brochures decorate the coffee table. Are they still debating between Costa Rica and Alaska for our family vacation?

"We were going to ask you the same question." Bernard frowns, his hands on his hips.

They know about Jude, but how?

Sheldon turns me around as Bernard pushes aside the drapes and jabs his finger toward the window. "What in the world is that?"

I look outside.

Oh, no.

Katie's text message now makes sense. It had nothing to do with Marcus and his wings.

My mouth falls open as I stare at the brand-spanking new dark blue car that screams, *Officer, I'm a teenage driver. Please pull me over.* Shiny and gorgeous, adorned with a humongous red bow on top with words written in gold script, so large I can read them clearly from the apartment, *Happy Belated Birthday, Lucy.*

My entire nervous system buzzes with panic. Subtlety is not Jude's strong suit.

I feel the weight of my uncles' stares.

"Something you want to share with the class, Luce?" Sheldon asks.

I wrap my arms around my stomach. Forget butterflies, I've got a violent case of hornets swarming in my belly. "Yeah, that's a tough one."

"There's a sixty-thousand-dollar vehicle sitting outside with your name on it. Give it a try," Bernard pushes.

Sixty thousand? I'm torn between wanting to pummel Jude and melting into a pool of goo under my uncles' hot glares.

I jump at the sudden knock at the front door. Another shot of adrenaline jolts through my body. My father couldn't wait ten minutes?

Neither of my uncles move. A second knock rings out, this time more urgent. I rush to answer it, relieved to get away from Sheldon and Bernard.

It's Marcus, and he looks unhappy.

"Um, hi..." I nod subtly toward my uncles. "Not a good time."

Marcus glances over my shoulder. "Just stopped by to see what you're doing today." He bends to hug me. "Persephone called. The ravens are going berserk. She had to set them free to keep them from injuring themselves trying to escape."

Persephone lives in the third-floor apartment. She's also a witch and was Gram's best friend.

"Why? What's wrong?" I whisper in his ear.

"Marcus, do you know anything about this car?" Sheldon calls out.

"I haven't been outside yet. What car?" Marcus pushes past me into the apartment.

My uncles pull the drapes back to expose the sweet sixteen birthday gift.

"I see," Marcus says stiffly, turning back to me. "I'm guessing he wants to talk to you."

That's when I notice his twitching, the strain of his muscles as he tries to suppress the urge to morph. *Duh.* Marcus knows Jude is here. He can sense him. This is going to be bad. Sheldon and Bernard will be furious. I'll be grounded forever, no longer allowed to spend time on the roof with Marcus. Will they insist I quit my nanny job with the Douglas family? Will they kick me out for being the world's biggest liar?

"Who gave you the car, Lucy?" Bernard asks in a huff, on the verge of losing his patience.

"Well..." It suddenly feels like a hundred degrees in the room as a droplet of sweat trickles down my back. "You see..."

Marcus's jaw is clenched, and cords stand out on his neck. He's fighting the change. This is torture for him. I have to tell my uncles and get Jude out of here, for Marcus's sake.

"It's a gift from my father," I blurt out. My mind races for an abbreviated version of the truth. "He contacted me recently. He knew all kinds of stuff about me. And Momma. And Gram." I pull my hair over my shoulder and twist it. "I wasn't sure if I wanted to see him after all these years, but I did meet him...over ice cream." My voice trails off at the looks of confusion and astonishment on Sheldon and Bernard's faces.

Sheldon pulls at his bottom lip. "Your father? He's back?"

What was it Sheldon told me last year about Momma and Jude?

"She seemed to lose her mind. Literally. Her life revolved around him, and when he left, it was like her mind," his voice faltered for a moment. He swallowed and forced himself to continue, *"It was like her mind and her will to live went with him."*

Bernard pulls the dishtowel from his shoulder, his eyes coming into focus for the first time since I dropped the bomb. "Lucy, this is big news. Did Marcus say the man is outside? If that's the case, you should invite him in. He can have breakfast with us and introduce himself." His gaze slides from me to Marcus. "Marcus, you're welcome to join us as well."

"I don't think Marcus can stay." I put a hand on Marcus's arm and give him a firm shove toward the door. Being in Jude's presence will only torment him more. Even now, he's trembling, and his skin is hot beneath my fingers.

Marcus ignores me and nods at Bernard. "I'd love to. Thanks."

I can't think of a way to argue with Marcus that won't involve my uncles finding out I've hidden other things from them, too. Why can't Marcus listen to me for once and go back upstairs to his own apartment? It'll be bad enough having breakfast with Jude and my uncles, but Marcus and Jude together in one room could be a disaster. They hate each other too much.

Sheldon and Bernard stare at me expectantly.

"Would you like me to go with you?" Sheldon asks, gesturing toward the door. "To invite your father in?"

There are a hundred ways this could go horribly wrong, but I can't think of an objection that will sound reasonable to my uncles. I shake my head, trying to keep the alarm from my face. I need a couple of minutes alone with Jude. With tremendous effort, I force my legs to move and I walk outside to Jude's fancy black sedan. I refrain from giving it a swift kick.

Jude rolls down the window. "What do you think?" he asks. I ignore the shark-like smile on his face. "I chose blue because it favors your coloring, but if you prefer something else, just name it."

"We had a deal. You were supposed to stay away from my uncles."

"I grew tired of waiting." The smile is still on his face. "Besides, with your horrible commute to school, I thought you could use a more convenient method of transportation. Also, I believe fathers giving daughters a car for their sixteenth birthday is traditional."

"Yeah, you're going to win Father of the Year, Jude." I glare at him. "Is it normal in the demon world for fathers to hang out in their daughter's bedroom? Because in the human world, it's creepy and inappropriate."

"I like to watch you sleep. It's the only time you look peaceful. If you lived under my roof..."

He's been in my bedroom before today? A white-hot ball of panic surges inside of me. Is he going to force me to move in with him? What does that mean for Sheldon and Bernard?

"That's not going to happen." Maybe I should put bars on my windows? Right, like that would keep him out. But it's the hard look in his eyes, the savage curl of his mouth that knocks the breath out of me. Like he would do whatever it took to get me to move in with him.

Sheldon and Bernard. My fingers start to tingle. Heat races down my arms. I could blast him right now. Torch his car. Better yet, I could torch his birthday present. I funnel the heat to my fingertips.

The foyer door opens behind me. *Crap.* I gulp in air and tamp down hard on the heat.

"Lucy?" Sheldon calls out. He sounds nervous. I can't blame him. For all he knows, Jude will drive me bonkers, just like he did to Momma.

My uncles stand on the front porch, both wringing their hands.

8

I turn back to Jude, my tone sharp as a knife. "My uncles want to meet you. I'm supposed to invite you in for breakfast. If you screw this up for me, or harm them in any way, I—"

"I would be delighted." In the blink of an eye, he's out of the car. Way too eager.

His window is down. I glance up at the sky, hoping for a storm to come and ruin the interior of his expensive vehicle.

Jude strides ahead of me and thrusts his hand out to Sheldon. I follow like an afterthought, my insides frothing as if I've just made a deal with the devil which, actually, I have.

"Sheldon Meyers. Vera's brother." Jude smiles broadly as they shake hands. "It's great to meet you." He turns to Bernard. "You must be Sheldon's partner, Bernard Goldman. You've done a wonderful job with Lucy. She adores you both."

Charisma pours off Jude in waves, coating my uncles and sucking them in. They fall all over each other, grinning as they quickly usher Jude inside. This is not the Jude I know and don't love. These aren't the uncles I know and do love, either, treating Jude as if he's some hotshot celebrity. I'm embarrassed for them, and I'm angry at Jude for making them act this way.

Jude pauses in the living room. His attention lingers on every single detail—the built-in bookcases loaded with books and knickknacks, the framed artwork, some of which is older than me. Some of this stuff belonged to Gram. I wonder if Jude recognizes anything.

"I hope you'll stay for breakfast," Bernard gushes.

"We've made an egg casserole, but if there is something else you prefer, we can whip it up in no time," Sheldon adds.

Jude isn't listening. His gaze locks on a series of framed photos arranged on the far wall—Gram and Grampa looking serious, standing tall and stiff, Momma goofing around, making her younger brother, Zack, laugh. Momma was fourteen in this photo. Sheldon tells me sometimes that I wear her same smile.

The photo of Momma riding on Sheldon's back when she was eight is one of my favorites. So is the black and white shot of Gram and Uncle Zack. Bernard took this candid picture one night when Zack, who was around eleven at the time, danced with Gram in the living room of the old house while listening to records. They both wore carefree smiles. Gram told me once that with most boys, that was the age they stopped wanting anything to do with their mom. Zack was different. He never liked being far from her. Her eyes had filled with tears. They always did when she talked about him.

A spot on Jude's temple throbs. He leans in, as if drawn to the photographs. He doesn't blink or breathe. I touch his arm, zapping him in the process. He tears his attention from the photographs. His gaze meets mine, black and threatening. His lips curve down into a hellish snarl before he turns away and follows my uncles into the kitchen.

Something in those photos upset him. A tremor of terror ripples down my back. It's never a good thing when Jude's upset.

CHAPTER TWO

– Lucy Walker –

"Great. Just great," Jude grumbles under his breath as he eyeballs Marcus in the kitchen.

"Marcus, this is Jude Morgan," I talk over Jude, trying to keep the edge from my voice.

Will Jude play along? What if he tells my uncles that we first bumped into each other the day I arrived in Chicago, that we've met several times since then? My uncles would kill me. Or worse, they'd give me that look. The one where Sheldon cocks his head, his hazel eyes large and full of hurt. Bernard would simply focus on something else, like the sink full of dishes, the weight of disappointment causing his posture to bow.

I glance at Marcus, hoping he'll give me that secret smile, the one that says everything will be all right. No such luck. He looks like a tightly wound spring about to buck loose at any moment. Guilt slams into me immediately. I have no right to expect Marcus to comfort me when he's miserable. I follow his scowl, which is directed at Jude.

My father sits at our twenty-year-old butcher-block table in a kitchen that is one quarter the size of his, clutching an Earth Day coffee mug. He takes in the old table, the walls covered in green paint and white wainscoting, Gram's homemade curtains on the window; then his eyes move back to the table. His annoyance at Marcus's presence evaporates. He's basking like a contented cat in a ray of sunshine.

Sheldon clears his throat. "I'm puzzled that you're just coming into Lucy's life now."

Jude nods. "I understand your concern. Vera, Lucy's grandmother, made it quite clear she didn't want me to be part of Lucy's life. I attribute that to the fallout between Donna and me. There were hard feelings." He takes a sip of his coffee, then another. His temple throbs again. The happiness I witnessed moments ago is gone. His posture grows rigid. The grip on his coffee cup tightens. "They kept me from my daughter."

I eye my uncles nervously.

Marcus stirs. I can see he's dying to call Jude out. His face flushes with the effort it takes to keep his mouth shut and his spasms under control.

"I was given bits of information through the years. I suppose I should be grateful for that." He turns to me, his dark gaze softening a bit. I force a smile. I need to keep his mood as light as possible. "All I ask is to be a part of your life now."

"But a car?" Bernard's face twists with disbelief. "I—we—get that you probably want to make up for lost time, but that's pretty extravagant."

"Never mind that I've been working and saving up to buy my own car." I want to make it clear that I don't need his help.

Jude suppresses a smile. "Bernard. Sheldon. Lucy is sixteen years old. I would feel better knowing she had a dependable car. I know Lucy's safety is as important to you as it is to me." There it is again. Charm. Loads of it. He uses that chummy tone, as if he, Sheldon, and Bernard are all on the same team, fighting the same cause. I can see my uncles are buying it, too.

Jude wants to keep me safe? Kind of a funny statement given that he's the most dangerous thing in my life. And I suspect my uncles are the opposite of safe now that they've made his acquaintance.

Bernard nods, clears his throat again. "But—"

"I am a wealthy man, so this isn't a hardship for me." Jude holds his hands together as if in prayer and bows toward my uncles. "Please allow Lucy to accept this gift."

Something about the way he says the word *please* sounds suspicious. Then it hits me. Jude is hypnotizing my uncles. My fingertips burn.

I slam my hands on the table. "Jude, that's enough!"

A tiny spark spits off my left index finger and finds its mark on Jude's hand, distracting him just enough from eye contact with my uncles.

"The egg casserole!" Bernard gasps. He sets his coffee cup down with a thud. Brown liquid sloshes over the rim and spills onto the table. I mop it up and glare at Jude. He shrugs at me, his sly smile still in place.

I don't want Jude's present. The last time I accepted a gift from him—a beautiful homecoming dress—he wound up kidnapping my boyfriend. What will this car cost me?

"I'm sorry," I announce. All faces turn to me. "I can't accept this. I'm not even close to getting my license."

Jude smiles. It's a dangerous smile. Goose bumps break out on my arms.

"It's bad manners to reject a gift, Lucy," Jude says evenly. His eyes are hard as marbles. I see the warning in them. What is he trying to tell me? Accept the gift or Marcus is no longer safe? Or he will take his anger out on the kids I nanny for? What will he do to my uncles?

"Lucy, say *thank you*," Sheldon urges, a look of surprise on his face, although whether by my lack of graciousness or by this ridiculously generous gift, I don't know.

Bernard nods at me.

Marcus's eyes burn holes into me, and I know he's disappointed by my silence. I can't imagine the super human effort he's making right now.

"Thank you," I say stiffly.

After breakfast, Sheldon, Bernard, and Marcus stand on the porch as I walk Jude to his car. "I can't believe you were hypnotizing my uncles. Don't you dare do that again. Ever."

"So long as they fall in line, it won't be necessary." Jude slides into his car. "Speaking of which, I recommend you talk your uncles out of the vacation they're planning."

We didn't talk about the vacation in front of Jude. Then it hits me. He saw the travel brochures.

"That's my girl," Jude says. His car purrs to life.

"I am not your girl," I say as he drives off.

Back inside the apartment, my uncles return to the kitchen to clean up.

"That's some car," Bernard says.

"I can't believe Lucy has to go to the Lexus dealership for a lesson," Sheldon says.

I grimace as they *ooh* and *ah* over the unwanted gift.

"Jude was furious when he saw the photos," I whisper to Marcus, nodding at the collages on the wall in the living room. "And I'm not allowed to go on vacation with my uncles. Or else."

"Sorry!" Marcus, pale and sweaty, smacks his hand over his mouth and races from the room.

CHAPTER THREE

– Lucy Walker –

"Not my finest moment," Marcus says an hour later. He paces his apartment, shirtless, his white and gray wings pulled tight against his back. I press my hands against his chest, forcing him to stop.

I jerk my hands away. "You're burning up."

"It's normal." He shrugs. "Fighting the change causes my body temperature to sky rocket."

"You should've left us and come here. Or gone to the roof. You could've changed earlier, and no one would've seen you. Why put yourself through that?"

He grimaces. "He's dangerous, Lucy. Do you really think it's wise having him anywhere near your uncles? What if they decide they don't like him and forbid you to see him?"

"You act like I invited him over," I complain, plunking down on the couch. Marcus's apartment is the opposite of my uncles' place. While Sheldon and Bernard have photos and art decorating their walls and bookshelves and a coffee table loaded with books and precious items they've collected over the years or inherited,

Marcus's walls are white and bare. His coffee table is decorated with graphic novels and albums—actual vinyl. His couch is the color of rich dirt, the kind that's purchased from a garden store, and the adjacent chair reminds me of the hot chocolate Bernard makes for me on occasion in a pan on the stove after the whipped cream has melted into it.

Marcus won't admit it, but this isn't just about Jude and my uncles. He doesn't want Jude anywhere near me. He's upset about the gift, too.

"I didn't want the stupid car," I mutter.

"It's not about the car," he says. "Although it did bug me that you gave in so easily."

"Like I had a choice. You don't get it. The whole conversation, the purpose of his visit...it was a veiled threat to me to cooperate."

Marcus's stony expression tells me I'm being dense. "Lucy, he was getting to know your uncles."

I roll my eyes. "Well, duh."

"No, you don't understand." He sits on the couch beside me and his wings bounce. "Getting to know them in a supernatural way. He's a demon. By the end of the visit, I'm sure he knew things about them that *humans* wouldn't."

I don't like his ominous tone of voice. Nervous laughter bubbles up my throat. "Like what?"

"That their favorite city is San Francisco." Marcus ticks off on his fingers. "That Sheldon takes high blood pressure medication for which he needs a prescription. They drink a unique brand of coffee, which can only be found at one chain store. Their accounts are held at the bank two blocks from here. They drive an old

Volvo, which would need special order parts in the event of repairs." Marcus's eyes burn into mine. "If the three of you were to disappear, it wouldn't take much effort for Jude to find you."

I suddenly forget how to breathe. "You think Jude picked up on all that?"

"Jude's brain works like a computer. He absorbs everything, and it's forever embedded in his head." Marcus looks at me soberly. "This wasn't a social call. This was a reconnaissance mission."

* * * *

"Good morning, kiddo," Sheldon says as he breezes into the kitchen Monday morning. I pause with a spoonful of Cheerios halfway to my mouth, gauging his tone. Faux cheerful—not good. That means a lecture is soon to follow, and I'm pretty sure Jude will be the topic. I start shoveling cereal into my mouth.

By noon yesterday, suspicion had replaced my uncles' initial thrill over meeting Jude. There had been hushed conversations between them throughout the day. I tried to ignore it and stay out of the line of fire, but Bernard's face as he brings the newspaper to the table tells me that my avoidance tactics are at an end.

"That was quite a shock meeting your dad yesterday," Bernard says.

Sheldon sits down next to him. "We need to talk about how much contact he's going to have with you, Lucy."

I say nothing but increase my Cheerio shoveling speed.

"Are you happy here with us?" Sheldon blurts out.

I nearly choke on my breakfast. I look up from my cereal bowl and see how drawn both their faces are. Do they think I would leave them for Jude?

"I'm sorry for not telling you about him." The lies come a little easier than they used to. Whatever it takes to keep my uncles safe. "Because of his history with Momma and how she turned out, I didn't know how you would react."

Sheldon levels his gaze at me. "You have to know that secrecy is never the answer."

"You need to trust us, and we need to be able to trust you," Bernard adds.

"You're both right, and I'm sorry." I meet Sheldon's gaze head-on. "I have no intention of moving in with Jude if that's what you're worried about. This is my home. You're stuck with me."

"Good to hear, kiddo," Sheldon says with a heavy exhale, breaking into a smile.

I kiss them both, then deliver my bowl and spoon to the sink. My uncles exchange a look as I pass the table. Unease? Fear? Whatever it was, I wasn't supposed to see it.

CHAPTER FOUR

– Lucy Walker –

"How long is this supposed to take?" I ask, peeking into the pot of bubbling liquid. *Sulfur*. I wrinkle my nose against the horrible, rotten egg smell. The potion doesn't look like much, but if it works to vanquish Seamus—the demon who tried to kill me last year for the sake of his grudge against Jude—then I don't care. Not that I'm in a hurry for him to show up again any time soon.

"It's your first day of practice and already you're impatient?" After setting two mugs on the counter next to the simmering teakettle, Persephone reaches over the sink and pushes up the window to air out her kitchen. From the look of her blue, green, and black paisley top and maroon stretchy pants, you would never know she's a powerful witch.

Persephone's trademark frown is in place, but there's also a twinkle in her eyes and the corner of her mouth twitches. Both fall away when she looks at me.

"Lucy, you can't race home to watch over your uncles every minute of the day. I'm keeping an eye on them. I can sense if Jude is near, which he isn't. I will let you know if there's something you need to worry about." She arches an eyebrow sharply. "Or are you trying to get out of your lesson? You said you were ready to learn the craft."

Am I being hypersensitive about Sheldon and Bernard? I don't trust Jude. Persephone doesn't get it. He's been excluded my whole life, and since our bizarre breakfast together, I worry that his grudge didn't die with Gram and Momma. I think it's now targeted at my uncles, who he perceives as the latest barrier between him and me. "As long as you promise to help keep an eye on them," I say, trying to shake my uneasiness.

"Of course." The deep lines leave her brow as she turns back to the rows of herbs laid out on her kitchen counter. She hands me a bundle. "Now tell me. Can you identify these?"

The leaves look like a hand with pointy fingers. Five fingers. I remember them from one of Gram's books, can picture her narrow scrawl in the margins. "Mugwort?"

"Correct." Persephone smiles and nods her encouragement. "What's it most commonly used for?"

I nibble my bottom lip for a moment and absently twirl the bundle between my fingers. Mugwort. Was it used for charm spells? Healing? Memory loss? There are so many herbs, so many uses, and a lot of them are similar. What's worse is there are ten different herbs that could be used for the same purpose. How am I supposed to memorize them all?

"For protection spells?" My voice raises an octave, giving away my uncertainty.

"It can be, yes," Persephone says. "However, it's most commonly used to strengthen divinatory abilities."

I set the bundle of herbs on the counter with a heavy sigh. I remember it now. Persephone probably thinks I'm slacking off on my studies. She wouldn't be entirely wrong.

"You're distracted," Persephone says as she pulls the whistling teakettle from the stove, using the blue and white dishtowel as a makeshift hot pad. She delivers a metal tea infuser and steaming hot water into each of the two mugs. She hands one cup to me, and I study the yellow-colored water. "It's made from dried mugwort."

I make a face at the bitter smell. "Sure I'm distracted. Do you blame me? I own a car I can't drive that I don't even want. My uncles are worried I'll move in with Jude." I frown, something I've been doing a lot lately. "Then there's this whole vacation thing."

"Vacation thing?"

"Jude warned me not to go on a trip with my uncles, to talk them out of it. It goes right along with what Marcus said. Jude's worried my uncles are going to steal me away."

"I would be careful if I were you, Lucy," Persephone says, her eyes meeting mine. "Jude's behaving right now. He's maintaining open lines of communication with Henry and me. Even Aiden has noticed he's less volatile."

It's a big deal for Jude to make an effort with Gram's two best friends and fellow witches. As far as Marcus's pseudo brother, Aiden, I don't put a lot of stock in anything he has to say. He doesn't like me and the feeling is mutual.

Persephone blows a dark brown curl from her eyes. "I agree that leaving town is a bad idea. See if Sheldon and Bernard will go without you. Tell them the Douglas's can't do without you. I will look after you." She nods at the herbs on the counter. "Now, back to mugwort and its common uses."

How will I convince my uncles to go on vacation without me? Sheldon's going to blow a gasket for sure. I pick up the bundle again, turning it over in my hand, holding it to my nose. The scent of mint is unmistakable. Too bad the tea doesn't smell the same.

I hear Persephone's irritated sigh, but I can't make myself care with so much swirling in my brain.

"How about Henry and I cast a spell on them?"

I snap my head up. "Don't you dare."

A small smile plays on Persephone's lips. "You know I wouldn't, but I see I finally have your attention, young lady," she chastises. "Besides, if Jude hypnotized them like you said, it's best not to tinker with their minds right now."

My heart drops. "What's wrong with their minds? Does Jude have some sort of control over them now? Can he read their minds, manipulate them somehow?" I lower my voice. "Will they go crazy like Momma?"

Persephone considers me for a moment. "Demons utilize hypnosis for two reasons. To manipulate, but also to get a foothold into someone's mind."

I struggle to keep myself from freaking out. "What do you mean by foothold?"

"He can sift through their thoughts."

"Why would he do that?" My voice is nearly a growl.

"In the event they decide to take you away—which they won't—he can track them and you."

Heat races down my arms like a violent spasm. I flex my fingers to ease the white-hot sensation.

Persephone leans against the counter. "Look at it from Jude's point of view. He finally has you in his life after sixteen years."

"Are you defending him?"

"No. I'm trying to enlighten you about a father's love for his daughter. Jude's determined never to lose you again." Her words act like a bucket of cold water, effectively dousing the heat in my arms and hands.

"A father's love," I echo. Could it be that simple? Who am I kidding? With a demon for a father, there's nothing simple about it.

My shoulders slump and I return the herbs to the counter. "It's not just that. There's the matter of Dylan, too."

"You're still worried about him?" Persephone asks.

Ever since Jude turned my good friend Dylan into a sort of demon, nothing's happened. For four months, Dylan had been, *well*, just plain Dylan. Lately, though, his bouts of temper and his amped up performance in the weight room are clear signs something's changing. It's like Dylan is on steroids, but he swears he's not.

"Have you talked to Marcus about it?"

I shrug. "I tried. He dismisses my observations and claims Dylan is fine."

"Keep an eye on him and report back to me any other changes," Persephone says. She nods toward my cup of tea. "Drink up. We're going to discuss divination and dream analysis through the use of mugwort tea."

24

I blow into the cup of hot liquid as I bring it to my lips. Would it be possible to gain insight into what's going on with Dylan? "How does divination work? Do I have to focus on a specific situation?"

"For today, just drink the tea and report back to me about your dreams tonight and your thoughts over the next few days."

I glance over my shoulder as the pot of bubbling liquid on the stove hisses and burps.

Persephone shakes her head. "Don't even think about it. That potion is out of your league as a beginner."

"Do you think I'll ever be as powerful as Gram?" It's a huge relief to voice the doubt that's been eating at me since I discovered I was a witch. "That I could take her place and join you and Henry? You know, the power of three?"

"I'm certain of it," she says, "although, your goal will be to form a trio with witches your own age. For now, focus on developing your powers. You are going to be a great witch, Lucy."

How can she be so sure? I glance at my cup of tea. Is it possible Persephone has seen the future? With a burst of enthusiasm, I gulp down half the mug. With my cheeks full as a chipmunk hoarding nuts, I rush over to the sink and spit the liquid out.

"Hot! Way too hot! And disgusting!" I pant into the sink. I dump the rest of the bitter tea down the drain and fill the cup with cold water. I drink it all in two gulps. "Are you trying to poison me?"

"You know better than to swill a hot beverage." Persephone frowns at me.

"So gross. And I think I have blisters running down my throat."

"Let's call it a day," Persephone announces, wiping her hands on her maroon pants. She wraps the herbs in damp paper towels and stores them in the vegetable crisper. "Spend more time with your books, Lucy. I need you to step up your commitment. We'll meet again next weekend."

I'm about to mention finals and how much studying I need to do, but I don't want her to think I'm making excuses. Besides, my mouth and throat are on fire. Persephone's right. I was distracted. Lesson learned. I need to pay attention. "Okay."

As I descend the stairs, I can't help but wonder if Persephone was wrong when she said I was destined to be a great witch like Gram. I have the gene and the powers transferred from Gram's raven, Lola, but does that really guarantee anything? So far most of the powers I've displayed are the evil kind I inherited from Jude.

My foot hits the bottom stair at the same time someone knocks on the front door. My body stiffens. With everything that happened last year, the foyer door now stays locked and doorbells have been installed on the exterior of the three-flat building for each apartment. Maybe the doorbells aren't working?

I cross the foyer and peek out the peephole. Can't be too careful given that Seamus is out there, and once he figures out I'm alive, he'll hightail it back here to finish me off.

But it's not Seamus. I open the door and stand face-to-face with a woman whose wavy hair runs a few inches past her shoulders, the color of which is hard to describe. Maybe it had been brown once. Based on the red and golden streaks running through it, the deep golden skin, and the freckles decorating the bridge of her nose and cheeks, she spends a lot of time in the sun. Deep crinkly lines form at the corners of her eyes and mouth when she smiles at me. She appears to be roughly the same age as Katie's mom, Ms. Stevens I have a difficult time tearing my attention from her eyes, which are a startling deep blue.

"Can I help you?" I ask.

Her lips turn up at the corners in a lopsided way. Something about it is familiar.

"I sure hope so. I'm looking for Gabriel Turner."

CHAPTER FIVE

– Lucy Walker –

Gabriel. She called him Gabriel.

"Are you Marcus's *mother*?" I take a step backward and stumble. I grab the doorknob and jerk upright, saving myself from an embarrassing fall. She must think I'm a total klutz. Marcus hasn't said much about his mother. Just that she's the only person in the world who ever called him Gabriel and she left when he was very young.

"He goes by his middle name now?" Her forehead creases like an accordion. She cranes her neck to look inside the foyer. "He lives here, doesn't he?"

Marcus's mother? Is this a surprise visit? Or have Marcus and his mother been in touch? Would he keep something that huge a secret from me? "Is he expecting you?" I ask.

If her eyes were weapons, I'd be a pile of dust on the foyer floor. "No," she says icily. "Is that a problem?"

It would be rude to slam the door in her face. Should I lie and tell her Marcus doesn't live here? Again, bad idea. Marcus may actually want to see her.

28

"No." I open the door wide and point up the stairs. "Apartment two, second floor."

She maneuvers around me, plants one foot on the bottom stair, and pauses.

"He's not home, but Aiden, his roommate, will let you in. You can wait for him."

"Thank you," she says over her shoulder. I catch a look of uncertainty on her face.

Her steps are slow as she makes her way to the second floor. Maybe I should walk her up and wait with her. I mean, she is my boyfriend's mother. I should probably try to make a good impression or something. Then I think about trying to make small talk with this stranger and Aiden. I chicken out and text Marcus instead.

My fingers shake, and I have to retype my brief message twice. *What time will you be home?*

I pace the foyer. Back and forth. Back and forth. What else did Marcus tell me about his mother? *Nothing.* I had pretty much assumed she was dead. Is he still mad at her? Or does he never talk about her because he no longer cares?

I jump when my phone vibrates against the palm of my hand. *Half hour. Why? What's up?*

Marcus is always on edge, worried Seamus will come for me. I drum my fingers on the banister while I figure out how to word my message. Is it my place to tell him his mom showed up? Or should I let her surprise him? I try to put myself in his shoes. Would I want to be surprised by a parent who bailed on me? Nope.

A woman claiming to be your mother is here. She's waiting in your apartment with Aiden.

Five seconds later, Elvis Costello's voice croons from my phone. Marcus's ringtone.

"Hello—"

"Is this some kind of joke, Lucy? Because it's not funny." His words come out in sharp, angry bursts.

"It's not a joke, I swear." How could he think I'd do that to him? I feel super offended by his words and his tone for several seconds, then shake it off. He must be completely freaked out. "She just showed up asking for Gabriel Turner. Should I have lied? Told her you don't live here?"

There's silence on the other end. Finally, he murmurs, "No."

"Do you want me to be there, at your apartment, when you get home?"

"No. I've got this." His voice sounds flat. Is he in shock?

"You're sure?"

"Positive," he says crisply.

Marcus disconnects without saying goodbye. I shove my phone into my pocket and head into my apartment. Absently, I follow the buttery scent of something fantabulous into the kitchen, all the while the image of Marcus's mother's face is burned into my brain.

"Hey, kiddo," Sheldon says. "Homemade pot pie tonight. Just for you."

"Not those frozen things. Trying to find a vegetarian pot pie at the store that's any good is impossible," Bernard huffs as he shoves the clean rolling pin in the lower cabinet.

"You're the best." I wrap my arms around Bernard and kiss him on the cheek.

30

Sheldon raises his bushy eyebrows and taps his cheek. "Hey, what about me?"

I cross the kitchen and plant a noisy kiss on his cheek. Figuring I should add my efforts to the cause, I wash my hands, then grab plates, glasses, and silverware and set the table. Why did Marcus's mom decide to show up now? Did it take her this long to find him?

Bernard pulls dinner out of the oven and distributes the pies onto our plates. We all stab the tops of our pies to release the steam and heat. I pick off bits of crust, blow on them then pop them into my mouth. We eat in silence for a while.

"What's going on with Dylan?" Sheldon asks as he opens a bottle of red wine. I wrinkle my nose as the sour smell hits my nostrils. "He hasn't come around in a while."

It's true. Dylan usually stops by once a week for dinner and to suck up to my uncles. It's an ongoing rivalry he has with Marcus.

"I'm not sure, but I plan to call him after dinner. I'll find out."

"See if he wants to come over for dinner one night this week. We like your mood when he visits," Bernard says. "You laugh more when he's around."

It's true. Dylan does make me laugh. However, given his demon-esque outbursts lately, I really don't want him around my uncles.

"Sure. I'll ask him," I lie.

"If he doesn't show his face more around here, his ranking may slip below Marcus's," Sheldon says. He and Bernard both chuckle.

My face grows hot. The fact that they consider Marcus and Dylan on the same playing field annoys me. Marcus is my boyfriend. Dylan is my good friend. There's no contest.

Speaking of my boyfriend, I discreetly pull my cell from my pocket and check for messages on my lap. Why hasn't Marcus texted me? What's going on with his mother?

* * * *

I dial Dylan while unloading my backpack onto the desk in my bedroom. The sooner I finish all of my studying, the sooner I can meet Marcus on the roof. That is if he calls or texts me. He was there for me when I discovered Jude was my father. Will Marcus let me be there for him?

"Tennessee." Dylan's voice comes across the line like a slow purr. "How's it going?"

"The more important question is...how are you?"

He laughs. "I'm doing great. Better than ever, actually."

He's always been cocky, but his voice seems edgier than normal. After Dylan's powers awoke and we found out his father had made a deal with Jude all those years ago for extreme success and wealth in exchange for his first born, Dylan and I made a pact to keep each other from turning evil. I can't let the change in him slide. I have to be on guard, for his sake.

"Why's that?" My attempt to sound nonchalant fails, and instead, I sound suspicious.

He blows out a noisy breath. "I had a great day. That's all."

"If it's no big deal, then tell me about it."

"You're a pain in the butt, you know that?"

I knew it. Marcus was wrong. Dylan's demon powers *are* changing. But there's no way I'm talking with Marcus about this. Never mind that he's upstairs right now facing his long-lost mother. He'll blow a gasket like he always does whenever I bring up Dylan.

"Something happened. Tell me. Now," I say.

"Really, it's not a big—"

"Sure. No big deal. Spill it."

I hear the rustle as he shifts the phone to his other ear.

"Get this." His voice is low, excited. "I shot hoops with several of the guys earlier today. It's not my strong suit like football, but man, I was on fire. I wish you were there, Lucy," he gushes. "I still don't know how—but it was like, all of a sudden, I had tunnel vision. It was just me and the net. I was unstoppable." Dylan pauses in his rapid-fire explanation to take a breath. "Did you hear me? *Un-stop-a-bull.* I sunk the ball more times than I could count and I tore the net from the rim on my final shot."

I swallow past the uneasiness creeping up my throat. "Must be all your practicing," I say weakly, knowing Dylan would no more take time away from his football training for any other sport than Jude would become an angel.

Dylan chuckles. "Yeah, right. I became LeBron James, Kobe Bryant, and Kevin Durant all in one today. Michael Jordan, too. It was all me. One guy. I was awesome. I told the guys we're doing this again next weekend."

"You don't normally play basketball, right?" Is it possible that Dylan's naturally talented at all sports? Or is this part of his demon genes awakening?

"Hey, I know where you're headed with this and I have two words for you. *Buzz. Kill.*"

After I hang up with Dylan, I wonder if I should talk to Aiden about my suspicions. I still don't know if he's trustworthy, but he is a demon and he seems to know more about demon transformation than anyone else. Except Jude. But Jude would be excited by the prospect of Dylan embracing his demon side or whatever is going on. I make a mental note to call Aiden after I know Marcus's mother is gone.

I open my biology book. As I flip through the pages, my mouth goes dry. This can't be right. I turn to the prior chapter, scan the highlighted information, the notes in the margins. I close my eyes tight, then open them again. I know we covered this information already. Had a test on it. And yet it's not familiar. I can't breathe. My chest is tight.

I rustle through the pages to the next chapter. We've studied this material all week. I've read every page. Why don't I recognize any of the information?

I'm just barely managing to keep the B average my uncles insisted on if I want to keep all my privileges, a decline from the A average I maintained at my school in Lexington, Tennessee. If I don't do well on this test, will they tell me I can't see Marcus anymore? Will I have to give up my weekend job babysitting for Dylan's brother and sister? What if Sheldon and Bernard refuse to let me see Jude until I bring my grades up?

I try to focus on the diagram explaining how photosynthesis works, but the words blur and swim around the page. I'm checking my phone before I know it. Nothing. I try to read the text beneath the neat green diagram, but it might as well be in another language.

Finally my phone buzzes.

Meet me on the roof?

CHAPTER SIX

– Lucy Walker –

Marcus beats me to the roof. He doesn't stand at the railing ready to take my hand as I climb over. Instead, he sits on the ground, slumped against the short wall. I take a seat next to him. A fresh breeze chills my skin. I wrap my arms around myself. My teeth chatter, more out of nervousness than the cool night air.

"I can't believe she showed up like that." His voice is quiet as he stares at his hands clenched in his lap.

Marcus has never looked so miserable. What can I do to make him feel better? Nothing comes to mind. I hate feeling helpless.

"How long has it been?" I ask.

His laugh sounds more like a bark, harsh and loaded with pain. "She left when I was four."

I take hold of his hand and gently unfurl his fist, one finger at a time. "How was it seeing her? Talking with her?"

Marcus looks away from me. He pulls free from my grasp and rests his unclenched hands on his thighs. "I freaked out when you called. A hundred questions went through my head at once." His voice sounds flat, monotone. "It was a shock seeing her. A total shock."

That answered one of my questions. They hadn't been in touch before Camille's visit. Even in the dark, as close as we are, I can see his face. It holds no expression. As if it was wiped clean of all emotion.

"Of the hundred, which questions did you ask her?"

Marcus pulls his knees up, his shoes scraping against the hard surface of the roof. "I asked her why she left."

Straight to the point. I don't think I could have been that brave. "What did she say?"

He swings his head back to me, his eyes narrow, searching. I work hard to keep any sign of judgment off of my face.

"She—Camille—didn't want to leave. She thought she could change his mind about me."

I sit up straighter. "What do you mean? Change whose mind?"

"My real father—not the man I thought was my father—is special like me."

"Your *real* father? But your dad..." Marcus had told me how his dad had left him at church service one Sunday. Just took off and left him, unable to deal with Marcus's *extra abilities*. Father Bill at Old St. Pat's Church had connections with Persephone and my grandmother. In the end, my grandmother became Marcus's legal guardian.

"Nice, right? I'm a candidate for one of those stupid daytime talk shows featuring messed up families." Marcus shakes his head. "My real father left when he found out she was pregnant. He had a political career path, and children didn't play a role in his plans."

36

"So, he bailed?" My entire body tenses, my muscles quivering. What's wrong with these people? Part of me feels sorry for Camille, since Marcus's father took off when she was pregnant, but she did the same thing to Marcus.

Marcus nods. "She thought they were hardcore in love. Soul mates." He rubs the palms of his hands on his knee, silent for a long moment. I wait, not sure if he plans to continue. "Then the guy I thought was my biological dad came along." Marcus sighs, scratches his jaw. "Camille's car had broken down on the side of the highway one day, and he happened to stop. He fell in love with her on the spot and pursued her until she gave in."

"Did he know she was pregnant?" I ask. The tension oozes off of Marcus. More than anything, I want to take his hand, to touch his arm or his thigh, to show him I care. A little voice in my head urges me to give Marcus his space.

"Yes, but he didn't care. He wanted a life with her," Marcus says.

After a heavy, silent pause, I repeat my question, "Did she tell you why she left?"

Marcus nods, his lips pressed into a thin line as he focuses on a point across the roof. "Turns out my biological father contacted her. He wanted to reconcile."

"Why didn't she take you with her?" Miss Twenty Questions. That's me.

"Apparently, being a protector, even one as powerful as my mother claims he is, has its disadvantages. There are supernaturals who seek to kill them. Thugs for hire."

Alarm surges through me and I gasp. "Who's out to kill protectors?"

Marcus raises both eyebrows. "I'll give you one guess."

My skin tingles and my fingers twitch. My body's not going to produce a fireball. It's more of an energy overload. Suddenly, it dawns on me.

Who hates Marcus more than anyone else? Who tried to destroy him on the night of homecoming?

My father. "Demons."

Marcus nods, his expression grim. "Hired muscle. Demons with no other talents. Higher-level demons hire them to take out my kind. Garret—my father—thought it was safer for me to remain off the radar for a while."

"That would've been fine if demons couldn't sense what you are, but they can. Jude can. Who was supposed to protect you? Your human stepfather couldn't."

Marcus snorts.

"Are you saying that Camille up and left when Garret contacted her?"

Marcus rests his arms on his knees. I scoot closer and lean my cheek on his shoulder, sliding my arms around him.

"Camille was sure she could change his mind once she spoke with him face-to-face," he says.

That didn't happen.

"What now? What does she want?" I force the words from my mouth, my tone filled with bitterness.

"She wants to be a part of my life and..."

I can barely breathe and I close my eyes tight. "And?"

"To introduce me to Garret."

I suddenly feel dizzy, breathless. I raise my head to study his profile. "Why? What good is that now? They dumped you, made you fend for yourself all this time, and now they want some happy reunion?"

Marcus turns to meets my eyes, his face once again void of expression. "Camille wants us to be a family."

CHAPTER SEVEN

– Lucy Walker –

I make it through my first couple of periods at school on Monday in a daze. Marcus is going to meet with his mother again tonight, probably tomorrow night, too. I might as well get used to it. I'm going to lose him. A part of me wonders if Jude helped orchestrate this. He'll get his wish to have Marcus out of my life. By the time I join Katie and the girls at lunch, I'm feeling miserable.

"What's up with you?" Ella looks over at me, a teasing smile on her face. "Someone kill your cat. Wait, you have a bird, right?"

Lola and Serenity, Gram and Persephone's ravens haven't returned since Jude's visit to the three-flat. Of course, Jude tried to kill them last year, so it's understandable why they took off, but it doesn't make sense that they're still gone. "Not today, Ella," I say quietly.

Katie bumps my elbow, giving me a questioning look. I shake my head and pick at my cheese and pickle sandwich.

"What-*ever*." Ella responds in an annoying valley girl voice.

My relationship with Ella is hard to describe. She doesn't like me and goes out of her way to make sure I know it. While Katie's my best friend and Suzy and Cloe are close seconds, Ella's a thorn in my side. Caroline's not as bad, but she's Ella's BFF and is pretty annoying, too. There's not much I can do about it, though. The five of them have been friends since grade school. I'm the newbie, having started at St. Aquinas at the beginning of the school year. I don't want to rock the boat. Ella and Caroline were surprisingly nice to me after homecoming when I was so depressed over my boyfriend's absence. Of course, they didn't know he was turned to stone and camped out on the roof of my apartment building. But their kindness ended once they realized Dylan and I were spending time together. Ella's got a crush on Dylan, who pretty much ignores her these days, and Caroline goes along with whatever Ella dictates.

Ella smirks at me before she turns to Caroline. "Let's talk about something fun. Is everything still on track for your party?"

Caroline nods. "It's four weeks away and the guest list is nearly complete. The menu, too."

"Menu?" Cloe looks confused. "You said you planned to serve chips and dip, snacky stuff, right?"

"I like to be organized," Caroline points out. She flips through her spiral notebook and runs her finger down the pages. Her party notes? Ella peers over her shoulder.

"Do you really think people are going to respect a guest list?" Suzy asks, dipping her French fries in a pool of ketchup on her plate. "You know how it is. Everyone will tell their friends, and you're going to wind up with a packed house."

Caroline tears her gaze away from her notes and glances at Ella nervously.

"All the better." Ella grins at Caroline. "There'll be a great selection of guys for me—*for us*—to choose from."

I'm guessing Ella will be the one inviting people not included on the list. She'll take Caroline's party and make it her own. I wonder if Marcus will still be here by then.

He's going to leave you, the little voice in my head says. I close my eyes as a wave of despair washes over me. Lunch is no longer appetizing, and I push my food away. I pull my phone out of my purse to see if Marcus texted. No message.

"What's wrong, Lucy? One of your boyfriends ignoring you? Maybe you need a third. Oh, wait, there's Shawn, too, right?" Ella asks, her voice dripping with sarcasm.

Anger flares inside of me, and I dig my nails into my palms. I envision shooting a fireball at Ella, watching her go up in flames. The satisfaction is short-lived as I remember my promise to Persephone and Henry to keep my powers a secret. Turning Ella into a crispy critter doesn't bother me nearly as much as it should. Maybe I'm more like Jude than I thought.

Suzy points her fork at Ella. "Why do you have to be such a witch? Leave Lucy alone and leave my boyfriend out of this." Suzy winks at me across the table. Shawn's class ring dangles from a chain around her neck.

Katie pokes me in the arm as the bell rings. "See you after school. Fill me in then?"

I nod and head over to throw my lunch away. What's the deal with Marcus? He always texts me over lunch. *Always.* I try not to let it get to me. Once I make it to gym class and change into my uniform, I pull out my phone and text him.

I hope you're okay. The roof tonite?

* * * *

When I get home from school, I immediately dump the contents of my backpack onto my desk and tackle homework. If I finish studying before dinner, I'm free to see Marcus as soon as I've eaten and cleaned the kitchen.

Halfway through my Spanish assignment, my phone vibrates. Not just once, but continuously. It's Jude.

"Hi, Jude. Haven't learned how to text yet, huh?"

"What are your plans for the weekend?"

No hello or how are you? No fatherly love, not with Jude.

"I'm working for the Douglas's on Saturday, then going out with my friends. I have plans for Sunday, too. Why?" I don't tell him I'm spending Sunday morning with Persephone, learning witchcraft, and the rest of the day with Marcus, assuming he doesn't cancel to spend time with his mother.

I hear the tapping of computer keys and figure he's forgotten about me already.

"Your Saturday has just freed up. Come to my home at noon."

Anger flares inside of me. "Did you cancel my babysitting job?"

"Pierce Douglas belongs to me. A fact you are well aware of and so is he."

Now the pause for tapping made sense. Jude just instant messaged Dylan's dad and cancelled my job. Sparks fly off my fingertips, and I quickly pull my phone away from my ear to avoid burning myself. Plunking my phone on my desk, I hit the speaker button and turn the volume down so my uncles won't hear the conversation.

"But—"

"Saturday. Noon. It's time for you and Dylan to begin training with me."

My fingers keep shooting sparks. I pat out the red-hot flames on my schoolbooks before any serious damage is done. I clutch my glass of icy lemonade in my hands to quell the urge.

"Look Jude, you can't just cancel my job and—"

"Do I need to send a driver to pick you up?" The threat is clear. He'll make a scene in front of my uncles.

"A little more notice would've been nice," I complain.

"Shall we make it Saturday *and* Sunday?"

I grip my glass and curse the snapping of sparks from my fingers.

"Saturday is *fine*."

"Noon."

And he's gone. Unfortunately not forever.

As I make sure the call has ended—could anything be worse than having Jude listen to my private conversations? I shudder at the thought—a message pops up from Marcus.

Sorry. Can't meet tonite.

My insides sink, but I text him back. *OK. All good w-ur mom?*

Didn't see her today. Worked at St. Pats. Meeting 2morrow after school. Can u come?

He wants me to be a part of his meeting with Camille?

I'll be there.

I thought for sure Marcus was shutting me out. My chest swells with relief and happiness.

Before I forget, I type a quick text to Dylan, telling him about Jude's call and asking if he can pick me up for our training session.

Once my anger has faded, I slide my phone into my purse and head to the kitchen for dinner. There's no way I can tell Sheldon and Bernard I'm spending the day with Jude on Saturday. I don't want them getting any more paranoid about him than they already are. Maybe I should tell them I'm going to the mall with the girls on Saturday or to lunch and the movies. Or that Dylan and I are going to hang out for the day. They'd love that. I really hate lying to them, but the last thing I want is conflict. I can't risk it. Jude will always win.

"Have you given any more thought to vacation?" Bernard asks, as I dot a steaming corn muffin with butter, then take a bite.

I chew slowly as I consider my answer. "Don't you think it would be better if the two of you go away together? You haven't had alone time in a while. I can stay here. Persephone keeps saying she wants to spend more time with me."

Sheldon drops his knife. I flinch as it clangs against his plate. Bernard and I freeze, trying to gauge Sheldon's anger. Ever since Jude gave me the car and ate at our breakfast table, Sheldon has been grouchy.

"This is about *him*, isn't it?" Sheldon asks.

I'm not quite sure if he's referring to Marcus or Jude, but I play it safe. "If you're referring to Marcus, the answer is no. It has nothing to do with him."

Sheldon hasn't forgiven Marcus for the homecoming fiasco and for disappearing afterward without so much as a phone call. My uncles don't know the nightmare that really took place that night.

"It's ten days, Lucy. You'll see your boyfriend again soon."

It's true. Marcus is a factor in this, too. Part of me believes he'd be here, waiting with open arms when I return from vacation. Problem is, there's a part of me that isn't so sure now that his parents are around.

"Lucy," Bernard says, "the point is for the three of us to get away and have fun together as a family."

Family. The very thing I've always wanted. My throat clenches.

"But I have the job with the Douglas family. I can't take off and leave them high and dry."

I have to keep my uncles safe. I can't risk Jude viewing them as a threat.

No one talks for the rest of the meal. Sheldon slurps his soup and avoids eye contact with me, making it clear he's upset.

If they knew what Jude was capable of, what he did to Marcus last year, they would understand. But if I tell them, my uncles would take action to keep Jude and me apart. Then Jude would kill them.

* * * *

The next morning I'm at my locker, balancing my backpack on my knee while I switch out my books. Someone tugs on my hair from behind. *Could it be?*

"Tennessee."

I weave slightly as my entire body slumps.

Marcus attends St. Pat's, an all-boys private high school here in Chicago. Sometimes he blows off final period study hall and meets me at my locker, but there's no reason for him to be at St. Aquinas this early. I glance over my shoulder, and Dylan's face breaks into a mega-watt smile. I force a smile in return.

"I got a call from my favorite person in the world last night, just a few minutes after your text came through," Dylan says.

I close my locker and turn to face him. Dylan hooks his thumb in the pocket of his black pants, part of the St. Aquinas school uniform, and adjusts his backpack, which is slung over his shoulder. I try to ignore the outline of his muscled chest and shoulders through his white dress shirt. Dylan appears to be testing the limits of the shirt's seams and the buttons strain against the starched fabric. I'm tempted to ask if he's been working out more than usual, a stupid question since I already know that to be true, but I also don't want him to know I noticed. Then again, maybe he intentionally buys his shirts a size too small.

"What's so funny?" Dylan asks.

"Nothing. I figured Jude would call you."

"What if we blow it off?"

Based on his question, you wouldn't know that Dylan was with me when I stormed Jude's house after the homecoming dance. He helped me rescue the ravens and confront my father who had abducted my boyfriend. Jude was scary that night. I shake my head. "Bad idea. Jude's already got it out for my uncles. I need to keep the peace." I swing my backpack over my shoulder and Dylan walks me to class. "By the way, I'm telling my uncles that you and I are hanging out Saturday. Be a pal and don't say anything, okay?"

Dylan shoots me a quizzical look. "Why not tell them you're hanging out with Jude?"

"Let's just say Sheldon and Bernard are not huge fans."

It takes three minutes of speed walking to reach my destination. Dylan's going to be late for his class but he doesn't seem to care. Is he able to charm his teacher out of a demerit?

Dylan leans against the wall outside of my classroom. "I can't believe I'm the one saying this, but you're going to have to tell them the truth, eventually. Lying to your uncles...heck, lying to Jude...it'll come back to bite you. Let them deal with their own issues."

A morality lesson from Dylan? "I've seen how Jude deals with his issues. Plus, Sheldon's pretty upset with me right now. I think I'll give him some time to cool off first."

Dylan grimaces. "Problem is you're a terrible liar, and at some point they're going to bust you. Then they're going to be furious at you. What are you going to do when your uncles find out?"

"I'll just make sure they don't."

CHAPTER EIGHT

– Lucy Walker

Camille perches on the stairs leading to Marcus's apartment as Marcus and I enter the foyer after school. She's early.

Her gaze falls to our entwined hands. "Hello, Gabriel. Lucy."

Marcus shakes his head.

She flushes, her hands twisting on her lap. "Marcus...sorry."

"Hello, Camille," he replies. I can't blame him for not calling her Mom.

"Hi," I say, still unsure what to call her.

Camille studies Marcus, absorbing every detail. Thirteen years have passed. Is she comparing the grownup version of her son to the memory of the child she left behind? The tension between them is thick and uncomfortable. I don't belong in their conversation. "I'll let you two talk." I try to pull my hand free.

Marcus tightens his grip. "I want you to stay. Let's go upstairs."

Camille smiles at me. At least I think that's what her expression is supposed to be. Part of me feels sorry for her. I know she's trying, and I see the strain on her face, but there's another part of me that keeps wondering how she could have abandoned her son.

We file upstairs to my boyfriend's apartment. Camille and Marcus sit on opposite ends of the couch, their posture stiff. I sit in the chair, relieved to have some distance from the intense emotions rolling off of them.

"Thank you for agreeing to see me again," Camille says. She turns to him, her hands clasped on her lap. Her nails are cut short, and the cuticles are clean, not picked and ragged like mine. Embarrassed, I tuck my hands between my knees.

"I needed time to think," Marcus responds. He glances at her, his expression impassive.

On second thought, I wish I were sitting next to Marcus, so I could slide my hand into his.

Camille scoots a little closer to Marcus. She reaches out to him. "I'm sorry, Marcus. You know that, don't you?"

Marcus glances at her outstretched fingers. His hands remain where they are, one on the arm of the couch and the other on his thigh. "I don't understand. Why now?"

Camille's eyes shift from Marcus to me. Her face tightens, and I bristle at the hostility I see there. "I told you," she says.

Marcus pushes himself from the couch and crosses the room to the window. He focuses on something outside. I remember the two times I met Jude here. I did the same thing, using it as an excuse to put some space between us. "Yes, I know. My dad—*stepdad*—died. You promised him you would stay away until then."

"I wanted to come back sooner, years ago, but he wouldn't

allow it," she says the words quickly, urgently. "You have to believe me, Gabriel."

Marcus stiffens. "Now Garret wants to meet me." He snorts and shakes his head. I'm sure he's got a lot of pain going on inside, but I don't want Marcus to push his mother away, especially not before he knows her full story or before he gets a chance to meet his father. I would give anything to have talked to Momma once more before she died.

"Marcus," I say gently, perched on the edge of my seat. "If you don't meet with him, you could regret it later."

Marcus glances at me, his arms crossed over his chest.

"I love you, Marcus. I promise I will try to make it up to you," Camille says, her voice pleading. "More than anything, I hope one day that you can forgive me."

Marcus stands rooted to the spot, his jaw set stubbornly. Camille watches him with her hands on her lap, waiting. The silence is unbearable.

Camille sighs. "Garret wants to speak with you. Are you open to that at least?"

He glares at her. "Let's go back to the reason you left all those years ago."

Camille's face freezes. "Marcus, you have to understand."

He narrows his eyes at her. "Understand what exactly?"

"There were several attacks. Protectors were being hunted and slaughtered. Three in one year." She lets the words hang in the air for a moment before continuing. "As the next in line to lead the clan, Garret was a target. He didn't want you in harm's way."

"But you left with him." Marcus's expression darkens.

"Not initially." Camille steps around his statement. "Even though we were engaged to be married at the time, I wasn't permitted to go. As a mundane—*a human*—I was left behind."

Mundane? Even the word *human* causes her lips to curl in disgust. Camille catches my look of surprise before I can hide it and pauses. Her gaze lingers on me for a moment before she returns her attention to Marcus.

Marcus rubs his eyes with the heels of his hands. "You joined him later. What changed?"

Camille squirms. She pushes her hair from her face with an unsteady hand. Immediately, I feel for her. Just as fast, I wonder if it's possible to fake that gesture, her vulnerability. Camille holds her hair back, the cords of her neck straining, struggling with what she's going to say next.

"Garret had an opportunity to become head of the clan. It was an opportunity of a lifetime. A position of honor and power." A gleam flashes in her eyes—defiance? Did she feel the clan slighted Garret, that he should've had this position earlier?

"He had the ability to change the laws, so that protectors and mun—*humans* could be together. We could marry." Camille lets the words sink in, words that mean so much more to her than to Marcus. She chose Garret over her own son.

A stab of anger flares inside of me.

"I was only going to be gone a short while." She tries to convince Marcus. "I planned to come back for you."

Marcus narrows his gaze at her. "But you didn't."

Camille's gaze falls to her lap. Her fingers pick at the fabric of her jeans. "There was a constant threat of attacks against protectors. Garret felt it was best for you to remain outside of the clan."

Marcus's breaths come out in ragged, short bursts. "Outside of the clan," he echoes, a wild look in his eyes. "Did you agree with him that it was *best* for me to remain outside of the clan?"

"I...I..." Camille's mouth snaps closed.

"Let me ask you a question, *Mother*. How do you think it felt the first time my wings ripped their way out of my back?"

Camille curls into the corner of the couch, wrapping her arms around herself as if wounded.

Marcus rakes his fingers through his hair. He paces while remaining on the opposite side of the room, as if there's an invisible barrier between him and Camille.

"What did you think my stepdad was going to do when he found out I was a monster? Give me flying lessons?" His voice is raw, as the fiery words claw their way from his throat.

"It was the wrong decision. I'm so sorry."

"Why now? And don't tell me it's because my stepdad died." Marcus's face turns red. "I assume Dad told you he dumped me at St. Pat's several years ago, gave you Father Bill's number. Why didn't you come for me then?"

"Marcus, please..." she chokes out, about to rise from the couch and go to him.

Marcus gives her a death stare, and she stops, sinking back onto the couch. Her shoulders hunch, and she lowers her eyes. I watch him, the way he's perched on the balls of his feet, leaning toward her, holding his breath. I realize I'm holding mine, too.

"A protector—one who chose a life outside of the clan—was

slaughtered." Her voice gains strength. "That's never happened before. He should've been safe." She pushes herself off the couch. "I couldn't risk that happening to you. I needed to find you, make sure you were safe and..."

Marcus teeters, waiting. My chest burns, my breath held captive.

"To convince you to join us."

The air rushes from my lungs. Frozen, I watch Marcus for what feels like a very long time. Stars dance across my vision. With a heave, I fill my lungs with air. Camille keeps talking, but I no longer hear her.

My suspicions are correct. She's come to take Marcus away.

CHAPTER NINE

– Lucy Walker –

"Why did your stepdad forbid your mom to visit?" I ask Marcus.

Our jean-clad legs are intertwined as we lay on his bed, our faces inches apart on his pillow. Marcus twirls a lock of my hair around his fingers. He brings it to his nose and inhales. I trace the small scar above his lip with my finger. Does Camille know about the rumors spread by the boys who saw Marcus morph his first time? About all the fights?

Does she know anything about him? I catch sight of his guitar propped in the corner of his bedroom, below a poster of The Black Keys. Does she know he's a musician?

"I think my stepdad knew she wasn't going to come back. He was saving himself—and me—from spending our days waiting and hoping, like a couple of pathetic dogs with our noses pressed against the front window."

When he puts it like that, I get it. Momma refused to talk about my father, but it didn't prevent me from spending years wondering when he was going to show up and rescue us.

We fall silent for a little while, both of us lost in thought. If I put myself in Marcus's shoes, I'm not sure what I'd need to work through first, the resentment or the joy.

I swallow my own fear, pushing away the feeling of inevitability that Marcus may leave me to go with his family. He's always been here for me. Now it's my turn to be here for him. If he wants to go, I shouldn't stop him, should I?

"How did you know your mother loved you?" he asks suddenly. "Did she tell you? I mean, I know she had a lot of problems and wasn't very affectionate, but did she kiss you goodnight sometimes and tell you she loved you? Did she hug you on your way out the door to school and say it then?"

The questions catch me by surprise. It takes a moment to process, to gather the answers out of the mental vault where I store most of my memories of Momma. We were venturing into painful territory. If it was anyone else, I would have shut down or changed the subject.

"I'm not sure she did love me. She hated Jude, and I was a constant reminder of him." Unable to meet his gaze, I study the wall over Marcus's shoulder. "Sometimes on my birthday she would tell me she loved me. There were a few times while she was drunk when she would hug me and say it, but I don't count those times." I dare to peek at him and find his eyes glued to my face. The level of intensity causes me to gulp. "But Gram did all of those things you mentioned. During my summers here, she tucked me into bed and kissed me goodnight every single night. She made my favorite desserts and hung my drawings on the fridge. She told me she loved me more than once a day, as if trying to make up for Momma."

Marcus nods thoughtfully. "With my dad—stepdad—he never really said the words, but he would do things. When I got an A on a test, he would pat me on the back and take me out for a burger or a hot fudge sundae. When I loaded the dishwasher and took out the trash all month without having to be asked, he would take me to a movie or a ballgame." Marcus screws his face up tight. This time there's no pain in his eyes, just curiosity. "Stuff like that. To me, that was love."

I spent fifteen years wondering about my father. Dreaming about him. Praying he would find us and help us. Jude may not be the father I dreamt about, but I no longer have to wonder. It's like I was holding my breath all those years and I have finally been able to exhale. I close my eyes against the pain that surges in my chest.

"You have to meet him," I whisper.

"What?" His tone is knife sharp.

"Garret." My voice gathers strength. I can't think of myself. I have to think about Marcus. He deserves to know his father, to be loved. I don't want him to waste time wondering, and I don't want him to have regrets. I open my eyes and give him my most reassuring smile.

"I'm having a hard enough time with Camille." Marcus says curtly. "I'm not ready to face him right now."

Something inside of me snaps. "You know what? My dad wasn't there for me, either, but at least your dad is on the side of good. My dad's a frickin' demon, and I met him and put up with him and now I have to go to his house on Saturday for demon training. What do you have to complain about? What if this is a limited time opportunity? Maybe he's only here for a week or two. You owe it to yourself to meet him. Otherwise, the regret and the 'what ifs' will haunt you forever."

Marcus pushes himself upright and swings his legs over the bed. "Yeah, that worked so well for you, didn't it?"

I take a deep breath, then sit up. "Don't bring Jude into this."

"You brought him up, not me. And on the subject of Jude, when were you going to tell me about demon training?"

My mouth falls open.

"Let me guess." Marcus's voice is sweet as saccharine. "Dylan's going to be there."

"Don't change the subject." Did I really forget to tell him about training with Jude? Then again, when would I have told him? We've barely seen each other. I try to remember the point I was trying to make. "You need to meet with Garret."

"Sounds like Jude's getting his wish. When are you going to wake up and realize this is his ultimate goal? You and Dylan, together, and me out of the picture?"

I jump off of his bed and fling my arms out to my sides. "It's demon training, Marcus, not some twisted love fest."

"Keep telling yourself that, Lucy. Give it a couple of weeks. We'll see where things stand."

Angry tears burn my eyes as I storm from his bedroom, slamming the door behind me.

CHAPTER TEN

– Lucy Walker –

"I feel sick," Dylan mutters as he pulls to a stop at the massive gate outside Jude's creepy Lake Forest mansion.

"Something you ate?" I ask sardonically.

Dylan's mouth twists into a grimace as he surveys the house. "I think it has more to do with the fact that Jude's really bad for my health—yours, too. I spend a lot of time wishing he would just disappear. Then we could put everything behind us like a bad dream."

My eyes are glued to the dark gray monstrosity beyond the bars of the wrought-iron gate. I remember vividly the night of homecoming. The attack of the crows, their sharp beaks manically pecking my face, neck, and shoulders. Struggling to breathe as Seamus sent me soaring over the roof's ledge where I slammed into a tree. The sound of crunching as the back of my skull made contact with the solid, gnarly trunk. The branches tearing at my skin as I fell.

I wrap my arms around myself, so Dylan won't see me tremble.

"Let's get this over with." Dylan lowers his window and buzzes the house. Seconds later the gate clicks and opens.

Dylan and I fall silent as we drive up the entrance. I peer out the windows at the trees, looking for small dark shapes with red eyes. I know the evil crows aren't there anymore, but it still makes the back of my neck prickle.

Turn around, I want to tell Dylan. Let's go to the mall. Or the dentist. Heck, I'll go play football with him. Anywhere but here.

We come to a stop in front of the house. I'm paralyzed by the boulder-sized fear in my gut.

Dylan grabs my hand, his expression grim. "If things get out of control, we leave. Not one of us, both of us. We watch each other's backs. Okay?"

A loud thudding noise fills my ears, a heartbeat out of sync with my own. I nod vigorously and squeeze his hand. "I promise."

We exit the car and approach the front door. I'm relieved the shapeshifting Rottweilers aren't here. I'm not sure if it's a sign we've passed some sort of test or if Jude is simply trying to make us feel welcome.

I press the doorbell and glance at Dylan. I haven't talked to Aiden about Dylan's powers. Have any other unusual incidents occurred since the basketball game? Will there come a day when Dylan won't have my back against Jude? The thought makes me shudder.

Jude answers the door himself, a task usually delegated to his minions.

His eyes sparkle as he invites us in. I've seen him this happy one other time, when I stayed here briefly to recuperate after Seamus nearly killed me.

"Lucy and Dylan. So glad you could make it."

As if we had a choice.

He opens the door wide and beckons us in with a grand sweeping gesture. "Lunch is being served in the kitchen. I've made some of your favorites."

Dylan aims a curious look my way as we follow Jude down the hall. I think I can guess what he's thinking. How does Jude know our favorite anything?

A cold shiver races over my skin as we walk past the dining room. The ghost of my nearly dead self wraps her arms around me. I flinch at the sight of the mahogany table. Visions of my limp, bleeding body come flooding back to me. Jude's blood-soaked sweater propped under my head as Persephone spread some herbal gunk on my skin. The entire group: Persephone, Henry, Jude, Aiden, and Dylan circled around me as they chanted. Jude reached behind my head, cradled it as he worked his own healing magic on my cracked skull.

My legs give out, and I gasp as I relive the agony of that magic.

"Lucy!" Dylan catches me before I hit the ground.

Jude reaches my other side in an instant.

"You okay?" Dylan asks.

Jude's eyes—dark and intense—burn into mine. He expresses concern much the same way he expresses anger; he tries to read me. His gaze flickers toward the table then back at me. "Let's get her away from this room."

Jude is cruel, but every once in a while he surprises me with his understanding.

61

They each grab one of my arms. I try to push them away, embarrassed. "I can walk."

The two of them lead me toward the kitchen. I like this room. It's brighter and prettier than any other room in the house. An elaborate mural covers the wall to my right. How did I miss that before? It looks like one of those vintage French posters that are so popular. A plump man throws his hands out to his sides as if he's introducing circus acts to an excited crowd. The whole scene is loaded with rich shades of blues, reds, and yellows. On the other side of the room, the windowsill which runs the length of four spotless windows, contains pots filled with basil, oregano, cilantro, rosemary, and thyme. The smells remind me of Gram.

Once I'm settled at the stainless-steel topped table, Dylan scoots his chair close to me and sits down. Jude examines me again, as if to be sure I won't break or keel over. Then he retrieves two casserole pans from the oven. He sets them on top of the stove before he reaches back into the oven and pulls out a baking sheet full of crusty bread. The most amazing smells fill the room. Tomato sauce, basil, oregano, garlic, and cheese.

"You cook?" The words are loaded with more surprise than I intended.

Jude smiles wickedly. "Do you think I only spend my days plotting the demise of humanity?"

I blush and duck my head a little because yeah, I really only think of Jude as a killing machine.

Dylan's mouth falls open as we watch Jude squeeze lemons into a bowl, drizzle in some olive oil, add chopped basil, garlic, salt, and pepper, then whisk the ingredients together. He tosses the homemade dressing onto a large salad, then doles the salads onto small plates and delivers them to the table. He takes a seat at the head of the table.

Dylan and I look at each other, baffled. A demon who cooks?

As if reading my mind, Dylan mutters under his breath, "This would make for a great new series on Food Network. Ladies and gentlemen, The Demon Gourmet."

"It would give Hell's Kitchen and Cutthroat Kitchen a run for their money," I say.

We both burst out laughing.

Without pulling his attention away from his plate, Jude adds, "For the record, I would win. Now let's eat our salads while the lasagna rests."

Lasagna needs to rest?

I stab the lettuce and a tiny grape tomato. The dressing tastes delicious. The texture and flavor of the lettuce mix are more delicate than what I'm used to. There are garbanzo beans and little slivers of red onion. I try to take another forkful, but my plate is empty. I look up, coming out of my daze and see Jude and Dylan are only half done.

Jude takes my plate to the counter, refills it and returns to the table.

Is he still trying to convince me to move in with him? I thought I made it clear last time. I'll never leave my uncles.

After he and Dylan finish their salads, Jude rises from the table to remove the empty plates. He returns with a larger plate filled with layers of vegetables, noodles, sauce, and cheese oozing all over the plate. Buttery garlic bread, too.

"Yours is vegetarian." He nods as he delivers the plate in front of me. A moment later, he plunks down plates of meat lasagna for Dylan and himself.

Jude went to the trouble to make two different meals for us? "Th-thank you. This looks great," I say.

We eat in silence. I try to think of something to say, but come up with nothing. Dylan focuses on his plate, ignoring Jude. I stifle a smile when I notice Dylan devouring his food. It's impossible to hate the meal. Jude's a great cook.

Suddenly, a chunk of pasta lodges in my throat. I shouldn't be enjoying this, as if the three of us are one big happy family. We're not. Dylan and I are here against our will. My family—Sheldon, Bernard, and Marcus—are over at the three-flat.

"So, what's the plan for today?" I ask Jude stiffly. "Are we going up to the roof?"

Jude takes the cloth napkin from his lap and wipes his mouth. "No. Today we'll be working out back."

My insides tingle. "Doing what?"

"You and I are going to work on fireballs."

"But I already know how to throw them," I point out. "I want to learn something new."

"You're too emotional. You need to learn control. To engage and respond with confidence. Then I will teach you tactics." Jude turns his attention to Dylan. "You will work on your fighting skills."

Dylan leans back in his chair. "What? I don't get to throw fireballs?"

"Have you accidentally hurled any fireballs? Have you felt uncontrollable heat in your fingers, your hands?"

"No."

"Then mortal fighting skills will have to do for now," Jude says, smirking.

Dylan rolls his eyes but follows Jude and me out the back door.

The term *yard* doesn't do it justice. The grassy expanse that runs the length of Jude's property line is the size of St. Aquinas's football field. It has fewer trees than the front; although, they're still the giant, knotted kind, resembling petrified ogres. Chirping birds draw my attention to the treetops. Common sparrows. Common is good.

An all-too-familiar voice calls out, "You rookie demons ready to get dirty?"

Aiden. *Why is he here?* Aiden helped save me, and he's a good pseudo brother to Marcus, but I don't trust him.

The feeling is mutual, and he greets me with an unfriendly smile. "This should be fun."

I narrow my eyes at him then call out to Jude, "Please tell me I get to throw fireballs at Aiden."

Jude turns to Dylan, ignoring my sarcasm. "Aiden will be your sparring partner."

"Lucky you," I say to Dylan.

I watch as Aiden leads Dylan to the opposite end of the yard. If he hurts Dylan, I'll turn him to burnt toast.

"Ow!" I slap my hand to my face to smother the burning spark Jude shot at me. "Hey!"

"Do I have your attention?" Jude asks.

I rub at the sting. "You know, a normal father would just yell at me. Not try to burn my face off."

"We are not normal. Conjure a fireball."

My mouth falls open. I've never been asked to create a fireball on command. *This is cool!*

Across the yard, I hear bodies slam together. I flinch. The urge to turn and check on Dylan is strong, but Jude's expression stops me.

"A fireball, Lucy. *Now.*"

I focus my mental energy on Aiden. If anyone can inspire my anger, it's him. What if he hurts Dylan? My muscles quiver as heat flushes through my body. I hold up my palm. *Nothing.* Bodies slam behind me. Dylan swears at Aiden.

Need something more. I close my eyes and focus on a memory. Dylan in a hospital bed barely alive after Jude awakened his powers.

My fingertips start to tingle. Then my palms. I wiggle my fingers as the sensation runs back and forth, back and forth, growing stronger. I detect a low hum, and the current moves along my arms, to my palms and fingers and back again. I recall Marcus in his stone form on Jude's roof the night of the homecoming dance. Angry tears burn behind my closed eyelids.

"You want him, there he is," Jude said dryly. *"Take him. Just know that he will never be human again."*

Why not? My eyes darted from Jude to the gargoyle and back again. He was stone before, and it wasn't permanent then. What did Jude do to him?

"Turn him back!" I cried, my heart pounding painfully in my chest. Every nerve ending in my body screamed.

"Better take him soon, Lucy." Jude leveled his dark glare at

66

me. "I would hate to see what would happen if someone knocked him off the roof. My guess is he would shatter into a million pieces."

I gasp as fury rips through me. On instinct, I extend one arm in front of my body. I open my eyes, oddly startled by the fireball balancing on my right palm.

Jude suppresses a grin. "You want to throw that at me, don't you?"

I purse my lips and focus on the fireball, trying to gain control over my anger, but it's too strong.

"You nearly destroyed Marcus." I glare at him. "You tortured Dylan."

Jude's eyes darken. "The gargoyle is not worthy of your concern. As for Dylan, what I did was necessary to trigger his powers."

I shake my head, my body trembling with anger. The fireball glows yellow and red in my palm. Jude is only ten feet away.

"I begged you to turn Marcus back, but you wouldn't. It wasn't until *you* needed him that you changed him. Why?"

The fingertips on my left-hand tingle. Then my palm. I welcome the fiery sensation with dark pleasure. I roll it over my palm, bounce it from one hand to the other. I pull at the flame with my fingertips until it separates.

I reveal both palms. Two fireballs.

Jude ignores my question. "Better. Still too emotional, but you're starting to exhibit some ability to conjure."

"What the hell do you think you're doing?" Aiden roars behind me.

I spin around. Aiden's got Dylan face down on the ground, his arms pinned behind his back. Like a gunshot, I take off. I reach them in seconds and hurl the fireballs at Aiden, one after the other. He jumps off Dylan, effectively dodging both of my attacks. Dylan climbs to his feet, red-faced.

"What's your problem?" Dylan shoves Aiden.

Aiden steps toward Dylan, stops halfway, and looks at Jude as if called. Can Jude speak telepathically to Aiden, too? Aiden jabs Dylan in the chest with his finger. "The next time you try to remove my arm from its socket, I will tear you to pieces."

I tug Dylan by the arm in an attempt to break their killer eye contact. "What happened?"

Dylan's entire body twitches. His skin is hot to the touch.

"He attacked me," Dylan snarls. He lunges toward Aiden and I jump between them.

"Dylan, you can sit out the rest of the session. You're not ready to learn what Aiden has to teach you," Jude calls out.

"That's a load of crap!" Dylan yells.

"Lucy, we're not done with your session. Turn around. Your next target has just arrived," Jude says.

Dylan and I both whirl around as a large white-tailed deer enters the yard. It's a buck with eight points on its antlers. His reddish-brown coat twitches.

A block of ice settles in my stomach. I peer over my shoulder at Jude. "You expect me to kill it?"

He glances at his watch. "Today, Lucy."

How does killing a cute, furry animal help me train to kill demons?

"Lucy! Take it down or I will, just enough to maim it, so Dylan can snap its neck."

"What is it with people always telling me what to do?" My insides grow hotter; my heart beats faster. "If it's not Persephone, my uncles, or Marcus, it's *you*!"

"Exactly," Dylan growls in agreement.

I meet Dylan's gaze. The anger on his face mirrors my own.

He feels what I feel.

Dylan's irises turn black. Similar to Jude's but without menace. He holds his hand out to me. Power he wants to share with me. I grasp his hand. An energy, invisible and strong, moves between us. It's like drinking ten Mountain Dews, but better. An adrenaline rush courses through my veins. Is this what Dylan felt when he played basketball with his friends? The power stokes me. I feel...unstoppable.

Jude and Aiden argue, but I pay no attention. Dylan squeezes my hand, and another surge of energy courses through me. My heartbeat pulses through my body. I close my eyes as the throbbing sensation grows stronger. The sudden urge...the *need* to get rid of all this energy, this anger, takes over.

My eyes fly open. I want to *destroy* something. A hot, electrical current zings along my arms. I hold up my hand, palm side up. I grin at the large fireball resting there.

It's the biggest fireball I've ever made. I beam at Dylan.

"What are you going to do with it?" he asks.

Need to get rid of all this energy.

Take down the deer, Lucy.

I look around. Jude's eyes boring into me.

Get out of my head! I tell him.

I hurl the fireball at one of the ogre-like trees across the football field yard. It's enough to startle the deer who takes off, its tail raised in alarm. One word repeats in my brain as I focus on the tree. *Burn...Burn...Burn.* It takes a moment before I realize Dylan and I are chanting the words in unison. The knotted limbs snap and sizzle as they're engulfed in flames. Did my fireball catch that quickly? Or was it my magic, fueled by Dylan? I can't turn away. I'm enthralled by the blaze of red, orange, and yellow. The heat soothes me.

"Beautiful," Dylan whispers. I simply nod. There's no better word to describe it.

Fingers snap in front of my eyes, jolting me. Jude waves his hand through the air, and the fire is extinguished. Smoke swirls from the charred branches. Dylan releases my hand. The happiness and warmth are gone. My body suddenly feels like it's filled with lead. I sag against the weight of it.

"You're out of control. Both of you." Jude stares us down, his voice sharp as steel. "I asked you to do one thing. One thing. You disobeyed me."

There's no way I'm killing Bambi's daddy.

Jude yanks us both by the arm, blasting us with electrical currents so powerful my knees buckle. I fall to the ground.

"Let me go!" I try to pull my arm free, but I'm no match for Jude.

Jude yanks hard, dragging me until my legs start to function again.

"A load of crap!" Dylan mutters, his voice thick with fatigue.

I catch a whiff of burnt hair and realize Jude singed all the hair off my left arm.

CHAPTER ELEVEN

– Lucy Walker –

It's eight o'clock by the time Dylan pulls up behind Marcus's car at the three-flat. He meets me at the passenger side and pulls me from the car. We both slouch against the closed door.

"That was surreal," Dylan says, rubbing his eyes. "Aiden and I spent the day beating the crap out of each other. Do you know how amazing that felt?"

I shake my head. "Jude's right. Half right, anyway. You're out of control."

Dylan flashes a tired smile. "I wasn't the one who torched the tree, little fire starter. Do you think Jude was behind that? Manipulating your emotions?"

"Based on how mad he was, I would say no." I turn to Dylan. "Can you believe Jude was able to drag both of us across his yard? I mean, I'm sort of puny, but you're..." I gesture to Dylan's buff physique, "not. He's got superhuman strength."

Dylan frowns. "We should probably keep that in mind before we disobey him in the future."

I recall Aiden's furious expression before I hurled fireballs at him. "Speaking of scary. You need to be careful. I think you made an enemy today."

Dylan's eyebrows pull together. "Things started out really well. Aiden taught me some awesome techniques. I now know it's not just about brute strength, but also how I maneuver. It's about skill. Strategy."

There's no missing the excitement in his voice. "Then why were you trying to take him apart?"

Dylan crosses his arms over his chest. He's silent for a long moment, and I wonder if he'll tell me.

"He warned me to keep things platonic with you, that he has Marcus's back. Basically, he told me to stay away from you or else." He glances at me. "For the record, it wasn't my intention to try to rip his arm off. Things just...escalated."

My mouth falls open. I can't believe Aiden would stick his nose into my relationship with Marcus. Part of me is glad to see him acting like a real brother to Marcus, but another part of me feels indignant. Who does Aiden think he is, doubting my loyalty?

Is it possible Aiden caught Dylan watching me? Dylan does that sometimes. I ignore it. Dylan understands I'm in love with Marcus. Problem is Aiden won't ignore that.

"I should get inside." I push off his car.

Dylan pulls me into a hug, his hands rubbing my back. Just as I'm about to pull away, my arms and legs start to tingle. I jerk myself out of his embrace.

"Did you feel that?" I ask, startled.

Dylan nods. "Probably just a weird hiccup from earlier."

All those swirling emotions while Dylan and I connected at

Jude's house. Was it simply a matter of our demon powers merging? Or was it something else? "Yeah, probably," I eventually agree.

"Take it easy, and I'll see you at school on Monday." He walks around the car and pauses. "Think about what I said earlier. If you and Katie need a ride to school, call me."

"I'll get back to you on that. Thanks."

Dylan salutes me before ducking into his car. I wave, then make my way up the sidewalk, not sure what to make of that strange energy exchange. Is it possible it's some kind of demon thing, similar to Jude and me zapping each other?

A figure emerges from the shadows. I jump backward and swear under my breath when I realize it's Marcus.

"You really need to announce yourself or something." I press my hand against my pounding heart, willing it to slow down. I haven't seen or talked to Marcus since we argued. Not even a text.

Marcus glances down the street, in the direction of Dylan's departing car. His arms remain slack at his sides.

"Were you at Jude's this whole time?"

I nod. "It was exhausting and annoying." I decide not to tell him about the deer Jude wanted me to kill.

Marcus grimaces. "I'll bet."

My blood pressure rises. "Hey, Aiden was there, too. You can check with him if you don't believe me."

His lips press into a tight smile. "I believe you. I just don't like it."

I tuck my hairless arm behind my back. "There are lots of things I don't like. Trust me."

"Like when your boyfriend acts like a jerk?"

I take a step back, surprised. "Yes, that."

"I'm sorry. I'd tell you I'm struggling with a bunch of stuff right now, that I feel like I'm sinking, but I don't want to give you any excuses."

"I want to help, Marcus. Let me be there for you."

Marcus wraps his arms around me and gently pulls me to him while his lips brush against my forehead. I slide my arms around his waist and sigh.

"I've missed you." I snuggle against him and inhale the complex scent that is distinctly Marcus. A mix of mint and musk and a hint of something sweet.

Marcus pulls away and leads me to the porch where we both take a seat.

"I met with Camille again today. We had lunch then went for a walk along the lakefront."

"Were you off work today?" I ask.

"Yes, but I went to St. Pat's anyway. I took Camille to meet Father Bill."

My whole body stiffens. It took months before I got to meet Father Bill. His mom comes to town, and she meets him within a week?

"Does Camille know your history with Father Bill?" I try hard not to sound jealous, but I'm not sure I'm successful.

"I told her." Marcus doesn't take my hand. I consider taking his, but then I notice the two inches of space between our bodies. Marcus normally presses his body to mine whenever we're near each other. Is he angry about my long day with Dylan? Or does this have to do with Camille?

I force myself to sound upbeat. "Did you have a good time together?"

Marcus plucks a leaf from the step and twirls it between his fingers. I catch his smile in profile. There's no happiness in it. "During our walk, Camille filled me in on her life. She and Garret moved around a lot. They lived in Alaska and Vancouver for a while. Switzerland, too."

"Switzerland? Sounds exotic."

"Camille loved the chocolate there. She said my grandmother, who was French, used to complain about how bad American chocolate was, but that the Swiss knew how to do it right."

"I never knew you were French."

He laughs and his body relaxes. "When I was little and had trouble sleeping, my mother used to sing me this silly French song."

I wrap my hands around his arm and snuggle against him. "Sing it to me?"

He laughs again. "It's a stupid song, but I used to beg her to sing it over and over."

"Come on. I want to hear it."

"If you laugh..." he warns.

"I won't. I swear." To make my point, I draw an invisible cross over my heart with my fingers.

"Okay."

I don't believe him. I've asked him to play his guitar for me, to sing for me, and he never does. He's private when it comes to his music. But sure enough, his rich voice rings out as he sings the song. I make out only a few words, like *alouette*, *plumerai*, and *le bec*.

75

I hold it in until he's done, then I burst out laughing.

"You said you wouldn't..." he says. After a moment, he bursts out laughing, too.

The sound jars me. I try to recall the last time I heard him laugh, saw the brightness in his eyes. "It's the song. I recognize it. I heard it years ago, but I don't know what it's about," I say.

Marcus rolls his eyes and nods. "It's a dumb song about the body parts of a bird. Something about plucking the bird before cooking it."

"Seriously? She sang it to you to help you sleep? Nightmares anyone?"

"Never. Probably because I didn't know any French." He chuckles again, but it ends with a sigh. "It sounded fun the way my mom sang it to me." Marcus shrugs, and I sense his happiness is fading.

I imagine Marcus as a four-year-old, his mother lying next to him, stroking his hair as she sang to him. "I can't believe you remember it."

Marcus twirls the leaf in his fingers, then tears it in half and tosses it. "It's the last memory I have of her." He blinks, and the beautiful brightness is gone from his eyes.

"What's the plan?" I ask, trying to sound casual. "Is she—are they—moving back here? Or just visiting?"

"I don't know." Marcus frowns as he stares at the sidewalk. "Camille's going to arrange for me to meet Garret. After that, I don't know." He sniffs the air. He turns to me and raises a handful of my hair to his nose. "It's not my imagination. Why do you smell like smoke?"

Uh-oh. "It's nothing."

"When I ask Aiden about it, will he agree that it's nothing?" Marcus asks.

I tell him about torching the tree and how Dylan and I merged our powers.

His expression turns stony.

"There was this deer, you see and I didn't want to kill it—but as far as Dylan and me? That's nothing." Why is this coming out all wrong?

"Your hug with Dylan at the curb when he dropped you off? That was nothing, too, right?" I hate his gruff tone.

"We're friends, Marcus. We hug. It's not like when you and I hug."

How can I explain to him how much I relish hugs, whether they're from him, Dylan, my uncles, even Dylan's younger brother and sister, Ethan and Brandi? I need to know people care about me, that I'm not alone.

"I think hugs mean something different to Dylan," Marcus says.

I recall the feelings coursing through me earlier, while Dylan and I were merging our powers. I ignored it then, but could Marcus be right?

No. It was all about our powers. Marcus is wrong.

"Dylan knows how I feel about you."

"Why can't you and Dylan train on different days?" Marcus pushes. "You have different powers, so it makes sense."

"But Dylan is my buffer. It's not like I need protecting from Jude, but I don't particularly like being at his house alone."

"I'll come with you," Marcus offers.

I give him a wide-eyed look. "Are you crazy? Jude's effect on you is too painful. And let's face it, he likes the effect he has on you."

"I can take it."

I shake my head. "I would spend the whole time worrying about you. I'd get nothing done. Jude would get mad."

"Lucy..."

"Marcus, you don't get it. It was Jude who dictated Dylan and I train together, not me." I'm running out of arguments.

"I can't win with you, can I?" Marcus hops up from the porch and storms off toward his car. "Just forget it."

"Marcus, wait! What is that supposed to mean?"

He pivots on his heel and glares at me. "Meaning I'll be spending a lot of time with Camille, so go do whatever you want with whomever you want."

Is this his way of breaking up with me? "Wait, Marcus!"

His car roars to life, and he peels away from the curb.

I rush inside and slam the foyer door behind me. I gulp for air and blink away tears. Inside the apartment, my uncles watch TV—*were* watching TV. Now, their eyes are glued on me. I wave to them as I race to my room. "I'm going to bed."

"Trouble in paradise?" Sheldon says to Bernard, not bothering to lower his voice. "Maybe now she'll reconsider the vacation."

It takes superhuman effort not to slam my door. My uncles have a strict No Door Slamming policy. I really don't need Sheldon's sarcasm on top of everything else.

I pace the small space of my bedroom. All of a sudden Marcus's long-lost mother shows up, and she's golden? And where does he get off making all sorts of assumptions about Dylan?

A little trust would be nice.

I change into my pajamas and go to the bathroom to wash up. After I brush my teeth, I return to the living room to kiss my uncles goodnight.

"Did you and Dylan have a fight?" Bernard asks, muting the TV.

As if they didn't already know.

"No. Marcus and I did after I got home," I say glumly.

Sheldon and Bernard exchange a look.

"It's not what you're thinking. It had nothing to do with Dylan," I lie.

I kiss and hug them stiffly before I return to my room.

Sheldon calls after me. "Persephone stopped by. She said the two of you are supposed to get together tomorrow. Continue that closet project you were working on."

I press my hands to my temples. *Crap.* I forgot about Persephone. It doesn't matter. Marcus isn't going to want to spend the day we me tomorrow, anyway.

"Thanks for the reminder," I call back.

Once in bed, I stare at the ceiling. My freak-out mellows a little. Marcus and I had our second fight in a week. Is it possible he'll fall out of love with me?

Tap...tap...tap...

The sound is almost too faint to hear. It's not the rapid-fire pecking of the Jude's crazy red-eyed crows.

Tap...tap...tap...

I jump out of bed, my heart swelling with hope, and fling open my window. Without waiting for Marcus to say a word, I wave him inside. We stand there, face to face.

I speak first. "I'm sorry."

"For what?" Marcus asks.

I search my mind for an answer. For going off on him while he's dealing with the sudden reappearance of his mother? For not supporting him more? For hugging Dylan back?

Marcus exhales heavily and steps closer to me. "Lucy, you don't have to apologize. You didn't do anything wrong."

"But you left..."

"And I realized I was being a jerk, so I circled back." Marcus takes hold of my hands. "This stuff with my parents, it's got me all messed up. I shouldn't be freaking out about Dylan. I trust you."

"Don't take off like that again," I tell him, my insides so full of air I can't expand my lungs and my voice comes out a whisper. "I thought..." It's not like the world would end without Marcus. Right? My heart squeezes in response.

Marcus sighs. "I'm not going anywhere." He pulls me into his arms.

I swallow the golf ball-sized lump in my throat. Am I that transparent? I've always been able to hide my feelings. Not with him, apparently.

"It was a fight. That's all," Marcus strokes my hair.

The relief is immediate and euphoric. I tug at the collar of his shirt with one hand and pull his face to mine with the other. Our lips meet and I wrap my arms around his neck, pulling him closer still. The idea that I could lose him terrifies me. I kiss him, my desperation igniting something else, a longing deep inside. I groan as Marcus runs his hands along my hips, my back, until they simply clutch me against him.

Our kiss deepens. My fingers run through his hair, down his cheek, to his neck. I recall the night of my birthday when I was blown off the three-flat roof. The night I discovered he had wings. He saved me. He keeps saving me.

Marcus pulls away, his breath ragged. "We need to stop."

My body cries out in protest. "Marcus...no." I hook my fingers through the belt loops on his jeans, preventing him from pulling away further.

"Lucy, I came here to apologize. I said things I didn't mean. And..." Marcus rakes his fingers through his hair. "I want to do this, but I can't."

"You won't lay down with me?"

His eyes grow wide for just a second. "Uh, no. Bad idea."

He winds his fingers through mine and raises them to his lips. He kisses my fingertips. "I love you."

I'll never get tired of hearing that. "I love you, too, but I really wish you'd stay for a while."

Marcus presses his lips to my forehead. "Sweet dreams. We'll see each other tomorrow."

He turns and climbs out the window.

I slump onto my bed. It seemed so easy for him to walk away. My insides continue to churn as I imagine our kiss going further. I envision Marcus lying beside me, his fingers stroking my arm, my hip, giving me shivery goose bumps, before pulling me close.

Grabbing hold of my pillow, I press it to my face to muffle my frustrated groan. I relive our agonizing kiss over and over until I finally fall asleep.

CHAPTER TWELVE

– Lucy Walker –

"I decided that instead of having you bury your nose in your grandmother's books and memorize herbs, you might learn better through practical application." Persephone slides a white mortar and pestle to the center of her countertop. I remember standing at Gram's kitchen counter crushing dried herbs.

A cloud passes over Persephone's face. How many times did she and Gram work together, making potions and casting spells? She must miss Gram as much as I do. Maybe more.

"Today, we're going to assemble a few satchels," she says.

"Like the ones Gram used to make and stick in my dresser drawers?" I had assumed they were homemade potpourri.

Persephone nods. "What herbs are you most curious about?"

Contrary to what Persephone thinks, I actually did spend a lot of time over the past week with my face buried in Gram's books on herbs. "Just two at the moment. Dandelion and bay leaves."

"Okay, tell me why."

I pause, feeling silly all of a sudden. Persephone shows no sign she's going to laugh at me, so I continue. "Bay leaves to give me extra protection against Seamus."

Persephone nods thoughtfully. "Good choice. It's used to rebuff the magic of another supernatural."

"I figure that since Seamus teamed up with his daughter the last time, he's not going to work alone now or in the future. Marcus said demons follow patterns. My guess is he'll team up with someone else. He wants us to think he works solo, but he really doesn't."

Persephone looks at me in surprise. "I like how you think. Now tell me about the dandelion."

"I want the second sight."

She scrunches up her brow as she thinks that over. "For what purpose?"

This time I don't lower my gaze. This has to do with Marcus, and I don't care if she thinks it's crazy. I need to protect him.

"To see if Marcus's mother's intentions are good. I don't know if she's got Marcus's best interests in mind or Garret's, but something doesn't feel right. Maybe the herbs can help me figure it out."

"I feel I'm obligated to tell you this. I don't recommend you stick your nose into Marcus's family. He can handle this himself."

"I don't care," I tell her without blinking. "I've met her—Camille—and I don't trust her. I think she and Garret are up to something." I nibble my bottom lip and stare off for a moment, recalling Camille's sneer when she referenced humans as mundanes. "I don't believe she came here solely because Marcus's stepdad died. It's more than that. They're here for a purpose, and I think it's something big."

Persephone's lips twitch into a smile—a small one—and her eyes sparkle with approval. "Well, then, let's get to work. Your goals are specific, which is helpful. If you practice, strengthen your level of focus, and learn to heighten your awareness, you should have no problem achieving them."

Seriously? Persephone didn't laugh or tell me I'm paranoid. My chest swells with pride and I smile, but the smile quickly slips away. That means Persephone has the same fear. She doesn't trust Camille and Garret, either.

"Go into the pantry and grab the dried dandelion root. I'll show you how to make tea. Then we'll move onto bay leaves."

I do as she instructs, then watch as she dumps bits of dried flowers into the mortar.

"What's that?" I ask.

"Chamomile for the satchels," she grinds the flowers with the pestle, "for you to tuck away in your apartment. It removes hexes," she says, her expression grim. "I think you're right about Seamus. It's time we prepare for whatever heap of trouble is headed our way."

* * * *

After an hour of standing on the packed train on Monday afternoon, my feet hurt. It's another thirty minutes on the bus before I trudge up the sidewalk to my uncles' apartment building. I can hardly wait to get my driver's license. The thing is I need to get my behind-the-wheel time in first with Marcus or Bernard. Every time Sheldon takes me out for a lesson, he spends half the time harping on me about vacation. It will be summer before I'm able to drive myself anywhere.

In the meantime, Katie's all for taking Dylan up on his offer to carpool to school. On days like today, I like the idea, too, but I don't think Marcus would.

"Lucy, can you hold up a moment?"

I hold the foyer door open as Camille jogs up the sidewalk. She looks stylish in a long khaki skirt and a navy and white striped sleeveless top. Her long hair falls loose around her shoulders.

"It's good to see you again." Her smile doesn't reach her eyes.

It's obvious she doesn't like me much, like I'm the competition and Marcus is the prize. That's okay because I don't like her much, either. The nagging feeling is back, too. I ignored it the day Marcus and I met with her in his apartment. I know part of it is jealousy, but there's more to it. It's like I told Persephone. I have a feeling that Camille and Garret are going to cause trouble for Marcus.

I smile sweetly at her, injecting a question in my voice. "You, too, Mrs...Turner?"

"Call me Camille," she says evenly.

I nod.

"When we first met, I assumed you were simply Gabriel— *Marcus's* neighbor. But Marcus tells me it's something more, and it's serious."

I stand a little taller. "It is serious."

"Given your importance in my son's life, I would like to invite you to dinner on Friday. Garret, Marcus's father, will be there as well."

I'm being invited to meet Garret? I assumed Marcus's parents would insist this be a private family matter. Maybe now I can get a sense of what they're up to.

"That's very nice of you," I tell her. "I'll be there."

"Great. We will see you then." She smiles that fake smile again.

We stand there awkwardly for a moment.

"I'd like to see my son now."

My cheeks flush hot, and I scoot out of her way. "Of course. Sorry. I'll see you on Friday."

Camille climbs the stairs, then knocks on Marcus's door. The door opens and I glimpse a sliver of Marcus's profile.

"Hello, Marcus," Camille says. "Can we talk?"

I wonder if he'll take her to the roof, to our spot. I wonder if she's been in his room and if she's seen the posters on his walls. Has Marcus played any of his favorite CDs for her? Does she even know who the Arctic Monkeys or Elvis Costello are? Death Cab for Cutie? Will Marcus spend the whole evening with her?

I take a deep breath and roll out my shoulders. *Chill out, Lucy.* It's his mom, not another girl. I turn and enter my apartment, nearly colliding with Sheldon.

"There're leftovers in the fridge, kiddo. Persephone stopped down looking for you."

After spending half a day with Persephone yesterday, what does she want with me now?

"Where are you going?" I'm surprised to see Sheldon decked out in a suit.

"The play at Steppenwolf. You forgot?"

Bernard rushes into the room, adjusting the knot on his tie. "Don't wait up for us."

86

Sheldon tips his head toward the foyer. "Who was that woman? The one you were just talking to?"

"Were you watching through the peephole?" Bernard accuses with a laugh.

Sheldon's cheeks turn red. "I heard voices."

There's no sense lying to them. It's bad enough I kept Jude a secret. "Marcus's mother."

They look at each other, raised eyebrows on both their faces. Bernard glances at his watch and nudges Sheldon. "Clearly, there's a story there," Bernard says. "But we're running late."

I hug them both on their way out the door. Once they're gone, I change into a T-shirt and a pair of jeans. I reheat leftover stuffed peppers, following it up with two scoops of vanilla ice cream and a handful of pecans. Once I'm totally stuffed and the kitchen is clean, I make a cup of dandelion tea and take it to the living room.

Steam rises from the teacup. I drum my fingers against the coffee table as I wait for it to cool a little. How does this work? Persephone didn't say. Will my dreams contain visions? Deliver clues? Or maybe Uncle Zack will visit me again once I'm asleep and tell me what to do. Wishful thinking. I stifle a yawn and rub my eyes.

As I raise the cup to blow on the hot liquid, the smell assaults my senses. Dirt and mushrooms. *So gross!* What if I add some sugar or mix it with a tea that actually tastes good? No. I can't risk messing this up. I've got to figure out what Camille's up to. *Maybe she just wants a life with her son?* Maybe. And if that's all it is...

My lids droop. *So tired.* Maybe I'll just curl up on the couch, shut my eyes for a few minutes while the tea cools. Then I'll shut off my sense of smell and chug it down.

* * * *

Sunshine teases me awake. Birds *chirp, chirp, chirp.* A lawn mower roars to life. Only the fastidious Mr. Romano would mow his lawn this early on a school day. Fabric tickles my nose. I rub the smooth cottony fabric between my finger and thumb. Peeking out of one eye, I take in the white sheet decorated with bright colored coffee mugs. Compliments of my uncles? I stretch, big and lazy and slide off the couch. Pushing myself off of the floor, I sniff the air and head to the kitchen. No coffee yet? That's strange. A peak at the Golden Gate Bridge wall clock shows ten to six.

"Oh, good. You're up." Bernard rushes into the kitchen, making a beeline for the coffee maker. "What do you want for breakfast?"

I show him the box of cereal in my hand. That's when I notice the bags under his eyes. "Rough night?"

He lets loose an exaggerated yawn then shakes his head as if to clear cobwebs from his brain. "You could say that. What kind of tea were you drinking last night?"

The baby hairs on the back of my neck stand on end. "Chamomile, I think. Why?"

Bernard pulls a mug from the cabinet. "Sheldon finished it off for you. Then he tossed and turned all night, muttering the craziest things in his sleep. Bad dreams. You should avoid that kind in the future."

With my attention focused on filling my bowl with cereal and milk, I say, "I will, thanks. Is Sheldon okay?"

"He's fine. Just tired."

I don't want nightmares. Life is hard enough as it is. There has to be another way to figure out what Marcus's mother is up to.

CHAPTER THIRTEEN

– Lucy Walker –

By the time Friday comes around, I'm a nervous wreck. I'm nearly in tears as I try on the fourth outfit and model it for Bernard and Sheldon.

Sheldon pulls his attention from the computer and tries to take an interest in my wardrobe crisis. The rain forest and screecher monkeys on the monitor suggest he is winning the vacation argument with Bernard. Fortunately, he doesn't bring it up.

"That outfit looks beautiful, too," Sheldon says.

Bernard tosses aside the laundry he's folding when he sees my face. "Lucy, why in the world are you so upset?"

I press my fingers to my temples. "I'm having dinner with Marcus's parents tonight. I need to look respectable, pretty, and smart." I swallow past the painful lump in my throat. "What if they don't like me?" It's a stupid question given that I already know Camille doesn't like me. Despite that I still want to make a good impression.

Bernard takes hold of my hands. Over his shoulder, I catch Sheldon's look of alarm.

"Luce, Marcus adores you. I'm sure his parents will, too." Sheldon rises from his chair and walks over to pat my shoulder, glancing at Bernard nervously. He doesn't get it, but I love him for trying.

"What's the deal with them, anyway?" Sheldon asks, more to Bernard than to me. "I've never seen them before. I don't recall Vera ever mentioning them, either."

Bernard nods, looking equally curious. "Now they show up out of the blue?"

They both focus on me.

There's no way I'm going to explain that Marcus and his dad are protectors. "I don't really know. I guess I'll find out tonight."

"If you want my opinion, I think the purple top and the black pants look lovely on you," Bernard offers. He turns me around and gives me a gentle shove. "Now hurry up. Marcus will be here any minute."

Ten minutes later, the doorbell rings. I'm dressed in record time and rush Marcus out the door before my uncles can interrogate him.

"On a scale of one to ten, how nervous are you?" I ask once we're in the car.

He slumps in his seat. "An eleven. How about you?"

I run my sweaty palms along my slacks. "About the same. You can't even make me feel better by telling me your father will like me. I'm half-demon in case you've forgotten."

Marcus frowns. "Call him Garret, please. Skip Turner was my dad. This man is a stranger." He squeezes my hand. "You're not the enemy, Lucy."

Why do I think Marcus might be wrong about that?

"If he's rude to you, we'll leave. I promise."

I jerk my hand from his, my eyes wide. "What do you know that you're not telling me?"

Marcus laughs as we pull away from the curb. "You really need to chill out."

With traffic, it takes forty minutes to get to the condo where his parents are staying. We pull up to a high rise building on Green Street, one block past Halsted, and enter the parking garage. I'm impressed that Marcus found the building without using a GPS.

"Are their friends going to be here? The ones who own the condo?" I ask once we're in the elevator. Somehow I think that would be better than just the four of us. That way Garret won't freak out when he realizes his son is dating a demon. Correction, half-demon.

"Their friends are travelling. They're gone a lot, so Camille and Garret have an open-ended invitation to stay here."

Great. Deep breaths, four counts in and four counts out. Repeat.

The elevator doors open on the seventh floor, and we step into a quiet hallway decorated with beige walls and floral carpet. Marcus takes my hand and pulls me to him. His eyes look darker than normal, and his brows have been in a permanent frown since he parked the car.

"Tell me you love me," he says, his voice strained.

I place my hands on his shoulders. "I love you. I like you, too."

"That's something," he says, his face breaking into my favorite lopsided smile.

"Come here," I say as I pull him closer. My arms circle his neck as our lips meet. I press myself against him and our kiss deepens. For just a few minutes, I forget where we are and what's ahead of me and focus on Marcus. I run my nails along the tender skin of his neck and down the length of his back. Marcus shivers.

Marcus pulls away a couple of inches and smiles. "I'm glad you're here." He presses his forehead to mine. "Thank you for the kiss. I needed that."

My purse explodes with my favorite St. Vincent song, startling us both. "It's Bernard. Go ahead. I'll meet you at their unit," I tell Marcus as I dig my phone from my purse.

"I'm not going in without you." Marcus says before he turns to proceed down the hall.

I press my phone to my ear. "Hi, Bernard. Is everything okay?"

"We just wanted to check in with you. You were so upset earlier. Meeting your boyfriend's parents is a big deal. Not just for you, but for Marcus, too. Take a deep breath, Luce. Everything will be fine."

An argument erupts somewhere around the corner. One of the voices is Marcus's. *What's going on?*

"Bernard, I have to go." I shove my phone in my purse as I run down the hall toward unit seven-o-nine.

"Get inside, Marcus. Now. There's a demon in the building," a tall, broad shouldered man says as he attempts to shove Marcus behind him toward the apartment door.

"We're not in danger. It's only Lucy." Marcus struggles against the man who towers over him.

Camille tugs on the man's arm. "Garret, please take your hands off of him."

"What's going on?" I ask, edging closer. I'm with Camille. Garret needs to stop pushing Marcus around.

Garret's gaze lands on me and turns arctic. His hair is caramel-colored, with gray flecks throughout. He has dark brown eyes, like Marcus, and a large, misshapen nose, which I'm guessing has been broken once or twice. He wears black slacks and a white dress shirt untucked from his waistband. It's a stylish look; something I would expect to see on Jude.

"Marcus, do you mind telling me why you brought a demon to my home?" Garret asks, his eyes narrowed slits. His voice vibrates with anger.

As if beckoned, my palms start to burn and my fingertips twitch. *Oh, God, no. Not now!* I shove my hands in my pants pockets, forcing myself *not* to envision pitching a fireball at Garret's look of disgust.

Garret takes a hostile step closer.

Camille's wide eyes meet mine. "Lucy?"

Marcus dashes to my side and shoves me behind him. "Leave her alone."

Garret's eyes fix on Marcus. "Tell me I'm wrong—which would be a first. Tell me she's not a demon."

Camille glances uneasily down the hall. "Please, let's take this inside."

We follow her and Garret into the condo. The short entryway

leads into a living room. The exposed brick wall on one side and the deep red wall on the other are what I imagine a downtown Chicago condo should look like. The couch and two overstuffed chairs are brown leather, and a deep red wooden chest, which serves as a coffee table, has a delicate needlework draped over the top. The oak floors shine. A huge flat screen TV is mounted on the wall. I wish Camille would turn it on. It would be a welcome distraction from the tension in the room.

We move to the kitchen where takeout containers decorated with a red dragon symbol line the granite countertops. The room is stuffed with shiny stainless-steel appliances.

"Why did you bring her here?" Garret demands.

"She's *half*-demon," Marcus corrects him. "Nothing like—"

His father sneers. "She's a demon, the enemy of our kind."

Camille grabs the countertop to balance herself. Her gaze jumps from Marcus to Garret, then me. Her attention doesn't linger on me for long. I've fallen out of what little favor she'd granted me when we first met.

"Marcus, do you understand why your father's been on the run for so many years?" Camille pleads. "It's because of the demons who seek to destroy him and all of his—*your*—kind."

But I love him. How can she think I'd hurt Marcus?

"I've met the enemy, and she's definitely not one of them," Marcus hisses through clenched teeth.

"Demons and protectors are not—will never be—compatible," his father growls. "We've been enemies since the beginning of time."

I take a step from behind Marcus. "I'm half-witch," I tell them. Marcus tries to tuck me behind him again, but I push him aside and step forward. "I didn't even know who my father was until last year."

Garret scoffs. "That's impossible. Demons never lose track of their progeny. I can sense your bloodline. It's strong. Your father wouldn't allow you out of his sight."

Marcus grimaces. "Lucy, you don't owe him an explanation."

I reach for Marcus's hand and squeeze it. "It's okay." I turn back to Garret. "My grandmother cast a shrouding spell over my mother and me to hide us from him."

Garret considers this. "Your grandmother must have been powerful."

I raise my chin. "She was."

"She's dead," Garret says.

I want to smack the knowing look off of his face. "My father wasn't the demon who killed her," I snap.

Marcus tugs on my hand as he fixes Garret with a look of contempt. "Are you done with the inquisition? I think it's time for us to go."

Garret stares him down. "Lose the tone, Marcus. I'm looking out for our kind, as I always have. It's no wonder you're spoiled, given the carefree existence you've led."

Marcus clenches and unclenches his jaw. His hand grips mine tightly. "Carefree? You don't know anything about me or my upbringing. You dumped that job on a complete stranger a long time ago."

"Marcus!" Camille pushes herself away from the counter. "Don't you dare speak to Garret like that. You have no idea what our life's been like. Your father—" Marcus narrows his eyes at her.

"Garret is chief of our clan; he's responsible for keeping clan members safe. They're under constant threat."

"Something you know nothing about," Garret says, "with the soft life you've lived."

Marcus stiffens, his body trembling with anger. My mind races through memories in a matter of seconds. Marcus's back splitting open as wings erupted from his skin. The red, angry scars where smooth skin should have been. Marcus's pained expression as he told me about his ten-year-old self sitting alone in the middle of mass at St. Pat's, knowing deep down that his dad was never coming back.

Soft life?

Heat blazes down my arms, raging its way to my palms. *No. No. No. Not now, please not now!*

"Get down!" I scream.

Garret lunges across the room with lightning speed and throws himself over Camille. Fireballs hurl from my hands in opposite directions. One blasts against the huge TV, sending it crashing to the floor in pieces. Sparks and smoke fly in all directions. The other fireball blasts across the kitchen. Takeout containers explode, shooting Thai food in every direction.

"Garret, no!" Camille shrieks.

Garret bows deep before us, his eyes fixed on me. A low growl erupts from his throat. The wet tear of flesh fills the room. I stumble and slam into the refrigerator behind me as wings, black and veined, blast from Garret's back.

"What the..." Frantically, I reach for Marcus's hand.

Garret rises to his full height, dwarfing the room. The leathery appendages twitch and expand until they touch the opposite walls of the room. Dishes crash to the floor.

"No!" Marcus yells. He thrusts me behind him with one hand while his other extends toward Garret in a STOP gesture. My lungs seize at the sight of the massive creature advancing toward us. His eyes glitter like a wolf approaching bloodied prey.

"Once you've been with the clan a while, you'll look back on this and understand why I had to do it." Garret gnashes his teeth.

"Touch her and I'll kill you," Marcus warns. He hunches and grunts as his shirt flies off his body in shreds, buttons pinging from the fabric and skittering to the floor. The scars along his back break open, emitting a wet, ripping sound. His wings wriggle from his bloody skin like a newborn fighting to be free. I'm flung to the floor by the power of those wings as they slam into me.

Marcus roars as he charges Garret. The two collide, and I flinch at the sound of their violent tackle. Fists fly and claws swipe through the air. *Wait...claws? Marcus's father has claws?* Garret leans toward Marcus, his lips drawn back as he's about to sink sharp, pointy teeth into his son's shoulder.

I run toward them, about to plunge my fingers into Garret's eyes.

Camille hurls herself between Garret and Marcus, the weight of her body sending me backward. "Garret! Stop!" She clutches him by the shoulders. She cranes her neck, a desperate look in her eyes. "Marcus, get her out of here. *Now.*"

Marcus's wings retract and collapse against his back, very much like the swans I've seen at the zoo. His wings wiggle and slide into the slits in his skin.

My mouth falls open in amazement, but snaps shut as Marcus, shirtless, grabs my hand and yanks me toward the door. I wonder if later, when I replay all of this, if I will be able to digest what I've seen.

"Tell me something," Garret calls after us.

Marcus pauses. I want to turn around, curious to see if Garret put his wings away, but I mimic Marcus, who stares stonily at the door.

"Who's her father?"

Marcus responds with silence.

"Marcus..." Camille's voice sounds haggard. "It's important. Who is he?"

Once you've been with the clan a while, you'll look back on this and understand why I had to do this. Garret was going to kill me.

I saw the slash marks running across Marcus's chest, recalling Garret about to sink his teeth into his son's shoulder. Despicable for someone who calls himself a protector.

I turn to face them. "Jude Morgan is my father."

Camille's eyes bulge. "No!"

Marcus whips around, searching Camille's face. "What is it?"

Garret smacks his lips. The fangs are gone. "Well, my dear boy, Jude Morgan is the devil I've been sent here to destroy."

CHAPTER FOURTEEN

– Lucy Walker –

"Unbelievable," Marcus chokes as his eyes burn into Camille's. "You told me you came here to be a part of my life. You lied."

Camille stands rigid, frozen to the spot. "It wasn't a lie."

"My dad died at the same time you were given a mission to kill a demon in Chicago? I'm not buying it."

Garret looks at us like we're insane. "Not any demon. Do you have any idea who Jude Morgan is?" He shakes his head and flashes a look of confusion at Camille. "Besides, Skip died almost a year ago. What does he have to do with this?"

Marcus exhales sharply, his icy gaze fixes on his mother. Camille clutches her stomach and winces. Garret unknowingly ratted her out.

"So many lies..." Marcus mutters. He flings open the door.

Garret's voice sounds rough as gravel in the otherwise silent room. "I need to know if your loyalty lies with me, boy."

"My loyalty lies with Lucy," Marcus calls over his shoulder as he pulls me by the hand down the hall.

Once in the elevator, Marcus hits the button for the first floor.

The door doesn't close fast enough, and he punches the panel of buttons over and over. The little plastic globes crumble to the floor.

"Stop!" I lunge forward, take his clenched fist, knuckles bloodied, in both of mine.

Marcus's breaths come out in raspy bursts. His wild eyes meet mine.

"It's not worth hurting yourself," I tell him. "Not for them."

Marcus pulls his hand from mine and slumps against the wall of the elevator.

What kind of father—a protector no less—attacks his own son? I saw Camille's face that day in Marcus's apartment. She came to Chicago to take Marcus away. I didn't get that sense from Garret tonight. He's here for a very different purpose, and that's to destroy Jude.

I wait for the relief to flood my insides. I can finally be rid of Jude. My uncles will be safe. So will Dylan, Ethan, and Brandi. Marcus, too. But do I really want Jude destroyed? Relief doesn't come.

The doors open, and Marcus takes my hand and leads me out of the building to the car. As he peels away from the curb, I clutch the door handle and center console. I don't say a word.

Five minutes later, we pull in front of Old St. Pat's Cathedral. Marcus turns to me, his face in shadow. "I need to be here for a little while."

I hear the anguish in his voice and wish more than anything I could take it away.

"Then I need to be here with you."

He leans across me, opens the glove box, and retrieves a set of keys. "Let's go."

Marcus unlocks the heavy wooden door of the church, and I wonder if we'll get in trouble for being here. Then I remember Marcus telling me how he used to spend a lot of nights here alone before I moved to Chicago. This is where he practiced guitar for hours until it was time for him to return home and spend his evenings on the roof of the apartment building.

Once inside the dark sanctuary, we're met with a powerful silence. A streetlight illuminates the stained glass just enough to make out the Faith, Hope and Charity windows. While Old St. Pat's wasn't Gram's church, she'd been here several times and loved them.

The church is huge, and I crane my neck to take in the ceilings. Since I can't see them in the darkness, I imagine they go on forever.

A scene from earlier tonight comes back to me: Garret about to sink his teeth into Marcus's shoulder. That was after he slashed Marcus's chest with his claws. Had Garret punished Marcus for mixing with the enemy of their kind—me?

I turn back to Marcus. "What're you going to do now?"

"You mean now that I've been played by my mother?"

I shudder at the pain in his voice. "She hasn't gotten you to do anything yet."

I reach for him.

He pulls away. "Camille called me every day since her first visit, eager to meet with me," he whispers roughly. "She told me how much she loved me, what a terrible mistake she made leaving. She..." He clears his throat then continues. "All this time she was only doing Garret's bidding, trying to bring me into the fold...to what? Help him destroy Jude?"

I fold my arms over my chest, unsure how to help and scared by the intensity of his anger.

"I'm so sorry, Marcus."

Marcus spins on his heel and walks away. Does he want to be alone? If so, he could've dropped me off at home then returned here on his own. I pull my hair over my shoulder, winding it through my fingers as I debate what to do. By the time I decide to follow him, I realize there's no way for me to find him in the dark church.

I jump at the sound of a loud creak off to my right. I peer into the darkness, wondering if Father Bill is here somewhere. Then again, this is an old building. It's bound to make lots of noises.

Or maybe it's Garret coming to finish me off.

A chill passes over my skin as I listen, hyperaware of every little sound. Marcus is going to come right back, isn't he? I hug myself tightly as I listen for the sound of his footsteps. I could call out to him, but don't want to draw attention to myself if there's someone else here.

That's when I hear it. Marcus and his guitar. I try to pinpoint where the sound is coming from, but it's impossible. The enormous space fills with the echoey sound of Marcus's raging chords.

I fumble through the dark, my arms reaching out ahead of me until I reach a row of pews. I slide onto the hard wooden bench and listen. The only time I've heard Marcus play was after he had recovered from saving me the night of homecoming. After our weeks apart, I found him in my uncles' garage strumming his guitar. His soulful voice ripped my insides apart. Tonight's songs are different. Marcus is taking his anger out on his guitar.

Tears spill onto my cheeks, and I wipe them away, feeling hypocritical. Isn't this what I wanted? I thought Camille was here to make amends and take Marcus from me. As it turns out, she and Garret do want him, but not for a family reunion. They—or maybe just Garret—want his help to take out Jude.

I frown into the darkness. I don't like Jude, and I've had nothing but trouble since he came into my life, but that doesn't mean I want a life without him. *What do I want?* With a heavy sigh, I realize that I don't know.

I grab hold of my hair again and absently braid it, my fingers working rapidly. Jude fought hard to save me the night of homecoming. Of course, the whole mess was his fault to begin with when he conspired with Seamus's daughter to kidnap my boyfriend from the dance. Then Seamus showed up at Jude's house to kill me. Seamus got away that night. He's still out there. I'm learning to use my demon skills, but I'm not powerful by any stretch. If Garret destroys Jude, who's going to help me battle Seamus the next time he shows up?

The music changes. It's less bitter. My fingers release my hair and fall onto my lap as the gentle strumming fills the Church. Goose bumps break out along my skin when I hear Marcus's voice. The lyrics are no less angry. They ring with accusation as they describe an act of abandonment, betrayal. This has nothing to do with Garret. It's about his mother.

I pull my legs to my chest and wrap my arms around them. I rest my head against the back of the pew.

...dating a mundane is bad enough, but a demon?

It doesn't make sense that gargoyles consider humans inferior. Protectors—gargoyles—help humans. Besides, Camille *is* human. Why would she look down on her own kind? Has Garret brainwashed her into thinking she's one of the protectors?

But I'm worse than human in their eyes. I'm half-demon and unworthy of their son.

Will Garret and Camille insert themselves between Marcus and me now that they know I'm part demon and Jude Morgan's daughter? I don't think Marcus is in a hurry to see them again, but after seeing Jude's determination to wedge himself into my life, I suspect Camille and Garret are not going to give up on their son. It may not be love motivating their actions, but they're set on becoming part of Marcus's life, at least until they achieve what they came for.

I sigh and lie down on the pew. I try to clear my mind of Marcus's parents as I focus on the chords of his guitar, the sound of his voice.

I'm not sure how much time passes, but I jolt awake as a hand squeezes my shoulder.

"Lucy, we should go. I need to get you home."

Marcus sounds better than he did when we arrived. I know he's not fine, but the music helped to exorcise a lot of his anger. For now.

Once in the car, my head gradually clears of sleep. I study his profile. "What are we going to do?"

He glances at me briefly, his expression resolved. "I won't help them destroy Jude."

I breathe a sigh of relief. I needed to hear him say it. I knew he wasn't going to join Garret and Camille, but I also know how much he despises Jude.

"I'm tempted to tell Jude about their plan, but I know that's not the right answer. I texted Aiden from St. Pat's. He, Henry, and Persephone are waiting for us. We need to tell them about Garret's plan."

I check the time on Marcus's dashboard clock. "Let me check in with my uncles, then I'll meet you at Persephone's."

Marcus nods. He glances at me, his stern expression visible in the glow of passing headlights. "I'll never be a fan of Jude's, you know that."

"I know."

"Garret's right. Demons are the natural enemy of protectors. That was never explained to me, but I knew it by instinct." Marcus weaves his fingers through mine and holds my hand tight. With that gesture, I know we are rock solid and unified. "But I now know Jude didn't kill Vera. And he's training you to defend yourself against Seamus. If Jude's really going to honor our truce—allow us to be together without any more attempts to take me out—then I'll stick with my end of it. I won't come between the two of you. Whatever Garret has planned, I will stop him."

But is Marcus any match for Garret with his huge size, sharp teeth, and dagger-like claws? I wonder the damage the older protector could cause Marcus in a serious fight. I shudder and slouch against my seat, feeling very afraid for Marcus.

CHAPTER FIFTEEN

– Lucy Walker –

By the time I get to Persephone's apartment, everyone is waiting. Persephone pours tea for Henry who sits on the green and yellow couch. Marcus paces by the window, while Aiden talks to him in a low voice.

"Can we talk Garret out of this?" Persephone asks as she pours tea for herself. She takes a seat next to Henry.

Marcus turns and nearly knocks a sprouting glass off the window ledge. He glances at the dozen similar glasses along the sill and shakes his head. "Not a chance." He looks at the door as if eager to escape.

"You should've seen him. His eyes full of disgust as he figured out who—*what*—I was. Then he attacked Marcus..." I am full of dismay and revulsion all over again and a shiver races down my spine.

Persephone's expression twists with anger. "I've never heard of a protector doing such a thing!"

"He didn't look like a protector," I tell them, my eyes wide. "He had claws and fangs; things Marcus doesn't have."

Persephone blinks several times as if soaking that in before she glances at Henry. They exchange a baffled look. "Fangs? Claws?" she asks.

Aiden glowers at Marcus. Didn't Marcus tell them any of this before I arrived?

Marcus nods. "And he grew several inches when he morphed."

"How is that possible?" Henry's gaze locks on Aiden.

What would Aiden know about a protector? He's a demon. A pretty useless one as far as I've seen.

"I hate to ask this of you, Marcus, but is there any chance you could speak with your mother alone? See if there's any way to get Garret to back off and perhaps find out what he's done to become this new version of protector?" Henry asks.

From his position near the window, Aiden narrows his eyes at Henry.

Marcus erupts. "I'm not part of the clan, so I have no interest in anything having to do with them. They can all go to hell as far as I'm concerned." He storms out, slamming the door behind him. It takes superhuman effort not to follow him. One of us needs to be here.

Aiden grimaces. "You shouldn't have suggested that."

Henry pulls his glasses off and fixes Aiden with a hard glare. "Something big is brewing, and we need to get a handle on it before we have a catastrophe on our hands."

Persephone snaps her fingers, effectively interrupting the stare off between the two men. "We'll figure out another way." She turns her attention to me. "I told Henry about your training with Jude."

I flinch as car tires peel away from the curb outside. Clearing my throat, I nod at Henry. "Don't bother asking me to get out of it. He'll never allow it."

"I understand," Henry says, his expression grave. "But I would guess that Garret has a team watching Jude's house. He'll see you training with Jude, and he'll likely conclude you're training to kill protectors."

My heart drops. "I'd never..."

Concern flashes in Aiden's eyes. I know it's not meant for me. Maybe for Marcus if he loses me? Or Jude?

"Do we have any idea when Garret plans to take action against Jude?" Aiden asks quietly.

"If you saw his face, the way he talked. He hates Jude," I tell them. It's impossible to contain my fear and stress as I review everything that happened and what I learned at Garret and Camille's condo earlier tonight. "I'm guessing it's going to be soon."

"If only there was a way to convince Garret to see reason. I don't believe Jude has done the things Garret's accusing him of. After all, we're here." Persephone gestures to everyone in the room. "We're watching him. Have been for years."

I shrug helplessly. "Garret's hatred is so strong, his determination. It's like..."

"I imagine it must feel much like Seamus and his pursuit of you," Persephone finishes.

I nod wordlessly. The realization hadn't hit me until just now. My father and I have a common enemy in Seamus, who is hell-bent on killing me in order to hurt Jude. It turns out we have a second common enemy. Maybe if I hadn't been dating Garret's son, I wouldn't even register on his radar.

Henry slides his glasses back on. "We're going to need to consult with others. Persephone, what about Mirabelle and her coven in New Orleans? They might be able to help."

Persephone nods. "I'll contact her."

"I don't understand," I say. "Why consult with others? We're strong enough to take on Garret, aren't we?"

Persephone shakes her head, her wiry curls bouncing. It would be funny, except for her expression. I've never seen Persephone wear fear before. "If Garret came here to take out Jude, he's been preparing for a long time."

I swallow carefully because my throat just closed.

Henry turns to Aiden, visibly bracing himself. "You're not going to like this, but we're going to need to summon your old friend."

Aiden's eyes darken. "Bad idea, Henry."

"We can trust him, and frankly, we need the numbers," Henry says.

Persephone nods slowly. "Max? Good thinking."

I've never seen Aiden squirm before. "Who's Max?"

Aiden shakes his head stubbornly. "We should consider other options."

"Max comes from a powerful line of fighters," Henry points out. "Since Jude saved his life all those years ago, he's indebted to him."

"I remember all too well," Aiden says.

"What's so special about this guy that we need him? How can he help us?" I ask.

"He's hired muscle." Aiden watches Henry, daring him to disagree. "If chaos and slaughter are what you're after, you call Max."

Henry holds up his hands. "We're not looking to harm Garret. We simply need additional protection for Jude. If we want to intimidate, he's the perfect demon to have on our side."

"He's a hothead and conniving," Aiden counters. "And he's not known for his loyalty."

Persephone gives Aiden the look I thought was reserved solely for me, the one where her eyes narrow into slits and her lips all but disappear. That look scares the bejesus out of me. "Put your personal differences aside. We need him."

Aiden glowers. "You'd better hide everything of value before he shows up. Consider yourselves warned." He turns his back on us and focuses on something outside the window.

Henry sets his teacup on the table and pushes himself off the couch. "We'll keep searching for other allies. Whatever it takes to protect Jude."

Did I hear him correctly for the second time? "I don't understand. You both despise Jude. Why would you help him?"

"Lucy..." Henry's face softens. His green eyes appear deeper, more of a moss color, and I wonder if I'm seeing things.

"This isn't about Jude." Persephone sniffs.

"Then what is it?" I ask.

The room fills with oppressive silence. I look from Persephone to Henry and, clearly, neither of them are all that eager to clue me in.

Aiden turns away from the window and his stony expression fixes on me. "When a demon dies, so do all of his progeny."

It takes a moment for his words to sink in. Then my blood turns to ice. "No," I whisper. Aiden's lying, trying to frighten me. Persephone's eyes meet mine, desperate and afraid. *It's true.*

I could be wiped out of existence at any moment—Jude could be hit by a bus tomorrow or killed by Garret next week—or even if Garret fails, there will be someone else who wants to kill Jude. Scratch the bus squashing analogy. Demons are immortal. To destroy them is extremely difficult. Surely, Garret, the head of the protectors, knows how to get it done.

If Jude dies, I die, too. The words float around in my brain, vague and sort of cloudy, until they finally settle in with razor-sharp clarity. What about Chinese takeout night with my uncles? Ms. Stevens promised to take Katie and me to Margie's—the best ice cream parlor in Chicago—this summer. Will I still be alive when Katie and her mom decide on a date? Who will help Persephone take care of Lola, once she and Serenity return? Then there's Ethan and Brandi. Who will take care of them once I'm gone? What about Marcus? Garret will go after him. I have no doubt. Who will Marcus kiss after I'm gone?

It's impossible to catch my breath. My temples throb.

"Lucy?" Henry calls out. The sound of his voice echoes in my head and the room starts to tilt.

"She needs to sit down," Persephone says as she takes hold of my arm.

Henry appears at my other side. The two of them push me onto the couch.

"Deep breaths, Lucy." Henry's voice sounds far away.

"Does Garret know that by killing Jude, he'll kill me, too?" The words come out as little gasps.

"Of course he does," Aiden says, his voice full of acid. "It's efficiency in action. He gets rid of his enemy and the scandalous girlfriend chosen by his son. I'd bet his goal is to use Marcus to perform his dirty work, then he'll abandon him again."

My thoughts race. How much time do I have left? Will I finish sophomore year? Will I get to drive my new car? Will I make it to Caroline's year-end party? It suddenly feels important that I do. How many spells can I learn from Persephone? That's when it hits me. I turn to them, cautious but hopeful. "There's a spell that'll protect me, right? If Jude dies?"

It takes Persephone too long to answer. "Not that we know of."

With a noisy exhale, I slump against the couch cushion. *Jude's going to die. I'm going to die.*

Persephone hoists herself from the couch. She stands tall. "I will reach out to Mirabelle today, see if she knows of any protection spells that can help us." Her expression is determined and fierce.

"We're in a catch twenty-two. The only way to save Lucy is to warn Jude, but we can't. That would mean certain death for Garret. We can't risk the life of a protector, especially the head of the clan," Henry says. "So, for now, we work together to protect Jude."

I look across the room in time to see the distress on Aiden's face before he returns to the window.

* * * *

I blow my nose in a tissue, then shove it in my sweatshirt pocket along with the others. It's late and the street below is dark.

"So much for finally getting my wish to live in Gram's house," I turn away from the ledge and plunk down next to the stone gargoyle, "and having a best friend. Two if you count Dylan." I slide a sideways glance at Marcus, expecting a sarcastic remark. None comes, of course. "And what about you? Never in a million years did I think I'd have such an amazing boyfriend."

Tears fill my eyes again and spill onto my cheeks. "It's stupid, I know, but I really hoped we'd be together forever. You know?" I choke on my tears.

Who knows how much time I have left with him? I gasp and swipe at the wetness on my cheeks. What if Garret decides to kill Jude tonight? The realization hits me like a hundred-pound dumbbell. Back on my feet, I bend to grasp Marcus's concrete wings and shake him. It's more like a teeter.

"Marcus, I need you." I touch the prickly stone of his face, his head. "Come back to me, please."

I plant kisses along the cold, hard contours of his face. "Now may be all we have left. You've got to change. Right now." Can he hear me? Or do my desperate pleas fall on stone deaf ears.

I sink to my knees. My fingers brush against his cold, hard legs down to his paw-like feet.

Suddenly, Marcus shivers. Stone statutes don't—another tremble!

I look at his toes. It's not possible. *What the heck?* With both hands, I proceed to tickle the gargoyle's feet.

The stone statue tips sharply to the left. I grab him right

before he hits the ground and heave him upright. His left wing bends and flutters against my shoulder.

I gasp. "Marcus?"

His body ripples and shudders through the change. His wings transform from stone to feathers. His limbs no longer resemble a dog and a bear, but a man. The transformation occurs so fast, so powerful that it appears blurry. Because of our close proximity, Marcus's change into his protector form shoves me backward and I land on my butt.

Marcus arches his back and groans as his body elongates, his bones snapping into place. His chest heaves as he sucks in air to fill his lungs.

"Lucy," he wheezes. His wings tremble then retract against his back. "What's wrong? Who sent you?"

I scurry to my feet and dust off my jeans. "Sent me?"

His posture hunched; Marcus looks around the roof suspiciously as if ready for an attack. "Is Seamus here? Garret and his goons?"

I close the distance between us. "It's just me." I push damp hair out of his eyes. I kiss his flushed cheeks, his forehead, his lips. "Only me."

Marcus studies my face and after a moment, relaxes his posture. Great. With my puffy, red face, I'm sure I look gross.

His hands cup my cheeks while his eyes study me. "What's wrong?"

I cover his hands with my own, tears stinging my eyes. "What if we only have tonight, Marcus? What would you do?"

He grips my shoulders. "Stop it, Lucy. You're scaring me."

I wriggle free. I don't want the calming influence of his touch right now, whether it's intentional or not. "You're scared? What about me?" His baffled expression tells me I lost him. "Did you know about demons and their progeny? What happens when they die? What happens if Jude dies?"

Realization dawns on Marcus's face, followed by horror. "What are you saying?" His voice is low. His words choked. "Is Jude going to die tonight?"

My shoulders slump. "Why didn't you tell me? Why did I have it hear it from Aiden?"

Marcus's arms hang limp at his sides. "Because I thought I could fix this before it ever got to that point." He drops his gaze. "It was easier, you know, when Jude caused all the problems. When he was the enemy. I knew all along I would do whatever it took to protect you from him." Marcus sighs and his eyes meet mine.

"Marcus..." I want to throw myself into his embrace, do whatever I can to make the gut-wrenching sorrow leave his eyes.

Marcus's gaze hardens as he exhales noisily. "Now, my father is threatening your life." His fists curl at his sides. "He won't harm you, Lucy. I'll kill him myself."

CHAPTER SIXTEEN

– Lucy Walker –

"Lucy!" Brandi shrieks as she bounds into my arms. She's a vision this morning with her pink sweater, pink jeans, and pink socks.

I hug Dylan's younger sister like today's our last day together. Then I tickle her until she breaks into a fit of giggles.

"Guess what?" she asks, gasping for breath. She doesn't wait for me to respond. "My birthday is April tenth."

"Seriously?" I calculate the days. "That's in two weeks!"

Ethan walks into the room, his hair damp from a shower. In contrast to his sister, he wears khakis and a button-down oxford shirt the color of tangerine. He dresses the part of a little adult, a miniature Mr. Douglas.

"Yeah, I can't wait to have a houseful of screaming eight and nine-year-old girls." He frowns. "I suggested to our mom that she have the party at a restaurant. That way, I could stay home."

I narrow my eyes at him. "Ethan, that isn't very nice. Brandi's birthday is a big deal." My breath catches when it hits me. I may not be around for her big day.

"But I don't like her friends, and when she's around them, I don't like her either," he says. "You'd be the best nanny ever if you help make that happen."

When did the ten-year-old boy turn into a grumpy old man? I reach over and mess Ethan's hair. He frowns again and quickly finger combs it back into place.

"My friend Maria loooooooooves you," Brandi croons. "She says she wants to marry you."

Ethan purses his lips, pulling his eyebrows low. "Tell her to forget it. She's a spoiled little baby and she wears weird purple glasses."

I listen to the banter. Maybe it's because there's no anger behind their words and it's not headed for a fight. Or maybe it's because I may not have much time left with them. Suddenly, every second with them matters, and I want to sit back and absorb every detail.

A shiver passes through me as I recall Marcus's threat to kill his own father to keep me safe. There has to be another way to stop Garret.

Mrs. Douglas *click—click—clicks* her way into the room. She cinches the belt of her buff-colored designer dress around her tiny waist and grabs her bowling bag-sized Gucci purse from the counter. I never understood why she carries something so large. It's not like she eats, so I know there's no snacks inside. "Lucy, I need you to go to the printer and pick up the invitations for Brandi's birthday party. They called yesterday to let me know they're ready."

She waves a sheet of paper at me. "Here is the guest list. Address the envelopes and get them in the mail. Use your best handwriting, *please*. I don't want these people thinking the children wrote them out. Also, the baker's number is on the counter. Can you call and get the cake ordered? Make sure to have them repeat the instructions back to you. They're the best baker in the city, but they've been known to make mistakes. I don't want to be embarrassed in front of our guests."

Her condescending tone hits me like a dozen poisonous darts, each word stabbing into me. It's like I mean nothing at all. Was I kidding myself to think I had become part of the family?

My head bobs automatically, acknowledging my duties. A part of me wonders what it would be like to tell her off. Just this once. What does it matter if I'm not going to be around long anyway?

"You're an ungrateful, ugly woman, Mrs. Douglas. I work my fingers to the bone for you—and so does Charlene, your loyal housekeeper—and you treat us like crap. Your children get more affection from us, the hired help, than they've ever gotten from you. Why have kids if you're not going to love them? Or spend time with them? It seems cruel to keep them around if you're only going to resent them."

But then I glance at Brandi who clenches her hands to her chest, a huge smile on her face at the preparations being made for her big day. Ethan shifts from one leg to the other, quiet but impatient, his eyes glued to his mother. It's what I call the Ethan dance. It stops only when Mrs. Douglas bends down to give him a hug. Then the deep crease between his brows relaxes, and his pursed lips ease into a small, satisfied smile.

I clench my jaw, biting back my words, and wait for the door to close behind her. Then I check out the list on the table.

I gasp. "Thirty kids are coming to your party?"

"You agree it should be held at a restaurant?" Ethan raises his eyebrows at me.

I pat him on the shoulder, careful not to mess his hair again. As much as he acts like a mini adult, he's still such a little boy. Once again, I notice his big brown eyes. He and Dylan have the same eyes as their father. Same with the hair. Brandi, however, looks more like her mother with her fair skin and blue eyes. I'm guessing Mrs. Douglas's hair color looked more like Brandi's dishwater blond before she started dying it to its current peachy blond.

"What're you staring at me for?" Ethan grumbles. "Fine. I'll stop complaining about the stupid birthday party."

"You're the best, Ethan." I give him a big smile.

He rolls his eyes at me.

"I was thinking we'd go to the pool today," I say.

Ethan and Brandi both jump up to high-five me. "Yes!" They shriek in unison.

"Call Dylan! I want him to go, too!" Ethan's eyes bug in anticipation.

Where did Mr. Grumpy go?

"Actually, he texted me last night. He'll be here in an hour."

"Sweet!" Ethan punches the air.

As the kids run off to pack their swimsuits, I join Charlene in the kitchen and give her a hug.

"Did you hear about the birthday party?" Charlene collapses onto a stool, blowing a damp lock of hair from her eyes. She's not wearing any makeup, and there are dark circles under her eyes.

"You would think we were planning a party for the president."

"That's insane. Why don't they hire someone to help you?" It's not like they can't afford it.

"She's invited all these ladies she knows from the club. Brandi doesn't even hang out with their kids. Those little girls are sharks. They're going to eat her alive at her own birthday party." Charlene leans forward, her gaze meeting mine. "For a while, Mrs. Douglas was acting like a real mom to them. Playing games and tucking them in bed at night." She shakes her head. "I should've known it was too good to be true. She's back to being her normal self."

Mrs. Douglas thought she was going to lose her kids to Jude last year. I noticed the change, too, and had hoped it would be permanent.

Just then, Ethan and Brandi race back to the kitchen and take their seats. While they eat breakfast, I call and order the cake. The woman at the bakery probably thinks I'm a loon after I reviewed the cake decorations and inscription three times with her. I set the notes on the counter near the phone to go over with Mrs. Douglas when she gets home tonight.

I quickly braid Brandi's hair while she finishes eating.

"Do you want more eggs?" I ask Ethan as he scrapes his plate clean.

"Nope. I'm full."

"You're sure?"

Ethan screws his face up tight and shakes his head at me.

As Brandi climbs off her stool, she teeters. I race to her side and grab her glass before it falls from her hands.

"Dylan's here!" Brandi calls out.

Charlene grabs hold of my arm and tugs me backward. "You're acting like a nervous mother hen. What's going on?"

My breath hitches. What if Ethan, Brandi, and I never work on another jigsaw puzzle together? Or snuggle on the couch and watch a movie? Or bake cookies? What if I never feel their arms wrapped around me in a tight hug? Or smell Brandi's strawberry shampoo?

I turn away from Charlene and take a deep breath as I face the kids. "Do you two have your swimsuits?"

Ethan holds up his backpack, and I'm relieved it's a fraction of the size of his normal swim bag. "In here, along with my towel, goggles, and fins."

"Me, too!" Brandi squeaks, holding up her pink backpack.

Dylan strolls into the kitchen. "I have mine on. Do you want to see?" he leans in and whispers in my ear.

I roll my eyes. "I'll pass."

I hand the order receipt for Brandi's party invitations to Dylan. "We need to stop and pick these up after we're done at the pool. Is Arnold in the car?"

"I'm driving. I told Arnold to go meet up with his buddies at the coffee shop for a few hours."

I pause, knowing Mrs. Douglas doesn't like any deviation from the schedule or the rules. And she's not a big fan of Dylan. "Are you allowed to do that?"

"What my step-monst...my *stepmother* doesn't know won't hurt her." He stares menacingly at Ethan and Brandi. "Right?"

They both giggle, mimicking Dylan as he draws his fingers across his lips like a zipper.

* * * *

By the time we reach the pool, it's crammed full of shrieking, splashing children.

Brandi clings to my side as Ethan and Dylan hurl themselves into the deep end. "I can only swim in the shallow end."

"Of course."

She grips my hand tighter. "Don't let go of me."

"I won't."

Brandi and I make a game of sinking to the bottom of the pool, flapping our hands frantically to help keep us submerged, then jumping up from the water.

"We're like mermaids," Brandi says excitedly.

My heart swells so large my chest hurts. "You can be Ariel," I tell her.

"You can be one of her sisters!"

After a while, Dylan joins us, leaving Ethan to hang out with a bunch of his friends from the swim team.

Dylan leans close. He glances at us, then to the deep end, his voice low so only Brandi and I can hear him. "Brandi, I have to warn you. I heard there are sharks in this pool."

Brandi's eyes grow as large as fifty-cent pieces.

"No..." Her voice is a whisper.

He mimics her solemn expression and points to the deep end. "I thought I saw one down there."

She squints hard as she searches the water. "I don't see—"

Dylan slips under the water, his hands skimming the surface, mimicking a shark fin.

Brandi jumps and shrieks before lumbering away in a fit of giggles. Dylan swims back and forth in the shallow end, chasing her while I stand in the corner and watch. Several other kids Brandi's age join in, racing through the water, splashing and giggling, trying to escape from the killer shark. If Mrs. Douglas could see this, she'd cease her crusade to keep Dylan apart from his brother and sister.

If I die, will Brandi and Ethan lose Dylan?

Two hours later, family swim is over, and we're back in Dylan's car. The kids are asleep in the back seat, snoring softly. Brandi's head rests on Ethan's shoulder, and his head tilts against hers.

My vision blurs and my throat burns. What will their lives be like without me? They live in their museum-like house, with an emotionless mother and a workaholic father. All the toys in the world aren't going to compensate for a lack of love and attention.

I have to stay alive for them.

Dylan breaks the silence. "Spill it."

I blink away tears as I pull my attention away from the kids. "What?"

"You can't stop staring at them. Ever since I showed up this morning, you've been acting like...like my mother did last year when I came home from the hospital." He slides a dark glance my way. "What are you afraid of? Is Jude going to come after them again?"

"I told you he'll never come after them—or you—again."

"Then what is it? And—"

"It's nothing," I say.

"I was about to say...and don't tell me it's nothing."

"I adore them." I glance at the sleeping figures in the backseat. "That's all."

I'm dying to tell Dylan about Garret, but I can't risk him telling Jude. Guilt twists like a knife in my heart. Garret might come after Dylan too. He deserves to know. But can I trust him with Jude's life? With my own?

"Whose life is in danger now?" His tone is sharper this time.

"You're so dramatic!" I force a laugh. "Nothing's going on."

Dylan's grimace tells me he doesn't believe me, but he leaves it alone as we pull into the parking space at the printing company. I grab the order receipt from the dashboard and dash inside to pick up Brandi's party invitations, relieved to get away from his probing stare. My phone buzzes, and I slide it from my pocket. My eyes nearly pop out of my head as I read the text message. *Marcus has a sister?*

CHAPTER SEVENTEEN

– Lucy Walker –

Marcus paces across the living room of his apartment. "Her name is Selima Kanaan Bergmann. Camille told me about her," he explains to me.

I'm guessing Bergmann is Garret's last name. Is that Camille's last name, too? Or did she keep Turner so she and Marcus would have the same last name?

A car with a loud muffler roars down the street. Marcus slams the window so hard the glass rattles within its frame. I sit stiffly on the couch. Camille, Garret, and now a long-lost sister. Marcus's life has turned into one of those soap operas Momma used to watch when I was young.

I think back to the last time Marcus met with his mother, before that horrible night at the condo. That was a couple of weeks ago. "Why are you just telling me about Selima now?"

Marcus stops his pacing and faces me. His expression shifts from fear to panic. "Because she's coming here. On Monday. After school."

I roll my eyes. "That doesn't really answer the question."

Marcus rakes his fingers through his hair. "I should've told you. I'm sorry."

I really thought we were past the point of secrets. "I'm more curious *why* you didn't tell me."

Marcus collapses onto the couch next to me, his expression strained. "My mother left me. My stepfather bailed, leaving me at St. Pat's in the middle of Sunday service. I find out my biological father supposedly didn't want kids." He struggles to make eye contact. "Then Camille tells me about Selima, the daughter Garret adores from his first marriage. I'm struggling with that."

I slide my arms around him. "I'm an idiot. Sorry for giving you a hard time."

"You're not an idiot." He pulls back. I see the worry in his eyes. "Will you go with me? To meet my sister?"

There are lines around Marcus's eyes, and he's wrenched his hair into a crazy mess. After all he's been through, I should cut him some slack. But is it safe to meet with Garret's daughter?

"What do you know about her?" I ask.

Marcus rubs his eyes with the heels of his hands and exhales. "If you're worried about her coming here to attack me, don't be." He stretches his lips into a partial smile. "She seemed more nervous about the meeting than me."

I give him a dubious look.

"Okay...equally nervous."

We both laugh. I relish the sound. We haven't had much to laugh about lately.

CHAPTER EIGHTEEN

– Dylan Douglas –

I wait until Marcus pulls into the gas station before I climb out of my car. Rain streams down my scalp, diluting my gel. *Great.*

Marcus emerges from his car and remains standing beneath the gas station canopy. He doesn't bother meeting me halfway. His hair stays dry. *Jerk.*

"This better be important, Dylan." It drives Marcus crazy that Lucy and I are close. If I had it my way, she'd leave him in the dust. Some day—and I'm hoping it won't be long—she'll realize I'm the better choice. I make her laugh. With all the scary drama in her life, that should mean something.

I recall Lucy's expression last weekend, as she watched Ethan and Brandi sleeping in the backseat of the car. I know that look. I've felt the exact same way, fear you wouldn't see them again. I've asked her about it twice since then, and she keeps dodging the subject.

I nod at Marcus, trying to look grim. *Need to be convincing here, D-Man.* "Lucy told me what's going on."

Marcus tries to mask his surprise as he shoves his keys in the pocket of his jeans. It feels pretty damn good to watch him fumble. His eyes narrow. "How much did she tell you?"

I grin inwardly. I like getting under that brooding exterior.

"Everything." I lie. "The question is...what are you going to do about it?" I fake a dramatic sigh and stare off for a moment. "And what can I do to help?"

"You? What makes you think you can do anything?" Marcus's voice and expression are loaded with incredulity. I want to punch that look off of his face.

"You have a short memory. I was there for her that night at Jude's house. I did whatever was asked of me, for her sake."

Marcus frowns, unable to dispute that. He starts to say something, then stops. He glances at the ground, then back at me. It takes a lot of effort not to laugh at his sheepish expression. "You haven't told her about that night, have you? I mean...I figured you haven't. I'm not sure she could handle it."

I cross my arms over my chest and rock back on my heels. "I haven't said a word to her and don't plan to." I pause for effect. "But you might want to think about this. Lucy's powers are growing. And she's smart. Don't you think she's going to wake up one day and realize a simple embrace from you isn't enough to save a girl near death?"

Marcus's Adam's apple bobs.

"She's going to figure out there was more to her magical recovery, and when she does, she's going to be furious we kept it from her."

Marcus nods thoughtfully. "You have a point. I did what I had to do and I do owe her the truth. Eventually."

Lucy's going to freak. A part of me feels bad for him. I'm grateful to Marcus for saving her, but he should've filled her in a long time ago. Besides, I'm sick of holding onto his secret. But that's not why we're here. "What're we going to do about the current situation?"

"I don't know." Marcus suddenly looks tired and sad at the same time.

Guilt starts pulling at me and I give myself a mental left hook. *Can't worry about him. Lucy is my priority.*

Marcus's tone turns to a whisper as if he's talking to himself. "I wish I knew when Garret plans to move. We've got Jude's power on our side. Destroying the demon won't be easy."

It takes effort to restrain myself. Kill Jude? This is great news! But that doesn't make sense. Lucy seemed so sad. Marcus looks ready to explode. What am I missing?

Marcus nods at me, his gaze turning fierce. "If you want to help, figure out a way to keep Lucy alive." He turns on his heel, climbs into his car, and peels out of the parking lot, fishtailing on the wet pavement.

I stare after him, ignoring the rain. Lucy's life is in danger again. Still? First Seamus, now Garret. Who the hell is Garret, anyway? What's the connection to Jude? Is there one?

Who am I kidding? All life-threatening problems involve Jude. The question eating at me is...why is Lucy keeping this from me?

CHAPTER NINETEEN

– Lucy Walker –

The smell of coffee fills the kitchen. It's a happy smell. A comfortable, snuggly smell. I kiss my uncles goodbye, ignoring their silly smiles.

"Tell Dylan hello for us," Sheldon calls after me as I head out the door. It's Sunday. My second day of demon training.

It's odd for Dylan to miss an opportunity to brown nose my uncles in person, but his text said to meet him outside. I want to tell him that Marcus has a sister and we're going to meet her tomorrow night—something that scares and excites me. That would be difficult, though, since I haven't said a word to him about Camille and Garret.

I slept with my fingers curled around the feather—Marcus's feather—tucked beneath my pillow, praying Selima isn't here to hurt Marcus and that she isn't a part of her father's plot to kill my father and me.

As soon as I climb into his car, Dylan shifts gears, an angry grinding sound, and speeds off down the street.

"Hey, chill out!" I grip the dashboard with both hands. "You're going to piss off my uncles."

"You're going to die?" His face twists. "What was it you said? Oh, yeah. *Dylan, don't worry. Nothing's going on.'* Isn't that the load of crap you fed me?"

I open my mouth to explain why I didn't want to tell him, then close it again. My reasons would only make him angrier.

Dylan pounds the steering wheel with his fist. "Do I matter to you at all? Or is this your way of keeping me out of the way? Reminding me how useless I was last time?"

He's driving too fast. It's scaring me. "You weren't useless. How...how did you find out?"

"Does it matter?" he yells. Within the interior of the car with the window rolled up, his voice booms. "I expected more from you. Aren't you the one who hates secrets?"

I've never seen him this angry.

Dylan throws a determined look my way. "We need to have a sit-down with Jude today. Screw his stupid lunch, bonding like we're some kind of freaky-happy demon family. Let's tell him about this, so we can take action. Save you."

"No!" I grab his arm. "You don't understand. If we tell Jude, he'll kill Garret."

Dylan shakes off my hand. "So what? I'll take Garret's death over yours—whoever the hell he is."

"Garret's important. He's a protector, like Marcus. He's Marcus's father." I nearly gag on the words.

Dylan's eyeballs look as if they're going to pop out of his head. He's silent for a moment as he takes in my words while watching the road. "A protector? Why's he planning to kill you?"

I slide low in my seat. "You have your facts wrong." I almost ask again where he got his information, but I'm afraid he'll rip my head off. "When a demon dies, his descendants die right along with him."

Dylan processes the information in seconds. All anger slips from his face. Slowly, he nods. "He's after Jude."

I cross my arms over my chest. "If you tell Jude, he might attack first. Garret has backup."

"Why? I mean, how does it work? Is there any way around it? You dying?" Dylan's frantic gaze bounces between the road and me.

"Henry says that when Jude dies, fifty-percent of my DNA, what I inherited from him, immediately goes poof. It literally dissolves. Then I'll die." I pull my bottom lip between my teeth, holding my breath as I wait for Dylan to digest this information.

I flinch when Dylan punches the steering wheel again, harder this time. It's not going to withstand much more from his fists.

"This is a load of crap!"

"It's not just me I'm worried about," I tell him.

"What do you mean?" Dylan glares at me for a second before returning his attention to the road.

"The deal your dad made with Jude all those years ago. He drank a goblet of Jude's blood. You carry some of Jude's genes, too."

"My parents are my parents." Dylan glowers. "I may have a very small amount of Jude's genetics inside of me, but not enough to kill me if he dies. Not like you. Dammit!" Dylan whacks the dashboard this time.

I reach for his arm, but stop myself. With his demon genes expressing themselves, he's unpredictable. He could lash out and punch me. "Dylan...you need to hold it together when we get to Jude's. You can't let on that anything's wrong."

"Great. More pretending. Like I do with my dad, pretending everything's fine when he's married to the biggest social-climbing witch on the planet. And that something's changing in me, a Tasmanian devil running loose inside, but hey—" His expression twists into a mad scientist kind of grin as he holds up jazz hands. "Look at me, everything's JUST GREAT!"

The car in front of us isn't moving fast enough for Dylan. He jerks the steering wheel, then stomps on the gas pedal and races around them. I nearly flop out of my seat. While I get that he's hurt I kept the Jude and Garret thing from him, his anger has escalated too far. Is this a side effect of his demon genes coming to life?

"Maybe you should take a pass today. Drop me off and go to the gym, work this off," I suggest, my own temper flaring.

"Yeah, right. Leave you vulnerable in case this Garret guy shows up to assassinate Jude?" Dylan snorts. "No way. From now on, I'm stuck to you like glue."

If he wasn't acting like a psycho, I'd laugh at his play on words. Instead, I clutch the dashboard and my door handle and keep my mouth shut.

Once again, Jude meets us at the door, and I wonder if Darcy, Jude's fashionista-like assistant, suffered a similar extermination like the red-eyed crows.

We eat a quick, awkward lunch, then head out the back door

to the yard. I stop short when I see Jack and his two thugs—the shapeshifting Rottweilers who Jude sent to terrorize Dylan and kidnap Marcus last year. "What are they doing here?"

"Aiden couldn't make it today," Jude says.

"But..." I begin, scanning Jude's massive yard. Garret's probably watching us now. Aiden is supposed to be here to help protect Jude. This doesn't make sense. Did Jude order him away, worried Aiden and Dylan's dislike for each other would interfere with training?

"It was my suggestion," Dylan says behind me.

I whirl around to face him. "Are you crazy?"

His face breaks into a cocky smile, a smile that contrasts with the glaring accusation in his eyes. The fury is still simmering below the surface.

"When Jude told me Aiden couldn't make it, I thought this might be..." Dylan nods at Jack, Troy, and Matt, "fun."

I whirl to face Jude, my muscles twitching. "I can't believe you agreed to this. After everything these dirt bags did last year..." I bite my tongue. "If they hurt Dylan, I'm done with you."

Dylan laughs. The sound sends a chill down my spine. What's wrong with him? Does he have a death wish? These guys are strong, and there are three of them. Dylan jogs across the huge yard to get started on today's training.

The three creeps utter a low growl in unison, anticipatory smiles on their faces. The way they clap each other on the backs, they act as if they've already won. Three against one isn't fair. Dylan isn't thinking straight. My stomach churns painfully. Jude won't let this go too far will he?

It doesn't matter. I'll be watching them. The first hint that Dylan's in trouble, I'll chase the mutts off.

I glare at Jude. "Do I get to shoot fireballs at you again today?"

Jude glances across the field at Dylan, his expression thoughtful. Is he curious how this sick match is going to turn out?

"No, today is defensive work. I'm going to throw fireballs at *you*. You're going to learn to deflect them."

Jude spends the next thirty minutes demonstrating various maneuvers. I check over my shoulder every time I hear someone swear or yelp. I cry out at one point as I watch Jack, Troy, and Matt circle Dylan, their teeth bared like a pack of wolves ready to attack. Heat surges along my arms, throbbing all the way to my fingertips. I'm about to rush to Dylan's aid when Jude grabs hold of my elbow.

"Let me go!" I thrash against his vice-like grip.

"Just watch."

I hold my breath, my heartbeat pounding in my chest all the way to my ears. Dylan crouches in a defensive position as Jack and his two friends continue to circle. The heat settles in my palms. I restrain the overwhelming urge to hurl fireballs across the yard at the three losers. There's no way I could throw that far.

"Dylan!" I cry as Troy lunges at him from behind. Jude's grip tightens. I consider firing off at him in order to get loose. Electrical impulses scream through my body. The urge is strong. The burning in my hands is too much. I need release.

Jude meets my look of rage and desperation with his steely black gaze. "Don't even think about it."

The high voltage zap he dispenses to both of my arms short-circuits my entire nervous system, causing my knees to buckle. Jude releases me, and I flop to the ground.

My father just tased me? I try to stand, but the spasms in my leg muscles make it impossible. I struggle to shoot a sarcastic remark at the man towering above me, his hands shoved casually in his pockets, but my tongue fails me.

Another grunt and a cry of surprise pierce the air. I turn back to Dylan in time to see Troy lying on the ground. Jack and Matt move in from opposite sides. Dylan sinks his elbow into Matt's midsection. Matt hunches over, gasping. Dylan reaches for Jack, grabs him by the arm, and spins around. He flips Jack over his back and slams him onto the ground with so much force the earth shivers beneath me.

Dylan scowls as he whirls around to face Matt, who is upright and swinging. Matt tries to fake Dylan out by lunging right. Matt's fist connects with Dylan's face. Blood spurts from Dylan's mouth as his face jerks to the right. Matt punches Dylan again and again. Dylan stumbles to his knees, disoriented. Matt goes in for another attack.

"This is insane!" I pull my legs under my body and struggle to push my body upright. "Help me up! Call Matt off of him!"

Jude's gaze never leaves the fight. "Your lack of faith in your partner is disappointing. If you were focusing, you would know Dylan is restraining his powers."

Jude's wrong. Why can't he see what I'm seeing? Dylan's going to lose this fight. Jack, Matt, and Troy had it out for Dylan last year. It's clear they're still out for blood. I groan and tell myself to look away, but I can't. Instead, I crawl, grasping handful after handful of grass to help pull me along. Can I make it across the field and roast Matt before he kills Dylan?

Matt's fists continue to pummel Dylan. With every punch delivered, my fury grows. My trembling arms barely support me as I pull my body along. My muscles quiver and seize. My face connects with the grassy earth.

Damn Jude! Then it hits me. What did Jude just say? Focus? I aim my hands toward Matt. All of my anger and fear condense within me. I wait for the heat, for the electricity to fill me. I visualize a human fireball. Nothing comes. I focus harder, extend my arms until my muscles ache. My powers are dead. I cry out in frustration.

My stomach flips with a sickening twist as Matt is about to drive his knee into Dylan's face. Will he shatter Dylan's nose? Jam it into his brain? Suddenly, Dylan jumps up, tackles Matt around the midsection, and slams him into the trunk of a tree. Matt flops to the ground, emitting little squeaky noises as he struggles to regain his breath.

Jude's feet appear in my peripheral vision. "Dylan has incredible strength. He's clever, too." His voice swells with pride. He pulls me to my feet. I teeter on unsteady, spongy legs. "Enough distractions. It's time to resume your training."

Once again I wonder how Jude's death would affect Dylan. If Aiden were here today, I could ask him.

"Think fast."

Before I register Jude's words, he hurls a baseball-sized fireball, which slams against my arm. Heat sears my skin.

I clutch the burned skin as I stumble backward. "Are you insane?"

"Relax. Inspect your arm."

I'm about to insult him on his parenting when he nods at my limb.

"Look at it."

I hold up my arm, which doesn't hurt as much as it did when the fireball first hit me. The deep red mark on my skin fades just a little. There's no swelling or blisters. How is that possible?

"This can't be real."

"Another benefit of being a demon. You're welcome."

You're welcome? I hold my arm up to show him. "You burned my hair off, Jude," I snap. Now both of my arms are temporarily hairless.

"Are you paying attention now?"

"You could've just asked the question. You didn't need to burn me."

Jude takes one step toward me. "Check the attitude, Lucy, or I'll show you the kind of training I endured when I was your age. Suffice it to say I doubt you would survive." His steely tone sounds dangerous.

Goose bumps race down my arms and legs. *He won't really hurt me, right?*

"Now that you've experienced what it feels like to be hit with a fireball, you want to avoid being hit by another one. A series of fireballs could do real damage. If your clothes catch, the damage would likely be fatal." Jude holds his palm up and a fireball appears. "Think of the two D's. Deflect or dodge."

Jude hurls the fireball at me, and I fall to my knees. Sharp bursts of pain explode in both knees and I cry out in pain and frustration.

"That certainly qualifies as a dodge, but it's not the most effective." Jude stands still as a stone as he raises his palm and presents another fireball. Before I have time to move, he hurls it at me. I shriek in alarm as the fiery ball burns through my shirt and scorches my shoulder. "When you land on the ground, you have no leverage. You're stuck and an easy target. It's better to squat or shift low, lunge from side-to-side." He watches my face to see if his instructions sink in.

Psycho. I bite back the word before it spills from my mouth.

Jude nods. "Let's try it again."

I grit my teeth and struggle to my feet. *This sucks.*

The fireball balancing on Jude's palm catches my attention and I stop my internal complaining. Without any verbal warning, the fireball comes at me. I resist the urge to drop to the ground and instead veer to the right.

"Crap!" Hair sizzles against my ear, and I quickly pat it out. The smell nearly causes me to wretch.

There's no time to dwell on that before Jude sends two successive fireballs my way, forcing me to lunge to the left, then back to the right again. He has me practice that maneuver until my thighs scream with fatigue.

"Another defensive tactic is the drop and roll," he says.

"I really need a break," I tell him as I struggle to catch my breath. Sweat drips down my back and along my skull beneath my hair making my skin itch. "And some water."

Jude takes several steps toward me. "If Seamus were here, would he grant your requests for a break and some water?"

I make a face, not caring if Jude sees it.

"Drop and roll is an effective power move," he continues.

If Garret kills Jude, then I would be free of him. Oops. Then I'm a goner, too.

"Can you demonstrate?" I ask with a straight face, hoping he won't pick up on my delay tactic.

"I can." With a wave of his hand, Jude invites me to throw a fireball at him. I grin, only too happy to oblige.

Jude drops to his knees and immediately rolls to the left three times, then leaps to his feet, effectively avoiding my fireball. Without being asked, I hurl another. He repeats the maneuver, this time rolling to the right.

Jude leaps to his feet and brushes off his hands. "Your turn."

He launches a fireball at me as if he's pitching for the major leagues. My cry of surprise gets lodged in my throat as I drop to my knees and immediately roll to my right. My aching thighs refuse to cooperate, and instead of leaping up from the ground, I wheeze my way upright.

"Let's try that again. This time with a little enthusiasm," Jude says dryly.

I catch the smile on his face as he lobs another fireball at me. *My father's a nut job.*

There's no masking my cry this time. Fiery pain erupts from my knees as I connect with the ground. Dots dance across my vision, and I whimper as I curl and roll to the left. It takes several moments before I manage to climb back to my feet.

"It looks like you get a short day today," Jude announces.

I shield my eyes from the sun and spot Dylan walking toward us, his chest puffed out and a sly grin on his face. Jack, Troy, and Matt follow behind him, limping and sullen.

"Team Dylan wins." He jerks his thumb toward the mutts. "I'll need stiffer competition next time."

I don't understand. Although Dylan's face is bruised and there's blood smeared along his jaw, he doesn't appear to be tired. He doesn't look happy, though, and that cocky grin is as grim as when we first arrived.

Once inside the house, I grab my bag and limp my way to the bathroom to change. My hands are caked with dirt and scorch marks. No blood. I turn my hands over, intrigued. On the days when I'm throwing fireballs, my skin turns a dark red. I threw only a couple fireballs today. Jude explained the red skin is my body's protective mechanism kicking in, so the heat from my own fireballs won't hurt my hands.

I'm glad Jude keeps clothes here for me, so I don't have to train in my good clothes. My shirt is burned in a dozen places. My jeans are ruined, too. True to Jude's word, my wounds heal quickly.

As I pull on the clean jeans I arrived in, I notice my legs are red, too, like they're sunburned. Same with my arms. The burns marks are gone, though.

I jump as someone knocks at the door. "I'm in here. Go find another bathroom."

"It's Dylan. Open up a second."

I open the door a crack. "This house has to have more than one bathroom."

He laughs and pushes his way in. "It's not like you're naked or anything." He closes the door behind him.

"Can you believe how trashed those guys were?" He gloats, leaning against the wall.

"It was so weird. Jack came at me, grinning like a crazy person and something inside of me It's hard to explain. I was in the zone again."

He cocks his head, and suddenly, our eyes lock. I try to look away, but can't. His energy seeps into me, spreads through me.

"Something came to life inside of me. It took over. I don't know any other way to explain it."

I feel myself grinning like a crazed hyena right along with him. If only I could've found that zone while I was training with Jude.

"Jack used to scare the crap out of me. He's bigger than me— all of them are. But today...it never occurred to me to back down or to be afraid. I slammed him onto the ground before he realized I had him off his feet. I've never been able to move that fast. Never had that kind of power."

The thrill of his fight courses through my veins. My body trembles with exhilaration.

"We went round and round like that. I tried every move Aiden taught me. But these guys fight dirty." Dylan's eyes grow wide, and I can't tell if it's with awe or fear. "This is going to sound messed up, but the harder they came at me, the more charged up I felt."

I'm guessing if one—or all three of them—was here now, Dylan wouldn't hesitate to engage in a re-match.

"The biggest bullies we know are no longer a threat," I say. A fit of laughter bubbles up inside of me.

Dylan closes the distance between us. I hold my breath as he reaches for me. A smile plays on his lips as he strokes my cheek. Then he uses his fingernail against my skin.

I turn to the mirror and frown. I missed a couple of soil smudges on my face. Jude wins Dad of the Year again for shooting fireballs at me, causing me to land face-first in the dirt. I grab the fluffy, white washcloth off the sink and hold it under warm water.

"Ugh. I look gross." I stare at my reflection as I scrub at my skin. There's no washing away the blush coloring my cheeks, however. *What was I expecting him to do?*

"You look like a girl who just kicked somebody's ass." Dylan takes the washcloth from me and tosses it in the sink. He grasps my chin, forcing me to meet his gaze. "You'd think you've been training for years. I was pretty impressed."

I inhale sharply as warmth spreads through me. My pulse quickens, more out of embarrassment than anything. "You must've missed all those times I landed on my butt. Or my face."

Dylan takes my hand and holds it palm side up. He caresses my skin with his thumb. "Your secret weapon. You have no idea how jealous I am."

His touch makes me nervous. The room grows warm, and yet I'm overcome with the need to move closer to him. Much like my need to hurl fireballs, it builds quickly, urgently. I don't understand *this*. I can't control it, and honestly, I don't want to.

Dylan pulls me against him—or did I lunge at him?—and his

mouth crushes against mine. My breath hitches as energy rages between us, something I've never felt before...or maybe I did. The night Dylan and I torched Jude's tree. I felt it then. But this is stronger. The heat between us sizzles. We're pressed so close together that we're one, but it's not enough.

A sudden memory pierces my thoughts. The night Marcus and I sat together on the front steps of the three-flat. He sang a French song about plucking feathers from a bird.

I shove Dylan away, gasping.

"Come on, Lucy. This is amazing. You and me." Dylan leans in and presses his lips to mine. My body betrays me, leans into him.

What am I doing? I push against Dylan's chest. He laughs and pulls me closer. Does he think I'm playing around? I push him again, but it does little good. Panic bubbles up inside of me. *I don't want this.* I pull my hand back and slap him as hard as I can. A red mark forms immediately on his cheek.

Dylan's eyes widen as he takes an uneven step backward. He opens his mouth, but no words come out.

I fling open the door and flee from the room.

CHAPTER TWENTY

– Dylan Douglas –

Dumb. Dumb. Dumb. What was I thinking? I wasn't, and that's the problem. I close the door after Lucy and splash cold water on my face. *What the hell was that?* It was hot, sure, but kind of insane, too.

Closing my eyes, I'm right back there, feeling her lips against mine. She was kissing me back. It made me lose my head. I've never felt desire like that before. Not even with my ex, Rachel, and I didn't think it got any hotter than Rachel.

But the look on Lucy's face before she ran out of here. Disgust? Guilt? Betrayal? Who am I kidding? It was probably all three. There go my chances of getting her away from Marcus.

Maybe.

I'm her ride home. She wouldn't risk asking Jude for a ride, not when she's trying to keep him away from her uncles. What can I do to make her see I'm a good guy, still the same old Dylan?

After I scrub off the dirt and blood and change clothes, I track Lucy down in the kitchen where she's sitting at the small table drinking hot tea. Her gaze lands on me like a deer in the headlights. A very scared deer.

Pain twists in my gut like a knife. I don't want her to be afraid of me.

"I'm sorry," I tell her, glancing around the room for Jude. If he heard this conversation, he'd probably skin me alive then set me on fire. "I didn't mean for that to happen." It felt great. I don't regret it. Sorry, but I don't. But I have to go easy. Lucy can handle herself against Jude and all sorts of scary, but when it comes to sexual stuff, I get the sense it terrifies her.

Lucy scrapes her chair back, washes her teacup in the sink, dries it, and returns it to the cabinet. She crosses the kitchen and pauses, a good five feet between us. "That won't happen again. Ever."

The look in her eyes knocks the wind out of me. Cold and distant.

CHAPTER TWENTY-ONE

– Lucy Walker –

"Thank you for agreeing to meet with me." Selima waves Marcus's hand away and hops over the railing. She surveys the roof of the apartment building. "I'm sure it's been a lot to take in with Garret and Camille showing up out of the blue."

"You could say that," Marcus replies evenly. He turns and gestures to me. "This is my girlfriend—"

"Lucy!" Selima flashes me a dazzling smile and shakes my hand.

I gasp as her grip nearly brings me to my knees.

"Selima!" Marcus takes my hand and inspects my throbbing fingers.

Selima cringes, her face flushing red. "I'm so sorry. I...I don't shake hands with many humans these days." She touches my arm, but her attention is directed to her brother. "Is anything broken? I will heal her."

"I'm okay." I force a smile and attempt to bend my fingers. "You said my name as if you knew about me."

"Camille told me about you. I couldn't wait to meet you."

I wonder what Camille said about me. Did she refer to me as demon spawn? Cheater can be added to the list now, too. The kiss with Dylan flashes through my head and my shoulders sag. Marcus doesn't need more disappointment.

I shake off thoughts of Dylan and focus on Selima. Her appearance catches me by surprise: nose and eyebrow piercings, dark brown hair cut short and spiky, heavy black eyeliner rimming striking brown eyes. She's dressed in black from her tank top all the way down to her combat boots. In contrast, she has full, sensual lips.

After my last run-in with Camille and Garret, I can't help but be suspicious. I check her fingers for claws and try to get a look at her teeth.

I glance at Marcus, whose hands are stuffed in the pockets of his jeans. He shifts from one foot to the other, eyeing her.

"Not what you were expecting?" she says with a throaty laugh.

"You and Marcus look nothing alike," I blurt out. "Are you really brother and sister?"

"We have different mothers," Marcus murmurs.

I knew Selima was Garret's daughter from his first marriage, but I still expected to see some family resemblance. There's none. I notice Marcus keeps his distance from her. His expression remains closed off.

Selima blows out a long breath and smiles at me. "My little brother's pretty broody. What's up with that?" She waits for me to agree.

I narrow my eyes at her, feeling extremely defensive on Marcus's behalf. After everything that's gone down recently, her attempt at humor is wholly inappropriate. "Do you know Garret attacked Marcus recently?" *And I kissed another guy?*

Selima's upbeat mood fades. "I do and I'm sorry about that." She reaches for Marcus.

He stands stone still, his hands tucked away.

"Can you tell me what happened? I heard Lucy hurled a fireball in the kitchen and trashed the place."

My mouth drops open.

Marcus chuckles bitterly. "Of course Garret would tell you that part. If you're here on his behalf, you should go."

Selima holds up her hands in surrender. "I'm not judging. Please don't send me away. I'm here because I want to meet—and get to know—my brother. There's no alternative agenda."

Marcus raises his eyebrows. "You swear?"

"I swear."

The moment feels heavy with intention. It reminds of all those times Momma and I made pinky promises. Momma rarely kept hers.

Marcus relaxes and turns to me. "She's good. Protectors can't lie."

A vision of Garret about to sink his dagger-sharp teeth into Marcus's neck has me leery about the virtues of protectors.

"Why are you here?" I blurt out.

The corners of Selima's mouth curve up. "To meet my brother, like I said. I was hoping to meet you, too."

"Who sent you?"

"Just my conscious."

Marcus tugs on my hand. "I think we're good, Agent Walker. No further interrogation is needed."

After a moment, I return his smile. I want more than anything for Selima to be good. For Marcus's sake. Especially now that I've proven I'm not.

Selima sits in one fluid movement. Her stretchy black skirt accommodates her movements, and her top hugs her torso. She moves like a dancer, but I have a feeling her training is along the lines of something far more dangerous. Maybe her intentions are good, but what kind of girl has a crushing handshake?

According to Camille, Garret didn't want children. Was that because he already had Selima? What's so special about her that he couldn't love another child?

Marcus sits down opposite Selima. The moment I sit next to him, he gently clasps my bruised hand in his. If he knew about yesterday, I doubt he would be so tender. "How old are you?"

"Nineteen. You're seventeen, right?"

Marcus nods. "So...Garret dated Camille after he and your mom split?"

"Their marriage ended." Selima raises her shoulder, then drops it. "While Garret technically left my mother and me, he still took care of us. My mom supports Garret as clan leader."

"Do you support him?" The question is out of my mouth before I can stop it. I turn to Marcus. "Sorry, I guess I'm not done with the interrogation."

He strokes my hand with his thumb. "It's okay. You have a stake in this, too."

"Depends on the agenda." Selima squirms. "Listen, I love Garret. He's my father. But we have our issues. He tries— unsuccessfully—to order me around."

"You don't strike me as someone easily ordered around," Marcus says, the hint of a grin on his face.

"I work and go to college in northern Wisconsin. In exchange for my services, my employer covers my tuition, and room and board. Garret doesn't like who I work for and is constantly on my case to quit and go to school someplace else with other protectors."

She's working and going to college? What's Garret's problem? "Who is your employer?"

Selima meets my gaze, raising one eyebrow, and I suck in my breath. How many times have I seen that same gesture on Marcus's face? I shake it off and force myself to pay attention.

"I work for a group of demons."

I lurch forward at the same time Marcus throws his head back and laughs.

"How is that possible?" I ask. "You...you're a protector."

"Scandalous, isn't it?" Selima grins slyly. She leans forward conspiratorially. "They're different. They aren't, for example, like your father."

I gape at her in surprise.

"Oh, yes, I know all about Jude Morgan. He's Enemy Number One in Garret's eyes." She rolls her eyes. "Garret's very dramatic, in case you didn't know."

Marcus's grin falls away. "Dramatic? Vicious is more like it. Are you aware that Garret's here to kill Jude and by extension Lucy?"

Selima nods solemnly. "Do you believe Jude is guilty of the crimes he's accused of?"

"Killing protectors?" Marcus inhales then exhales slowly.

"Jude's evil. I know that for a fact. He's got it out for me, but that's because I'm a protector who's dating his daughter. Otherwise, I don't think he'd pay a second of attention to me."

Selima eyes him suspiciously. "Even though you're the enemy?"

"According to Aiden—"

"The demon you live with?" Selima asks.

"Yes. Aiden told me about the treaty Jude and Grayson signed all those years ago."

"I've heard about the treaty," Selima says. "But no one has ever been able to find a copy of it. Who knows if it's real?"

"Or maybe it goes against the current agenda so it's been hidden," Marcus says. "I'm sorry. I'm not trying to pick on your father, but according to Henry and Persephone—"

Selima's eyebrow shoots up quizzically.

"They're witches," I clarify.

She nods, unfazed.

"Jude hasn't slaughtered any protectors under their watch."

"How long have they been watching him?"

"Since the day I was born," I tell her.

Selima nods thoughtfully.

"You trust these witches?" she asks Marcus.

"With my life."

"That's good enough for me," Selima says, her voice full of determination.

"What do you mean?" Marcus and I ask in unison.

Selima's face breaks into a smile. "I'm going to help keep Lucy alive."

Chapter Twenty-Two

– Lucy Walker –

Persephone yanks open the door after my first knock. She's been waiting for me.

"I heard you met the sister?" she says as she leads me to the kitchen. "What do you think of her?"

"Marcus trusts her. With his extrasensory powers and the whole protectors can't lie thing, I guess I trust her, too. At least for now."

Persephone chuckles. "Trust doesn't come easy for you. Not such a bad thing."

Do I tell her about what happened with Dylan three nights ago? I've done a good job at pretending it never happened. I avoid Dylan at school and ignore his text messages. Any mention of him at the lunch table and I tune out.

Is it really considered cheating if I kissed another guy? I remember how it felt with Dylan, the fire between us. That kind of intensity didn't seem possible. It was dangerous. Besides, the whole pretend game isn't helping. I toss and turn at night, the guilt eating at me and robbing me of much needed sleep.

With considerable effort, I force myself to focus on the task at hand. Persephone and I need to figure out a way to save Jude. It'll be hard for me to beg Marcus for forgiveness if I'm dead.

"Do I need one?" I nod at the bottle of water in her hand.

"This is plenty. Did you bring the business card?" Persephone asks as we stand beside the kitchen table.

I pull Jude's business card from my pocket, the one he slipped into my book at the airport when I arrived in Chicago last year. I set it on the table next to the bottle of water.

Persephone holds up two hunks of black, shiny stone, roughly the size of golf balls. "Whoa, Nellie!" she twitches and giggles as if tickled.

"What are those?"

"Black tourmaline. They give off quite a zing—their energy. Your grandmother never sensed energies from precious gems. You may not, either. Want to give it a try?"

"Sure." I take the two stones from her, holding one in each hand. They're heavier than I expected. I wait a moment, then shrug. "I don't feel anything."

"Give it some time." Persephone catches me eying two dark brown slim branches sitting on the table. "They're from a birch tree. I prefer ash, but with the damage done by those nasty beetles throughout the city, they're scarce."

I frown at the branches. More like large twigs. "They don't look like much."

"They'll do the trick," Persephone says over her shoulder as she crosses the room and climbs onto a stool to investigate a top shelf of her cupboard. Glass bottles clank against each other as she searches for something.

"Here we go," she mutters as she retrieves two small bottles. She closes the cabinet and climbs off the stool gingerly. "Why don't you grab the branches and follow me? Let's get to work."

After I stuff Jude's business card in my pocket, I tuck the sticks in the crook of my elbow, while clutching the black tourmaline stones. I still don't sense anything.

Persephone leads the way down the hall, around the corner and up the stairs. Her steps are slow and heavy as we make our way to the attic, and for the first time, it occurs to me that she's old. A quiver of fear works its way from my belly to my throat. What would I do if I lost Persephone? She's the only mother figure I have left. Without her around to train me to be a witch, would my demonic powers take over?

I draw in a sharp breath, and Persephone pauses mid-step. "You okay?"

I cough into my hand. "A-okay."

She nods and continues on. Once at the top, she lifts a thick chain from around her neck. There's a key dangling from the end of it. She holds the key in mid-air. I peer around her and see her eyes are closed. A rush of whispered words flow from her lips.

She opens her eyes, inserts the key into the lock, and the door opens with a slow, eerie creak.

"Very few people have ever been in here, mostly just your gram, Henry, and me," Persephone says as she closes the door behind us. She taps the doorknob with her index finger twice, and the lock clanks in the tumbler, no key necessary.

I want to learn how to do that.

"Lights," Persephone calls out. Light floods the attic.

Whoa!

"Aiden used to come here, too." Persephone titters at my shocked expression. "Vera was fond of Aiden. She believed in his good side, wanted to train him in our ways."

How did Aiden fool Gram?

"While he dated Daphne, she talked him into bringing her here. She tricked Aiden into practicing dark magic. Can you imagine? Dark magic within these sacred walls? The two of them damn near blew up the house." Persephone purses her lips at the memory. "Aiden's memory of this space was erased. He hasn't been up here since."

She crosses to the center of the room, walking around the circle drawn on the floor, so she enters it from the east. I mimic her actions exactly. After what I read in Gram's books, I'm afraid one little misstep might cause a catastrophe.

Persephone sits down on a moss-green cushion and gestures for me to sit on the cushion next to her. It's yellow, Gram's favorite color.

"Was this Gram's?"

Persephone's face softens. "It was. Now it's yours."

I smile and fold my legs Indian-style. Something flutters inside of me. It feels strangely familiar, like the energy I felt that night at Jude's house when Lola transferred Gram's powers to me. I cock my head as I wonder if...No, it's not possible. A cushion doesn't hold any power. Besides, I couldn't sense energies in the black tourmaline.

Suddenly, I remember the warmth of Gram's hugs, the smell of her floral perfume, and the tug against my scalp as she finger-combed tangles from my hair. I brush my fingers against the edges of the cushion beneath me. Would this be something different? Is it possible to connect with a magical object if it belonged to Gram? Or is my mind playing tricks on me?

"This is my altar." Persephone interrupts my euphoria. She nods at the wooden table in front of us, which sits several inches off the floor on thick legs. She pulls matches from the single, slim drawer and lights a dark purple candle, which sits at the center of the altar. "The candle will enhance magical powers, which in turn will help us with our spellcasting."

She touches the match to the incense stick set off to the right.

"What are those?" I point to the carved wooden figures that stand on each side of the candle.

"This is the Goddess Demeter." Persephone points to the figure on the left. "And this is the Goddess Gaia. The choice of the Goddesses you will pray to is a very personal decision." In front of each figure sits a small bowl. From reading Gram's books, I already know what's in the first bowl. Salt. In the other bowl, Persephone pours an inch of water from her bottle.

"You are about to witness your first ritual. Pay close attention," Persephone says calmly. Her face is absent of the usual deep lines. Her posture is relaxed. Her voice doesn't carry its normal stern tone. I think I'll like spending time with Persephone here.

Before starting the ritual, Persephone opens her drawer once more. She retrieves a knife and sets it before her on the altar. It looks really old. The ornate, golden handle is decorated with the image of a winding oriental dragon. I wonder if it's real gold.

"It's an athame, one of our four elemental tools. It represents fire. Beautiful, isn't it?" Persephone fingers the carved metal, a small smile playing at the corners of her mouth. "It's one of my most treasured..." She trails off, and I hold my breath, waiting for her to continue. "I purchased this on a trip with your Gram, years ago, after Zack's death."

I grind my teeth. Heat flushes through my body. There were so many things Persephone got to do with Gram, so much I was excluded from, while I was stuck back home taking care of Momma. My shoulders droop at the familiar stab of guilt.

I admire Persephone's knife—*athame*—and grudgingly wonder if I'll ever have something that interesting and unique for my altar.

Persephone slides a sideways glance at me and frowns. Has she picked up on my anger? My guilt? This is a sacred room of magic. Maybe there are no secrets here. I swallow and flex my fingers until they relax.

"Let's get to work on that spell," Persephone suggests. She struggles to her feet and grabs a broad metal tray from a cabinet behind her, which she sets on the floor beside the altar. She moves her cushion to one side of the tray; I move mine to the other.

Persephone wiggles her fingers at me, beckoning. "Jude's business card? He wrote on it, didn't he?"

I pull it from my pocket and show her the note scrawled on the back.

Lucy,
It's very important we meet. Call me, please.
Jude Morgan

It's hard to believe it's been a year since Jude and I first met. Well, collided is more like it.

"Set it in the middle of the tray. It will serve as a representation of Jude."

I do as she says.

"I hope it's really Jude's handwriting and not something he dictated to some assistant at his office. Will the spell work if Jude didn't write the note?"

"If he went to the trouble of running into you at the airport, I have to believe he took the time to write the note," Persephone says.

"Good point."

"Place the black tourmaline on the tray," Persephone instructs. I grab the black gemstones and set them on either side of the business card. Persephone separates the wooden branches and arranges them on the tray, so they, together with the stones, form a sort of square-ish circle around the business card. "As I said, the business card represents Jude. The sticks and stones represent protection."

Persephone uncorks the first bottle and pours a small amount of liquid into a shallow dish. I recognize the stems inside the bottle. Rosemary. She pours liquid from the second bottle into the second small dish, and the rich, earthy smell of cedar hits my nose.

I watch intently and try to keep my hands from fidgeting. I wish she would let me do something.

Next, she retrieves what appears to be a sewing needle from her altar drawer and twirls it over the flame of the purple candle.

"Now we need to activate the protective oil by adding a couple drops of blood."

She raises her eyebrows at me. It takes me a minute to get it.

"You mean mine? Sure, okay." It never occurred to me blood was used in good magic. I thrust my hand at her, palm side up, and try to sound braver than I feel. Needles make me think of Momma.

Persephone swiftly pokes my index finger, then squeezes it to draw out the blood. She steers my hand over the two small dishes, clutching my finger until three droplets of blood land in each dish of oil. As soon as she releases my finger, I stick it in my mouth and suck on it to stop the bleeding.

Persephone swirls the two small dishes to distribute the blood throughout the oil. She anoints the gemstones and the birch branches with the rosemary oil. Then she anoints Jude's business card with the essential oil of cedar.

"It's important to note—and you'll come across this as you continue to study your Gram's books—that you should avoid protective herbs that are also traditionally used in exorcism, like sage, frankincense, and myrrh."

"Exorcism?"

Persephone frowns at me like I'm a total moron.

"Jude's a demon. The spell would be a disaster."

I shudder. We've had enough of those.

"Now we need to visualize a protective circle around Jude," Persephone says, staring intently at the contents of the tray. "Can you do that?"

I nod and focus on the sticks, stones, and our representation of Jude. I imagine huge boulders and the ogre-like trees in Jude's yard surrounding him, creating a barricade so no one can get through.

I didn't realize how hard I was focusing until Persephone's voice startles me. "Deep breaths, Lucy. I don't want you passing out."

I take a deep breath in, then exhale.

"Now repeat after me," Persephone's calm voice washes over me and I relax even more. "Sticks and stones forge together to protect Jude Morgan."

I wonder if she's making this up on the spot or if she wrote it ahead of time and memorized it.

"Lucy!" Persephone hisses.

Oops. Focus. "Sticks and stone forge together to protect Jude Morgan."

"No matter what conclusions are foregone or cast on."

Foregone conclusions? Does she think this is a lost cause? Is Jude going to die no matter what? Am I? I give myself a mental shake, then repeat the line before Persephone can chastise me.

"Keep him safe from all opposition."

My shoulders have crept up to my ears. I roll them out to regain my relaxed state and repeat the line.

"Remove all suspicion, regardless of his position."

Position? I'm about to repeat the line when an old, creepy voice echoes through the attic.

"Jude holds the rank of king among demons, and he is said to have been created second only to Lucifer."

Who was that? Where did that come from? Was that part of the spell? I glance up at Persephone, but she's just glaring at me.

162

"Did you hear that?" I ask. "That voice?"

Persephone's eyes narrow as she peers at me.

"I heard a voice, I swear. Some old guy talking about Jude and Lucifer."

Persephone's complexion grows pale. She clears her throat. "Let's finish this."

I nod.

"Remove all suspicion regardless of his position," she repeats, her voice firm.

I repeat the words quickly.

"Form a barrier against those who mean harm."

I'm relaxed. I'm relaxed. I'm relaxed. I repeat Persephone's words.

"Stay arm in arm, sound the alarm then unarm."

The words come out slow as they're a bit of a tongue twister, and I don't want to get them wrong. What happens if you get a spell wrong? Does the opposite happen? Or does it ruin the whole thing and you have to start over? I'm pretty sure Persephone would be mad either way.

"Until the threat is gone."

I repeat the words without delay. Silence. Are we done? I peek out of one eye at Persephone. There's a look of annoyance on her face. I'm guessing I didn't do so well.

"I'm impressed with your ability to rhyme," I tell her, trying to suck up a little.

"Shhh!"

I press my lips together and watch as Persephone looks around us, waiting, listening. The spell didn't work. She fixes me with a look, eyebrows pulled low, her mouth an upside-down smile that clearly says it's all my fault.

Jude holds the rank of king among demons, and he is said to have been created second only to Lucifer.

Lucifer. I shiver and swallow. "Should we do it again?" I ask meekly.

"Do you think you can focus?" Her tone is not harsh so much as exasperated.

I nod. "I'm sorry. I'll do better."

"It's not just about focusing," she says, her voice gentler this time as she adjusts her position on her cushion. "It's about visualization. You need to imagine the gemstones and the branches fusing together around Jude in your mind. Spells are all about manipulating energy, and visualization is a stronger form of energy." Persephone waits for some acknowledgement that I get it.

I nod.

"Use visualization to control and direct the magical energy. You must see it in your mind in order for it to work. Does that make sense?"

"I think so."

Persephone takes several deep breaths. I do the same. As I repeat her words, I imagine the black tourmaline turning to liquid and melding with the birch branches. They become one, then grow tall and wide, like a wall surrounding Jude.

I gasp when I realize that in my vision, Jude's wearing the same outfit he had on the night of homecoming. The shirt that wound up soaked with my blood. I shake off the image. I focus on the wall, the impenetrable barrier. It grows taller and thicker. Jude is safe.

"Until the threat is gone." I open my eyes as I state the final words of the spell, my attention still focused inward on my vision.

Persephone nods at the tray on the floor between us. I inhale sharply as a glowing ball of energy swirls around Jude's business card. It picks up speed. I focus on my inner visualization, afraid that if I stop, whatever this is will stop. I'm guessing this is supposed to be happening or Persephone would've done something about it. I continue to imagine the wall of stone and wood growing thicker and taller.

Suddenly, the magical orb speeds up, racing faster and faster around Jude. It bounces off the larger of the two gemstones and ricochets across the room, smashing through the small, octagon-shaped window.

"What was that?" I gasp.

Persephone smiles. "The magical spell is headed over to Jude's." Then her smile falls away. Both goddess statues on her alter lay broken in half. "A consequence."

Uneasiness swirls inside of me. I never heard the statues break. Maybe it happened at the same time the ball of energy shattered the window? "What do you mean? Why?"

"I used good magic to help someone evil."

CHAPTER TWENTY-THREE

– Lucy Walker –

On Thursday I come home from school and stop short when I find my uncles talking with Camille in the foyer. The three of them huddle together, their voices low.

I move close as Sheldon takes her hand in both of his. "It's lovely to meet you, Camille. You and Marcus should join us for dinner."

"I'd like that," she says.

I close the foyer door behind me noisily.

All three of them turn to me.

"How was school, Luce?" Bernard asks, sparing only a moment's glance my way.

First, Jude shows up unannounced and uninvited, forcing a meeting with my uncles. Now, Camille. It's bad enough she stood beside Garret after he attacked her son. What does she want with my uncles?

"Um...fine, I think."

Camille's eyes are red. What did she tell them? Did she reveal the truth about Jude? I take in Sheldon's watery eyes, his bottom lip pushed out. Bernard nods eagerly, looking a little distracted. I bet he's already planning the dinner menu.

But neither of them are freaking out. So she didn't tell them anything. Not about demons, witches, and gargoyles, anyway.

Camille moves to shake Bernard's hand, and he pulls her into a hug.

"I look forward to seeing you soon." He pats her gently on the back. "Come for coffee anytime."

"It's the best coffee I've had since my days in Seattle." Camille's lips pull into a crooked smile. Marcus's smile.

Hostility burns inside of me. Jealousy?

"Hello, Lucy." Camille acknowledges me as she pulls out of Bernard's embrace. "It's always nice to see you." She moves to hug me.

I take a step back and open the foyer door so she can leave. This is the same woman who abandoned Marcus, and who even now sides with Garret over her son. She can burn in hell for all I care. Maybe I should ask Jude to put in a special request for her.

"What's up with the love fest?" I demand to know once she's gone.

"Such a remarkable woman," Sheldon says, following Bernard and me into the apartment as he wipes his eyes with a white handkerchief.

Bernard nods. "So brave, revealing the ugliest parts of her past."

"What exactly did she tell you?" I'm sure she left out the part where she stood by while Garret was about to sink his nasty fangs into Marcus's shoulder.

"That she left Marcus and his stepfather all those years ago. Did you know about that?" Sheldon asks.

She told them some of the truth. Interesting. But why? What's her angle? "I did...I mean, I do. Are you mad I didn't tell you?"

"Of course not." Bernard pats my shoulder. "Poor Marcus. He's been through a lot. Now his birth father wants to reconnect with him, too, on the heels of his stepfather's death? That's a lot to take in."

I stuff my hands into the pockets of my black pants and focus on my shoes. Then I go and kiss Dylan. Add that to the list. Maybe I'm more like Momma than I thought. What if I don't live long enough to make it up to him?

"Lucy, go call Marcus and see if he wants to join us for dinner," Sheldon calls over his shoulder as he follows Bernard to the kitchen. "We're making burgers and your favorite, tater tots."

"O...okay." I resolve to tell Marcus tonight. He deserves to know the truth.

I head to my room and dump my backpack on my desk. I pull my cell from my purse, swallow hard, and call my boyfriend.

"Hey, stranger." Happiness washes over me the second I hear his voice, followed by more guilt. "I was beginning to think you're avoiding me."

I mentally run through our recent conversation. Marcus knew I had to work with Persephone last night. We texted Monday over lunch and after school. Yesterday? Nothing.

He's going to know something's up. An image of Dylan and me pressed against the bathroom door at Jude's flashes through my thoughts. My skin tingles with excitement. *Stop it!* I tell myself.

I slump into my desk chair, squeezing my eyes closed as guilt consumes me.

Marcus bursts out laughing. "Are you still there? I'm just kidding. Relax."

I finally find my voice. "My uncles are making burgers and tater tots for dinner. You're invited to join us."

"Hmmm...Dylan's usually the one who gets invited to dinner."

"I know. I have to be honest..." I almost choke on the word. "They spoke with your mom today. The three of them had coffee. She just left. I think she shared the whole story with them."

He pauses on the other end of the line. "The *whole* story?"

"Not the part about you and Garret being protectors and not about Jude or how Garret attacked you," I say quickly. "The other part, about her taking off. Sheldon and Bernard called her brave."

It takes him a while to respond. "Interesting."

"I thought so, too." I wait for him to say more, but he doesn't. "If it helps you to make a decision, I'm told Sheldon makes the best burgers." I immediately regret saying it.

"Let me guess...by Dylan?"

"Please come." There's a part of me that wouldn't mind if he declines, and I hate myself for it.

"Sure. I'll come. I can't believe I haven't kissed you since Saturday. How is that possible?"

My laugh sounds robotic. "I don't know."

So lame.

An hour and a half later I'm done with homework. I brush my hair, apply cherry lip balm, and join my uncles in the kitchen.

"I'll set the table." I volunteer as Sheldon takes a platter of raw patties and a separate plate with a veggie burger outside to the grill.

While the smell of tater tots baking is delicious, the heat from the oven is oppressive. I jump as water hisses on top of the stove. Bernard lifts the lid on the steamer and fills it with broccoli.

He glances over his shoulder at me. "Put all the condiments on the table, too, will you?"

"Sure."

When the doorbell rings a few minutes later, I move on leaden legs to the living room and open the door for Marcus.

He smiles at me, and I'm torn between feeling like the happiest girl alive and the worst girlfriend ever. He pulls me into his embrace.

"I've missed you." He buries his face in my hair.

I wrap my arms around him and inhale his amazing smell. That familiar stirring comes to life inside of me. The kind of attraction I feel for Marcus makes my heart swell and my toes curl. When his arms are around me, I feel safe, loved, and excited. With Dylan, it's dangerous and desperate. It's the wrong kind of hot, like we're going to catch fire. "I've missed you, too."

"Yeah?" The word comes out soft and slow. His eyes burn into mine.

Our lips meet and my arms automatically circle his neck. These are the lips I know. His kisses are gentle, probing, loving, not hard and demanding like Dylan's.

Marcus winds his fingers through my hair. "Thank you for that," he says, a satisfied smile on his face.

I tug on his arm. "Come on in. You're a VIP at our table tonight."

"Maybe I should've told them my sad tale a long time ago," Marcus teases as he follows me to the kitchen.

My uncles decline Marcus's offer to help and direct him to a chair. I pour lemonade for everyone.

Marcus lifts his glass and looks curiously at the green stems in the liquid.

"It's rosemary," I tell him.

"Herbed lemonade is all the rage right now," Bernard says, taking a long draw from his glass. "Lucy learned about it before I did, if you can believe it."

Marcus studies me over his glass. I wink back at him. My original intention with the rosemary was to help my uncles keep their cool when we talk about the vacation—something I learned in Gram's books—and now it's their favorite beverage.

"Marcus, we met Camille this afternoon. She's an intriguing woman." Sheldon carries the platter of cooked burgers in through the back door.

"She is." Marcus dips a tater tot in ketchup, then pops it in his mouth. Our eyes meet and I suspect he's wondering the same thing as me. What's Camille up to? Maybe she's trying to get to Marcus through my uncles? I'm not sure what good that would do.

"She mentioned she's a fan of the arts. Do you think she'd be interested in joining us at the opera next month?"

"Maybe. You'd have to ask her," Marcus says with a shrug.

My uncles seem to pick up on Marcus's reluctance to talk about his mother and, fortunately, there's no more talk of her through the rest of the meal.

While my uncles and I clean up the kitchen—they forbid the

guest of honor from helping—Marcus offers to grab my hoodie from my bedroom for our trip to the roof. I bite my lip and turn away as he leaves the room.

I need to tell him. I can't keep it inside any longer. If someone as awful as Camille can be brave and confess to my uncles how she abandoned her son, then I can be brave and tell Marcus about my kiss with Dylan.

Half an hour later, Marcus is quiet as he helps me over the railing.

He knows something. But how? I study him out of the corner of my eye. I move around him and am about to sit down in our normal spot when he clears his throat. I look up. He hands me my cell phone.

"It kept buzzing when I was in your room." Marcus's expression is pinched. "Someone was eager to get in touch with you. I thought it might be Jude, that he'd get upset if he couldn't reach you."

My heart sinks like a lead weight. It's impossible to read his expression, but his detached tone scares me. Not cold, exactly, more like he's talking to a complete stranger. He gestures for me to take the phone. "Text messages. You should read them."

Three messages and they're all from Dylan. I don't want to read them, but what else can I do while Marcus's eyes burn holes into me?

I lick my lips nervously. I glance at Marcus, see his unwavering stare, then look back at my phone.

I click on the first message. *You can't hate me forever, you know. I'm sorry about the kiss.*

Okay. Not so bad. I can explain this to Marcus.

I click on the second message. *But tell the truth. It was incredible. I know you felt it, too.*

I try to inhale, but my lungs won't cooperate. I glance at Marcus. "I can explain..."

Marcus narrows his eyes. "Please continue." His voice drips with sarcasm. "The last one is my favorite."

Jude's right. We're meant to be together. It's time to dump Marcus.

My stomach spasms as fear rips through me, fear that Marcus is going to dump me here on the roof. I slip my phone into my back pocket with an unsteady hand.

"So this whole time you and Dylan..." Marcus spits out the words. "Demon training?"

"We *have* been training." The words sound defensive. Will he mistake it for guilt? Then again...I am guilty. I kissed Dylan back. I felt what he felt. I didn't want to, but I did.

"Right," he grinds out the word. "And plenty of other stuff, too, apparently."

"Marcus, please. It didn't mean anything. I swear." Tears burn my eyes, my throat. "I love you—"

"What about Dylan? Do you love him?"

"No! I mean, as a friend, yes, but not romantically. Not anything close to how I feel about you. It was a mistake."

Marcus rubs his eyes with the heels of his hands. "I have to go."

I reach for him. "Wait, Marcus!"

"Don't you get it? I can't be around you right now," he chokes. "If only you could see your face."

He swings his leg over the ledge and jumps off the building.

CHAPTER TWENTY-FOUR

– Lucy Walker –

"What happened to carpooling with Dylan in the mornings?" Katie complains.

I slam my locker door and sling my backpack over my shoulder as we head to lunch. "Dylan and I aren't talking right now."

She grabs my arm and yanks me out of hallway traffic. "What happened?"

I can't look her in the eye. The heat of a blush burns my cheeks.

Katie gasps. "You didn't."

Am I that transparent?

"Did you two make out or something?"

I pull my hair over my shoulder, twist it over and over as I will the tears not to come. Finally, I nod, not trusting my voice.

Katie's eyes nearly pop out of her head. "Holy crap! Does Marcus know?"

I nod again, my eyes brimming.

"How mad is he?"

I sputter and roll my tear-filled eyes at her.

"Okay. Dumb question. Did he break up with you?"

"I...don't...know." I hiccup. "He's...not...talking...to...me."

Katie clutches my hand. "What're you going to do?"

Tears slide down my cheeks. Pulling my hand free from Katie's, I wipe them away quickly and turn my face away from the students racing by to their next class. I swallow several times, struggling to get myself under control.

"I don't know. Dylan likes to visit his brother and sister on Saturday when I babysit." I pull a tissue from my purse and blow my nose. "I texted him, told him not to come this weekend. He's mad at me, too, since I slapped him." I shake my head miserably. "Now he's not responding."

"You slapped Dylan?" Katie does that thing again with her eyeballs. "Is he furious?"

"I don't care," I snap. "He knows I have a boyfriend. He shouldn't have started it."

I see the look on Katie's face. I just admitted to her a few minutes ago that Dylan and I made out. This isn't all Dylan's fault. But she's too nice to point that out right now.

My shoulders slump. "I'm a bad person."

Katie hooks her arm through mine and leads me down the hall. "What I mean is...let's face it, it's Dylan. The cockiest guy we know. You're choosing Marcus over him. *That's* why he's so mad." She squeezes my arm. "I don't think you're a bad person, but if you think so, fix it. Make things right."

* * * *

That night I call Dylan and, luckily, get his voicemail.

"Hey, Dylan. It's Lucy." I pause for a moment, then remember this is voicemail. I don't want to be cut off. "First, I want to apologize. I shouldn't have slapped you. What happened at Jude's...it was my fault, too, so I'm sorry." I cross and uncross my legs. Finally, I shift, pull my feet onto my bed and pick at the chipped dark blue nail polish on my toes. "Um, next, I'm not sure if you got my other message, but it would be best for you to skip your visits with Ethan and Brandi on Saturdays for a while. I'm sorry. I know how hard it is for you to see them when Alana's around, but this is best for now." I re-read the piece of paper on my bed and write a check mark next to the first two items. "I'd love to skip going to Jude's house on Sunday, but you know I can't. So, I need you to stay away for a while. Jude's totally going to freak, but I'll deal with him. I'll check to see if he wants you to train on another day."

I check that item off my list, and suddenly, I'm unsure how to end the call. Dylan's one of my best friends. My throat constricts at the thought of losing him. I blink rapidly at the oncoming tears.

"No one knows you like I do, Dylan," I whisper. "You're an amazing person. Ethan and Brandi are really lucky to have you. I'm going to miss you."

I click to end the call and flop back on my bed. I close my eyes and inhale—four counts in—and exhale—four counts out. I repeat this several times. It works to keep the crying fits away. The call to Marcus is going to be so much worse.

After a few minutes, I climb off my bed and grab the glass of water from my desk. I down the whole thing, then pick up my phone.

I'm not sure which scares me more, Marcus answering the phone or getting his voicemail. I get his voicemail.

"Marcus, it's Lucy again."

I relay my voicemail message to Dylan. "I'm not taking him up on his offer to carpool to school, either, although Katie's upset about that."

Trying to insert something light into the message sounds dumb. I go for honesty.

"I'm sorry, Marcus. I have no excuse for what I did. I'm begging you to forgive me. Maybe I don't deserve it, but I'm asking anyway...because I can't imagine my life without you. It wasn't much before I met you. Even though it's a big hot mess right now, having you in it makes it special. For the first time since Gram died, I look forward to my future...because you're in it." Even though that future is iffy.

I end the call and climb under the covers. Sliding my hand under my pillow, I curl my fingers around the delicate feather. Marcus's feather. The one I've kept in the medicine cabinet for months. Over the past few days, I've needed a piece of him near me. It won't mean much if Garret kills Jude. I need to fix things with Marcus before it's too late.

* * * *

A persistent vibrating noise pulls me from sleep. My hand flops around my bedside table in the dark until it connects with my phone. With one squinty eye, I focus on the readout and bolt upright.

"Marcus?"

"You forgot to tell me you love me." His voice sounds sad, far away.

I stare off into the dark space of my bedroom, the cobwebs of sleep slipping away. "What?"

"In your message. You forgot to tell me you love me."

I squeeze my eyes tight as I try to recall the message I left on his phone. "How's that possible? I feel like I'm always saying it." I stop myself. "I love you, Marcus. More than anyone can love another person."

"That's a lot," he says softly.

"I know."

"I love you, too."

My throat threatens to close as my vision blurs. "I wasn't so sure anymore."

"You hurt me, Lucy."

My heart constricts painfully in my chest. The sleepy fuzz is replaced by shame. "Will you ever forgive me?"

"Eventually."

What did I expect?

"Aiden explained something to me. You'll find it interesting."

"I don't know about that." My cheeks flush hot. I can't believe Marcus told Aiden.

Marcus sighs. "Just listen. He said when demons reach puberty—*emanation*—their hormones drive them to mate. It's pretty intense and, as Aiden put it, they sort of lose all self-control. They turn into horny beasts."

Emanation? "What are you saying?"

"That you're a horny beast, but that it's not entirely your fault. It's partially your fault, so you should feel really, really bad. Horrible actually, but..."

I almost laugh, but stop myself. "Demon puberty... *emanation*...is a real thing?"

"It is, but you're not allowed to kiss Dylan again."

"You're the only person I want to kiss."

"Can you please tell me it didn't go past that?" I hear the strain in his voice. "Aiden made it sound like it's kind of impossible to stop once it starts."

"I promise you that's all that happened," I say quickly.

"His hands never...?"

"Never."

"You swear?" His voice comes out tight and strained like a taught rubber band.

"I swear."

"Okay." He sighs after a long pause. "Then I don't have to kill him."

I shudder. "Please, no killing."

"I'm going to let you go. I don't want to, but we've got school tomorrow. I haven't slept in a while."

I clutch the phone with both hands. "How long is a while?"

"A few days."

"Marcus!" I cry out in alarm. I slap my hand over my mouth, hoping I didn't wake up my uncles.

Marcus hasn't taken his stone form at night on the roof for days? According to Persephone, the nightly ritual is required. Otherwise, his abilities as a protector and a healer suffer. His own health suffers.

"Don't worry. I'll be fine," he says. "'Night Lucy."

"Marcus..."

"I'll be fine."

All of this is my fault. "Goodnight. I love you."

"I love you, too."

CHAPTER TWENTY-FIVE

– Lucy Walker –

"What do you mean Dylan's not coming?" Jude roars.

"I told him not to." How's he going to punish me today? Tase me? Throw more fireballs at me? I try to look on the bright side—something I'm able to do now that Marcus is speaking to me again—at least Jude and I are both alive. I'm hoping the protection spell is hard at work.

I clutch the edge of the kitchen counter. There's a pan covered with foil sitting on the stove. It smells like chipotle peppers, tortillas, and cheese. Enchiladas? My stomach growls.

"That's not your decision to make." His tone is especially sharp on that last word. "Call him and tell him to get over here. *Now.*"

"No." I frown at him. "We can't be here together. I promised Marcus."

"What does the gargoyle have to do with this?" Jude's eyes narrow into slits. He jerks his head toward the hall as if he heard something, and he storms from the room. I scurry after him to the front door. He wrenches it open.

Marcus stands there, twitching and jerking, his expression murderous. "Leave her alone, Jude. From...now...on...she trains alone."

Is Marcus crazy? Jude gave our relationship his blessing after the whole homecoming fiasco, but he still despises Marcus.

I jump between them and press my hand flat against Marcus's chest. "I told you to go home. Pick me up later."

"What's he doing here?" Jude spits through clenched teeth.

"Was it...your intention for this to...happen?" Marcus grunts, perspiration streaming down his face.

"Marcus, *please*."

It's torture seeing him like this. He won't be able to control it much longer. Why didn't he listen to me just this once and leave after he dropped me off? The teams of landscapers at work in Jude's yard don't need to see Marcus sprout wings.

Jude's gaze slides to me, baffled. "Intention? What's he talking about?"

Marcus laughs bitterly. "Don't...act so...innocent." He turns to me, grabs my hand. "Let's go."

Jude smoothly yanks me from Marcus's grasp and shoves me behind him. "She's not going anywhere. It's you who needs to leave."

"Marcus..." I try to wiggle my way around Jude. "Please don't do this. Come back and pick me up later. Five o'clock. Okay?"

Before Marcus can respond, Jude slams the door in his face.

"What'd you do that for?" I yell.

"Enough of this nonsense. We will sit down and have lunch, like a proper family. Then we'll get to work on your training." The words come out sharp as glass. His grip on my arm hurts. I'll have a bruise later. "No more distractions."

He drags me toward the kitchen. I look over my shoulder, fearing Marcus still stands on the other side of the door.

"You shouldn't have done that." I try to yank my arm free.

An explosion booms through the air. I dive to the floor. Jude whirls around in time to see the remnants of his front door land on the floor in pieces. The steel hinges clank like bullets into the wall across the room.

Jude growls, eyes cold and glittery, lips drawn back to expose his teeth. He's ready to lunge. Marcus stalks across the threshold. I gasp at the sight of his naked torso, the muscles of his chest and arms ripped and taut, the cords of his neck standing out. All of that pales in comparison to the gray and white wings twitching and eager to expand. Is his shirt in shreds on the front porch? So much for discretion.

Jude and Marcus take a predatory step toward each other.

Jude raises his hand. A fireball balances is his palm. "It's time for you to go, gargoyle. Permanently."

I scramble to my feet and lunge between them.

"Stop it already. This is stupid."

"Get out of the way, Lucy," Marcus snarls.

Jude's eyes lock on Marcus. "Lay one finger on my daughter, and you're dead."

Marcus glowers. "If you care about her, then you wouldn't force her to mate with Dylan against her wishes."

Jude cocks his head; the fireball in his hand fizzles out. "Dylan is trying to mate with my daughter?"

"Like you didn't orchestrate it," Marcus mutters with disgust.

Jude's eyes fix on me like laser beams. "Did Dylan force himself on you?"

I hang my head, my cheeks burning with heat. "Not exactly, but things are happening that I don't want to happen."

"Aiden explained emanation to me. Don't act like you don't know," Marcus growls at Jude.

How many times will I have to live through the humiliation of my actions with Dylan? I peek up at Marcus, expecting to see judgment on his face. There's only anger, and it's directed at Jude.

"You're sixteen?" Jude asks.

I nod.

"Is this the age most human girls...*copulate*?" His face twists with distaste at the word.

"Some, but not most," Marcus glowers. "Lucy will not be *copulating* with Dylan."

Enough with these two talking around me. I rise to my full height. "I can speak for myself."

Jude's lips curl into a sneer. "Have you and the winged one...?"

My cheeks burn even hotter. I wish the floor would split open and swallow me whole. "Uh...no," I whisper, red-faced. "Not that it's any of your business."

Marcus takes a step toward Jude. "If Dylan tries anything with her again, I'll rip him to pieces."

Based on the fury in his eyes, I believe him.

Jude bares his teeth in a cruel smile. "I appreciate that you'll battle on behalf of my daughter's virtue, but you are outmatched.

Dylan's strength has multiplied tenfold. You wouldn't stand a chance against him, gargoyle."

I shake my head in frustration. "His name is Marcus. Why is that so hard for you to—"

"Lucy, let's go," Marcus snaps.

"Lucy made a deal. She stays," Jude says firmly.

"The deal's off, demon." Marcus grabs my arm and pulls me toward the door.

* * * *

"Jude's right. I can't bail on my end of the deal," I say once we're in the car.

"Well, you are." Marcus clicks his seatbelt into place. I do the same, reluctantly. His wings are gone. I caught a glimpse of the angry red scars running the length of his back before we got into his car. His shirt, what's left of it, is tossed on the backseat.

"Marcus, you don't understand. He'll go after—"

"Dylan?" Marcus's dark gaze meets mine. His nostrils flare. "Don't even go there."

My own temper flares. "It's not just Dylan. What about my uncles? I have to keep up my end of the deal. I have to keep training with Jude. He's behaving. We need to keep it that way."

Marcus grips the steering wheel so tightly all the blood leaves his fingers. "You're not training with Dylan."

"I understand that, but you can't chaperone me, either. It's torture for you to be near Jude."

"That's my problem."

If only I could blink and fast forward through time, I would have my license and could drive myself to Jude's. Then again, if the protection spell doesn't work, fast forwarding would bring me closer to death. Since he hasn't been able to recruit Marcus, Garret is no doubt working on a new plan to kill Jude.

"Did Aiden happen to mention how long emanation is supposed to last?" I ask, eager to change the subject from Jude.

Marcus's jaw clenches and unclenches. "Until mating has occurred."

CHAPTER TWENTY-SIX

– Dylan Douglas –

I pull the door closed behind me as I follow Jude into the backyard. It never fails to amaze me that his yard is bigger than the football field at St. Aquinas. It seems a waste. I think of Ethan and Brandi stuck in the condo downtown. They'd love to have a yard like this.

"What are you doing here?" a familiar voice asks.

I shield my eyes against the blaring sunshine and spot Aiden next to the tree Lucy torched.

My entire body tenses. Jude called me; said I need to make up my missed training session from yesterday. Now Aiden's here too? I was hoping this would be quick. I have a paper due tomorrow.

I shrug, keeping my cool.

"He's here at my request," Jude says.

Aiden studies me, his brows drawn low. He turns to Jude, curious.

Jude stops dead center between Aiden and me. I can't read a thing from his expression. What's he up to?

"Dylan, are you learning enough in your sessions with Aiden? Are you becoming a better fighter?" Jude asks.

"I've learned a lot."

My gaze moves past Jude to Aiden. His expression twitches.

"But not enough," Jude says. It's not a question.

I shrug again. I really thought Aiden would be a tougher opponent, but I keep that to myself. There's something going on here I don't understand. Best to keep quiet.

"Don't do this..." Aiden's dark eyes bore into Jude.

"What if I told you Aiden has been holding back?"

I lean in as if I heard Jude wrong. Aiden gave it his all. He said so.

I whirl around to face Aiden. "Is that true?"

It's all over his face. He thinks I'm weak.

My pulse speeds up. My muscles quiver.

"Dylan, do you want to become a great fighter? A warrior?" Jude asks.

"I am a great fighter." I grind the words out. "I proved that with your mutts last weekend."

Jude smirks. "Then why is Aiden babying you?"

Aiden's glare shifts from Jude to me. "I was taking it easy on you until—"

I don't hear anything else. He thinks I'm inferior to him.

Adrenaline floods my veins. Black dots dance across my vision, then clear. "You better figure out a way to take me out." I squat a few inches, anchoring my body, then throw the first punch.

Chapter Twenty-Seven

– Lucy Walker –

"We heard you got a new car," Suzy announces at lunch as she plunks her tray filled with chicken nuggets and French fries onto the table and sits down across from me. "This is huge news."

"Yeah." I shrug and focus on my lunch. "Kind of weird, since I don't even have my license yet." My cheeks burn as Ella, Caroline, Suzy, and Cloe stare at me expectantly.

Katie is unusually quiet as she focuses on her lunch, chewing methodically and avoiding eye contact. It's not hard to guess who spilled the beans.

"You're in driver's ed. You'll have your license soon enough," Cloe says, grinning. "Congratulations!"

"I wouldn't call a fully loaded Lexus *weird*," Caroline says. "Let me be the first to call shotgun when we all go out together. I love new car smell."

"No way!" Katie says. As my best friend, she's entitled to permanent shotgun. Her protest falls away when she sees my look of annoyance.

"Who's the gift from?" Ella asks, blunt as ever.

The table falls silent. This is exactly why *I* never brought it up. I'm not ready for the world to know about Jude. It's bad enough he showed up at my uncles' apartment. Now they're vulnerable. He can get to them anytime.

Jude was my secret and not Katie's to tell. Did she also tell them about Dylan and me? That Marcus and I had a huge fight?

"Ouch!" Katie says as I kick her under the table.

The girls glance at Katie for only a second before they return their attention to me.

"It's a long story." I squirm.

"We've got the whole lunch hour." Ella smiles sweetly.

I raise my gaze from the table and focus on Suzy and Cloe. They truly are my friends. They won't judge. "It's a gift from my father," I say.

"I knew it!" Ella smacks the table with the flat of her hand.

I bounce on my seat, surprised. "Knew what?"

"That the whole poor southern hillbilly thing was a lie. A ploy to gain sympathy." Ella scoffs. "It worked on Marcus and Dylan, so I guess you pulled it off."

Anger boils inside of me. I refuse to give her the satisfaction of getting under my skin. I just roll my eyes. "Whatever."

"Speaking of Dylan," Suzy says as her gaze skims the lunchroom. She leans in a few inches. "Did any of you see him today?"

I've been doing my best to *not* see Dylan.

Ella and Caroline look at each other questioningly. They shake their heads.

"No, why?" Caroline says.

"Don't tell me he's back with Rachel the skank or I'm going to puke," Ella says.

Suzy's eyes are as big as saucers, her voice barely loud enough for us to hear in the noisy lunchroom. We all lean in close. "Someone did a number on him. Beat his face to a pulp. Bruises, stitches. It's horrible."

A shiver races down my spine. Suddenly, what little I've eaten threatens to reappear. *Please God, tell me Marcus didn't do this to him.* My boyfriend—a protector—would never do something so awful.

I jump up from the table. "I'm sorry. I think I'm going to be sick."

My legs barely move fast enough. I make it to the girl's bathroom and heave my lunch into the toilet.

Once the episode passes, I rinse my mouth and pat my face with a cold, wet paper towel. With shaking fingers, I pull my phone from my purse. I call Dylan's number, but go directly to voicemail. His phone must be off. Or he diverted my call. I take a deep breath and dial Marcus. His phone rings five times before voicemail kicks in.

"Hey, it's me. Just checking in. Some of the kids here at school are talking about Dylan. He was beat up. It's bad." I take another breath. "Please tell me you didn't do this. It was only a kiss, Marcus. I promise to spend the rest of my life making it up to you. Please tell me you aren't the one who did that to him."

I replay the message. When the robotic voice asks me if I want to send the message or delete it, I hit delete. I record a new message, telling him about Dylan.

Marcus is a protector. He would never hurt Dylan. The question is...who did?

Chapter Twenty-Eight

– Lucy Walker –

"Lucy Walker, as your teacher, I have to tell you that you're getting a big fat 'F'."

I duck to avoid Persephone's glare and slip around her into the apartment. Sheldon and Bernard aren't home yet, and I couldn't stand being home alone, not with the howling wind and the rain pelting the windows. Besides, Marcus hasn't called me back, and Dylan's still dodging my calls.

"Persephone, I need to talk to you—"

Thunder claps so loudly the walls rumble and the lights dim. I slap my hands over my mouth to muffle my shriek. We stand still as mannequins, both of us mid-gesture, until the lights flicker back to normal. I *hate* thunderstorms.

"Enough already." Persephone waggles her finger midair.

"Who are you talking to?" I glance furtively at the window as shadowy branches *rat-tat-tat* against the glass.

"The goddesses," she grumbles.

"They're behind the storm? They're mad we're helping Jude, aren't they?"

"Either that or Seamus is tinkering with the elements again."

The night the violent winds blew me from the roof. I shudder. That was Seamus's doing. "You think he's back? Or could it be Jude? He was furious when I bailed on training the other day. Just when I thought Marcus was safely off his radar."

Persephone glares out the front window. It's like she's daring whatever force is at work to bring it on.

As if in response, a new wave of splattering raindrops begin their suicidal descent from the clouds, driving in sheets against the windows. My teeth start to chatter and I wrap my arms around myself. "Maybe we should go to the basement?"

"Why didn't you come to me about this emanation?" Persephone asks, waving off my concern. "Why did I have to hear about it from Aiden?"

My face flushes. "Of course Aiden's blabbing about it. I'm sure he loves spreading the word. Anything to humiliate me."

"Honey, for your information, he was asking for my help. It seems Marcus is determined to keep you from going back to Jude's house. A bad idea as you and I *and* Aiden know all too well."

I nod solemnly. Just this once Aiden doesn't have it out for me. He's looking out for his pseudo-brother. "That's what I keep telling Marcus."

"Marcus is stubborn. It would be better to cast a spell over you and Dylan to eliminate any attraction between the two of you."

"I'm not attracted to Dylan." My glare disappears as thunder assaults my ears like a cannon. I swallow a whimper and pray the roof doesn't cave in.

"Of course, dear. Now come on over here," she says lightly as I follow her into the living room.

Did she just roll her eyes?

"You don't understand. My relationship with Marcus was almost ruined. It still might be."

Persephone nods sympathetically and pats my shoulder. "We're going to fix this, okay? Arrange for Dylan to meet you here Saturday night."

"I don't know if I can," I whisper.

Persephone's expression softens. "Something's happened. Tell me. I'm guessing it's not just the storm that's got you all skittish."

I shake my head and take a deep breath. "Something bad has happened, and Marcus may be responsible. It's all my fault."

"Near as I can tell, just about everything is fixable. Why don't you tell me about it?"

So I tell her about Dylan's beating, and with every word, I fear I will launch dinner all over her coffee table.

When I'm done, Persephone studies me. "That doesn't sound like Marcus."

"I didn't think so, either, but who else has a grudge against Dylan? The timing," I say. "Just a coincidence?"

"Have you talked to Marcus about this?"

"We've been trading voicemails and texts. Marcus has been spending time with Selima."

Persephone purses her lips and stares off. "As you said, who has a grudge against Dylan? You would know this better than me."

"Dylan's popular. He has more friends than anyone I know. Guys either respect him or worship him. They want to be him.

Girls, well, Dylan's got a lot of fans."

"Has he gotten in any other fights this year?"

"Nothing at school. Outside of school? Wait!" Why didn't I think of this before? I'm such an idiot. "Jack, Matt, and Troy. The bullies from school. Jude's shapeshifter flunkies. Dylan beat the crap out of them in our training session two weeks ago."

I'm filled with relief. Of course, Marcus wouldn't do something so horrible. What was I thinking? I smack my forehead with the palm of my hand.

"You'll get Dylan here Saturday night?" Persephone asks.

"I'll get him here." I try to sound more confident than I feel. After my last message to Dylan, I'm pretty sure he wants nothing to do with me. Besides, how am I going to explain emanation to him?

The wind gusts, rattling the windows like a haunted house. I wish Marcus were here. With his arms around me, I'm not afraid of storms. Or anything else. I have some major making up to do.

"Earth to Lucy."

I shake my head and give Persephone my full attention.

"Did you distribute the satchels around your apartment? Have you been burning the incense we made?"

I nod.

"Good. Then let's pull out the Book of Shadows and look for spells to break whatever's going on between you and Dylan." Persephone sits down on the couch, and after a moment of stunned silence, I plop down next to her.

"The Book of Shadows really exists? I thought it was a myth."

"It exists and I think you're now ready to see it." Persephone fixes me with a stern expression. "It's important that the existence of the Book of Shadows stays between us."

I make a face. "I won't tell anyone."

"When I'm not using it, I keep it in a secure place." Persephone hoists the enormous book from beneath the coffee table. It lands with a heavy thud at the same time lightning flashes across the night sky. Thunder crashes so loudly, the walls tremble. I nearly jump onto Persephone's lap.

"What's the consequence for ticking off the goddesses?" I ask, casting another nervous glance at the window.

Persephone pats my shoulder, tucks a lock of hair behind my ear. "We should focus on finding a spell to help you and Dylan. We'll worry about the goddesses later."

I nod and turn my attention to the massive book. I fight the urge to reach out and touch it. Instead, I study the worn leather cover, with a design engraved on the front. It's so faint I can barely make out the three interlocking oval symbols contained within a circle.

I point to the emblem. "What does it represent?"

Persephone runs her fingers over the engraving and releases a heavy breath. "The power of three. In our case, one oval for each of us: your gram, Henry, and me."

"Does that mean I can't use it?"

"You can use it. More importantly, once Henry and I are gone, this book will become yours. You can work the spells on your own, but eventually, you will need to find two more witches to work with. Spellcasting is optimal when performed by the power of three."

How am I supposed to find witches? Is there a database online, some kind of Match.com for witches?

Persephone opens the cover and flips through thick, yellowed pages. Some pages are stained. They make a crinkly sound as she turns them.

"Now, let's see about that spell," Persephone murmurs.

There are words I can't pronounce on some of the pages. A bunch of the spells are written in another language. "Are some of these in Latin?"

"Many of the old ones are. You have to be careful with those. To mispronounce words can have dire consequences. It's best to stick to the newer spells until you become familiar with the language. St. Aquinas offers Latin, doesn't it?"

"They do. I'll sign up for a class in the fall."

Persephone continues through the book, her fingers running down the pages as she looks for an appropriate spell to break what's going on between Dylan and me. The handwriting from page to page is different. I recognize Gram's. The others are probably Persephone's and Henry's.

As she fast-forwards to the middle of the book, I catch sight of a spell titled Reverse Memory Erasing Spell. When Persephone took away my memory of the night Seamus poisoned me in Marcus's apartment, I felt violated. She took something that belonged to me without permission. I don't care how painful it may be. It's mine and I want it back.

"Here we go." Persephone plunks her finger on a page. "This is the one." She pats my hand. "We'll get rid of your demon lust. Don't you worry."

I smirk at her. Persephone's sense of humor sucks.

Persephone scans the spell. She pauses.

"What is it?" I ask.

Her eyes narrow and she leans closer to the book. Her expression pinches as she reads the text written in the right margin. I can't make it out from where I sit.

"Persephone, will this work?" I lean over to get a clear view of the tight scrawl.

She clears her throat and snaps the book closed. "Of course."

I catch the waver in her voice. Lightening streaks through the room like the blinding flash of a dozen cameras, followed by a deafening thunderclap. I shriek and burrow against Persephone. This isn't good. Not good at all.

* * * *

As soon as I get home from Persephone's, I head to my bedroom and pull out my cell phone. No word from Dylan. I pace my bedroom. He's not going to answer. He probably hates me. If he ignores me, how am I supposed to get him to come over on Saturday night? How can Persephone cast the spell? This crazy attraction has to end. It's going to ruin our friendship. It's going to ruin Marcus and me.

Stop being a wimp. Call him!

My heart pounds in my chest as his phone rings. Voicemail again. "Dylan? Can you please call me when you get this message?" Will he listen to this? Or simply hit delete? "This is going to sound weird, but Persephone has a solution for our *problem*." Darn it. He doesn't know about the emanation. I recall his ex-girlfriend, Rachel, in one of her many slutty outfits. I'd bet these crazy puberty feelings are normal for *him*. "Please. This is important."

I know I was the one who told him we couldn't train together and he had to stay away from his dad's house on Saturdays, but it hurts he's ignoring my calls. I miss him.

I'm halfway through my geometry homework when my phone vibrates. Dylan's actually calling me back. How mad will he be?

"I'm really busy, but you said it's important. What's up?"

It barely sounds like him, more like Dylan with a mouthful of cotton. I imagine the three mutts beating the crap out of my friend.

Fury forces heat to throb along my arms. "Did Jack and his loser friends hurt you? I'm going to make them pay, Dylan. I'll talk to Jude. I'm going to torch all three of them. They won't get away with this!"

Dylan mumbles something.

"What? I couldn't hear you."

"They didn't do it," he says.

It wasn't Marcus. He wouldn't do something so brutal.

"Then who did?" I demand.

"I don't want to talk about it."

"But I do. We can't let whoever did this—"

Dylan cuts me off. "You called me about something else. Either we talk about that, or I'm hanging up."

"Why are you being so secretive?"

"Hmmm. There's a lot of that going around."

I guess I sort of deserve that. Or maybe not. "To make a long story short, I found out you and I are encountering some sort of demon puberty. It's causing us to, well...you know."

"No, I don't know."

I ignore his pissy tone and tell him everything.

"I don't want someone casting a spell on me. Hell, I don't want that done to you, either. There has to be another way to make this go away."

That's a good sign. Dylan cares about what happens to me. He doesn't totally hate me.

"Dylan, I don't think you get it." I struggle to find a delicate way to put it. "The only other way is to...uh, *do it*. That's not going to happen."

"Oh." He clears his throat then winces. "If this is the only way then...okay."

As a sort-of demon, Dylan has speedy healing powers. How long before he's out of pain? There is one benefit to Dylan being out of sorts. He could've used this opportunity to be Dylan the Jerk. Or he could've responded with a crude joke. He's experienced, so this probably isn't as big a deal to him as it is to me.

My bedroom suddenly grows too warm as a vision of Dylan and Rachel comes to mind. My entire body tenses and hot electricity shoots down my arms and settles in my palms.

Jealousy? I wipe my damp palms along my jeans. *Oh, man, that came out of nowhere.* I down half my bottle of Vitamin Water and change the subject. "We have to train together at Jude's. He's furious you didn't make it on Sunday—which is totally my fault. Then Marcus smashed in his door, and he was doubly—"

"Fine."

"Wait. Don't you want to hear the rest of what happened?"

"Let's talk about the spell."

I lean back in my chair, stung by his curt attitude. *Cut him some slack, Lucy. The guy's been beaten.* True. *I'm determined to find out who did this to him.*

"Persephone wants you to come over on Saturday night, once I'm home from taking care of Ethan and Brandi."

"This Saturday?"

"Yes. Something about the waning of the moon."

Dylan clears his throat. "Do you trust this, Lucy?" His voice is low and serious, even through the cotton-effect. "What if something goes wrong?"

"I trust Persephone. You should, too." I close my eyes, my entire body clenched. He needs to understand how important this is to me. To us. "Besides, this is the only way to save our friendship."

Dylan exhales heavily. "Then I guess I have to trust her, too." A heavy silence falls between us. I feel bad laying it on so heavy about our friendship, but he needs to take this seriously. He has to show up for the spellcasting. "Does that mean I can come over and spend time with my brother and sister during the day on Saturday?"

My heart squeezes painfully at his hopeful tone. "Not a good idea. Next week should be okay, though." I promised Marcus I would stay away from Dylan until we fix this. "Besides, based on what I've heard about your face, you would scare Ethan and Brandi."

Dylan exhales. "That's the last thing I want to do. Then I'll see you Saturday night, especially now that I don't see you at school anymore."

The line goes dead.

The spell has to work. Persephone was nervous. I caught her pinched expression when she thought I wasn't looking. Are we messing with things we shouldn't by mixing witchcraft and demons again? Goddess statuettes broke the last time. What's going to happen this time?

CHAPTER TWENTY-NINE

– Lucy Walker –

Sheldon turns off the lawnmower and wipes the sweat from his brow with a yellow bandana. "Thanks," he says as I hand him a glass of lemonade.

"If you teach me how to use the mower, I can help," I offer.

Sheldon walks over to the back porch and sits down. He pats the spot next to him and I plunk myself down.

"Not necessary. You've taken on enough of the household chores." The ice cubes clink in his glass as he gulps down half of his beverage. "How was school today?"

"I aced my Spanish quiz, and I'm working ahead in geometry. I'm thinking of taking Latin in the fall."

Sheldon raises his bushy eyebrows in surprise. "That's my girl." He takes another sip from his glass. "Your Gram took Latin, too. She was the brainy one in the family."

She was also a witch who needed to be able to read those old spells.

I inhale deeply. Fresh cut grass. "Hmm. Nice." The smell makes me think of summer break and Gram. So do the lilacs, which are in full bloom. What was it Gram always said? They smell fresh and clean and sweet and innocent. There's no better description.

As the sun washes the backyard in a late afternoon glow, glimpses of all my summers here with Gram glide through my thoughts like a digital photo album. My dream came true, just a couple of years too late. This is where I belong, and since I can't have Gram, Sheldon and Bernard are the best substitutes.

Sheldon reaches over and pats my leg. "I can't believe it's nearly been a year since you moved in with us. It's been good, hasn't it?"

I squint against the sun beaming over his shoulder and smile. "It has been." I lean into him and tuck my arm through his. "I'm happy here. I don't think I tell you that enough."

Sheldon swallows hard and clears his throat. "Thanks, kiddo. We're happy you're here, too." His eyes water a bit as he looks out across the yard. "You'd tell us if you weren't happy wouldn't you?"

I follow his gaze and notice a spotted tail bobbing through the tiger lilies lining the edge of the yard. The stalker cat is back, probably coming after our house sparrows and finches. I'll chase him off if he starts to cause trouble.

I return my attention to Sheldon. "Is this about Jude? Because you and Bernard have nothing to worry about. This is my home. I don't want to move in with him."

"Sometimes we worry whether we're doing this right, this pseudo-parent thing. Are we too strict? Not strict enough?" Sheldon turns to me, his lips pulled down at the corners. "Then I remind myself that you have a solid head on your shoulders. You grew up faster than most kids your age. I have to trust you, something Bernard is much better at doing."

I pull away from him. "You don't trust me?"

"Lucy," he sighs. "If you only knew what we—your Gram, Bernard, and I—went through with your mom when she was younger. Her obsession with your father and all the trouble he caused. Now he's back. I'm scared as hell, to be honest with you."

"I think it's different for me than it was for Momma." Jude's ability to hypnotize me has faded. Or maybe he doesn't try anymore, since his other methods for manipulating me have worked so well.

Sheldon seems to accept this for now. "Your Sundays with Dylan are good for you; although you and Marcus tend to wind up in arguments over them."

I bite my lip. If my uncles knew where Dylan and I went every Sunday, what Jude put us through, they'd really freak. I wonder what I'll be in for this upcoming Sunday after taking off with Marcus last weekend. Will he tase me again? What will he do to Dylan for missing his session?

"We're working through that. It's going to be okay."

Sheldon blows out a breath that rattles his lips. "They both want the same thing. You. One of them will win and the other will lose."

I tune Sheldon out as I think back to Jude. What will Jude do to us for missing our session?

"Someone did a number on him. Beat his face to a pulp. Bruises, stitches. It's horrible."

Did Jude schedule a makeup session for Dylan? What if Dylan lied to me and Jude pitted Jack and his mutts against Dylan in a re-match? Payback for missing training on Sunday. That would be very much like Jude to get back at me by hurting someone close to me.

Sheldon tugs on my arm. "Lucy? Are you listening to me? We need to make plans for your birthday. What would you like to do?"

I plant a kiss on Sheldon's cheek, then hop up from the porch. "Living here with you and Bernard is all I need for every birthday. Pizza and cake, too."

"Where are you going?"

"Dylan isn't feeling well. I need to check on him."

* * * *

Aiden answers the door. "Marcus isn't home." He proceeds to shut the door in my face.

I shove hard, catching Aiden by surprise, and enter the apartment.

"Try that again, and I'll blast the door into a million pieces," I tell him.

Aiden smiles. "I'd love to see you explain that to your uncles, little demon girl."

He's right and I hate him for it.

"What do you want?" he asks, his voice as welcoming as an iceberg.

"What happened to Dylan?"

Aiden studies me for a moment. "What do you mean?"

"You're going to stand here and pretend you don't know that

someone beat the crap out of him? It's bad, Aiden. Did Jude schedule a rematch with the mutts? Did he penalize Dylan for me bailing last weekend? It was me who told him not to go to Jude's for training. If Jude's pissed, he needs to take it out on me."

Aiden's chest rises and falls. His nostrils flare.

"Tell me what you know, Aiden."

His expression darkens. "I can't believe he would stoop that low."

With my hands on my hips and a stomp of my foot, I ask, "Who did that to him?"

"Jude." Aiden proceeds to crack his knuckles.

The apartment door opens, and I whirl around.

Marcus drops his backpack on the overstuffed chair and eyes Aiden and me. "What's going on?"

"Why didn't you tell me about Dylan?" Aiden snaps at Marcus.

Marcus jerks his head up in surprise. "Since when do you care what happens to Dylan?"

"Since I've been training him." Aiden's lips flatten against his teeth. He pushes up the sleeves of his shirt. "Jude told me to show him a lesson last weekend, and I refused."

A cold shiver passes over my skin. "Why did Jude want you to teach Dylan a lesson?"

"Jude's not one to explain himself," Aiden says. "But it probably has to do with you. What did you do?"

I clutch my head with both hands. Dylan paid the price for my actions. Jude, a powerful demon, beat Dylan. After several moments, I meet Marcus's eyes. "This is our fault—*my* fault. We never should've left last weekend."

Chapter Thirty

– Dylan Douglas –

"Thanks for agreeing to help me," I say, once Marcus ushers me inside his apartment.

Marcus grimaces at the sight of me. Who can blame him? I've stopped looking in the mirror. I follow him to the bathroom.

"Sit," Marcus orders, pointing to the toilet seat. "The blood will make you lightheaded. I don't want you to fall."

I can't believe I'm doing this, but I want to see Ethan and Brandi tomorrow. I'm one of the few normal people in their lives. Lucy was right. They would be horrified to see me this way. My demon genes aren't healing me fast enough.

"Aiden told me what happened," Marcus says.

I chuckle, but it sounds more like a fart through my swollen lips.

"Nice try. Aiden took off before this happened."

Marcus turns on the tap and lathers his hands and his wrist. I appreciate his efforts at hygiene on my behalf.

"We know Jude did this to you. The question is why?"

I avert my eyes and shrug. "Who knows?"

Marcus dries his hands. "You're lying. If you want me to heal you, you're going to have to fess up. Otherwise, forget it."

Is that one of his supernatural abilities? To detect lies? I bite my lip in frustration. Dumb move. The pain is immediate. After a moment, I mutter, "I've always had a high pain tolerance. Used to, anyway."

"You took a beating from Jude. A big difference from the shapeshifters and even Aiden." Marcus studies me. Is he gauging to see if his words sink in? "He held back. Otherwise, you'd be dead. Now, tell me why he did this to you."

"You wouldn't understand. You're a protector. A world of difference from a demon. Even a demon-wanna-be like me," I say.

"Are you saying you had to prove something to Jude?"

My temper ratchets up as I recall Jude's revelation. "Aiden was going easy on me during training. He thought I was weak. Jude confirmed it, told me I was an embarrassment."

"And?"

Why is it so hot in here all of a sudden? I try to swallow, but I choke instead.

Marcus fills a glass from the tap and hands it to me. I take small sips, and even those are painful, compliments of Jude's chokehold.

"What did you do, Dylan?" Marcus asks. He crosses his arms over his chest and leans against the sink.

"I told him to fight me, not to hold anything back."

Marcus's eyes widen at the same time he pushes away from the sink. "Are you crazy?"

I laugh, then break into a coughing fit. By the look on his face, he thinks that I'm a lunatic.

Marcus hands me a navy-blue towel.

"He wouldn't do it. At least, not until I egged him on."

"You're suicidal," Marcus says. "Lucy's going to ask you about this, so be prepared. Jude actually likes you." He shakes his head as he brings his wrist to his lips. He tears at the flesh and immediately thrusts his hand in my face.

I press my swollen lips awkwardly around his wound. My stomach convulses, and I fight the urge to wretch. I can't believe I'm doing this voluntarily. *Man up, D-man. Do this for Ethan and Brandi. For Lucy, too.* I don't want to scare her, either. It drives me crazy that she's avoiding me at school, that she won't take me up on my offers to carpool. I need to see her.

I close my eyes so Marcus can't see the longing in my eyes, the desire I feel for his girlfriend. As I grip his hand and forearm, I continue to suck on his wound, all the while distracting myself with thoughts of my brother and sister, of Lucy, of anything that keeps me from thinking about the fact that we're engaged in an act that feels intimate in a super creepy kind of way.

Suddenly, a rushing sound fills my ears. The room is oddly bright, even behind my closed lids. A sweet, floral smell floods my nostrils. There's a hint of mint, too. I've never smelled perfume or flowers or anything else like it.

For the first time in a long time, I realize everything will be okay. Ethan and Brandi will be safe. Jude won't go after them. Lucy will be fine. For now. Jude was going to punish her for bailing on her session last weekend. I made sure he wouldn't. A deal is a deal. I learned that from my dad. I need to keep Lucy safe. She fought for me last year. Now, it's my turn. Garret's after her and that white-haired freak, Seamus, is still out there. I'm going to help keep her safe. Maybe one day soon she will look at me as more than a friend.

"That's enough." Marcus pries his wrist from my mouth.

I stare at him dazed. There's a strange glow around his face. He looks like an angel.

Marcus wipes my mouth. I'm too out of it to be embarrassed.

"You okay?" Marcus asks.

I nod. At least I try to.

"Protector blood is intoxicating. Some people experience mild hallucinations." Marcus pulls me by the hands, hoisting me off the toilet. A minute later I'm sprawled out on a comfy couch. "You can crash here tonight."

CHAPTER THIRTY-ONE

– Lucy Walker –

By the time I arrive at the Douglas residence, Ethan and Brandi are already in the kitchen eating breakfast. Charlene grabs her keys and a grocery list and heads for the door.

"See you all in a couple of hours." She tugs my hair playfully as she passes.

"Lucy, my birthday's in one week! My princess cake will be done in time, won't it?"

I kiss the top of Brandi's head on my way to the fridge, where I retrieve the container of orange juice. "It will. It's going to be the prettiest cake ever."

"It's going to be boring," Ethan complains. "Pink. Everything with her is pink. Gag."

Brandi crosses her arms over her chest. "It's my favorite color."

"It would look cooler with Transformers crushing your stupid princesses, turning them from pink to red." Ethan grins wickedly. "Blood everywhere. Or better yet, zombie princesses!"

"Princesses don't bleed red. They...bleed...pink." Brandi squeaks as she stabs the air between them with a menacing finger.

"Zombie princesses don't bleed," he says, his eyebrows bouncing. "They eat Barbie brains."

"All this talk about brains is making me hungry." I grab an apple from the basket on the counter and take a big bite. The argument halts, and they both turn to me, eyes bugging out of their heads.

"Gross." Brandi scrunches her face.

"Cool." Ethan grins.

"What do you want to do today?" I ask between bites. "We could play tennis or go to Millennium Park."

Brandi pulls her troubled gaze from her brother. "Can we go swimming again?"

"Swim-ming, swim-ming!" Ethan bangs his fists on the table in time with the chant.

It's a great day when they actually agree on something.

"Okay. After breakfast, get your stuff together. It'll just be the three of us this time, though."

Brandi shoots Ethan a confused look. "But you said..."

"Dylan's coming, too," Ethan says defensively, his brows pulled low.

Why does he look as if I'm punishing him? "Sorry, Ethan, but he's not able to make it today."

There's no way they can see Dylan right now. Add to that the emanation issue. Not a good time for a visit from Dylan.

"That's not what he said in his text." His voice rises an octave.

I freeze. When did Ethan get a cell phone? Skip that. What's Dylan trying to pull? We had an agreement...or at least an under-standing. He's going to freak the kids out with his damaged face.

213

Dylan's here. Before anyone realizes it, before he even makes it around the corner and into the room, I feel him. A snap-crackly energy zips through my limbs. My nerves twitch like I pounded way too many Cokes.

What the heck *is* that?

Brandi jumps up from the table, throws herself at Dylan. Dylan kneels and she wraps her arms around him. Ethan strolls over for a one-armed hug.

"What happened to your face?" Ethan asks.

Brandi gently touches the faint bruises on Dylan's skin.

"Football practice got a little rough. No biggie."

The kids buy his lie and return to the table to finish their meal.

I try—unsuccessfully—to ignore the tingly sensation spreading through me as I meet his determined gaze. His face looks better than I expected. Much better. His demon genes must've healed him faster than I thought possible. "You came after all."

Dylan rises to his feet. He takes a couple of steps toward me. "I couldn't stay away," he says, his voice a mix of pleading and an apology.

Is that Dylan talking? Or his teenage horny demon genes? I swallow, aware of a sudden vibration passing between us. Not good. "You really shouldn't have come." I take a couple of steps away from him.

"I tried not to. I really did." A flash of confusion and guilt pass over his face. "But I wound up here."

"We're going to the pool again today, Dylan," Ethan announces. "Did you bring your suit?"

Dylan reluctantly tears his eyes from mine. "I sure did, little man." He ruffles Ethan's hair.

"You're coming to my birthday party next weekend, aren't you?" Brandi flashes Dylan her doe-eyed stare.

Dylan turns to his sister. I spot faint bruising around his throat. My resentment toward Jude grows. "Sorry, kiddo. It's a party for pip-squeaks your own age. I'm too big and a boy."

In other words, Mrs. Douglas won't let him. Lucky Dylan. I love Brandi, but I'm not looking forward to meeting her friends, or more specifically, their mothers.

The kids dash off to wash up and get ready. Not wanting to be alone with Dylan, I start to follow Brandi to help her pack her bag.

Dylan grabs my arm. "Don't push me away like that again."

I eyeball his hand gripping my arm. "Dylan..."

"I mean it." There's a sullen look in his eyes. His grasp tightens. "We're meant to be together, and you know it."

Alarm courses through me. Or is it excitement? I run my fingers through my hair, lift it from the warm skin of my neck.

Confusion flashes across his face again. He's struggling as much—maybe more—than I am. "I mean as friends."

"You really shouldn't be here. You know this is something we can't control."

Sweat beads on his upper lip. "I told you, I couldn't...*I tried.*"

"Why don't you leave now?" I whisper. "Please."

"I can't."

"You're impossible!" I yank my arm free and push past him to find Brandi. I won't risk what I have with Marcus, no matter what my body wants.

* * * *

Once family swim is over, the kids pile into the car exhausted but happy. I climb into the backseat with them. Two hours of fighting Dylan's advances and my own urges at the pool and I don't trust myself—or him—enough to sit next to him.

Back home, Charlene puts out a spread of sandwiches, fruit salad, and puffed cheese curls. I'm not used to treats at the Douglas house, especially those that aren't organic, gluten-free, soy-free, or taste-free. Charlene catches my look of surprise and leans in close to my ear.

"Mrs. D bought them and inhaled half the bag last night. She's stressed about the party. I was told to make the rest of the bag disappear."

"Can we play Wii after lunch?" Ethan asks.

"Whatever you want." Dylan reaches over and messes Ethan's hair. Ethan laughs. Why is it I get the evil eye when I touch his hair? "Today is all about what you two want to do."

"Can we have sundaes?" Ethan asks hopefully.

"Be happy you're getting chips," Charlene says as she takes a seat next to me.

"Oh!" Charlene taps the table. "I almost forgot. Lucy, your father stopped by looking for you and Dylan. I found it a little odd since you've never mentioned him. All I ever hear about are your amazing uncles." She winks at me. "I didn't tell him that, though. Didn't want to hurt his feelings."

She continues on, but Dylan and I stare at each other, neither of us breathing. Why would Jude come here? I assumed the

Douglas residence was off limits, but then, I used to think Gram's house was, too.

Dylan's gaze travels to his brother and sister. I know what he's thinking. I feel the same way. I don't want Jude anywhere near them.

"Is that all right?" Charlene asks.

"I'm sorry. What?" I smile and tap my head like I'm a space cadet.

"I told him the two of you took the kids to the pool, and you'd be back in a few hours."

"Sure, that's fine," I say with a little too much enthusiasm.

"Why haven't you talked about him before? He's charming and very good looking."

After the number Jude did to Dylan's face, what was his intention in coming here today? To dole out more punishment? Was he coming for me this time? Or was he intending to hurt me in a super effective way, by going after the kids?

Dylan jumps in. "They're reconnecting after some time apart."

"I understand. I had that with my mother. She was pretty controlling," Charlene says.

"Dylan tried to eat my leg at the pool."

We all turn to Brandi, who chomps down on a cheese curl for effect, and burst out laughing.

Twenty minutes later, Dylan and I watch the kids rock out to Just Dance, clutching the Wii controllers in their hands.

Dylan slides close to me on the couch. "What do you think Jude wanted?"

My breath catches as my entire body tingles. "He probably came to talk about training. How did he know we'd be here together?"

Dylan ponders that for a second. "Maybe he didn't. Maybe he came here to talk to you, out of earshot of your uncles and Marcus."

Didn't Charlene say he asked about both of us? "Now he's going to ask why we can't train together when we're both here now."

"If the spell works tonight, then it doesn't matter. We'll show up for training together tomorrow."

I hesitate. "What if it takes several tries before the spell works?"

"You never said it could take several tries." There's an edge to his voice. "I thought after tonight—"

"Your turn!" Brandi thrusts her controller at me.

I hold my hands up in protest. "Why don't you dance with your big brother?"

Instead, Dylan yanks me from the couch. He scrolls through the song selections and picks one he knows we both like. My body warms up quickly. In fact, I dance better than Dylan for once. Not a fair comparison, given his injuries.

As I sway my hips, I catch Dylan watching me. I blush furiously and focus on the TV screen. Dylan's arm brushes against mine, and a spark ignites inside of me. Heat zooms through my limbs and settles in my belly, leaving me breathless. I should stop, but I can't. Thankfully, after two songs, Ethan and Brandi demand the controllers back.

"Bathroom break," I announce. After closing the door in the powder room, I grab a cloth from beneath the sink and run it under cold water. My flushed reflection stares back at me as I press the cool cloth to the back of my neck, then against each of my temples. Dylan needs to leave. I can't handle being around him. Not until Persephone's spell takes effect.

I jump at the soft knock on the door. I press the cloth to my lips. *Please don't let it be Dylan.* What if it's one of the kids, needing to use the bathroom? I open the door and immediately regret it.

Dylan pushes his way inside and closes the door behind him.

"Get out." I back away from him and bump into the shower doors.

He grins playfully. "But I'm not doing anything."

"Stop walking toward me."

"I just want to make sure you're okay. You looked a little flushed." His expression grows serious. "Are you worried about Jude?"

"Yes. I'm also worried about your face and how exactly that happened." And I'm worried about the fact that there's only about two feet between us.

"I'm touched you care." He closes the distance between us and plucks a lock of damp hair from my cheek, twirling it around his fingers. My skin burns from his touch.

I press my hands against his chest.

"Why are you fighting this?" His words are velvety soft.

My eyes close without permission. "Because it's wrong."

"It wouldn't feel this good if it was wrong."

Momma said the exact same thing once when she was high as a kite on heroin.

My eyes shoot open, and I shove him as hard as I can. "It's *wrong*."

He removes my hands from his chest and pulls me against him. His breath warms my already too-warm cheek. His fingers sink into my hair as he draws my face to his. My eyes close again.

"Hey, where'd you guys go? It's your turn!" Ethan calls from the other side of the door.

My eyes pop open. I shove Dylan away from me.

"Hide behind the door," I hiss before I flush the toilet. "I'll be right out!" I call to Ethan.

I pretend to wash my hands while I shoot a nasty glare at Dylan in the mirror. I return to the living room. Dylan returns a few minutes later.

"You're not supposed to the use the bathroom in Mom and Dad's bedroom. No one can," Brandi says to Dylan, her eyebrows scrunched up tight.

Dylan glances at me. "Sorry about that, but Lucy was in the other one. Don't tell on me, okay?"

Brandi grins and makes a show of zipping her lips and throwing away the key.

"Dylan, didn't you say you had to leave?" I struggle to keep my voice casual.

He glances at the kids uneasily, then forces a smile. "I was having so much fun, I forgot."

Ethan and Brandi make a fuss, but Dylan kneels to hug them and promises he'll visit again soon.

Before he leaves, I whisper in his ear. "Meet at Marcus's apartment at eight o'clock."

He flashes his megawatt smile. "Why not your place? I'd like to say hi to your uncles, make sure they still like me better than Marcus."

I shove him out the door

CHAPTER THIRTY-TWO

– Persephone –

I end the call, and my gaze lingers on the phone. Good grief and goddesses almighty, Henry and I could've put an end to this emanation. Where is that man when I need him? Bailing Max's behind out of another mess, that's where.

Can I make the spell work without him?

There's a knock at the door. I glance at my watch. They are right on time. I make my way across the room and open the door. I blow a heavy curl from my eyes and survey Marcus, Aiden, Lucy, and Dylan.

"Let's get this over with. Quick," Lucy huffs.

"For once, I agree with her," Aiden says stiffly.

"It's good to see you again, Persephone." Dylan winks at me. "At least one of us brought our manners."

Lucy rolls her eyes and elbows Dylan in the side. Dylan doesn't look too bad for a guy who took a serious beating recently. I study the wounds on his face and neck. Maybe his chest bore most of the damage? Marcus appears surprisingly tolerant. Tonight may go better than I expected.

"Marcus, I need you to assist with the spell, to serve as the third supernatural in the spellcasting."

"No problem." Marcus says. His manner may be easygoing, but he's keeping an eye on Dylan. "I planned to stick around until this thing is done, anyway."

"Henry's not going to make it?" Aiden glowers. "Let me guess. Max?"

"Leave it alone, Aiden. We have a lot of work to do."

I lead the convoy out of my apartment and up the narrow, slanted stairs. The footsteps of the others echo behind me. I try to ignore the pain in my hip, a pain that's grown substantially worse since Lucy and I cast our protection spell on Jude. Is this simply a temporary punishment or the beginning of something much worse? Whatever it is, let it rest on my shoulders alone. That girl's got enough to bear.

At the top of the stairs, I run through my unlocking spell and lead the group into the attic.

Soon, Lucy will have her own key. At the rate she's training with Jude, her demon powers are going to overtake her witchcraft. I promised Vera that wouldn't happen. Once we resolve the emanation issue, Lucy must step-up her training.

"Lights," I call out. The room brightens.

Dylan whips his head around as the door locks behind us. His gaze narrows suspiciously at Aiden, then Marcus. The muscles in his arms flex. "Is this some kind of trick?"

Lucy touches his arm. "You're safe. I promise."

Dylan hesitates for a moment then relaxes. Something more passes between them and they exchange a private smile. Out of the corner of my eye, I notice Marcus watching them, his jaw clenched. I need to move things along. Fast.

I snap my fingers and all eyes fix on me. "Follow my footsteps exactly. Don't stray, please."

The energy pouring off of Dylan and Lucy fills the room and overwhelms my senses. I must apologize to Marcus later for not taking him seriously when he first came to me with the problem. Their energy passes through me, and I shudder at its strength. I feel Dylan's desperation, his longing. I feel Lucy's fear as she fights her desire. Her resistance is crumbling. I double over and grip my stomach as the emotions pummel me.

"Persephone, are you okay?" Lucy reaches for me.

I hold my hand up. "I'm fine."

Whispered voices swirl through my mind.

Would it be so bad?

Why not let nature takes it course?

They are the same. They're meant to be together.

Don't interfere!

Then a faint, yet familiar, voice calls out to me. A voice I haven't heard in four years. *You know what to do, Sepha. Don't allow the darkness to determine Lucy's future. It's about free will. Always has been.*

I gasp and stop suddenly. *Vera.* Pressing my fingers to my forehead, I beckon to her. *Vera, please. I could use your energy tonight. I've already angered the Goddesses. Please...*

"Persephone!" Lucy calls out. "What's going on? You're scaring me."

I open my eyes and meet Aiden's questioning gaze. "Can you do this?"

The voices are gone. From the corner of my eye, I catch Dylan's finger brush Lucy's arm. A sigh escapes from her lips and mine simultaneously. My skin tingles. Goose bumps break out over my arms. Marcus flinches, his muscles clench as he struggles to keep his anger in check.

"Of course," I say.

My chest aches and my limbs feel heavy from Vera's brief visit, a visit that comes after so many unsuccessful attempts to conjure her spirit. Why now? Is the decision of Lucy's future mate so vitally important that Vera's spirit finally came forth?

Aiden nods. "Let's move this along."

I cross to the center of the room, walking around the circle drawn on the floor, so we enter from the east. I gesture for them to sit on the four cushions arranged on the floor. My altar sits between them and me.

Marcus pulls Lucy toward him, his eyes blazing at Dylan. "If you touch her again, you're going to lose a hand." He is about to say something else, but stops himself.

I fix him with a stern look. "Not now. Not here."

"He's not sitting next to her." Marcus's voice is a growl.

"Of course not. Aiden..."

Aiden moves to sit between Lucy and Dylan. The spell could backfire if I can't keep all the emotions in check. Once everyone settles onto their cushions, I close my eyes. Anger burns inside of me. In order to move forward with our spellcasting and express my intent to the universe, I need to clear my mind and heart of all emotion.

Vera's visit caused me pain, but not anger. That means the anger vibrating through me isn't my own. I open my eyes and analyze the four faces across from me. "Marcus, please take a moment to relax. There's no room for your hostility here."

"Yeah, Marcus, chill out." Dylan grins.

"I'm going to rip you to pieces, I swear..." Marcus pushes himself off of his cushion. Aiden reaches around Lucy and puts a hand on the protector's arm.

"Please stop fighting," Lucy groans. Her sense of hopelessness travels through me and my body sags.

Aiden raises an eyebrow at me. "Persephone?"

"Yes, yes. Moving right along."

I lower myself onto my cushion, my knees creaking and cracking in the process. My left hip protests. I face my round, wooden altar and pull matches from the single, slim drawer. I light the black candle at the center to enhance the spell that will be cast before touching the match to the incense stick to my right. It's odd to see the empty spaces on both sides of the candle where the figures of my favored goddesses once stood.

"Please tell me you spoke with Jude," Aiden says. "Demon magic is his area of expertise."

"I did. He offered to help, but..." I harrumph. As if I would allow a high-powered demon into this sacred space. It's one thing to erase Aiden, Marcus, and Dylan's memories of tonight, but I don't have the power to erase Jude's. He doesn't know about the attic, and it's going to stay that way.

I'm not reversing a spell or releasing them from the magic of other supernaturals. Lucy and Dylan's natures are compelling their actions. Jude isn't sure such a thing can be reversed. It's unfortunate timing that Henry had to help Max tonight. But without Max and his partner, we don't have enough of a team to combat Garret.

"Let's get to work. Aiden and Marcus, the three of us need to form a circle around Lucy and Dylan. Lucy and Dylan, you need to turn and face each other and recite this spell." I pull the sheets of paper from my pocket and hand one to each of them. "The key is to focus on your intent. Put your emotions and belief behind the words you recite."

Lucy and Dylan nod as they review the words on the paper.

"Aiden and Marcus, our purpose is to enhance the spell. While I'm the only witch in our trio, this type of spell has always been done with the power of three, so I don't want to mess with that. Essentially, we're going to amplify their intent. Focus on every word spoken. Believe in it as if it's already the truth."

"What if it doesn't work?" Marcus asks, sliding a sideways glance at Lucy. "What if we can't stop this...emanation?"

Aiden rests his hand on Marcus's shoulder. "If you don't believe it will work, then it won't. Spellcasting one-oh-one." He gives Marcus's shoulder a squeeze. "It will work, little brother. I promise you."

Marcus releases a heavy breath and nods at Aiden. "Okay."

"Lucy and Dylan, you will need to hold hands while reciting the spell."

Marcus twitches as Dylan takes hold of Lucy's hand.

I hold out my hands to Aiden and Marcus, and we form a circle.

"Now recite the spell in unison," I instruct Lucy and Dylan. "Three times."

"I need you to mean it," Lucy says to Dylan. "Our friendship depends on it."

Lucy's voice shakes at first. Dylan sounds strong from the get go, his eyes glued to Lucy's.

I return what I do not want
Host body reject the emanation
Cease all temptation
Let friendship resume
Where once passion bloomed

I close my eyes and slip slowly, level-by-level, deeper into focus. I sense the scent of the oil I used to anoint the candle, the satchels of centaury and allspice to strengthen the spell, and the barberry to free Lucy and Dylan from the power and control of their demon urgings. My ears fill with the sound of blood rushing through my body. My heartbeat thuds rhythmically in my chest. My power surges.

For the first time I feel the full extent of Aiden's powers as they amplify my own. I retain my focus as our powers coalesce. I draw in a deep breath as I see dark edges, black swirling with red at the edge of his aura. I am momentarily distracted by the colors. I haven't seen magic of that color in a long time. Not since... no...that's impossible.

Suddenly, we're jostled and jerked to the side. Not just once, but twice. I open my eyes as my hands are nearly yanked free from Aiden and Marcus.

Marcus's attention is fixed on Dylan, ready to pounce.

"Get your hands off of her," Marcus roars.

"Marcus, we must finish," I command. "Don't break the circle."

As the two of them glare at one another, I see Dylan's sheet with the spell sitting on his lap. His hand, slightly hidden from view, strokes Lucy's leg. She trembles, a low moan rising from her throat. I feel her longing. The emanation is proceeding fast. Too fast.

Aiden squeezes my hand and turns to Marcus. "Hey, little brother, what would Elvis Costello do in this situation?"

Marcus's attention flicks to Aiden reluctantly, fleetingly, before he focuses on Dylan again.

"He'd beat the snot out of Dylan."

"He wouldn't have to," Aiden says with a hint of a smile, "because his fans would do it for him."

Marcus takes a breath, releasing his visual death-grip on Dylan. His jaw unclenches and his shoulders relax. "I remember when he shared that story. That was a great night, a great show."

Aiden nods slightly, relief passing across his face. "What do you think, Persephone? Should we start over?"

"Everyone, please close your eyes. Lucy and Dylan, from the beginning."

Lucy reluctantly grabs hold of Dylan's hands and delivers a look of utter disappointment his way.

I force myself to descend deep into my subconscious, faster this time. I look for the black and red aura, but it's gone. I know what I saw. How is that possible? Only one supernatural ever had that aura. I'll need to speak with Henry after he bails Max's butt out of trouble again.

There are no interruptions this time. Once the spell has been repeated three times, I open my eyes. It takes a moment to get my bearings.

"Let's test it out. See if it worked," Marcus says.

The magic has left my body. I struggle to my feet, pushing aside the hand Lucy offers to me. My face flushes from the effort.

Aiden stands guard between Marcus and Dylan. "How do we do that?"

I eye Marcus warily and gesture for Lucy and Dylan to step forward.

Dylan shrugs. "I don't feel any different." He reaches for Lucy's hand, a cocky smile on his face. "In fact, come here. Let's hug this out."

Marcus lunges. His fist connects with Dylan's face, which jerks to the left. In response, Dylan narrows his eyes and bares his teeth. His fist cuts through the air, aiming for Marcus's face. Aiden raises his hand in time to absorb the impact.

"Marcus, no!" Lucy yells. She grabs his arm, tries to yank him backward.

"I told you to leave her alone!" Marcus shakes Lucy off and lunges for Dylan again.

Aiden shoves Dylan aside then grabs hold of Marcus and pulls him back.

"You're an idiot, Dylan," Lucy cries out. "Are you trying to ruin everything?"

With Marcus's arms pinned behind his back, Aiden shoves him toward the door.

"Keep him away from her, Persephone," Marcus snarls over his shoulder. "I mean it. Don't let him touch her!"

CHAPTER THIRTY-THREE

– Dylan Douglas –

I'm out of control. It took staring at my bedroom ceiling for two hours to circle back to the same point. I'm an idiot. All I had to do was hold it together and read a bunch of rhyming stuff on a piece of paper. I failed.

This spell is the only way to save our friendship. Lucy said as much. One lousy spell and I probably blew it. What happens next? Well, duh. *That's an easy one, genius. You'll have to train with Jude on different days than Lucy. You won't be able to see Ethan and Brandi on Saturdays. Lucy will avoid you in the hallways at school. If Garret attacks at Jude's house, you won't be there to help Lucy.*

What about Marcus? The guy was generous enough to heal me, and this is how I repay him?

Emanation sucks.

This isn't what I wanted. Sure, I wanted Lucy to like me. But not like this. Not under the influence of some demonic mojo. I want her to like me for me, something Rachel never did. Lucy isn't all about status and parties and getting drunk. She's deeper than that. She loves Ethan and Brandi. She's fragile and tough at the same time. She can produce fireballs. How freaking cool is that?

I don't want to lose her.

Maybe we can try it again. I'll talk to Lucy about it tomorrow morning when I pick her up for training. Scratch that. If we're not cured of this thing, she'll be super pissed at me. She won't go to training with me. Besides, Marcus won't let me anywhere near her.

Maybe I should talk to Persephone, see if she'll convince Lucy to give this another try. I can't risk losing her.

CHAPTER THIRTY-FOUR

– Lucy Walker –

At eleven the next morning, Dylan pulls into the driveway. Marcus stands guard at my side. Aiden flanks Marcus's other side, his arms folded over his chest.

"I owe all of you an apology. I'm sorry about last night." Dylan extends his hand to Marcus. "No hard feelings, man."

"I'm the one with hard feelings," I snap. "Let's get this over with." I turn to Aiden. "How do we know if the spell worked?"

"Hug it out. See if you feel anything," Aiden says. He turns to Marcus. "Sorry, little brother."

Marcus grips my hand reflexively.

I squeeze back reassuringly. "We have to give it a try."

Dylan and I eye each other cautiously. I brace myself as I anticipate the familiar heat to race through me, for my nerve endings to snap, crackle, pop, and leave me trembling. So far... nothing.

Marcus and Aiden take a step closer. Is it possible I'm holding back my feelings for fear of a fight between Marcus and Dylan? I roll my shoulders and try to relax as best I can as my boyfriend and his pseudo-brother hover beside me.

I take a step closer to Dylan. Nothing stirs inside of me. In fact, standing this close to him annoys me. And that annoyance is growing. It makes sense after the crap he pulled last night.

Dylan embraces me stiffly. His grip is too tight, and I can't breathe. I shove him away. "Are you trying to suffocate me?"

The smell of Dylan's cloying scent kicks in my gag reflex. I reel backward and clamp my hand over my mouth.

Dylan bursts out laughing. "I don't feel a thing. You could be super ugly...not that you are." His laughter turns to panic and his eyes grow wide. "Because you're not."

"What's up with your cologne? You smell like Eau du Skunk," I say at the same time.

Did he just call me ugly?

"Like you're Prince Charming?" I ask. Heat rushes through me, but not the kind that leads to kissing. I shove Dylan so hard he stumbles and falls.

"What was that for?" he asks, sprawled on the sidewalk.

"Yeah, exactly," I grind out through clenched teeth.

Dylan aims a baffled look at Marcus. Marcus merely stands there, arms crossed over his chest, a grin on his face.

"I'd say it took, little brother." Aiden claps Marcus on the back, beaming. It's the first time I've seen him smile.

Dylan pushes himself off the ground. "Whatever. Let's go and get this stupid training session over with."

I fan my hand through the air as he walks past. "Just promise you'll roll down the windows."

Why am I stuck having to train with him anyway? Suddenly I

remember what Jude did to Dylan. As much as I detest Dylan right now for nearly sabotaging the spellcasting last night, I plan to have it out with Jude. Once that's done, I will see if he'll allow Dylan and me to train on different days. Dylan didn't care enough to fully invest in the process last night, so why should we invest in training together.

Marcus pulls me backward and embraces me. He turns me around and plants a kiss on my lips.

Desire blazes through me like a lightning bolt. I grab fistfuls of Marcus's hair and kiss him hard.

Marcus finally stumbles away, breathless. He blinks several times, his eyes full of surprise. "Lucy…"

What's gotten into me? Maybe a side effect? Could terminating the emanation cause my hormones to go into overdrive for Marcus, my true love?

Aiden squeezes Marcus's shoulder, effectively breaking the intimate connection between us. "Everything is good here. We need to go deal with Max."

My brain struggles out of its heavy fog. "What's wrong with Max? Isn't he supposed to be here by now?"

Marcus shakes his head as if coming out of a daze. "Max tried to charm some people out of their valuable possessions. Henry bailed him out of jail." He glances at his watch. "They're probably back by now. Typical Max, right Aiden?"

"I say let him rot behind bars," Aiden grumbles.

I don't care what Aiden says. If Henry and Persephone believe we need Max, then Henry needs to work his lawyer magic and get the demon out of jail before it's too late.

Marcus flashes his crooked smile at me. The last thing in the world I want to do is go to Jude's house. I can think of so many other things I'd rather be doing. All of them include my boyfriend.

"Come back to me soon," he says, stroking my palm with his thumb.

"I will." I smile at him and notice for the first time the way the sun causes tiny flecks of green to sparkle in his brown eyes. How could I have missed that before?

Dylan sighs dramatically. "This love fest is super-duper touching and all, but Jude's gonna kill us if we're much later."

I squeeze Marcus's hand, then turn to go.

* * * *

Once in the car, Dylan glances at me. "Hey, I'm glad the spell worked."

"I'm super ticked off at you right now after what you pulled last night. You almost ruined everything. As far as I'm concerned we're not friends today," I hold up a finger, "but I'm going to let Jude have it for hurting you. I thought we were past his evil stunts."

"Just leave it alone, please. It's over," Dylan says uneasily.

"What's over?"

"Just leave it alone. Don't meddle," he snaps.

I make a face. "Don't be such a jerk."

Dylan shakes his head. "Whatever."

After forty-five minutes of staring out the passenger side window, listening to Dylan *chomp-chomp-chomping* on his gum and missing Marcus, we pull into Jude's driveway. I burst out the passenger side door the second he puts the car in park and fill my lungs with fresh, non-Dylan polluted air.

Lunch is a painful affair.

I can't tolerate the torture of his smacking lips any longer. "Can you keep it down over there?"

Dylan holds up his burger. "At least my food doesn't reek." He eyeballs my plate. "What is that slop? Kale and beans? If you fart in my car later, I'm kicking you to the curb. You can walk home."

My jaw falls open. My embarrassment turns to fury.

Jude flicks his fingers at Dylan, then at me.

"Ouch!" I rub my nose and cheeks to ease the sting.

"Toughen up, wuss." Dylan snorts. "You call yourself a demon."

I lean forward in my chair, my palms tingling. "Want to see what a real demon is capable of?"

"Enough!" Jude slams his hands onto the table. "Outside. Both of you."

"Thank God. I'll finally be able to breathe," Dylan complains.

Ignoring Dylan, I turn to Jude. "Are you going to beat us both like you did Dylan last weekend?"

Dylan gasps.

Jude narrows his eyes at me. "Is that what you would like me to do?"

There's an edge to his voice that makes me shrink in my chair. Jude's irises turn blacker than normal, which I didn't think was possible. He glances at Dylan.

"Did you explain to Lucy that you volunteered for our fight session last weekend?"

238

Dylan swallows. "I didn't tell her about it. She drew her own conclusions."

I force myself to take a breath and continue. I don't even like Dylan right now, but I have to do the right thing. "What's wrong with you? If you need to teach someone fighting techniques or if you are reprimanding them—someone you claim to actually care about—you don't do it to the extreme."

Jude leans forward, wearing a look that would normally stop me dead in my tracks. "You're going to lecture me on my parenting skills?"

"You're not Dylan's parent. I don't know why you beat him, but it was wrong. You want me to spend more time with you. When you threaten or hurt people I care about, I despise you for it." I gesture to Dylan. "You hurt Dylan. It was really bad, Jude."

Jude's temple throbs. His unblinking gaze burns into me for so long, I wait, breathless, for him to retaliate. I brace myself in case he goes berserk.

"Are you done?" he asks evenly.

"I am."

"Then let's go outside and train like civilized demons."

Dylan meets my gaze and mouths the words, *Are you crazy?*

You'd think the creep would appreciate that I've got his back.

Once in the yard, Jude stands between us. "I may regret this later, but the two of you are going to train together today."

Dylan stands too close, as if trying to annoy me.

"Back off!" I spat.

"There's three feet between us. Chill out."

I turn to Jude. "Do I get to set him on fire today?"

Dylan cracks his knuckles. "Do I get to knock her on her bony behind?"

Jude tries to ignore the verbal jabs. "We're going to start with defensive versus offensive moves. Lucy, Dylan is going to come at you and you'll need to outmaneuver him. For example..." He ushers Dylan off to the side and beckons for him to charge.

Dylan tucks his head. A smirk appears on his face as he charges Jude like an angry bull. I wonder if he has revenge on his mind.

When Dylan is roughly a foot away, Jude drops into a squat and extends his leg out to the side. Dylan trips over the leg and goes flying. He slams onto the ground, jumps up, and comes at Jude again. Jude faces him, legs rooted in a wide stance until Dylan is nearly upon him, then he directs a powerful blow to Dylan's solar plexus.

My mouth falls open as I watch Dylan fly backward and slam onto the ground. He doesn't rebound so fast this time. I feel bad for him. Then again, he did call me ugly.

"Who's the wuss now?" I call out.

"That...was...low," Dylan wheezes.

"Learn to anticipate," Jude says crisply.

Jude walks ten feet away then turns around.

"Lucy, Seamus is out there, and once he realizes you're still alive, he'll come back for you. We're going to reenact his attack from that night."

Alarm torpedoes through me. I open my mouth to protest, but seeing Dylan still trying to catch his breath, I want Jude to leave him alone for a few minutes.

I square my shoulders and plant my legs. "Okay, tell me what to do."

"You tell me," Jude throws back at me. "Recall the details. What was Seamus doing?"

I stare off, putting myself back on the roof. Seamus's daughter, Daphne, was a pile of ash on the ground to my right. Jude called out to me. Seamus appeared across the roof. His arms directed toward me. He was muttering under his breath. "He directed a spell at me."

"How do we stop him?" Jude barks as he paces.

My mouth goes dry. It takes effort to unglue my tongue from the roof of my mouth. How could he ask me to relive that night? "You...you threw fireballs at him. It didn't work."

"Tell me what you're going to do instead," Jude says as he continues to move between Dylan and me. "How do we disarm him?"

"It's about his hands, right? Why not break them?" Dylan wheezes.

"That's a great start," Jude says, "but if you're dealing with a powerful demon like Seamus, he can direct the spell with his mouth, his eyes, even a slight nod. Besides, he'd have injured—or killed—Lucy before anyone got close enough to his hands. Next option?"

It comes to me suddenly. "Knock him off his feet, break his focus on me."

Jude nods encouragingly. "How do we do that?"

"Someone charges him from the side while his attention is on me," I say.

"He'll throw a fireball, roast that second person, and in the blink of an eye you're back in his sights. Next?" Jude bellows like a drill sergeant, but instead of frustrating me, I feel exhilarated.

"You and I bombard him with fireballs, toast him like you did Daphne," I say.

"I'm the strongest demon around, and I wasn't able to take him out. With you helping me, no offense, we don't stand a chance. Next!" Jude clasps his hands behind his back as he continues to pace. His tension-filled expression sweeps between Dylan and me.

Fireballs won't do it. Breaking his limbs won't do it. A diversion won't do it. What else is there?

"If only there was a way to do to him what he was trying to do to Lucy," Dylan says, scratching his jaw.

Jude's face breaks into a self-satisfied smile. "Correct. A reflection spell."

Dylan mirrors Jude's smile. *Suck up.* Are the two of them best buds now?

"How do we do that?" I ask.

Jude rests his hands on his hips and nods over my shoulder. I turn around. Henry and Aiden cross the lawn toward us.

"A reflection spell is not a demon spell," Jude says.

"Witchcraft," I say under my breath.

"Henry," Jude says. The two men shake hands.

I resist the urge to hug Henry. Since I don't hug Jude, I suspect he would take offense at the preferential greeting.

Aiden surveys Jude warily. He glances over at Dylan, but says nothing.

"You're here to teach me a reflection spell?" I grin at Henry. "Cool."

Henry pushes his wire-rimmed glasses up his nose, and I catch the look of discomfort on his face. I'm guessing he's not too happy spending time at Jude's house. Having him and Aiden here assures me that nothing will get out of hand today.

"It's the perfect defensive tactic against a demon," Jude says. I shoot a quick glance at my father, surprised that he's sharing this information. "Or any aggressor."

"The key," Aiden says as he moves to stand beside Dylan, "is not to tip your hand."

"But he'll hear my spell. My hands will be aimed at him," I say.

"Whisper the words, so he can't hear you," Henry says.

I flush with embarrassment as soon as he says this. I've witnessed Persephone whisper spells on numerous occasions, but it never occurred to me to wonder why she whispered.

"The spell will need to be precise, and your focus has to be one hundred percent on target. Use your eyes, the subtle jut of your chin, nod your head, point your feet. One distraction and your opponent will best you," Henry says.

"Will that really work?" Dylan asks.

"It will. Let's run through it," Henry says. "For this example, Lucy will come up with a spell, and we'll pit her against Jude."

Great! I thrust my chest out as I step forward. "Poor Dylan. Left out again. If only you could conjure magic."

Henry frowns at me. I swallow and turn away.

"If you knew what she ate for lunch, you'd stay up wind of her," Dylan warns, then breaks into a fit of laughter.

"I'm going to lock the two of you in the basement if you keep this up," Jude warns as he and I face off thirty feet from each other.

Jude moves his lips, his eyes watching me intently. With a quick flick of his hand, which remains low against his thigh, I'm thrown off my feet. I slam onto the ground.

I grit my teeth and bite back a sharp cry as pain blasts through my hip and tailbone. "A little warning would be nice," I grunt.

Dylan bursts out laughing. "That was graceful."

Jerk.

"You're not going to get any warning from Seamus," Henry reminds me, gravely. He strolls between Jude and me, his movements graceful and his stride long. "You won't have time to get creative and rhyme. You're basically going to form instructions. Then you will repeat them over and over as you focus on your intent."

"Like a chant?"

Henry nods. "Have you put something together yet?"

That fast? I frantically shake my head as I start to think. If Jude's trying to throw me off balance and knock me off my feet—

My feet fly out from beneath me. I slam onto the ground.

"Give me a minute!" I climb to my feet, rubbing my throbbing tailbone.

Dylan laughs so hard he stumbles and nearly falls. Aiden crosses his arms over his chest, a smirk on his face.

"Work faster," Jude says dryly. "If I were Seamus, you'd be dead by now."

Pain radiates in my lower back and butt. As I shoot a dirty look at Jude, I notice his lips moving again.

Crap!

"Take his words and send them back. Take his words and send the back. Take his words and send them back. Take his words—"

Flat on my back, I gasp, pulling in one tiny sip of air after another. Dylan finds my repeated humiliation hilarious. He laughs so hard, clutching his stomach, that he nearly topples over. Without comment, I slowly flip over and pull my knees beneath my body. Ignoring the sharp pain that radiates from my back to the lower half of my body—at least I try to—I stagger to my feet. The pain will not last long, I remind myself. It's something I've learned from prior training sessions with Jude. As hellish as I feel right now, I won't feel as bad in a couple of hours.

"Think like a mirror, Lucy," Henry advises, eyeing me nervously. "Or remember that children's rhyme."

I consider his words for a second. Then it hits me.

"I'm rubber, you're glue, bounces off me, sticks to you," I whisper furiously. Jude's lips are moving, his eyes fixed on me. I return the stare, visualizing Jude slamming onto the ground. "I'm rubber, you're glue, bounces off me, sticks to you."

To my surprise, Jude's feet fly out from beneath him and he lands on his behind. My mouth falls open. It takes a minute to sink in that I made that happen. *Me. All by myself.* Without thinking, I raise my hand to Henry, and we high-five each other.

The sky is no longer above me as I'm thrown off my feet. I slam onto the ground. After a moment, I raise my head a few inches.

"Ouch!" Dylan cackles. "Gloat a little more, Lucy."

"Poor sport." Henry glares at Jude as he grabs my hand and pulls me to my feet. "You okay?"

I wipe the dirt off my jeans, buying time as I catch my breath and wait for the dazed feeling to pass. My head hit the ground hard that time. "Yeah."

The break lasts no more than a couple of minutes. Jude and I lock on each other. His lips move, but so do mine. As I whisper the spell, I visualize him falling. *Hard.* He flicks his wrist and I leap aside, dodging the spell as I focus harder.

Jude lands on his butt again.

Ha! See how *his* tailbone likes it.

"Again!" Henry calls out.

Jude hops to his feet. Is he immune to pain?

We run through the drill five more times, and all but once, my modified childhood rhyme works.

"Now, we're going to work on fireballs," Henry says.

"I'm growing mold over here," Dylan grumbles from the sideline. "Give me something to do."

All fired up over beating Jude, I conjure a fireball, balance it on my hand for a second to admire its beauty, then I pitch it at Dylan. I'm rewarded when his eyes nearly pop out of his head. He lunges to the left to avoid being hit.

"Still bored?" I tease.

"Play nice." Jude aims for a strict tone, but there's no missing the twinkle in his eyes. Demon pride?

Henry, on the other hand, glowers at me. "Dylan can't use spells yet or conjure fireballs. He can't defend himself. I expect better from you."

I thrust my chin in defiance. "I'm not apologizing. He's been a jerk to me all day."

"Cry me a river," Dylan balls his fists under his eyes, mimicking a sobbing baby.

I'm tempted to throw another fireball at him, but Henry stares me down. After a moment, he turns to Aiden. "Was there a problem with the spell last night?"

"According to Persephone, this is a possible outcome. It's temporary," Aiden says tightly.

"How temporary?" Jude asks.

"I assumed the four of you could handle this," Henry says.

"It was *your* bright idea to bring Marcus and Dylan together—with *her*—under one roof." Aiden stares Henry down. "You were needed here, not running around saving a worthless criminal."

Thank God, Aiden doesn't mention Max by name. Since Jude knows him, our plan would be blown wide open.

Henry glances my way, guilt flitting across his face. "We can fix—"

"Do I need to separate the two of you as well?" Jude's cold tone pulls my attention from Henry and Aiden.

There was a problem with the spell? Is it possible Dylan and I can go back to being friends without the crazy demon attraction and without the urge to strangle each other? And what about Max? Now that he's in town, what's the plan? I'm not so keen about saving Jude right now, not after what he did to Dylan, but I'd rather not bite the dust at sixteen.

Henry shifts his attention back to training. "Once again, we'll start with Jude initiating. Lucy, you have to physically respond to the attack this time. You're going to need to combat Jude's fireball. To do that, you have two options. You can ricochet it off your own power or throw a fireball at his fireball. They will collide and destroy each other."

"I don't understand the ricochet part. Can you show me?" I ask.

Henry moves to stand beside me. He beckons to Jude, who conjures a fireball instantly. Without delay, Jude hurls the fireball at Henry. I notice it's not at the speed he threw at Daphne that night on his roof. Henry holds up his hand as if to stop the fireball. "I'm visualizing a shield," he says, without taking his eyes off the ball of flame. "My hand represents the shield. If you lose focus, you'd better dodge it or you'll be hit."

The fireball pauses several inches from Henry's hand. He whacks the air and the fireball bounces back to Jude, who smacks the fireball to the side without touching it. It lands on the ground, sizzles and pops then dies out. Jude immediately lobs another one at Henry, this time with more force. Henry moves faster, throwing his hand up and whacking it back to Jude. It's like watching a game of table tennis, but with fire. They go at it for several rounds, picking up speed each time, dodging and lunging to avoid being burned. Finally, Henry nods at Jude and steps back.

"Remember, Lucy, visualize the shield. Focus."

Oh, great. How am I going to explain third degree burns to my uncles?

Jude holds out the flat of his hand and a fireball appears. He bounces it on his palm a few times then hurls it at me. I immediately put up my hand as if to stop it. I visualize a shield, more like a bulletproof vest, like the kind they wear on cop shows.

"Lucy, watch out!" Henry shouts.

I drop to the ground. "Ouch!"

Dylan cackles from the sidelines. Before I do something I'll get in trouble for, I turn my attention back to Henry and Jude.

"Your focus is weak," Henry points out. "Let's do it again. No distractions."

Easy for him to say. I nod and take my position, trying to ignore my throbbing knee.

Jude balances a fresh fireball in the palm of his hand. He lobs it at me, and I hold my hand up. Quick as lightening, I envision my hand as a brick wall. Big, strong, impenetrable. I imagine it swelling, doubling in size and strength. As the fireball comes within six inches of my hand, I step toward it and lob it back to Jude. The fireball moves toward Jude, but sputters out before it reaches him.

"Pretty lame if you ask me," Dylan calls out.

"Funny thing, no one asked you!" I snap.

"Again," Jude calls out. "This time put some power behind it."

We repeat it again. I struggle to ignore Dylan's taunts. What is it with him? Why won't Jude or Henry reprimand him?

I wait until the fireball is a couple of inches from me then whack it back at Jude *hard*. He lunges to the left to avoid being hit.

"Nice job, Lucy," Henry says.

"For a puny girl," Dylan adds.

Puny? Did he just call me *puny?* Fed up, I spin around and throw a fireball at him. It slams against his shoulder. He tamps out the flames and flashes a big grin my way. "Is that all you've got?"

I take a step toward him. "Keep it up. There's more where that came from."

Dylan laughs. "You've got nothing. Without Daddy to protect you—and everyone else—you're nothing."

Every inch of my body trembles. Heat surges through my limbs. My hands throb painfully. I raise both palms, awed by the twin fireballs seething and swirling in them. My chest swells with pride at the large, angry balls of flame I created. *What if?*

I bring my hands together and gasp as the fireballs merge, creating one larger fireball. The red and orange flames lick and hiss. Sparks shoot off and sizzle against the fabric of my clothes. A tingly feeling spreads through me as I rest my gaze on Dylan. A smile pulls at my lips as I step toward him and take aim.

"This is going to hurt," I tell him.

CHAPTER THIRTY-FIVE

– Lucy Walker –

Marcus pushes himself off the three-flat porch as Henry and I climb out of the car.

"We'll continue this conversation later. If I have any say in this, you'll be grounded from your powers," Henry says.

Grounded from my powers? As if Jude would let that happen. Why am I the one who always gets in trouble? Why doesn't Henry talk to Dylan, tell him to stop harassing me?

Marcus pauses on the sidewalk, meeting us halfway. "What happened?"

"Lucy attacked Dylan," Henry says, aiming another look of disappointment at me.

Marcus jerks his head in my direction, his eyes wide.

"Dylan was being a jerk to me the entire day. Somehow Jude and Henry overlook that part."

"There's a difference," Henry points out. "You're a supernatural."

"So is Dylan!"

Henry glares at me over the top of his glasses. "He's only a quarter of what you are. It's up to you to be the stronger person and ignore his taunts."

"Is he going to be okay?" Marcus asks. His concern annoys me.

"Because of his demon blood, he'll heal quickly, but that doesn't excuse Lucy's actions."

"I'm sorry, Henry." It's a big fat lie, but I tell him what he wants to hear.

"I'm going to speak with Persephone." Henry shakes his head as he walks away.

Marcus turns to me, eyebrows raised. "I can't believe you attacked Dylan."

I roll my eyes. "He deserved it, trust me. I can't believe you're siding with Henry on this."

Marcus grins and wraps his arms around me, pulling me close. "I'm not. I just wish you would've done it days ago."

Finally, someone's on my side!

"Does this mean that other thing is over with?" Marcus asks. The question comes out sounding casual, but I catch the underlying tone. He's tense.

"Yes." I fix my attention on his shoulder. I don't want to think about that other thing anymore.

Marcus lifts my chin, forcing me to meet his probing stare. Guilt gnaws at my insides. "Do you have any idea the effect that had on me? Knowing you were hot and heavy for Dylan? More than you'd ever been for me?"

"It wasn't real!"

He grimaces. "That's not exactly true."

"That thing with Dylan, it wasn't my choice. Left to my own

free will, I choose you every time," I tell him. "You're the only person I want to be with."

Marcus's eyes grow darker, and he looks away. "You were pretty close to giving it up for him."

"No, I wasn't!" I protest and that's the truth. Why is he doing this to me, anyway? To himself? "Dylan and I hate each other now. That should make you happy." Anger boils inside of me. After being attacked verbally by Dylan all day and physically by Jude, I don't need this.

"I have to go inside." I try to pull free, but Marcus restrains me.

His eyes meet mine. "I love you. You know that, don't you?"

I soften a little. Well, more than a little.

My vision blurs with tears. "I do, but you don't understand. My body was out of control. It literally had a mind of its own. Things were happening that I didn't want. It was intense. And scary." My voice falls to a whisper. "Then you acted like you hated me. I thought I'd lost you and..."

"Can you do me a favor?" Marcus asks.

I nod.

"The next time something crazy like this comes up, promise you'll tell me? Or if you can't handle telling me, talk to Persephone or Henry. I'd suggest Jude, but I still think he's hoping you and Dylan will end up together. Ask someone for help." Marcus's face pinches. "It was almost too late."

I recall the incident yesterday afternoon in the Douglas's bathroom with Dylan. Our lips nearly touched. The heat between us was tangible, the longing intense. Suddenly, I thrust Marcus away and fall to my knees. Violent dry heaves rack my body.

Marcus crouches over me and rubs my back. "Lucy?"

The nausea eases, leaves me trembling from head to toe. I run through what I'd eaten today. Scrambled eggs with veggies and cheese for breakfast. Kale and white bean soup at Jude's. Hours of training must've burned it all up because there's nothing in my stomach. I pull a tissue from my purse to blow my nose and wipe away the tears.

"Lucy...what were you just thinking about?"

Do I really want to tell him I was thinking about Dylan? Lying would be worse. "That kiss with Dylan. How guilty I feel." A half-truth. I can't tell him about yesterday. Besides, nothing actually happened. But I remember the need reflected in Dylan's eyes. The desire. I felt the same way. I wanted him more than I'd wanted anyone, even Marcus.

My stomach clenches and rolls. Another violent spasm racks my body.

Marcus breaks into a fit of laughter. I press a hand to my stomach, willing it to calm down.

I never thought Marcus was the type to laugh at me when I'm down. "Not...very...nice..."

"This is too good to be true!"

"What are you talking about?" I croak.

"Thinking of Dylan makes you physically ill."

I peer up at Marcus as he grins from ear to ear. I want to swat at him, but I don't dare for fear the violent heaves will start all over again.

CHAPTER THIRTY-SIX

– Lucy Walker –

"Is your brother going to be at your party?" Ella asks Caroline over lunch on Monday, each of them eating salads.

Katie and I roll our eyes at each other. When will Ella get over her crush on Caroline's brother?

"I doubt it. Why?" Caroline replies.

"Because I want a guarantee that at least one hot guy will be there. Let's invite him. We should play spin the bottle, so I can make out with him."

Caroline's expression twists with disgust. "Please stop."

"Since you convinced Caroline to invite half the student body, there will be plenty of guys for you to prey on," Suzy points out as she scans the music on her iPhone.

Cloe giggles behind her hand. She peers at the list of music Suzy is jotting down in her spiral notebook. "How is it you were put in charge of the music?"

Cloe and Suzy both opted for cheese pizza for lunch. It takes all of my restraint not to snag it from their plates. After training yesterday, my appetite is insatiable. I ate my veggie burger as soon as I sat at the table. My chips, too. My stomach grumbles, wanting more.

Ella frowns at both of them. "Good question. That should've been me."

"What about Dylan? Maybe he'll show up," Caroline's obviously trying to steer the conversation away from her brother and the music, "especially now that he's famous."

"Famous for what?" I ask, tearing my eyes from the ignored pizza on Cloe's plate.

Ella and Caroline grin at each other.

"His fight. How many guys do you know who can take on three guys at once and win?" Ella asks, her voice full of admiration.

Caroline scrunches up her face. "He looked pretty gross, but he still won."

"Amazing," I deadpan.

Ella clutches her hands to her chest and fixes me with a pleading expression. "Can we ask Dylan to the party? Would that be okay with you, Lucy?"

I shrug. Ella's not going to get under my skin. Not today. "Do what you want. I don't care."

She blinks several times then brightens. "Seriously?"

"It's Dylan we're talking about, right? Not Marcus?"

She nods, looking at me strangely.

"Invite him. Hopefully, he'll make it." *You two deserve each other.*

A slow smile spreads across her face. She smacks her lips for effect. "Hopefully."

I can't help but think Ella would make a great demon.

Caroline turns her attention to the rest of us. "You're each allowed to invite a couple of people. Let me know who you want to invite and I will add them to the list." She points to her notebook with her purple glitter pen before aiming a pointed look at her BFF. "I don't want troublemakers showing up. My parents will freak. Be selective."

"We'll have plenty of girls," Ella points out, ignoring Caroline. "You should probably focus on guys and, specifically, the good-looking ones."

Caroline presses her fingers to her temples, her face scrunched in a frown. I'd have a headache, too, with Ella as my co-party planner.

Katie elbows me in the side. "Wasn't she panting over Dylan a minute ago?"

I don't think five Dylans would be enough for Ella.

"If anyone asks, no booze, no cigarettes. And no weed," Caroline says, her eyes closed, still massaging. In the noisy cafeteria, I can barely hear her weak instructions.

The wicked grin returns to Ella's face. Caroline doesn't catch it.

Not my problem.

CHAPTER THIRTY-SEVEN

– Lucy Walker –

Five minutes into Brandi's birthday party and I realize Charlene was right. This party is for Mrs. Douglas, not Brandi. The music is my first clue. I'm sure the string quartet wasn't Brandi's choice. These kids aren't Brandi's friends; they're the children of Mr. Douglas's business associates and Mrs. Douglas's country club friends.

Mrs. Douglas marches Brandi to one child after another, fussing over the child's parents but basically ignoring the kids, leaving shy little Brandi to fend for herself.

"Lucy?" Mrs. Douglas calls out to me. "Can I get a glass of champagne for Mrs. Canty? Oh, and one for Mrs. Modale as well."

I make sure to get a good look at the women she's referring to before I fetch drinks from the makeshift bar set up along the living room wall. I've never heard of a champagne and wine bar at a nine-year-old's birthday party. The bartender hands me two glasses of champagne, and I weave my way through the crowded room. I deliver them to the two women, along with cocktail napkins. In what world is it okay for an underage girl to serve alcohol to her employer's friends at a party?

Wait, where's Brandi?

I find her cornered by three girls, her hands twisted together and lodged against her tummy.

"*Tu t'appelles comment?*" says a little blond girl who is dressed like she's ready to strut down a catwalk. Well, a catwalk featuring outrageously expensive clothes for young girls.

"*Mon nom est Marie,*" says a redheaded girl with a narrow, upturned nose. Her hair looks like she spent the morning at the salon. That would explain her perfect manicure, too.

"Why don't you speak French, Brandi? Your mom told my mom that you're taking lessons. If you plan to go to The French School in the fall, you'd better spend the summer with a private tutor," says another blond girl, not quite as stylish as the other two, unless you count the Tiffany's bracelet on her wrist.

"You're already *way* behind," the redhead says in a snotty tone, squinting her eyes at Brandi.

The room is filled with a bunch of over-dressed phonies. Mrs. Douglas makes a big show of laughing at some woman's joke. She's oblivious to Brandi, who's backed up against a wall, on the verge of a panic attack.

I rush over to the girls. My heart breaks at the sight of Brandi's pale skin and trembling lips. Just a little flick of my finger and I could teach the little witches a lesson.

"Brandi? I've been looking all over for you! You're supposed to get photos with the cake before we cut it." I pluck her from the group. "Sorry, girls. I'll bring her back in a little while."

Brandi grips my hand for dear life. We make our way through the crowd and into the kitchen. Charlene stands at the counter, surveying appetizers with a man and woman wearing white aprons.

I pull Brandi to the opposite side of the room and kneel down. "Who were those horrible girls?"

Tears spring to her eyes and trickle down her cheeks. "I don't know."

I wipe them away and stroke her hair, which is pulled into a sleek ponytail and sprayed stiff with hairspray.

"Do you know any of the kids out there?"

Her bottom lip trembles more. "None of my friends are here."

"Why not? Couldn't they come?" I ask.

"My mom didn't invite them."

I look away and exhale noisily. What kind of mother would do that? It's Brandi's birthday. It should be special. She should *feel* special.

Charlene joins us after the caterers exit the kitchen with trays of food. "What's wrong, princess?"

"The girls my mom invited are mean."

Mrs. Douglas bursts into the room. I jump to my feet. Brandi clings to my leg.

Once the door closes behind her, Mrs. Douglas fixes her ice-cold gaze on Charlene and me.

"I have a house full of guests, and the girl of honor is missing." She stares down at Brandi, her words clipped. "Now be a good girl, get out there, and talk to your new friends."

Brandi grips my leg harder.

"I'm sorry, Mrs. Douglas," I say quickly. "I brought Brandi in here because we had an emergency. She nearly threw up on three little girls speaking French."

Mrs. Douglas blanches. "No..."

"I was just about to get a cold cloth for her forehead," Charlene adds, darting across the kitchen and pulling a washcloth from a drawer.

All three of us study Brandi, who looks positively wretched.

Mrs. Douglas backs away, her hands up as if to protect herself from her diseased daughter. "Whatever you do, keep her away from the guests. And the food. I can't have her making a scene or getting anyone else sick."

"Of course," I call after her as she exits the kitchen. Once the door closes, I kneel down and take Brandi's hands in mine. "How about we have our own party?"

Brandi's eyes regain a bit of their usual mischievous twinkle. "What kind of party?"

I look around the kitchen hoping for inspiration. Then it hits me.

"We need your iPad," I say as we leave the kitchen. "This is going to be good."

Five minutes later, we are watching Mrs. Douglas and all of her guests on Brandi's device, compliments of their security monitoring system.

I pat her leg as I slide off her bed. "You stay here."

She reaches for my hand in a panic. "Where are you going?"

"It's not a party without presents. I'm going to grab some for you to open." I wink at her before slipping out the door.

Back in the living room, I slink over to the pink tulle-draped table piled mile-high with elegantly wrapped gifts.

"Lucy." I cringe as Mrs. Douglas beckons from across the room. "Mrs. Weinberg needs a refill on her Chardonnay."

After I deliver half a dozen glasses of wine and champagne, I pass the group of little girls who were bullying Brandi earlier.

"This party is lame." Blondie covers a fake yawn with her hand. "Where's the DJ? Where's the photo booth?" The rest of the group agrees.

I come to a halt and turn around. *You want to act like a witch, then you should look like one.*

A shivery tingle passes over my skin as I zero my attention on the head of the brat pack.

Focus on intent, I remind myself.

"Whisper the words..." Henry had said.

Hair of golden blonde, it's time to wave my magic wand,
Allow me to respond to your yawn, evil spawn,
Let's liven up this scene, and turn your flaxen curls to green,
Your obscene mouth now smells like a latrine.

The chatter of voices falls away as I repeat the spell a second time. It's just Blondie and me. But nothing happens. Blondie still looks the same. I purse my lips and focus harder. Third time's a charm, right? I whisper the spell again. I envision the little girl's hair turning green, like the sickly skin color of the wicked witch from the Wizard of Oz.

...latrine.

"Lucy!" Mrs. Douglas's fingers curl around my arm in a vice grip. "There are empty glasses that need to be filled. Where is Charlene? We're running low on fois gras and the appetizers—"

A high-pitched scream pierces the air. The quartet screeches to a halt, the bass cutting off with a violent burp. I look around the room. Frantic murmurs spread like wildfire. Women are craning their necks to get a look.

"Oh, my God!" Mrs. Douglas grips my arm tighter.

I follow her appalled gaze and gasp. Blondie number two has her hands clamped over her mouth, one over the other, reminding me of the monkeys in a poster I saw one time titled: *Hear No Evil, See No Evil, Speak No Evil.* Her eyes are wide as fifty-cent pieces as she stares at Blondie number one.

"What?" The former blond girl shrieks. She turns in a circle, eyeing the shocked faces around her. "Why are you all staring at me?"

Her redheaded cohort pulls a mirror from her purse and, without stepping any closer, tosses the compact to her friend. "You can keep it." She shudders.

I'm unable to move as I gawk at her putrid colored hair. It's the most amazing thing I've ever seen.

"Rebecca!" A woman races over to the little girl, grabs her by the shoulders. She tugs her daughter's hair as if to remove a wig. "You need to stop whatever game you're playing. It's upsetting the guests."

"I didn't do anything, Mom!" she wails, eyeballing her reflection. "Fix it. Make it go away!"

The party guests crowd around Rebecca, smiling and clapping.

Do they think this is a party trick? This has gone far enough. I didn't mean to terrorize the girl. My mind races as I try to think of a spell to turn her back.

Greenie suddenly clutches her stomach and doubles over.

"Rebecca! What's wrong?" her mother moves to touch her hair, pauses, then rubs her back instead.

Greenie groans as her stomach gurgles and rumbles. A sound erupts from her body like a pair of angry tubas. Several party guests burst out laughing, then slap their hands over their mouths when Rebecca's mom stares them down.

The most horrible smell fills the room. It reminds me of summers back home when the tanker truck came to the trailer park to empty septic tanks.

Party guests back away, gagging.

"I'm going to be sick," the pointy-nosed redhead exclaims.

Blondie number two jerks the neck of her shirt over her mouth and nose and nods at the redhead. The two of them scurry across the room to their mothers.

"Oh, my! What did you eat?" Rebecca's mother's complexion flushes in embarrassment.

Partygoers shove toward the door like cattle.

My heart thunders against my ribcage. Reversal spell... reversal spell...I've never learned how to undo a spell.

Rebecca's mother whirls around to Mrs. Douglas. "I'm taking Rebecca to the hospital. If I find out she's been poisoned by your food or she's been subjected to some sick joke, your reputation will be mud. I'll see to it."

"Mona, I...I...don't know what to tell you. This is not my doing.

I don't know how this happened!"

Mona's eyes narrow until they're tiny slits. "Turn...her...back," she growls.

Tears stream down Rebecca's face.

My heart squeezes painfully. *What have I done?*

Maybe if I tinker with the original spell? Green...latrine? No, not that again. Blond, bond, wand? No, that doesn't work. I shake my head tightly. No time for rhymes.

Allow me to fix your plight, return things to right,
Let's restore your flaxen curls,
Change that sickly smell to yummy chocolate.
Let what's been seen to be unseen.

I focus with everything I've got on Greenie. I repeat the spell three times. But nothing happens.

I hold my breath against the putrid smell for as long as possible. Mrs. Douglas stands immobile beside me, her nostrils twitching with the tiny breaths she takes.

Charlene races into the room. "Here's some Kaopectate," she says as she kneels beside Rebecca. She spoons a dose of the liquid into the little girl's mouth. "That should help settle your stomach."

"Alana, a word, please." Mrs. Douglas releases her grip on my arm as Rebecca's mother pulls her across the room to speak privately.

Charlene sets the bottle of medicine and the spoon on the floor. She wipes Rebecca's tears away then caresses her hair. "It's going to be okay."

Leave it to Charlene to comfort the little girl. It should be her mother, who's now too busy threatening to kick Mrs. Douglas out of the country club.

I need to fix this. *Now.* With every ounce of energy I have, I focus on Rebecca and repeat the spell. I envision her hair changing from green to blond, for the gurgling in her stomach to cease, and the lingering smell in the room to evaporate and instead smell like a newly unwrapped Hershey bar.

I whisper the words faster and faster. My intention couldn't be clearer or stronger.

That's when it happens.

"Can I have a candy bar?" Rebecca asks Charlene.

Charlene raises her nose to the air. I notice it, too. It's as if we're on the train about to pull into Ogilvie station, when the train cars fill with the intoxicating smell produced by Blommer Chocolate Company.

I kneel down and retrieve the compact Rebecca had dropped. "Take a look."

Rebecca shrinks from the mirror.

"It's okay," I tell her. She looks at Charlene, who nods.

Rebecca takes the mirror and looks at her reflection. A smile breaks out over her face.

"Mom, look! I'm all better!"

Rebecca runs over to her mother, who bends down to hug her. "You look like your beautiful self. We need to go."

Charlene follows them to the door, where she takes a chocolate cupcake from the dessert table and hands it to Rebecca.

"I don't think so." Mona eyes the cupcake as if it's poison and tugs her daughter out the door.

"I have a migraine and am going to lie down." Mrs. Douglas heads out of the room with a heavy sigh. "We will never speak of this."

I smack my hand against my forehead. "Brandi!"

I race off to Brandi's bedroom. Both Brandi and the iPad are missing. I check her closet and under the bed. No luck. I head down the hall to Ethan's room where I find the two of them sprawled on the floor with her iPad and Ethan's cell phone between them.

"I don't believe you," Dylan's voice rings out on speakerphone. "No one farts that loud."

"It's true!" Ethan says. "I snuck out there. The smell was so bad, worse than rotten eggs."

"Since when are you an expert on rotten eggs?" Dylan's laughter causes me to smile, but then it hits me that they're laughing at poor Rebecca. A nine-year-old girl was humiliated in front of a room full of people. I did that to her.

I push off the doorframe and enter the room. "Everyone's gone. Why don't you two come and check out the dessert table?"

"Hey, Lucy. Sounds like that was some party," Dylan says, his tone clipped. The easy warmth from a moment ago is gone.

I hear the accusation in his voice. He knows.

"You could say that," I tell him, my cheeks burning with shame.

"Is that little girl okay?"

Rebecca and her tears flash through my thoughts, her panic and fear. I've broken the golden rule. I used magic publicly. And I used it to teach someone a lesson. A little girl, no less.

"She is now." I clear my throat. "But everyone's gone, and Charlene and I have to clean up."

"Her hair really was green, Dylan!" Ethan interrupts.

"Sounds pretty magical, little man. Pretty magical."

CHAPTER THIRTY-EIGHT

– Lucy Walker –

"Why did I allow you to talk me into this?" Marcus rubs the back of his neck as he paces beside me. It's impossible to read his expression in the near-darkness.

"Relax," Selima says. "You're going to love it."

Marcus moves to the other side of the clearing. A chorus of nighttime sounds ring out through the woods, the skitter of nocturnal animals moving over a blanket of twigs, leaves, and brush. Two owls *hoot, hoot* to one another.

"I tried this before. Twice. It was a disaster." He clears his throat. "Maybe I can't fly. You know...like...some protectors can and some can't."

"Why didn't I think of that?" Selima says, her tone mocking. "While every protector I've ever known can fly, you're the one exception. Silly me."

I burst out laughing then clamp my hand over my mouth, certain Marcus is glaring at me through the darkness.

"Let's get this over with," Marcus mutters.

"That's the spirit, little brother!" Selima says. "I need to change. Lucy, can I have my other shirt?"

I toss Selima what can be best described as part T-shirt and part string bikini.

I thought it would be better in the dark, not seeing them go through the change. Marcus groans, and I visualize the skin splitting along his back, feathers scraping muscle and bone as they struggle free. I imagine his pain and shudder. Selima whimpers once. Did she just morph instantly?

"You ready, little brother?" Selima calls out.

Sliding my cell phone from my pocket, I select the flashlight icon and wave it like a wand in front of me. I gasp as Selima is illuminated in the faint light. While Marcus's wings are gray and white, Selima's are white with what appears to be a large, black spot on the left wing.

"Beautiful," I murmur.

Marcus moves into the light and studies his sister's wings. "It's like you have an extra eye." He points to the black spot. "Creepy."

Selima shrugs. "You ever hear of the evil eye? This is the opposite. It keeps me safe."

"Says the girl who works for demons," I say, grinning.

Selima grins back at me before returning her attention to Marcus. "I want you to forget what you've tried before. Assume it's all wrong."

Marcus snorts. I expect him to come back with some smart aleck remark and am relieved when he stays quiet. Why's he fighting this? Doesn't he understand how lucky he is? He can heal people. He can control other people's emotions. He's strong and fast.

Now he's going to learn to fly.

I study the sky, disappointed I can't see many stars. Too much light from the city, I suppose. The sky in Lexington was always full of stars.

"Watch what I do. Stay grounded for now," she says. "The important thing to remember is your wings need to propel you. You've never flown before. This is much different than using them as a landing device when you leap off a roof. No coasting. You've got to pump them. *Hard*."

I move closer to Selima with my makeshift flashlight. *Mental note to self: bring a real flashlight next time.*

She crouches in a low squat, her face pointing skyward. Her wings draw in tight against her back, twitching. She inhales noisily. With a grunt, she vaults her body into the air.

My mouth falls open as I attempt to trail her trajectory. Catching a glimpse of her back, the makeshift shirt makes sense. While the sleeveless design covers her front, the nearly non-existent back accommodates her wings.

"This isn't real," I whisper as Selima soars above me. I shiver, feeling awestruck.

"She can really fly," Marcus murmurs beside me.

I arc my phone over my head, trying to illuminate her movements. Other than an occasional glimpse, it's useless. I shut off the phone and return it to my pocket. Instead, I listen to the sound of her wings as they beat against the air.

"Amazing..." Marcus breathes, his gaze following his sister's movements.

"You can see her, can't you?" I ask.

"Yes."

I shake my head. His list of abilities continues to grow. I consider my own skills. Fireball creator. The ability to blast through doors. Deflect spells. Knock people off their feet. In the midst of training, I thought I was pretty badass. Now, not so much. Oh, yeah. I also have the power to humiliate a little girl in front of her friends. Compared to Marcus and Selima, I'm lame. Once Garret and his team come after Jude, do I stand a chance against them? How am I supposed to protect my father?

Just then, Selima's throaty chuckle cackles above us. I raise my face toward the sky, searching for her in the darkness.

"Over here," she calls out, far to the left.

She's fast.

"Enough showing off." Marcus stalks the ground below his sister.

What would it be like to fly? To move through the air without a parachute or a bungee cord? To feel the breeze move through my hair? Who am I kidding? My lungs would seize from terror.

"Boo!" Selima plunks down beside me, her wing brushing my back.

I gasp, startled. "Not funny!"

Marcus jogs to my side. "That was amazing, Selima. You've got to show me how it's done." He drums his hands against his abs in rhythm to a song only he can hear. His wings bounce in time to his movements. I've never seen him so excited.

"Come on," Selima says, waving him over to the spot where she launched the first time.

I pull my phone out again and aim the bright light at the two of them. Marcus mimics Selima's stance, squatting low and pulling his wings in tight against his back. He flexes his biceps, fists his hands.

"Remember to pump your wings as hard as possible."

"Got it." Marcus nods tightly.

"You ready?" Selima asks.

Marcus nods again.

"Envision a pole vault. It's all about the power in the legs," she says, her gaze leaving Marcus to focus on the dark sky. "Be fearless."

Marcus glances at me. A slow smile spreads across his face.

"Be careful," I tell him.

Selima launches herself into the air. Her white wings—majestic and beautiful in the glow of my cell phone—immediately expand. I forget to blink, mesmerized by the *WOMP, WOMP, WOMP* of her flapping wings as she climbs higher into the night.

"Here goes," Marcus says under his breath.

I peel my attention from Selima and point my phone toward Marcus. He mimics his sister's low squat then launches himself into the air with a loud grunt. He flaps his wings hard and fast, but doesn't climb. Instead, Marcus tumbles onto the ground.

"Come on, little brother. You can do better," Selima teases from above. Her wings are silent. It's like she's floating.

Marcus releases a heavy sigh and punches the ground.

"You okay?" I offer him a hand up.

"I'm fine," he says tersely and ignores my hand.

"You're such a mom, Lucy." Selima laughs. "Marcus, is she always like this?"

My body feels hot from head to toe. "What are you talking about?" I sputter. "I don't mother Marcus."

Marcus chuckles. "Yeah, you do, but it's okay...most of the time."

"Clearly, he likes that about you," Selima says.

"I do not mother him," I mutter.

"You do it to Dylan, too," Marcus says.

Why are we talking about this in front of Selima?

Back on his feet, Marcus resumes the squat position and tucks his wings tight against his back. He takes a deep breath and holds his arms in front of his body, fists clenched. He bounces low. Then with one swift pump of his arms, he thrusts himself skyward. His gray and white wings expand and beat down against the air as they elevate him higher. His grunts carry across the mild breeze.

Marcus doesn't fall. Relief floods my insides as I hear the powerful *WOMP WOMP WOMP* of his wings. I realize I'm holding my breath and finally exhale.

"Come and get me if you can," Selima sings out.

Marcus struggles to climb, or maybe he's simply struggling not to fall to the ground again. Selima calls out instructions to him. After several moments, Marcus begins to climb.

The air above me moves, and I thrust my cell phone above my head to spot which one just flew by. Low battery flashes across the screen of my phone. I power off and shove the cell into my pocket as I peer into the darkness above. I wish I could see them.

"Ouch! Not fair!" Selima cries out. "No feather snatching."

"Not so tough now, huh?" Marcus taunts.

They chase each other, tossing jabs back and forth, for a long while. It stinks to be left out. I'd give anything to have wings so I could fly with them right now. *You'd give up fireballs?* The little voice in my head asks. That's an easy one. Flying is so much cooler than throwing fire. Why couldn't I be a protector instead of a demon?

"Whoa! Oh, no!" Marcus tumbles onto the ground. "Oomph!"

"Way to go, genius." Selima laughs as she lands on her feet beside me and trots over to Marcus. "Slow down *before* you land next time."

"Now you tell me." Marcus arrives at my side, grinning. He picks bits of grass and leaves out of his hair.

"It sounded like you two were having a good time." I try to keep the jealousy out of my voice.

"Guess what? Marcus *can* fly, just like all other protectors." She teases. "Little brother...the next time you pluck one of my feathers, I'll take five. Consider this your only warning."

"Watch it." Marcus elbows her. The two of them get into a jabbing match, both of them laughing.

I sense their euphoria and wish I could be a part of what they experienced tonight. I'm happy Marcus has connected with Selima, but they spend so much time together. At least I was included tonight.

The sound of crickets suddenly rings out. Selima looks around curiously.

"It's my phone," Marcus says, pulling his cell from his pocket. "Henry," he says as he turns his back and walks to the opposite end of the clearing.

"I'm going to help him," Selima says, closing the distance between us. "Show him the ways of the protectors, what he missed out on."

"That's great, but what about keeping him safe from Camille and Garret?"

Selima sighs. "I think you're wrong about their intentions. Camille adores him. She won't hurt him. Garret just needs to get used to the idea of sharing Camille."

If she'd been there that night at the condo, she would realize how wrong she is about her father.

Marcus returns a moment later. His wings are gone, and his shirt is back on. He grabs me by the arm. "We've got to go," he says tightly.

I race to keep up with his stride. "What's wrong?"

"The ravens are back."

Lola and Serenity are back!

"Are they okay? Did Jude do something to them again?" I ask, trying to pull my arm free of his vice grip.

"What would Jude do...?" Selima asks.

"No. They alerted Henry and Persephone to some unusual activity in the woods." Marcus's words are clipped. "About a mile from here. We need to go."

"What kind of activity?"

"It's not Garret, is it?" Selima asks. She moves around Marcus, blocking his path. "You're scared. Who are we running from? Tell me so I can help."

A spasm racks my entire body. "Seamus?"

"Yes." Marcus bulldozes past Selima, nearly knocking her over.

"Who's Seamus?" Selima asks. Her stride is long and smooth like her brother's, while I trot to keep pace with the two of them.

Once at the car, Marcus opens my door and tries to shove me inside.

I push his hand away. "I've got it."

He rushes to the driver's side and climbs in. Selima's in the car behind us, her headlights illuminating the interior of Marcus's car.

"Are we going to meet with Persephone and Henry and come up with a plan?" I ask.

"I'm going to get you home. Aiden and I will guard the three-flat while Henry and Persephone inspect the woods. Then we'll switch in a few hours." Marcus tears out of the parking lot and takes an immediate left turn.

I nearly slam into the passenger side door. "I don't need guarding. My uncles do, though, so I'll protect them. Or I can help Henry and Persephone," I tell him. "Jude's been training me to protect myself. To fight Seamus. I'm ready."

Marcus snorts. "The fact you think you're ready tells me you're not. You're going home. The four of us can handle this."

I glare at him through the darkness. "You don't think I'm good enough to help? How can you say that? You haven't seen me in action."

"It's not about that. I can't risk you getting hurt."

"I've been getting my butt kicked every Sunday, working hard and eating crow. This is what I've prepared for. Now you're telling me I have to sit this out." My temper flares with every word out of my mouth. "No way!"

Idling at a stoplight, Marcus turns to me. The headlights of oncoming traffic illuminate his expression. I study the hard set of his mouth, staring at him stubbornly.

"Fine. You can guard your uncles from the inside. I'll be on the roof, and Aiden will tour the parameter." His tone is icy, clipped. "You don't step foot outside. Got it?"

This is as big a win as I'll get tonight. I'll take it.

CHAPTER THIRTY-NINE

– Lucy Walker –

Marcus stands guard at my locker after final period on Monday. His hooded gaze surveys the crowded hallway. Once he spots me, I wait a beat for his expression to soften, for that crooked smile that's meant only for me. Instead, his jaw clenches.

"You think Seamus will come after me here?" I ask once we're inches apart.

Guarding my uncles on Saturday night proved uneventful. Bernard, Sheldon, and I watched movies late, then I pretended to go to bed. Once I heard their bedroom door close, I stayed up, pacing the house, avoiding those areas where the floor creaked, and making sure all the windows were locked. I drank three Cokes in order to stay awake. Seamus never made an appearance.

Marcus grabs a lock of my hair, and my fingers pause on my locker combination. I wait for him to wind it around his finger and bring it to his nose.

"I need you to text Katie, let her know you're running an errand with me today." He releases my hair, pressing it flat against my shoulder as if to safeguard it. "You should let your uncles know you'll miss dinner, too."

The noise of hundreds of students and locker doors slamming can't compete with the thunder of my heartbeat. "What's going on?"

"We're going to do some investigating," Marcus says.

He's including me? This is a big change from his attitude on Saturday night. Did he finally realize I can help? I nod and open my locker. Marcus looks around, searching the halls.

"Seamus wouldn't come to my school. Would he?" Then I remember we have more than one enemy in town. "Or are you looking for Garret?"

"I'll tell you in the car," he murmurs. He glances around again, standing close.

My heart pounds harder. Mentally, I review the maneuvers I've practiced at Jude's house.

On the way to the parking lot, I notify Katie and my uncles about my change of plans. Once we're in the car, I turn to Marcus. "Is it Seamus or Garret?"

"We've been studying the woods since Saturday night. Seamus has spent a lot of time recently in one area in particular, Bunker Hill Forest Preserve. He's been practicing magic."

Seamus is back.

"We're going to confront him?" I remind myself I'm ready. Would Jude agree?

"It's been quiet in the woods for the last ten hours, so we believe he's moved on."

"Why are we going to the woods if he's not there?" I ask.

"To see what he's been up to, and if we're lucky, to get a sense of who he's working with."

"Just to be clear, he's gone from the woods, but he's not gone from Chicago?"

Marcus's face darkens and he looks away. "We're not sure."

I struggle to catch my breath. It's difficult since my lungs refuse to cooperate.

"We're ready for him," I say, more to myself than to Marcus.

Marcus reaches for my hand. "I won't let him hurt you. Jude knows better than to interfere this time. You'll be safe."

Seamus wants me dead. Garret wants me dead. *I'm screwed,* the little voice in my head says. *No, I'm not,* I snap back. I refuse to believe all of my training has been a waste.

"You should let Jude know," Marcus says.

I wish Jude texted. He probably knows how and only pretends not to. He answers on the first ring.

"Lucy, I hope you're not calling to cancel training this weekend. Dylan already tried. I offered to pick up Ethan in his place."

"You wouldn't!" I hiss.

"Try me."

Jerk.

"I'm calling to tell you Seamus is back." I'm met with silence. I wait several seconds, pull the phone from my ear and read the screen to ensure the call is still live. I return the phone to my ear. "Hello?"

"I know," Jude says.

"What? You knew and you didn't bother to tell us?"

"Since when do I have to report to my daughter?" The hard edge in his voice would normally make me back down. Not today.

"How am I supposed to protect myself if you keep secrets—big secrets—from me? Seamus came here to kill me!"

"Where are you?" Jude asks.

"On our way to Bunker Hill Forest Preserve."

"No," Jude replies. "Tell Marcus to take you home. Now."

I roll my eyes. "According to Henry, Persephone, Marcus, and Aiden, the area has been quiet for the last ten hours. It's safe. If he does show up, I can defend myself. Plus, so long as you don't disable the other person best qualified to help keep me safe, I'll have the protection of my boyfriend."

Marcus shakes his head, but I don't care. I had to make my point to Jude.

"I'll meet you there."

"But..."

The line goes dead.

I glare at Marcus. "Great. He's meeting us there."

"Not a horrible idea."

"Says you."

We drive in silence for a while.

"I hate to do this, but it probably makes sense to bring Dylan in on this, too."

I cross my arms over my chest. "Forget it. It's bad enough Jude's showing up."

"Lucy, put your personal feelings aside. The more supernaturals we have involved, the more successful we'll be taking Seamus out if he shows up."

My heart leaps into my throat. "But you said he isn't there. Besides, what good is Dylan? He's barely supernatural."

"His brute strength could come in handy."

"He'll never be able to get close enough to Seamus to use his fists. That's not how this works. With Seamus, it's all about fireballs, disarming him, and strong defensive tactics," I tell him.

Marcus raises an eyebrow, an expression I now associate with Selima. It sets me off.

"What do you think I do at Jude's house every Sunday? Play checkers? Take cooking lessons?"

"It sounds like your training is paying off. I'm impressed," Marcus says patiently. "Take the compliment."

"I'm sorry, but I feel like you don't give me enough credit, especially when spending every Sunday at Jude's house is the last place I want to be."

"I do get it," Marcus says. "Well, wake-up call, I don't like it, either. In case you forgot, I promised your grandmother I'd keep you two apart. For me to break that promise is huge. Protectors don't break promises."

I study his clenched jaw. I hate that the subject of Jude causes us to fight. I'm sure the subject of Dylan doesn't help. "I'll call Dylan."

Marcus rattles off the location of the forest preserve. "It shouldn't take him long if he's at home."

I pull out my cell phone and call Dylan, curious how Marcus knows where he lives.

Dylan picks up on the second ring. "Looking for another chance to barbeque me? What do you want, Miss Firestarter?"

"Seamus is back in the area. Marcus and I are meeting Jude at the woods over by Harts Road and Caldwell Avenue."

"And you need fresh meat to grill?"

I grit my teeth and resist the urge to disconnect. "Marcus says you should be included. Can you meet us there?"

"Let me guess. *You* don't want me there."

"Of course I do."

"You're a terrible liar. It's one of the few things I actually like about you," he says. "Jude just called me, too. I guess he thought you'd be an idiot and leave me out. I'll meet you there."

Blood surges to my temples. Where does Dylan get off insulting me? He's an inferior demon, a loser mutant. "I'm an idiot? How exactly are you going to help?"

"I'm going to kick Seamus's ass. Do you really think Jude believes you can handle a demon that powerful? Wake up and smell the coffee, hillbilly girl. He's got the rest of us on board to save your butt."

"I can't wait to see you. I'm going to roast you until you're well done."

Marcus reaches over and plucks the phone from my fingers.

"Dylan? It's Marcus." He's silent as Dylan blabbers over the line. "I hear you, but all of us are really tired of the fighting. Give us a break for one night, please. After tonight, you two can scream at each other all you want. Great. Thanks."

Marcus hands the phone back to me.

I punch the end call button and shove the phone into my purse.

Marcus's lecture immediately puts me on the defensive. Try

walking in my shoes. Or Dylan's. We don't want to be like this. It was the stupid spell.

We pull into the forest preserve parking lot, and Jude glides into a spot next to us two minutes later. How did he get here so fast? Is it possible he knows Garret is in town and is spying on him at the condo? If protectors can sense demons, is the opposite true, too? Or did Aiden spill the beans? Would Jude kill a protector? That's a stupid question. He would kill Marcus if not for our pact.

Marcus's body trembles and twitches beside me. *Damn you, Jude.*

I slide out of the car as Jude lowers his window.

"Dylan's on his way here. Any chance we can split up into two groups?" I glance over at Marcus, who's using super human effort to keep his body under control. "This is torture for Marcus."

Jude's gaze flicks toward Marcus. "I can show you real torture if you'd like."

"I can disappear from your life." I shoot back.

Jude's black eyes return to me. The shock zaps me instantly and I flinch. I miss the days when he actually had to touch me to shock me. At least then I had some warning.

"Very well," Jude says. "Dylan and I will scour the area to the east while you and the gargoyle work the west side. Call me if you find anything."

I return to Marcus and relay Jude's instructions to him.

"Perfect. Let's get moving."

Marcus's face drips with sweat as his body twitches. I'd suggest he allow the change, but the forest preserve is open to the public until dusk, and there are several cars parked in the lot. He can't risk it.

Marcus takes a map from a wooden dispenser and unfolds it as we approach the path. "We're going to head this way." He runs his finger along the west loop on the map. "The trails mean nothing to Seamus, but I'll be able to pick up his aura."

The path travels at a decline, and the further in we go, the denser the foliage. My senses register the earthy smells of decaying wood, grass, and a mix of lavender and sage.

Marcus makes no sound as he leads the way along the path. As quiet as I try to be, I can't avoid crunching acorns and branches beneath my feet. A blue jay screeches overhead. Then again. By the third time, I pause on the path to glare at the noisy bird. Is it trying to give us away? Could it be a spy for Seamus? If the demon was able to control Jude's red-eyed crows, he could do the same with one loudmouth bird.

Marcus stops and holds up his hand. His eyes narrow as he zeroes in on at an area to our right. I follow his gaze and see an open area through a dense cluster of trees.

I shiver as I follow him off the path, the branches scratching at my skin. The hair on the back of my neck prickles. Is this where Seamus practiced magic?

Upon entering the clearing, Marcus turns in a slow circle. He takes everything in, his nose raised to smell the air.

As I walk the clearing, I spot unusual scores on three trees bordering the open area. I run my fingers along the charred impressions. A supernatural was definitely here. Are these marks from Seamus's fireballs? Or was he practicing something more dangerous?

A huge tree is toppled over approximately thirty feet from where I stand. My spider senses suddenly go bonkers. The air crackles with electricity. "Do you feel that?" I whisper.

Marcus nods.

I walk over to the tree with Marcus on my heels. The break point looks fresh. The tree wasn't cut down. Seamus blasted it. Was he imagining me, the grandchild of Vera, his lost love, and Jude, the man who stole her from him, when he did that? There are dark markings on the tree. Scorch marks?

Before I can get a closer look at the scores in the tree, I am startled by the sound of breaking branches behind us. I whirl around to see Dylan enter the clearing, followed by a soundless Jude. I meet Dylan's tight expression and every muscle in my body grows more tense.

He doesn't belong here.

"Seamus's aura is all over the place," Marcus announces. "I'm guessing he was here for a week to ten days, same as the other two locations. He's moving from place to place to avoid being caught."

"What other two locations?" I ask. Why didn't he mention that to me sooner?

"Yet you didn't hone in on his aura until he was gone?" Jude asks.

"Do you honestly expect Marcus to know what's happening in all of Cook County?" I ask, exasperated.

287

Marcus nods at Jude, before he turns to me. "The point Jude's making is that Seamus is somehow able to cloak himself."

Seamus has another trick in his magical tool kit? Great. Just great.

"He's gone," Marcus says, mostly to Jude and Dylan, since they just joined us. "The question is where did he go?"

"Can we track him?" Dylan asks.

"He'll have so many protections in place, you'll never be able to," Jude says. He walks across the clearing and stops beside me at the giant tree lying on its side. Jude runs his fingers along the burn marks, the same ones I observed. He bends down to scoop a handful or dirt or ash from the ground. He draws his hand to his nose.

"I know what Seamus is up to," Jude announces. He dumps the contents from his hands. He turns to face us, his expression grim. "He's recruiting."

"How?" Marcus asks, and all three of us line up along the tree and study what I previously thought were scorch marks.

"Recruiting who?" Dylan asks.

In the fading light, the marks are difficult to see. I pull my cell phone from my pocket and use the flashlight function to brighten up the trunk.

"Originally, I thought these were random, a result of Seamus hurling fireballs," I say and lean close.

Marcus peers at the markings. "They're symbols."

There are three symbols in all. One looks like a teepee with a line through the middle, another that looks like the outline of a Christmas globe ornament with a plus sign on top, and the third looks like an upside down cross with a swirly tail.

Dylan and I scoop some of the ash from the ground beside the fallen tree. I bring it to my nose. Visions of Daphne erupting into flames last year on Jude's roof come to me and my stomach convulses.

"What does it smell like to you?" Jude asks us.

"Awful." I choke, feeling spooked as I thrust my hand away from my body.

Dylan's face twists. Did he have the same flashback? "Like burning hair, but so much worse."

Eyeballing the pile of ash mixed with bits of stone or some other hard things, I glance at Jude. I don't dump the contents. I'm not sure why, but I don't. "What is this?"

"A virgin lamb, most likely."

I fling the gritty dust from my hand as if burned. Big mistake. It becomes airborne. In a panic, I pull in a sharp breath. I drop to my knees, retching.

"You okay?" Marcus is at my side in an instant.

After a few minutes, I am back on my feet. I swipe my mouth with the back of my hand, unable to shake the vision of an innocent little lamb brought into the woods and slaughtered.

"What does all this ritualistic stuff mean?" Dylan asks.

Why isn't he as affected by the sacrificed animal as I am? Has he become immune? Or is he trying to be stoic to impress Jude? What happened to the Dylan I used to know?

"Is this all part of him recruiting a new partner?" I ask.

"It's a form of soul magic," Jude says. "Seamus must sense a supernatural in the area, or maybe a human he believes is both useful and malleable. Likely a young female, someone to replace his daughter." Jude studies our surroundings, the tree, the pile of dust, before he returns his attention to the three of us. "Seamus will summon her and I would bet he plans to tether her magic to his or, if she is human, he will feed off of her soul in order to strengthen his own power."

"But a human needs her soul to live," Marcus protests.

"If Seamus chooses a human, she will be dead once he is finished with her," Jude says.

Where is his anger? The indignation? Instead, Jude's face is expressionless, his words matter of fact.

"Seamus is gone," Dylan says grimly, gesturing to the surrounding area with his hands to signify the woods. "Do you think he connected with this girl?"

Jude's eyes turn dark, glinty as he surveys the area. "Perhaps." His gaze shifts to me and I shiver. "I want you to move into my home."

Seamus knows where I live. *Sheldon and Bernard.* My knees quiver and I lock them. "If he comes to the three-flat, my uncles will be in danger. They can't defend themselves," I say. "There's no way I'm leaving them."

"Persephone, Aiden, and I can protect your uncles," Marcus says through clenched teeth. He jerks and trembles as he fights the change. Suddenly, he cocks his head.

"What is it?" I ask.

"The last hiker just left the forest preserve." Marcus glances at Jude, then strides out of the clearing. A loud THAWUNK rings out. Marcus returns moments later, shirtless, his massive wings tucked tight to his back.

"Feel better?" I grab his shirt, which hangs from the rear waistband of his jeans and tuck it in the crook of my arm.

"Much."

Dylan heaves a sarcastic sigh and rolls his eyes before he turns his attention back to Jude. "What's our strategy?"

"Are you familiar with a two-front war?"

Dylan nods. "I know my history. Why?"

Jude glowers at Marcus. "In addition to taking on Seamus, we're going to eliminate the gargoyle's father."

CHAPTER FORTY

– Lucy Walker –

"This can't be good." I drop my backpack on the floor of the old library at St. Aquinas. Selima perches on the upper catwalk, clutching one of the many musty smelling books in her hands. I'm curious how she got into the building, which prides itself on having tight security. Then again, she's got the same killer charm as her brother. Maybe all she had to do was ask someone. "Jude knows Garret's in town."

Selima returns the book to its spot on the shelf. Ignoring the ladder, she steps off the ledge and drops twenty feet. I brace myself. A one-story jump is nothing for a protector, even one who hasn't morphed, but I still fear she will twist her delicate looking ankle. Instead, she lands in a deep squat, her fingers brushing the ground. It reminds me of all the times I leapt off the roof at Jude's house during my initial demon training.

"Demons don't have exceptional senses like protectors, but I'm guessing Jude's known about Garret for a while," she says. "Demons are territorial, and they always keep track of their enemies."

"Jude's going after him," I tell her.

Selima's dark, troubled gaze locks on mine. "Rumor has it Garret's planning an attack on Jude."

I swallow hard. "How many protectors?"

"Fifteen...maybe twenty."

Jude, Henry, Persephone, Aiden, Marcus, Dylan, me. Seven. With Max and his partner, that's nine.

"The odds aren't good," Selima says, coming to the same conclusion. "But I have an idea."

Suspicion careens up my spine. "You're willing to help me, a half-demon? Garret won't be too happy about that."

"Just because Garret's my father doesn't mean I automatically side with him. Unlike most of the others, I have a mind of my own."

I take a seat on the bottom stair leading to the catwalk and shiver against the chill of the air conditioning. "Why are you so eager to betray your father? Aren't you afraid of what he'll do to you if he finds out?"

"I can take care of myself. It's you who's in danger," Selima says sharply. "I don't care how powerful Jude is. It's about the numbers. Against Garret's team, he—and *you*—don't stand a chance."

Could this be a setup? Is Selima manipulating me? Maybe that's the real reason she's talking to me here and not the apartment building roof with Marcus present. He would see through her lies. But what if she's telling the truth? Could she really be here to help? To warn us? If everything she says is true, Jude and I are goners.

Selima shoves her hands in the pockets of her denim jacket and glances around to make sure we're alone. "Marcus told me Persephone and Henry are calling in favors from other demons and witches." She scrunches her brow. "It won't be enough."

She's right. We're all kidding ourselves. Jude may be unstoppable against Garret. I believe he would win against the protector, but not when Garret's got a small army behind him.

So far everything she's saying could be discussed in front of Marcus. Persephone and Henry, too. Why the secret meeting here at my school? Something about this doesn't feel right.

"What do you suggest?"

Selima squats before me and lowers her voice. "I have an idea. It's going to sound crazy—beyond crazy—which it is, but hear me out."

My entire body tingles. I'm not going to like this. "I'll consider anything at this point."

Selima chews her lip for a moment. "Who's the biggest, most powerful demon you can think of?"

I don't even have to think about it. "Jude."

Selima gives a small shake of her head. "Think bigger."

Bigger than Jude? Not Seamus, that's for sure, although, he's mastered the art of surprise. I only know one other demon and that's Aiden. He's small potatoes compared to Jude. So small that he has zero effect on Marcus. For all I know, he's like Dylan and only has the ability to use his fists. There's Max. He's nothing more than hired muscle, according to Aiden. "There's no one bigger than Jude. Even Garret said so."

Selima's pupils are so large her irises disappear. *Fear?*

I lean back a couple of inches, unable to do much more from my seat on the stairs, my spider senses on high alert. "Where are you going with this?"

"You're his namesake, Lucy," she whispers.

A pool of ice settles in my belly.

Jude holds the rank of king among demons, and he is said to have been created second only to Lucifer, said the voice that came to me in the three-flat attic when Persephone and I cast the protection spell on Jude.

"No," I whisper. "You can't mean..."

Selima's eyes meet mine. "He'll help you."

"Namesake?" I say, breathlessly.

Lucifer...Lucy...

Selima clutches my hands in hers. She doesn't crunch my fingers this time. "It's time you have a serious talk with your father."

* * * *

"I want to learn more about you," I blurt out over lunch with Jude and Dylan on Sunday.

Dylan chokes on his chicken and immediately guzzles half his glass of water. It's Sunday and our weekly meal together before demon training. Today we sit in the kitchen, which is much brighter with the light filtering in through the windows. I prefer this room to the dining room with its heavy drapes and massive dark wooden table.

Jude regards me calmly, chews his food then swallows. He dabs his lips with a blood-red cloth napkin. "What brought this on?"

"I've been thinking about my name. Is it a coincidence that Lucy and Lucifer are so similar?" Dylan's eyes nearly bug out of his head, but he stays quiet. My hands twist the napkin on my lap into a furious knot. My food sits untouched on my plate. Maybe Jude will pack the parmesan polenta and roasted vegetables for me to take home later. It smells amazing, but my stomach is way too quivery to tolerate even one bite.

Jude cuts another piece of his chicken scaloppini, chews then swallows. His eyes never leave my face. He takes a sip from his wine glass. "You came up with this all on your own?" he asks.

"It's not that big of a stretch." I'm offended he thinks I'm not smart enough to figure it out.

"Lucifer was my mentor. There is a hierarchy where I come from. I sat at his right hand, so to speak."

Where he comes from? "Was I named after him?"

He nods finally. "You were."

"Do you two keep in touch?"

Jude's eyes narrow. Dylan kicks me under the table, but I push on.

"You're my father. Can't I ask questions about you?"

He takes another drink from his wine glass, watching me over the rim. "Of course. I'm just curious why you're asking now. Are you up to something, Lucy?"

I force a laugh. "I guess I was too afraid to ask before. You're not all that approachable."

I can tell by his expression he wishes I still felt that way.

"He and I haven't communicated in a long time."

"Because Lucifer lives in hell?"

Dylan spits water a good foot across the table. "I'm sorry," he gasps.

Jude looks at him, appalled. Dylan jumps up from his chair and moves dishes around, so he can mop up the mess.

Jude returns his attention to me. His face looks drawn all of a sudden. "We'll call it that, for the sake of discussion."

"Is it possible to visit?"

Jude tosses his napkin at Dylan, who uses it to clean up the rest of his mess. He scrapes his chair back, and I can tell I've reached the end of his patience. "Where are you headed with this, Lucy?"

"I know nothing about you and where you come from. I know all about Momma. I'm curious is all. You have this huge, successful business or enterprise, whatever you call it. Did Lucifer teach you all of that? Was he your father figure? A mentor? Does he run businesses in hell? What does he do? It's not like he can retire, right? Because your kind, you, uh, live a really long time."

"My kind," Jude mutters. He crosses one leg over the other. "He's the head of a very complex political structure, societal faction. It involves business, but not like you know it here."

"He's *important*."

"You could say that," Jude says dryly.

"Will he be in that position forever or does it get handed down to you at some point?"

"Will you shut up already?" Dylan hisses.

Is he worried I'll tip Jude's anger and he will go after Dylan again?

Jude's expression pinches. "Is this some kind of homework assignment? A family tree or something?"

"Family tree." Dylan snorts. Jude shoots him a dark look, and Dylan returns to wiping the table.

"No, it's just me trying to understand my family." I'm unable to stop the frustration from creeping into my voice.

"There is some pressure for him to step down from his responsibilities, to finally designate a successor."

I lean forward. "Would that be you?"

Jude's face scrunches distastefully. "If I was interested, which I'm not."

"Why not?"

"Because I don't want the responsibility. I don't like all the positioning. And I live *here*. Are we done?" His tone makes it clear that we are, in fact, done.

"I thought you'd like me taking an interest," I grumble.

Jude rises from the table and beckons for Dylan and me to follow him. It's time to train.

* * * *

Later that night, I meet Marcus and Selima on the roof of the apartment building.

"How did it go with Jude today?" Selima asks. She plops down and crosses her legs in front of her. I catch a glint as light reflects off the tiny gemstone piercing in her nose.

Marcus looks from Selima to me, eyebrows raised. I take a seat across from her and Marcus joins me. "How did what go with Jude?" he asks.

"I played the role of the curious daughter, asking questions about you know who and their relationship. Jude didn't like it. He finally asked if I was working on a family tree for school," I say with a grin.

Selima throws her head back and laughs.

Marcus peers at us, his brows pulled together tight. "What are you two up to?"

"He didn't pick up on the real reason for your questions?" Selima asks, holding up a finger to Marcus to indicate he should wait a minute.

Marcus studies my profile. I feel his impatience. I focus on Selima.

"No, and I'm determined to figure out a way..."

Marcus shakes his head as if to clear the cobwebs. "Figure out what? A way to what?"

We both turn to him. Selima's eyes dance with excitement.

"Figure out a way to get Jude to go below ground," I tell him.

"If he can't be found, then he can't be killed," Selima says. "Then we only have Lucy to protect."

"We?" Marcus blinks at his sister.

She smiles at him. "Yes, *we*."

I roll my eyes. As if she cares one iota about me. It's great that she's helping me, but I still can't trust her motivation.

Marcus's gaze bounces between the two of us. "What about Garret? He'll be furious with you for getting involved, for siding with the *enemy*." He uses air quotes on that last word.

She sighs. "I work for demons, remember? I'm already in the doghouse with Garret."

Marcus shakes his head and exhales with frustration. "You're naïve. They're using you."

"No one uses me, little brother," she says, piqued.

"What do you do for them?" Marcus asks, not willing to let the subject drop.

"I work as part of the kitchen staff, which is sort of a ruse. My real job is to guard them. There are other demons—the nasty kind—who are a threat."

"Do you fight for them?" Marcus asks, an edge to his voice.

"No. When I sense trouble, I sound the alarm." She nods her head toward me. "Can we get back to the problem at hand?"

Marcus nods reluctantly.

"The point is to get Jude underground," she says. "Then to help protect Lucy, who's done nothing wrong. She's an innocent. It's my role as a protector to keep her safe."

"According to Garret, it's your role as a protector to kill Lucy because she's half-demon," Marcus says.

"She's also half-witch," Selima counters.

Marcus looks unconvinced. "Garret doesn't see it that way. Besides, Jude isn't going to leave Lucy."

This is the part that scares me to death. Am I crazy to go along with Selima's plan? What's in it for her?

"We're going to enlist some assistance," Selima says. She rests her hand on my leg, her eyes never leaving my face. She's going to help me with Jude. Maybe she's not a spy for her father after all. A sense of calm spreads through me.

Marcus narrows his eyes at Selima and plucks her hand from my leg. The sense of calm slips away. "I don't like this," he says.

What happens if we tick off the granddaddy of all demons? Fire...death...mass destruction? Images of Sheldon and Bernard glide through my thoughts. Ethan and Brandi, too. What if I fail to keep them safe? My chest tightens.

Focus, Lucy. Get Jude below ground. Then worry about the others.

Selima snaps her fingers, and it's enough to pull me from my grim thoughts. "We need to talk to Persephone and Henry. We're going to need their help," she says.

"Lucy?" Marcus turns to me, an edge to his voice. He cups my cheek and leans in close. "Tell me what you're planning, please."

Doubt tugs at me. Are we going about this all wrong? But what else can we do? What else can *I* do? Garret and his team are not going to rest until Jude is destroyed. We're outnumbered. I have no choice. I have to do this.

"We're going to summon Lucifer."

CHAPTER FORTY-ONE

– Lucy Walker –

"It's irresponsible." Henry flushes, his voice a mix of panic and disappointment.

Selima perches calmly on Persephone's couch. Aiden studies me with a thoughtful expression.

"Not an option!" Persephone huffs. "It's too dangerous."

I knew this was going to be difficult. Maybe even impossible. Marcus leans against the wall, his arms wrapped tightly over his chest.

"It's a stupid idea," he grounds out.

"It's the best idea so far to ensure Jude's safety and mine," I counter.

"We have a plan, Lucy." Henry pulls at his tie. He had come directly from his law office. "We've got other resources. Max is on board, and he brought a trusted partner. These are *reasonable* demons." He nods at Persephone. "What about Mirabelle?"

Persephone frowns. "She's in South America. I can't track her down."

"Regardless, we only work with supernaturals we can trust," Henry says, his stern expression directed at me.

Selima snorts and every pair of eyes land on her. She shakes her head, her lips twisted in a smirk. "I'm sorry. Two demons and your group? That's what?" She counts on her fingers to make a point. "Seven of you. Eight when you include Jude. Nine when you include me." She shakes her head, her expression rueful. "Your few supernaturals, no matter how powerful, will be overrun by Garret's team of twenty to thirty. Jude will be destroyed. Lucy will die."

Henry pushes his glasses up his nose, his expression pinched. "But...Lucifer?"

"Jude's not going to listen to anyone else," I tell them. "This is the only way to put him outside of Garret's reach."

"Lucy, you don't conjure a demon without consequences. With one as powerful as Lucifer...you're taking your life in your hands," Persephone says, her head twitching with every word. Her dark curls bounce, and I'm reminded of the jerky movements of Serenity and Lola, her and Gram's ravens, when they're agitated. "You're likely to anger him in a colossal way. We can't allow you to face off with the most powerful demon in existence."

Henry shakes his head. "It's too risky. Forget it."

I'd rather die trying to fix things than sit here and wait for Garret's army to kill everyone I love. Maybe if Persephone and Henry had seen Garret that night he attacked Marcus, the monster he morphed into, they could be persuaded.

Marcus and I meet each other's eyes. "Are you going to back me up on this?"

Marcus shakes his head. "I agree with Persephone and Henry. I'm sorry, but I'm not willing to risk your life."

That's it, then. I'm dead.

CHAPTER FORTY-TWO

– Lucy Walker –

Lola flaps her wings hard as she climbs higher. I shield my eyes with my hand as I watch her glide through the air. Her elegance and majesty leave me breathless. She repeats the same maneuver, climbing and soaring several times, then returns to me. Her talons are gentle, but firm, as she grips my gloved hand.

Filled with guilt, I recall Lola's excitement when I took her out of her cage this morning. I've neglected her. I stroke her around the head and neck, rubbing her cheek in soft circles. She deserves better.

Startled, Lola flaps her wings and erupts in a burst of chatter as she shoves off of my wrist. I turn as Aiden crosses the yard in my direction.

"Marcus must have left the building," he says, "for you to emerge from your apartment."

I shrug. "He's your roommate. You should know."

"I've been at work, so, no, I don't know." He peers up at Lola, who is perched on a branch of the oak tree, her gaze fixed on him as she continues to screech. "How long do you plan to keep avoiding him? Persephone says your uncles are worried, that you rarely leave your cave of a bedroom."

My face flushes as I glare at him. "There's a good chance I'm going to die soon. Forgive me for being depressed."

"Have a good cry about it if you need to, then do something about it. Fight."

I turn away and focus on Lola, who's spreading her wings and cawing in agitation. "If you don't mind, I'd prefer you leave us alone. Besides, you're upsetting Lola."

Aiden cranes his neck to study the raven. The silence between us grows, and I'm confused why he's still here.

"It was my fault," Aiden admits, "what happened to Lola and Serenity."

My hands fist at my sides. "You helped Jude capture the birds?"

"No," Aiden says. "But I'm the reason Daphne knew about them. It's bad enough I nearly blew up the house when I took her to the attic, demonstrated some of what I knew."

I narrow my eyes. "Persephone told me she erased your memory. How do you know about that?"

"Daphne." Aiden pulls his lips into a grim smile. "Persephone never erased *her* memory."

The raven's incessant squawking is giving me a headache. "Lola, stop!" I call up to her. The noise ceases. Lola's attention remains trained on Aiden.

"I told Daphne about the ravens and their powers." Aiden struggles to continue. "Including what happens when a witch dies."

"I can't believe you!" Marcus has always defended Aiden, even though he's been unfriendly to me since I arrived. Reformed demon? Not a chance. Now to find out he was responsible for Lola and Serenity nearly dying last year?

I stumble backward as a sudden blast of heat races down my arms and settles in my hands. I raise my hand, palm side up, and show Aiden the fireball resting there.

"Don't confuse my remorse for stupidity," Aiden warns. "If you attack me, I will retaliate."

I glance up at Lola. It's no wonder she despises him. I toss the fireball into the grass where it sizzles and dies. "Why are you telling me this?"

"I have an offer for you."

I square my shoulders and raise my chin. "What can you offer that I would be interested in?"

His dark eyes fix on me. "I can show you how to conjure Lucifer."

My skin tingles, and this time it has nothing to do with fireballs.

"To be clear, I'm not advocating this crazy plan or even condoning it, but if you're going to conjure a demon and you do it wrong, the consequences can be deadly."

"I'm touched you care." I smirk.

Aiden looks at me coldly. "I'm not doing this for your benefit. And I expect something in return."

I nod toward Lola. "You mean this isn't simply an opportunity for you to relieve your guilt?"

The vein in his forehead throbs. "For some reason I can't fathom, Marcus has chosen you as his life mate."

I cock my head. "What do you mean?"

Lola starts chattering again. Aiden and I both look up as she fluffs her wings, her eyes beading down at him.

"She really doesn't like you."

"Stop avoiding Marcus. Your pout fest is over. Do whatever you have to do to put a smile back on his face." His words come out clipped. I'm guessing Aiden doesn't want to be here talking to me anymore than I want him to be. "You and Selima should meet me out here tonight. I'll explain what you need to do. Then you can let me know if you want to proceed."

"What about Marcus? Aren't you afraid he'll see what we're doing?"

"He and Henry are on surveillance duty in the woods tonight. Meet me out here after sun down," Aiden says. He turns to walk away, then pauses. "If your grandmother were in your shoes, she wouldn't be hiding out in her bedroom, waiting for death. She would fight." The branches in the oak tree shift and sunlight dances across his face. Aiden squints against the brightness. "She never gave up on anyone or anything."

CHAPTER FORTY-THREE

– Lucy Walker –

A breeze moves through the trees and caresses my skin as I stand at the rooftop ledge. It's been a long time since I spent time up here alone. The nighttime air is filled with the sweet scents of late spring flowers in bloom. It's after midnight and most of the houses on the block are dark. Persephone's windows are open a little, and the muted sound of jazz drifts up to the roof.

Back in Lexington, I felt afraid all the time. Life in the trailer park with Momma was dangerous. Between her drunken boyfriends, the booze and drugs, the thieving neighbors, and the constant threat of losing our trailer because we were behind on rent—never mind how little we had to eat—everything was out of my control. The only things I was any good at were school and taking care of Momma.

Since Momma died, Sheldon and Bernard have given me stability and love. But with Jude's entrance into my life, I've got a whole new set of things to fear—demons, angry goddesses, and gargoyles.

Jude's trying to teach me to defend myself, but will it be too little, too late? Can I defeat Garret or even Seamus? It's unlikely, but I can use my powers to make sure the people I love don't die with me. Aiden has shown me the path. I'm no longer powerless and that's an incredible feeling. Until tonight, I thought all my fear was about dying. It turns out that was only partially true. Just as I felt responsible for Momma's life in Lexington, I feel responsible for Jude's here. Everyone else's, too. Now that I'm able to save them, a lot of my fear has subsided.

"Protectors are different than humans, who may fall in love over and over throughout their lives. Once a protector finds his life mate—his soul mate—that's it. There's no one else ever," Selima said earlier tonight. "Why do you ask?"

"Just curious," I told her. I wanted to ask her who Garret's life mate is, Selima's mother or Camille. Then again, maybe Garret is an exception and has two.

I kneel beside my turned-to-stone boyfriend and place a CD case near him—the music mix I've been working on for more than a month. I kiss his cheek. The stone is cool and rough beneath my lips.

"Someday you'll forgive me."

CHAPTER FORTY-FOUR

– Lucy Walker –

Music throbs from Caroline's house as Marcus and I approach her front door. The party is in full swing.

Marcus's hands are shoved in his pockets. He made no attempt to hold mine on the drive over.

"You've been quiet tonight," I say over the Taylor Swift song playing.

"We haven't talked in several days. Our first night together and we're coming *here*." Marcus turns to me, his expression pinched. "Tell me one thing. Have you and Selima agreed to let it go?"

"We're not letting it go," I tell him, meeting his pointed gaze with my own. "Have you decided to help us?"

"It's a suicide mission," Marcus snaps. "So, no, I'm not going to help you."

This party was a mistake. Marcus was right. We shouldn't have come, or maybe I should've come with Katie and Trevor instead. After all, this could be my first and last party ever.

Marcus and I stare stonily at the handwritten sign on the door that says to come inside. We follow the music to the basement.

Katie and Trevor rush over.

I push aside my bad mood and nod appreciatively at Katie's hot pink Guess shirt and skinny jeans. "Love your outfit," I tell her.

"You look great, too," Katie says.

My white wrap blouse has a flattering V-neck, giving the illusion that I have some cleavage. I paired it with my darkest blue jeans. Has Marcus uttered one word of a compliment? Nope.

"You're going to die when you see Caroline and Ella." Katie grabs my arm and pulls me across the room, which is finished with white walls, beige carpeting and folding chairs set against the walls. There are colorful Japanese lanterns dangling from the ceiling. "They're giving Rachel a run for her money in the who can dress sluttier contest."

I don't want to look, but I can't help myself. I peer over Katie's shoulder and see Caroline dressed in a skin-tight white T-shirt and a short black skirt. The deep V-neck leaves little to the imagination. One look at her overly bright smile and the can of Red Bull in her hand, and I wonder how many she's had tonight.

Ella...well, I shouldn't be surprised. She's wearing a halter-style dark green shirt cut extremely low and tighter-than-tight black stretchy pants. One wrong move and her boobs will burst free. She's clutching a can of Red Bull, too.

Their makeup and hair are impeccable and way overdone for a house party. I catch Marcus staring at them, and my stomach sinks. What was I thinking with my lame-Jane outfit when I'm up against crazy hot?

Trevor pops his gum. "Smokin', aren't they?"

Katie punches him in the arm. Trevor laughs.

"They dress to get noticed. Cut me some slack." He presses a noisy kiss against Katie's cheek. "Don't act so innocent, Katie. I've seen the way you check out guys at the mall."

"Discretion, Trevor. It's something you need to learn." Marcus steers him off to find beverages.

I make a face at Katie. "Can we leave now?"

"Because of them?" She jerks her head toward Ella and Caroline. "No way. We're going to pig out on Caroline's food, drink her pop, and dance to her music. Tonight will be fun."

Why can't I be more like Katie? "You promise?"

Katie holds her fist out to me and extends her pinky straight up into the air. "Pinky promise."

I burst out laughing as I grab her pinky with my own. Marcus and Trevor return and hand us each an ice-cold can of Coke. My laughter dies away at Marcus's grim expression.

I pull him aside. "If you want to leave, go ahead. I can get a ride home with Katie and Trevor."

He pulls his eyebrows low in a grimace. "Two hours, tops. Wasn't that our agreement?"

I nod. This is going to be a rough two hours.

By eight o'clock, Cloe and Darick arrive. Within minutes, Darick joins Shawn as DJ for the night.

"I can't tear Shawn away from the stereo. He's taking his responsibilities very seriously," Suzy says with a heavy sigh, taking a break from her own DJ duties.

"Great job on the playlist. The music's awesome," I tell her.

After Caroline's parents load up two card tables with food, we head over and fill our plates with chips and salsa, jalapeno poppers, popcorn, pizza, and chocolate chip cookies. I notice Caroline and Ella throw jean jackets on while Mr. and Mrs. Appleberg are in the room. I also notice their cans of Red Bull disappear only to reappear once Caroline's parents return upstairs.

By nine o'clock, there are so many people in the basement it's difficult to move. Our small group moves to the other side of the room where we can stand without getting claustrophobic.

"Much better," Katie yells. "If one more person elbows me or steps on my toes, I'm going to punch them."

"I'll massage them for you later." Trevor grins, his eyebrows bouncing wickedly.

"I'm totally going to take you up on that," Katie says before planting a quick kiss on Trevor's mouth.

Marcus twists to look at the doorway leading to the stairs. His gaze narrows.

"What's wrong?" I mouth the words to him when he returns his attention to me. Why is he so edgy? Can't he try to relax and have fun? Is he that desperate to escape the party?

Marcus touches my arm. It's the first contact we've had tonight. "I have to check something out. Stay down here."

"Marcus..." But it's too late. He's already worked his way through the crowd toward the stairs.

Katie leans in close to me. "He's not having a good time?"

"Not really," I respond with a shrug.

Would I have had more fun without Marcus? I scan the crowd as I listen to the music. Trevor leans past Katie to high-five a redheaded boy wearing baggy cargo pants. A lime green skateboard decorated with decals rests against the boy's leg. Does he go to school at St. Pat's with Trevor and Marcus?

Just then Ella rushes past us. "You came!" She throws her arms around Dylan as he steps off the bottom stair. Several others yell out a greeting to Dylan and he grins and waves in response.

Dylan unwinds Ella's arms from his neck. After scanning the crowd, he spots me and makes his way over to our group. Ella trails behind him wearing a full-on pout.

"Your boyfriend almost knocked me over on his way out the door. Something about getting some fresh air. I guess he's not a fan of the music," Dylan says loud enough for the group nearby to hear, then leans in close. "We've got company. Not the friendly kind."

My breath catches and I immediately tense. I take in Dylan's demeanor. Grim. He's not freaking out, though, so I know it's not Seamus. Who could it be? There's no way Garret would confront Marcus and me at a teen party. Would he?

"I'm sorry. I don't think he's having a good time." I smile and play it casual as Katie and Suzy watch our exchange. No easy task. After a moment, I lean close. "Garret?" I whisper.

"Dylan, do you want to dance?" Ella asks, tugging on Dylan's arm.

"Sure, a little later," he says, without looking at her.

With a sulky expression, Ella stomps off.

"Is it too late to join in on the fun?" We all turn to the sound of a loud, unfamiliar voice. The crowd parts as a tall, blond man with spiky hair enters the room. He looks to be in his late twenties and his black short-sleeved T-shirt, black jeans, and boots scream villain.

My spider senses suddenly go haywire. Goose bumps spread along my arms like wild fire.

"Ronan, tell me they're *not* playing truth or dare." A deep English accent rings out and a guy with brunet, shoulder-length hair stops beside Ronan. He looks older than the blond but not by much. "I do love a good game of truth or dare."

Dylan and I exchange a dark look. I survey the room.

"Yum! Where did they come from?" Ella says from the couch. "Caroline, who are they?"

Shawn lowers the volume on the music. He and Darick watch the new guests, curious, just like everyone else.

"Who...who are you?" Caroline asks weakly from her slouched position next to Ella. She's looking a little green. Too much Red Bull? Or was she indulging in something higher octane?

A strange vibration starts in my legs and creeps up my body. I catch Dylan watching me, a surprised look on his face. Does he feel it, too? Where is Marcus? This is a really bad time for him to take off.

Ella rises from the couch and delivers her sexiest smile. "Hello. I'm Ella, the co-host of this party." Leave it to Ella to flirt with complete strangers. "The game's not over if you'd like to join."

"What do you think, Flynn? Want to play with the mundanes?"

Mundanes? These guys are protectors? *Garret's men.* My breaths come out in shallow little bursts as I look around for Marcus again. Still no sign of him.

Dylan confronts the party crashers. He doesn't appear afraid of the newcomers at all. "You two need to leave."

Several people watch the exchange, but most of the crowd has turned back to their own conversations and their food. Trevor and Darick both shrug and Trevor jacks up a Macklemore and Ryan Lewis song.

"Dylan, don't act like a jealous boyfriend." Ella laughs and waves him off.

"Yes, Dylan, back off," Flynn says, a dangerous edge to his voice. He and Dylan eyeball each other in a hostile way, and my gut says Ronan and Flynn aren't here for the appetizers.

The vibration inside of me revs, making me feel like a human power plant. The sensation races up my spine, all the way to my head, making my molars ache. I grit my teeth against the pain.

These guys need to go before anyone gets hurt. I move to Dylan's side and gesture toward the stairs. "Dylan's right. You should leave. This is a private party." I attempt a smile, to convey friendliness. Just then a high-pitched whine slams into my brain. "You...weren't...invited." I clutch my head.

Am I out of my mind? I'm not the confrontational kind. I cringe as the sound clamors louder in my head. Gritting my teeth, I press the heels of my palms to my temples and will the noise and the pressure to cease. The party music and conversations sound far away, muffled.

"Just who we came to see." Ronan laughs as he claps Flynn on the shoulder. "You thought this would be difficult."

"What do you want with *her*?" Ella asks, crossing her arms over her chest in a huff.

"Don't worry your pretty little head about her, love," Flynn says with a wink, his voice velvety soft. She relaxes, blushes even. "You and your friends continue on with your party. Have a grand time. We just need to have a chat with this one outside."

Yes. Outside. We need to get these guys away from the basement full of innocent people. I nod toward the stairs. The grinding noise throws off my equilibrium and I teeter.

"Fine. Let's go," Dylan says. He casts a nervous glance my way. "You okay?" He takes hold of my arm to steady me.

"Actually, friend, we need to have a chat with your girlfriend alone," Flynn says.

"She's not my girlfriend, Brit Boy." Dylan's temple throbs. "But she's not going anywhere with you. Not without me. Let's go outside."

Ronan and Flynn study each other for a moment. Flynn nods. Telepathic communication? The metallic grinding noise claws its way through my skull. I clench my teeth and lock my knees to prevent myself from collapsing.

"A little under the weather, love?" Ronan smiles wickedly.

"Enough already," Dylan growls, sliding a sideways glance my way. Was that worry flickering across his face?

Where's Marcus? Did Ronan and Flynn do something to him before joining the party in the basement? I lead the foursome up the stairs, clutching the railing for support. Maybe Garret decided to skip Jude and sent these guys to kill me instead. Then he, Camille, and Selima can take Marcus back wherever they came from and act like one big happy family.

Or will Garret hurt Marcus once I'm out of the way?

Why tonight? One more day, that's all I need. Aiden, Selima, and I will conjure Lucifer and none of this will matter anymore.

Once outside, I release an unsteady breath, grateful as the noise and pain in my head subsides. Ronan ushers us behind a row of tall, narrow bushes. *What's he planning to do to me?*

As if reading my mind, Flynn holds up one hand. "We're here to talk."

Dylan snorts. "Yeah, good one. Your lies, along with your hairdo, need some work. Neither are doing much for me right now."

Ronan takes a step toward Dylan. His fists curl at his sides. I look to see if he's got claws, but it's too dark.

Did he just growl?

"What do you want to talk about? And why come here to do it?" I ask, trying to deflect the tension between Dylan and Ronan.

"Garret wants to meet with Jude. We need you to relay the message," Flynn says.

Doubt nags at me. "Why come here to tell me that?" And what's up with the headache-inducing skull torture?

Ronan shrugs. "Garret's orders."

Marcus told me protectors don't lie. Or did he say they *couldn't* lie? I decide to test my theory.

"That's not the real reason you're here, is it?" I ask. Quickly, I run through a list of possibilities. Would these two really come here to kill me? I can't imagine someone as savvy as Garret would authorize a public bloody scene. Were they here to abduct me? Again, too many witnesses. Threaten me? Order me to break up with Marcus or else? Or does this have something to do with Jude?

"Our orders were simply to serve as a messenger. Nothing more." Flynn levels his gaze at me. "You have my word."

"They're lying," Marcus shouts behind us.

Dylan and I spin around as Marcus and Selima jog toward us from around the corner of the house.

"Sorry I went MIA," Marcus says once he's beside me. "I sensed other protectors nearby and went in search of them. I called Selima for backup."

"Garret only sends his deflector soldiers when exterminating demons." Selima cocks her head and arches an eyebrow as she surveys the two party crashers. "What are you boys up to?"

"Garret will be very disappointed to learn you're here, mingling with mundanes and...worse." Flynn eyeballs me and his expression twists as if he just smelled something rotten.

The high-pitched noise ramps up again, piercing my brain. I clutch my head and clamp my jaw tightly as the grinding hum vibrates through every bone in my body. "Make it stop," I cry out.

Someone thumps to the ground and groans behind me. I turn and see Dylan kneeling on the ground, his body bowed as he punches himself in the head.

"Dylan, no!" I force myself to ignore the screechy-grinding noise, to ignore the pain that radiates along my jaw, stabs my brain. Before I can reach him, Selima is at his side, pulling his fists away from his face. She whispers in his ear.

A flash of movement darts past me. Marcus. He lunges toward the two protectors. Ronan steps in front of Flynn, and Marcus tackles him.

Flynn slides a cell phone from his pocket. Is he calling Garret to tell him this mission—whatever it was—failed? Why would he need to report back so quickly? My gut says this is some kind of ploy and again my thoughts circle back to my father.

Heat surges down my arms and settles into my hands. My fingers twitch, and in an instant, a fireball appears in my palm.

Flynn presses the phone to his ear. Before Garret—or whomever he's calling—answers the phone, I hurl the fireball at him.

Flynn ducks smoothly. He also drops his phone, shooting a look of annoyance at me. "You're going to pay for that." His English accent makes him sound even more menacing.

As I'm about to conjure another fireball, someone grabs my arms and forces them to my side. I thrash against the steely grip.

"People are watching," Marcus says low in my ear.

I stop fighting him and pull my attention away from Flynn. There's a crowd of people standing just outside Caroline's front door.

"Just a misunderstanding. Show's over." Dylan waves everyone off. "Go back inside."

Marcus takes another step toward the protectors. "You should leave."

"Garret's grand disappointment." Ronan's lips curl as he looks from Marcus to me.

The two of them stalk off. A moment later a car roars to life and peels off down the street.

I whirl around to face Selima. "Who were those guys? They... the pain in my head. It was like they were drilling through my skull. It was horrible."

"Horrible," Dylan echoes in agreement.

"Assassins." Selima shakes her head. "I can't believe Garret sent them. The two of you might be strong enough to defend yourselves, but humans." She gestures toward the house. "People could've gotten hurt tonight."

"Assassins?" Dylan asks.

"But their powers—their effect on Lucy and Dylan," Marcus says. He glances over his shoulder, keeping his voice low. I follow his gaze and notice most of the crowd on the porch has gone back inside. "Those weren't typical protector powers. What was that?"

I think back to the night Marcus and I met his mother and father for dinner. When Garret morphed, he looked nothing like Marcus and Selima when they change.

Selima studies us grimly. "Remember when I told you Garret may be up to something horrible?"

Marcus and I nod.

She fixes her attention on her brother. "The reason I followed him and Camille to Chicago—in addition to wanting to meet you and find out why you weren't living with the clan—was to find out their secrets."

"And?" I urge her.

Keeping her voice low, Selima says, "Garret has been experimenting on a group of protectors, including Ronan and Flynn, enhancing their powers and giving them new ones."

"Experimenting how?" Marcus asks through clenched teeth.

Selima struggles to make eye contact with her brother, her expression twisted with revulsion. "They're blood drinkers."

Dylan swallows hard and darts a glance at Marcus. Marcus looks stunned.

"Whose blood are they drinking?" I ask, struggling to swallow my disgust.

"Demon blood," Selima says, her voice barely a whisper.

Demon blood?

"That doesn't make sense," Marcus says. "Camille told me that Garret wants to wipe out all demons. If he succeeds, there's no more blood to drink."

"There are demons who are cooperating with Garret," Selima says.

"Serving as a blood bank? Voluntarily?" Dylan sputters, his eyes wide.

Selima nods.

The cooperating demons wouldn't be destroyed, so Garret and his gnarly minions would continue to have blood donors.

I squeeze my eyes shut for a long, long moment, letting it all sink in. When I finally open them again, I ask, "Why is Garret really after Jude? To get his blood?"

Selima's dark gaze slides to me. "Garret's soldiers were killing demons and draining them. Garret *acquired* the assets belonging to the dead demons." Her expression droops. The more Selima learned about her father, the more it pained her. "I heard Jude traced the deaths back to our clan. He retaliated. Garret wants Jude out of the picture, so he and his group can continue."

"Blood drainer and a thief," Dylan mutters.

"Unbelievable!" Marcus hisses. "Camille said Jude was slaughtering protectors for no reason, that the clan had to take action to protect itself. More lies." He rakes his fingers through his hair and takes several steps away from us. He spins to face us, frowning. "Selima, why do you think Ronan and Flynn came here tonight?"

My stomach clenches. "Are they after my blood? Dylan's?"

Selima frowns. "Neither of you are pure bloods—same reason neither of you have an effect on protectors—so I doubt that."

They didn't come for our blood, so what were they after? If Garret's mission centers around Jude, this has to have something to do with him.

"Could it have been a distraction?" I ask to no one in particular. With a sinking feeling, I believe I'm right.

Marcus touches my arm. "A distraction from what?"

Quickly, I look at each of the three in turn, desperate. "What if these two showed up to ensure we were out of the way if they attacked Jude tonight?"

"No offense, but why would Garret care? Compared to Jude, our powers are just a nuisance," Dylan says.

I ignore Dylan's insulting assessment of my powers. I'm stronger than he's giving me credit for. Does Garret feel the same way about my abilities? Since he's never witnessed me in action, he may. His underestimation of my powers is a good thing. It means I have the element of surprise.

Marcus and Selima study me, waiting for me to continue. "I trust my gut and my gut says Garret has a team of soldiers at Jude's house. We have to get to Lake Forest. Now!"

Tomorrow night, I plan to conjure the greatest demon of all, which won't help at all if Jude and I die tonight.

CHAPTER FORTY-FIVE

–Lucy Walker –

Jude's front gate is open. That's our first clue something's wrong.

"Demons and their mansions," Selima says from the backseat. "Such a cliché."

I drum my fingers on the dashboard of Marcus's car, afraid of what we'll find inside. That's when the darkness hits me. I peer out the window, looking skyward. "What happened to the lights along the driveway?"

A breeze rolls through the car as Dylan rolls down his window and leans out. "Uh, guys? There's broken glass out here."

"It's hard to see intruders on the security cameras in the dark," I point out.

"Garret's men are here," Marcus says. "I can sense them."

"I can, too," Selima murmurs.

Is that fear in her voice? I swallow hard.

Marcus pulls into the spot usually used for Dylan. I'm relieved to see my boyfriend twitching and shaking in the driver's seat.

That means Jude is alive. Then again, the fact that I'm still alive says something, too.

Dylan leans forward from the back seat, thumping the headrest impatiently. "Should we split up? Selima and I could go around back."

"No." Marcus thrusts the gearshift into park. "Let's get inside—together—and see what we're up against."

We hurry to the front door. As I slide between Marcus and Selima, I notice Selima isn't trembling at all. I shouldn't be surprised, given that she works with demons. Will Marcus ever become immune?

With all my training, how was I oblivious to the real reason for Flynn and Ronan's visit to Caroline's house tonight? Garret's entire army could be out back torturing Jude right now. What does it take to destroy a demon, a being that otherwise would live forever? Garret's been slaughtering demons for their blood for years, so he's an expert.

I shove myself to the front of the pack. Heat races down my arms, then settles in my palms. The energy coursing through my body throbs painfully. Dylan puts a hand out to stop me as he lowers his shoulder, positioning himself to ram Jude's new door. He thrusts his body against the steel door with such force, it breaks free of its hinges and slams into the opposite wall. The sound is as loud as a thunderclap and I wince. He may as well have telecast our arrival.

Dylan glances over his shoulder at Selima. "You mentioned the plan. What exactly is your father's plan?"

Selima levels her gaze at him. "To create a race superior to all other supernaturals."

What would happen if that day came? What would be in store for demons? For other supernaturals? Worst of all, what would happen to the humans? I feel sick. Garret is no protector.

The four of us pause in the foyer. I close my eyes and focus. My mind crawls along the hallway to Jude's office. It's empty. Next, I move to the kitchen and dining room. Again nothing. Same thing with the living room and family room. I push my mind further out to the backyard.

Where is Jude? He has to be here somewhere.

In my continued training with my father, I've come to learn that he has the ability to close his mind to me. When Jude wants to communicate mentally with me, he can. Otherwise, he locks me out and becomes invisible.

"What is she doing?" Selima asks.

"She can detect those she's connected with," Dylan says. "Jude, me, the ravens."

That's not entirely true. Since Persephone cast her spell over Dylan and me, our connection is gone. I'm sure Dylan knows that.

"Ravens?" Selima asks.

"Anything?" Marcus asks me, ignoring Selima.

I shake my head.

"They can't hide their auras from me," Marcus says. "They're here. Several of them."

"I see them, too," Selima says, her gaze traveling down the hall.

Dylan scowls. "What are we waiting for? Let's search the house."

Lucy!

I stumble backward and gasp as Jude's voice fills my head.

"What is it?" Marcus grabs my arm.

"Jude." I squeeze my eyes closed and focus harder.

Leave now! I flinch as my father's voice booms in my head. *It's too dangerous for you here!*

I relay his message.

"We're not going anywhere," Dylan says, scowling. "Not with a team of nutjobs here to destroy him." He leaves off the second part of that statement, the part where I would die, too.

"They're out back. Let's go," I tell them, rushing down the hall. The three of them on my heels.

Marcus and Selima skid to a stop outside of Jude's office.

"The auras are pretty dense here," Marcus says to his sister, nodding at the closed doors.

"They spent a lot of time..." Selima's voice trails off. Her face turns ashen.

"Doing what?" I ask.

"Cut the protector telepathy crap," Dylan snaps. "Talk out loud."

"The color, smell, and density of an aura is affected by emotion," Selima says haltingly. She moves her hands slowly through the air, as if her fingers and palms can help her to decipher the auras. "There was a lot of rage here."

I push past the two of them, Dylan close behind me.

"Lucy, wait!" Marcus grabs my arm. I shake him off.

I throw open the doors. Panic zigzags inside of me as I take in the state of Jude's office.

"No!" I cry out.

Bookcases tipped over and books, shredded to bits, cover the floor like oversized confetti. Jude's desk had been split in two as if Godzilla had karate chopped the dense furniture. The computer and security monitors lay broken on the floor.

Dylan touches my hand. It's the first sign of tenderness he's shown me in a long time. "Come on. Let's go outside," he says.

The four of us reach the back door in a matter of seconds. My heart pounds in my chest; adrenaline floods my veins. I'm ready for a fight.

"Leave Garret to me," Selima says.

Marcus starts to protest.

"He won't hurt me," she says, meeting his eyes.

"Are you ready for this?" Dylan asks me.

"This is what we've trained for," I tell him, pushing open the back door.

All four of us stop cold.

To our left, Jude hurls fireballs in quick succession, fending off three approaching monster-fied protectors.

"Max is here." Marcus points to the right where two demons hurl fireballs at a group of Garret's soldiers, evident by their naked torsos and massive bat-like wings.

The taller of the two demons clenches his head with both hands and drops to his knees. The shorter one swipes his hand through the air, and a protector loses his balance and slams onto the ground. The taller demon pushes himself upright and hurls an oversized fireball at the offending protector, engulfing him in a ball of flame. I look away.

In the middle of the football field-sized yard, two bodies lie immobile, consumed by flames. I choke on the stench of burning flesh as I charge toward Jude.

"Lucy, wait!" Marcus calls after me.

"Marcus, go with Selima. We've got Jude," Dylan yells over his shoulder as he runs after me.

Behind me I hear a sharp *THAWUNK*, followed by another. Marcus and Selima have changed form. Are they prepared to battle their own kind?

Dammit, Lucy. I don't want you here! Jude's voice blasts through my skull, rattling my teeth.

White-hot energy zooms across all of my nerve endings at once. *I'm here to keep us both alive!* I respond, not sure if he receives my telepathic message.

With a sweep of Jude's hand, one protector's legs fly out from beneath him. He slams onto the ground. Dylan grabs the second protector from behind in a chokehold. I conjure a fireball in each hand and hurl them in quick succession at another protector about to charge Jude, his hands sporting razorblade-like talons. The protector dodges both fireballs and continues toward Jude at high-speed. I conjure another fireball and am about to hurl it when the protector collides with an invisible obstacle.

"Oomph!" He grunts, his face squishing as if connecting with something hard. There's a cacophony of crunches as his fingers smash against the invisible blockade. Blood oozes from his flattened nose, and shattered teeth splinter from his mouth as he slumps to the ground.

Jude and I look at each other baffled. What just happened?

Then it hits me. The protection spell Persephone and I cast on Jude. The impenetrable wall. Could that be it? I only assisted Persephone, but suddenly I feel like there's hope for me as a witch after all.

The protector in Dylan's grasp falls slack. His gurgling noises fade away. Dylan releases him, and the lifeless body slides to the ground. As Dylan turns away, the body bounds upright.

"Dylan!" I shriek.

The protector faked Dylan out. I rush to close the distance between us, conjuring a fireball and hurling it quickly. Then another. It's too late. The protector pulls Dylan against his chest and sinks his teeth into Dylan's neck from behind.

Fueled by rage, I smack the air forcefully. The protector's head jerks back, a trail of bloody saliva flying through the air. He releases Dylan who falls to the ground. I hurl three fireballs at Dylan's attacker. Two of them land on target, and the protector screams as he turns into a writhing ball of flame.

The third protector throws his head back and roars with fury. He flexes his razor-sharp talons and stomps toward me.

"I've got this one," Jude says.

He wrenches his hands in a violent gesture. A wet snap rings out. The protector drops to the ground, his head twisted at a sickening angle. Quickly, I swallow the bile rising in my throat. With no more monsters coming for Jude and me, I rush to Dylan who is on his knees. His breathing is shallow and erratic. His eyes glaze out of focus and he teeters.

"Dylan! Stay with me!" I clutch his shoulder and peer at the blood pulsing from his neck at a sickening rate.

"Jude!" I cry out.

Jude reaches my side in an instant. "The gargoyle bit him in the jugular." He tears Dylan's shirt away to study the wound.

"How do we stop it?" I ask.

Jude takes Dylan's shredded shirt and presses it against the gash. His eyes, black and fierce, fix on me. "Get your gargoyle over here now!"

Fear and determination fuel me as I sprint across the massive yard. Marcus and Selima battle the two remaining protectors.

"Marcus," I yell. "Dylan's been hurt. We need you!"

Marcus cranes his neck in my direction, and one of the protector's lunges at him, slashing his chest.

"No!" I cry out.

Before Marcus can retaliate, Selima jumps into the air, her feet climbing invisible stairs and connecting with the protector's face. I hear a series of crunching sounds as his nose and left cheekbone collapse beneath the force. Blood spurts from his face, temporarily blinding him.

The protector chokes and gurgles on blood and snot. Another wet snap rings out. The protector collapses onto the ground, silent. I turn and see Jude, his fists twisted in the air. He's killed another protector.

I pull on Marcus's arm, aware that he's bleeding now, too.

"I've got this. Go!" Selima pushes her brother away.

Blood streams from his chest wound. Marcus has healing powers, but can he heal himself?

We reach Dylan and Jude.

"It's the external jugular; otherwise, he'd be dead already,"

Jude says. He removes the blood-soaked shirt he had been pressing against Dylan's neck.

Marcus crouches beside Dylan's unconscious body. I watch in horror as Marcus tears at his own flesh, opening the skin of his wrist. This is what Dylan witnessed the night of the homecoming dance. The night Marcus saved my life for the third time.

My stomach flip-flops nauseously. Jude wipes the fresh blood away from Dylan's throat. He holds Dylan's head firmly to the side, while Marcus applies his own blood to Dylan's wound. After several applications of protector blood, Dylan's wound appears to cauterize itself.

"How is that possible?" I sputter. "Wait! What are you doing?"

Jude's fierce glare stops me as Marcus holds his bloody wrist to Dylan's mouth.

"You must drink, Dylan," Jude orders. "This is going to save your life, son."

I doubt Dylan can hear Jude in his unconscious state, but he starts sucking the blood from Marcus's wrist anyway. Maybe it's a demon order Dylan can't refuse?

I whirl around as running footsteps approach. Selima. Max and the other demon follow, but in less of a hurry.

"How's he doing?" Selima nods at Dylan.

I glance past her, across the length of the lawn. No one is left standing. The yard is littered with lifeless bodies, some burning and some not.

Selima shoves past me. "Marcus, let me take over."

Marcus pulls his wrist from Dylan's mouth. Like a hungry infant, Dylan's lips continue to suck at the air.

Selima tears at her wrist and presses it against Dylan's demanding lips. "I never saw Garret, but his aura was inside the house," she says.

"After the battle in the office, he took off."

We all look up at Max, whose flaming red hair is cut short and spiky. He's the shorter of the two demons.

"It's a good thing, too, because he would've freaked seeing his warriors bouncing off of Jude like he was surrounded by some kind of force field." Max grins.

"Yes, I found that curious," Jude says.

I peek up at him to find him watching me intently. Does he know Persephone and I put a protection spell on him? Could he detect white magic?

"Lucy, that's Max, Aiden's friend," Marcus says, introducing the red-haired demon before he lowers his chin to inspect his chest wound.

Max throws his head back and laughs. A sound I find completely inappropriate given Dylan's condition. "Friend? Not a word I would use where Aiden is concerned."

Selima—who is bent over Dylan—and I both take in the giant, bald demon towering over Max. He appears to be almost seven feet tall and broader than a truck.

"This is Warrick." Max jerks his thumb toward his sidekick.

"I'm going to search the house. Make sure no one's lurking," Warrick says in a gravelly low voice.

Neither demon seems shocked over the healing going on. Have they seen this before? Or maybe horrific and gross are normal for them?

"He's stable," Selima announces, pulling her wrist from Dylan's mouth.

Jude presses his fingers to the unwounded side of Dylan's neck for a moment. He murmurs something in Dylan's ear, and Dylan stops sucking at the air. "His pulse is already improving. Thank you Marcus and..."

"Selima," she says. "Marcus's sister. Friend to Lucy."

That's to be determined.

Jude nods.

Dylan's going to be okay. I no longer care what started our fight in the first place. Instead, I recall Dylan, the adoring older brother to Ethan and Brandi. His bravery on Jude's roof the night of homecoming last year. All of his visits to my house after I nearly died, trying to act casual, but unable to hide his fear and worry.

I choke back a sob at the realization I almost lost him.

"We saw your office," Selima says to Jude. "Is that where the protectors initially attacked?"

"That's where I found them when I came home," Jude says grimly. He checks Dylan's pulse again. "They were searching for information on my computer."

Persephone told me Jude is rich. Bill Gates kind of rich. What was it Selima had said? That Garret steals the assets of those demons he slaughters? "Were they accessing information about your businesses? Your finances?"

"They attempted to, but it's impossible to breach the security on those accounts," Jude says. He tears his attention from Dylan's face and focuses on me. "They copied the file I have on you."

His accounts are guarded like Fort Knox, but information about me isn't?

"What kind of information?" Marcus asks.

"Everything I've compiled since the day Lucy was born. The gargoyles forwarded it all to two email addresses, both of them untraceable."

"Garret met me," I point out. "He knows what I look like. Camille has been to my house and has met my uncles. What more do they want to know?"

After several moments of silence, realization dawns on Marcus's face. "Your school."

"Why would Garret care about that?"

Jude's expression tightens. "After Seamus's attacks, Persephone, Henry, and I put several wards on the three-flat. It prevents entry to those who mean you harm. As a second layer of protection, they render demons powerless."

"But..." I say, panicked. Does that mean if Jude came to my apartment to help in a crisis, he would be unable to use his powers to help me? Marcus is still able to morph, so I'm guessing his powers are intact. Persephone and Henry's, too.

"It was a fair exchange and meant you'd be safe from harm, particularly from Seamus," Marcus says. "But your school is another story."

"What do you mean?" My gaze lands on Dylan's still body and Selima's hand resting on his arm.

"Henry and Persephone put a shrouding spell on your school, similar to the one your grandmother had on your home in Tennessee. Supernaturals would never find you there." There's an edge to Jude's voice. Gram hid me from him all those years, and he's still not over it.

Marcus closes his eyes. "Garret now knows where you go to school. St. Aquinas is too large. It's impossible to ward."

I jump to my feet, envisioning the school's crowded hallways between passing periods. "It's a public place. Would Garret actually make a scene in front of the student body? He's a protector. He wouldn't hurt a bunch of helpless high school students, would he?"

"Anyone going to address the elephant in the room?" Max rocks back on his heels, his hands tucked in the pockets of his jeans. "Garret and those assassins he deployed tonight are not normal protectors." He displays his teeth and wiggles his fingers at Marcus and Selima. "Do either of you develop fangs and claws once you morph? I've never seen those hideous, bat-like wings before, either."

We all turn to Selima. It takes her a moment to respond. She glances around our small group. It's one thing to confess what she's learned to Marcus, Dylan, and me. I'm guessing she isn't visibly sweating over Max's presence. Her eyes dart over to Jude. "There are rumors that Garret and certain members of his army are supplementing."

"It is true," Jude says. He shakes his head and exhales, gestures so human, it's easy to forget he's a demon. "Grayson, the former head of the gargoyles and a man I respected, informed me of the rumors before he was killed," he nods at Selima and Marcus, "that some of your kind were drinking demon blood."

All to build an army of assassins.

Marcus catches me inspecting his chest wound. "It'll be fine. It's already healing, see?"

Sure enough, the gash is closed and no longer bleeding. Accelerated healing is a handy power to have.

"What about the mental torture earlier tonight at the party by Ronan and Flynn? What was that?" I ask. Just thinking about it makes my molars hurt.

"Part of their new powers?" Marcus asks.

Selima sighs. "I don't know."

"Combining the best of both species. Clever. No doubt they're stronger, faster, and we know about their bitey, scratchy fixations," Max says, cracking his knuckles. "Where do I find them?"

"Lucy's school would be a good guess," Marcus says, his arms flexed at his sides. "The question is when?"

"My blood isn't pure, so what does Garret want with me? Will he kill me just to hurt Jude?" I ask.

Selima gives a tight shake of her head. "You're dating Marcus. It's an embarrassment to Garret and, in his words, an affront to the clan."

Marcus jumps to his feet, and I notice the gashes on his chest are only welts at this point. "I don't care what Garret thinks and as far as the clan—"

Selima holds her hands up in surrender. "It's not *my* opinion."

Marcus glances at Dylan's still form. He raises his eyes to Jude, a question on his face.

"Go," Jude says. "Once I know he's out of danger, I'll meet you at St. Aquinas."

"I'll stay, too," Selima says. "Just in case."

"I'm going with you. I want another chance at the head of the freakazoids," Max announces, a smile spreading across his face. It's the smile of a killer.

CHAPTER FORTY-SIX

– Lucy Walker –

"You're not going to find him," Max says from the backseat of the car.

I glance at Marcus. His curious expression mirrors my own.

"Daddy Gargoyle is political," Max says. "He won't be hanging around Lucy's school tonight."

I crane my neck to study Max. He doesn't look like much—short, compact—but I have a feeling if provoked, his strike would be fast and deadly.

"Do you think he's taken off to regroup?" Marcus asks, eyeing Max in the rearview mirror.

Max nods. "Garret's not particularly bright, but he's savvy enough to surround himself with people who are. He wouldn't make a move without strategizing with his team. He's also going to need to restock his little army given the casualties at Jude's."

"Since there won't be another fight tonight, why did you come with us?" I ask, confused. More than anything, I want to be alone with Marcus right now. We have to talk. I can't shake the image of Marcus tearing his own flesh, applying it to Dylan's wound then putting his wrist to Dylan's mouth for him to drink. Assuming that's what Marcus did to help heal me the night of homecoming, I want to know why he kept it a secret.

Max shrugs. "I know Jude. He'd make me dispose of the bodies. Besides, I want to see my good friend, Aiden."

There's no missing his sarcasm.

There's no point being angry about his presence. I swallow my frustration and try to relax against my seat. Jude and Dylan are safe for now.

"We need to talk to Persephone and Henry. Fill them in," Marcus says.

* * * *

"When Grayson led the clan, he always thought of what was best for the clan. He didn't report to others. He was trusted and respected by the protectors." Henry says as he takes the last seat at Persephone's kitchen table. "The structure has changed. Garret's a mouthpiece for a high-powered cabinet who doesn't have the best interests of the clan as their priority."

"How long have you known about Garret and his clan?" Marcus asks Max.

Max glances at Marcus for a moment then over at Aiden who leans against the counter. Max and Aiden are dressed similarly in short-sleeved black T-shirts and jeans. Like Aiden, Max's black irises are a dead giveaway he's a demon.

"Demons and protectors are natural enemies. We've always known about each other," Max says.

"Then why don't you know more about Garret's circle?" Persephone asks.

Max leans forward. "Garret's slippery. So are the others. He never stays in one place for long, so it's hard to learn what he's up to."

"The protectors claim that's a necessity because demons are slaughtering their kind," Henry points out.

"Of course they do," Max sneers, his fist curling on the table, "but it's a bald-faced lie. Demons and protectors, while they were never *friendly*, they coexisted peacefully for a time. Grayson and Jude created the treaty. There were no attacks by either side during that time." Max relaxes his fist. He intertwines his hands and bends his knuckles back in one swift movement; a series of snaps and cracks rings out. His glances over at Aiden again. "It all went to hell when Grayson was murdered."

"You have a big mouth, Max," Aiden says sharply.

Max aims an icy smile at Aiden. "I don't subscribe to the theory that everything needs to be kept secret, buddy. Secrets are toxic. They'll eat you from the inside out."

Max and Aiden eyeball each other in some weird standoff kind of way. Whatever's between them, neither one is going to spill.

"It's our understanding a demon killed Grayson. Are you saying that's not true?" Persephone asks.

Max looks at each of us in turn, a small smile playing on his lips. He leans back in his chair, rapping his knuckles on the table absently. "When Garret took the throne, so to speak, rumors swirled about elections being fixed, demon thugs hired to lean on anyone speaking out against Garret. Then a couple of years ago we hear about protectors with new powers. They're stronger than ever. They've got fangs and claws, and they operate without a conscience. Tonight was the first time I've seen Version 2.0 up close and personal." He rests his elbows on the table, his biceps bulging. Max's gaze locks on Aiden. "I don't think Grayson was killed by demons."

"It's not just the soldiers who are dosing, either. Marcus and I both witnessed Garret under the influence of demon blood. Fangs, razor-sharp claws, and oversized."

Max nods grimly. "Grayson never would've condoned such a thing."

"What if Garret has all of you fooled into believing he's got these shadowy figures backing him up?" Aiden asks. "What if it's just him?"

Max shakes his head. "Someone else is pulling the strings." He pushes his chair away from the table. "I'm going back to Jude's. He's probably got things cleaned up by now."

"Can you call us when you get there, let us know how Dylan's doing?" I ask Max as he makes his way to the door.

Max waves over his shoulder. "Sorry. Dylan's not my problem."

"You may want to remember who her father is," Aiden points out, his tone icy.

Did Aiden just defend me?

"Fine." Max sighs. "I'll check on the faux demon and get back to you."

"Thanks," I say.

Max glances at Aiden, his hand resting on the doorknob. "Remember what I said. Secrets will eat you from the inside out."

CHAPTER FORTY-SEVEN

– Lucy Walker –

"Rise and shine, Luce. Rise and shine!"

Bernard noisily opens the blinds in my bedroom.

I wince and pull my sheet over my face to block out both the sun and Bernard's cheerful tone.

"Luggage is in the car," Sheldon calls from the living room.

Luggage?

I bolt upright in my bed.

Bernard tosses a pair of jeans at me. "Come on, sleepy head. Your breakfast is on the table. You need to see us off."

I rub sleep from my eyes. "Off where?"

Bernard exits my room, whistling some upbeat tune.

I throw on the jeans and a T-shirt. Two minutes later, I meet my uncles in the kitchen, where they're stuffing an envelope with cash.

"This should cover anything you need," Sheldon says as he tucks the money in the cookie jar.

I blink rapidly and try to clear the cobwebs from my brain. *Am I in the Twilight Zone?*

"Where are you going?" I ask.

"Vacation, silly," Bernard says. He and Sheldon exchange a look and smile. "We didn't give consideration to your job, which you take seriously, and to your relatively new friendships with Katie and Dylan. Besides, with everything Marcus is going through, we imagine it would be difficult for him to have you away."

I grimace at their placement of Dylan's name before Marcus, but let it go. Did they tell me they booked their trip, and I forgot? Have I been that wrapped up in my own problems?

"Persephone and Henry came by yesterday. They told us how much Persephone relies on you. We didn't realize that." Sheldon's voice is more relaxed than normal. Did they have mimosas this morning? A quick glance around the kitchen shows no sign of empty champagne flutes. "We're giving you permission to stay home while we go on vacation. We signed a temporary guardian form appointing Persephone in our absence. Katie's mom and Henry witnessed the document. It was all very simple."

"Simple," I echo with a robotic nod. *Too simple.* "You're sure about this?"

Sheldon pats my cheek, his eyes twinkling. "Only if you are, kiddo. If you decide you want to join us, we'll go online and book you for the trip."

I shake my head, donning my most solemn expression. "It's like you said. I have the Douglas kids to take care of, and I need to help Persephone with a couple of projects. Then there's Marcus, Katie, and Dylan."

"It's settled then." Bernard gives me a wink. "It just took Persephone and Henry to help us realize we needed to treat you with a little more freedom. Respect your obligations."

Persephone and Henry convinced them? Put a spell on them is more like it. Why didn't Persephone talk to me first? Is there a consequence to using magic on them? I whack my palm against my forehead. The dandelion tea. Did it make Sheldon more susceptible to their spellcasting?

"Grab your medication," Bernard reminds Sheldon, steering him toward the living room. "I've got our flight and hotel confirmations."

Sheldon pauses and taps the fridge with his index finger before allowing Bernard to maneuver him out of the kitchen. "Our itinerary. You can reach us on our cell phones or at the hotel."

I scan the sheet on the fridge. They decided on Costa Rica after all. I'll have to hide this information once my uncles leave. I don't want Garret or any of his team breaking in and finding out my uncles left town.

Could we have reached this point without manipulating their brains? Maybe. But if things go horribly wrong when we try to conjure Lucifer, at least my uncles will be far away and safe.

* * * *

Dylan picks me up an hour later. I fill him in on my uncles' sudden trip.

He nods with approval. "It's good they'll be out of the way when things blow up between the demons and the gargoyles."

And Lucifer. Can't forget him.

I clear my throat. "Gargoyles? You sound like Jude."

Dylan's expression darkens. "There's no way I'm going to refer to a bunch of killers as protectors."

The light beaming through the windshield reflects against the shiny patch on his throat. The wound scarred over in record time. It's the only outward evidence of Dylan's near-death experience. I can only imagine how freaked out he must be on the inside. His ordeal last year was bad enough. Now this?

"I'm sorry, Dylan. I know you're scared and..."

"Let it go. I'm going to work my butt off today and every day until this so-called battle goes down." Dylan's eyes narrow as he stares out the windshield. "I'm going to slaughter those freaks."

"Not every pro...*gargoyle* is bad. There's Marcus and Selima."

Dylan grunts. "You had the pleasure of watching me suck their blood. Good luck getting that out of your head any time soon."

The sight of Dylan drinking blood from Marcus's wrist has been replaying in my mind like a horror movie. I'm going to confront Marcus about the night of homecoming. He neglected to tell me the truth. I want to know why.

Silence falls between Dylan and me, which gives me a chance to think about tonight. Will Lucifer show up? Will he be willing to take Jude below ground? According to Aiden, Lucifer will look like a normal man, and not, as I suggested, like one of the creepy monsters from *Buffy the Vampire Slayer*. Will he be happy to see me? I would hate to face an angry Lucifer.

Dylan glances my way for the umpteenth time. I force myself to stop picking my cuticles and instead flip on the radio.

Dylan reaches over and turns it off. "What's going on?"

With effort, I force my expression into a neutral mask. "I'm in the mood for music?"

"You still think you can fool me? If something's going down, tell me."

I tuck my hands between my legs to keep from picking. "I'm just worried? We're outnumbered."

"Funny thing is, I'm not worried." The curl of his lips turns cruel. "I'm wondering how much it's going to hurt when I rip off their wings. Or how long they'll take to bleed out."

"Stop talking, please." My voice is sharp and loud, cutting off any additional sadistic descriptives he intended to add. I turn away and pretend to focus on the scenery whizzing by. Dylan sounds like a monster.

"Don't tell me you're squeamish. You saw what they did last night. To me. To Marcus." I turn back to him, notice the sweat beading on his forehead. "You told me how Garret tried to attack Marcus at the condo. Jude's a pussycat in comparison. Gargoyles are the monsters here."

"This isn't you," I whisper.

"Life isn't about hanging out at the mall or going to the movies. Cool cars, short skirts, and touchdowns? That's not our world anymore."

Dylan's describing his own world. "I get that. Trust me. I nearly died last year. I—"

Dylan shudders. "Don't go there. Just...*don't*."

If everything works tonight, Jude will be safe. I will be safe. Garret and his army, with no enemy to fight, will leave town—without my boyfriend, hopefully. Dylan can go back to being a skirt-chasing football star. I couldn't stand Dylan the Jerk, but I'll take him over this new, grim version.

CHAPTER FORTY-EIGHT

– Lucy Walker –

Selima and I close the door behind us. I wrinkle my nose. Fresh paint? It smells awful, like a mix of car exhaust fumes and fresh cut grass. I would suggest we keep the door open, so we can all breathe, but summoning a demon is probably best done in secret.

What used to be Gram's basement storage room now looks like it was taken over by an angsty boy listening to way too much metal. The walls used to be white. Now three of them are the color of steel gray, and the fourth is black. Some of the symbols painted on the walls look familiar, although I don't recall their meaning. A simple round wooden table sits in the center of the room surrounded by five chairs.

Aiden eyes the box in my hand skeptically. "A Ouija board?"

"You said I had to bring a spirit board. I didn't have time to make one, and I found this in the closet with the other board games." I turn to Selima, gently shaking the box. "You said this would work."

She touches my arm. "It's fine."

"Like you're an expert." Aiden glowers at Selima before moving to light the four black candles set on posts around the room. North, south, east, and west. "Let's hope it hasn't been used to conjure in the past. Otherwise, we could have a serious problem on our hands."

"How serious?" I ask, my voice nearly a squeak.

"Stop trying to scare her," Selima scolds him. She pulls the Ouija board and planchette from the box, setting them in the center of the table.

"Sit," Aiden says to us, taking the chair facing the black wall. He places several sheets of paper facedown on the table in front of him.

Selima and I sit on each side of Aiden. That leaves two chairs empty. "Are we waiting for others?" I ask.

Aiden mentioned that the more supernaturals involved in summoning Lucifer, the higher our chance of success. "It's all about intention—something you're familiar with," he explained the night he originally met with Selima and me. "The more participants, the more able we will be to move a powerful demon through the planes of existence."

My knees knock under the table. *Are we really going to do this?*

I bounce in my chair as the door bursts open. Max and Warrick stalk into the room.

"Are we late?" Max collapses into the chair beside Selima. Warrick nods at me. The wooden chair creaks as he lowers his giant body onto it.

"Another one of your many fine traits," Aiden mutters under his breath.

Selima narrows her eyes and glares at the two men. "This isn't the place or the time for an argument. Shelve it, boys."

"Thank you for helping me—us—with this," I say to the demons. As dark and strange as the circumstances are, I still want to show my appreciation.

"I'm not doing this out of the kindness of my heart, cupcake." Max winks at me, a mischievous look in his eye. "If we live through the next week, it'll be nice to finally be debt-free."

I glance at Warrick, curious if he knows what Max is talking about.

The oversized demon shrugs. "I was asked to help, so I'm here," his deep voice rumbles up from his barreled chest.

"Let's get started," Aiden says. He hands the papers to me facedown. "Pass these around." He issues a stern look to everyone around the table. "Don't turn them over until I tell you to. Our intent has to be unified and clear."

"Are we doing this in English or Latin?" Warrick asks.

"I'll recite the spell in Latin, while the rest of you read it in English." Aiden's hands tremble just a little as he fingers the paper in front of him.

I wonder for the first time if Aiden knows what he's doing. He's the one who warned me about catastrophic consequences. Maybe he's nervous because once Jude finds out he helped me, the two of us will be in big trouble. Maybe he's afraid of Lucifer? He'd be a lunatic not to be.

My insides quake. We're crazy to do this. Totally wacko. *But I have to do whatever's necessary to protect Jude and myself.*

Aiden pushes the sleeves of his black pullover up to his

elbows. He clears his throat, his frown touching on every face around the table.

He has my attention. A strange vibration starts in my belly. Nervousness? Or some kind of shared supernatural energy?

"Key factors to keep in mind." Aiden raises one finger into the air. "Focus. I can't say this enough. If your concentration falters at any point, we fail. Second." He jabs two fingers into the air. "The rules: we specify the demon we're conjuring. We extend a formal invitation. We enlist his assistance with taking Jude underground." His gaze sweeps the table again. "Any questions?"

Questions? I have a ton. Like, will this work? Will Lucifer be ticked off and blow up the apartment building, killing us all? Is Selima double-crossing me? Is Aiden? Will Jude sense what we're doing and somehow put a stop to it before we even begin?

With a sigh, I shake my head along with everyone else. *Nope. No questions.*

The vibration in my belly spreads until my entire body trembles. *Just nerves. Just nerves. Just nerves.*

"Take a moment to clear your mind. Close your eyes. Take several deep breaths and relax," Aiden instructs.

"Meditation? Nice. Maybe we can do yoga next time," Max chimes in.

"For a guy who wants to be debt-free, you don't act like it," Warrick rumbles.

Max slinks low in his chair and pipes down.

Aiden, Selima, and Warrick close their eyes. I follow suit. Hopefully, Max does, too.

I inhale long and slow, then exhale. I repeat, focusing on

quieting my thoughts. Right now, nothing else matters. *Protect Jude and me. Marcus too. Get Garret and his gang out of town.*

"In a moment we're going to flip the sheets of paper over." Aiden says, his voice relaxed.

My body tenses at his words. A million things could go wrong.

I take another deep breath. *Protect Jude and me and Marcus. Dylan too if Garret knows about him, which I'm guessing he does after Caroline's party. Get Garret and his gang out of town.*

"On the count of three," Aiden says calmly, "we will flip our pages over. I will read mine aloud in Latin. Lucy will lead you in reading the spell in English."

We need to get on with it.

"One...two...three. Flip," Aiden instructs.

My heart leaps into my throat and nearly chokes me. I flip my page over and take another breath.

The second Aiden's voice rings out I start reading. The others' voices fall in line with mine.

"Lucifer, your eminence,
We hereby request your assistance,
To save Jude Morgan, your right hand, and Lucy, your namesake.
Make no mistake, to ignore this request will mean to forsake those important to you.
We respectfully invite your emergence,
Your resurgence.
In order to avoid the demise of those you hold dear,
We ask that you take Jude Morgan and hold him near."

"Rest two fingers of each hand on the planchette."

I jerk my head back at the sound of Aiden's voice. I look around the table, feeling dazed. The now familiar vibration moves through my veins. *How deep was I?*

We all squish our fingers together onto the guiding device in the middle of the Ouija board.

"Now, we wait and see if he will grant us a response," Aiden says.

We sit like that, our arms poised over the wooden board until our fingers cramp. Droplets of sweat trickle down the back of my neck, beneath the weight of my hair, between my shoulder blades. *Was this a waste of time?* I double my focus, make my intention clear.

Lucifer, please, save him. Save Jude. He's the only parent I have left. If he means anything to you—and I think he does—don't allow Garret to kill him. Keep him safe. Take him back with you. Allow him to be your right hand again. Or promote him. Do whatever you want. Just take him. Please.

Nothing.

How can I persuade you? I think I get how this works. Whenever Jude gave me something—whether I asked for it or not—I owed him something in return. What will I owe you? I don't have much, but name it. I'll give it to you. Just promise that you'll keep Jude safe. Everyone else in my life, too.

Do I have to name them? Is that how this works? Here goes: my uncles, Sheldon and Bernard, my Gram's BFF and the only female pseudo maternal figure I've got left, Persephone, and Gram's other BFF, Henry. My own BFFs Katie and Dylan, and

Dylan's brother and sister who I babysit, Ethan and Brandi. They're precious to me. I've already mentioned Jude a few times. He's the reason I'm doing all of this. There's Marcus, too, my boyfriend. Garret may have it out for him, although I'm not sure if it's because Marcus is dating me, the enemy, or because of some weird jealousy issue over Camille's affections. Please keep him safe, too. Should I add Aiden to the list? He's helping me out, so I might as well. Selima, too, although I'm still not one hundred percent sure she's on my side or if she's serving as a secret agent for her father. Sorry for rambling. I'm nervous and I want to be sure to include everyone important to me. Anyway, just name it. Whatever you want from me to keep everyone safe...I'll give it to you.

The planchette trembles and a collective gasp rings out.

"Don't force it," Aiden warns.

I fear my slick fingers will slide off the device, but I don't dare apply pressure. The plastic apparatus wiggles slightly, then creeps across the board. I can't believe what I'm seeing. I study everyone's fingers, check to see if their nail beds are red from effort and their fingers stiff from applying pressure. No. They're all resting gently like mine.

The planchette inches over to the letters and lands on *H*. It shakes against the board then moves to *O*. The device pauses then moves to *W*. The lights flicker and I look to Aiden, then Selima, gulping down breaths to stay quiet. Neither of them pulls their attention from the board. The plastic piece suddenly lunges across the board and I struggle to keep my fingers in place.

D.

Is anyone else freaked out by this? I don't dare inspect their faces.

A.R.E.Y.O.U.

"How dare you?" Max whispers. "Oh, man. Aiden, what have you gotten us into?"

"It's still moving," Selima hisses. "Don't remove your fingers."

H.A.L.F.L.I.N.G.

My pulse throbs at my temples.

"Halfling?" Warrick asks.

Tears burn my eyes. Half-witch, half-demon. Being the namesake of Lucifer doesn't mean so much after all. In an instant, I'm back in Tennessee. Trailer Park Lucy with the drunk, addicted Momma. The one who wears clothes that none of the other girls would be caught dead in. I dared to think I meant something to the ruler of the underworld. This was my chance to save Jude—and everyone else—and I blew it.

The planchette falls still. Aiden pulls his fingers away. The rest of us follow suit. The vibrating energy is gone.

Halfling. Lucifer is angry.

I wrap my arms over my chest, suddenly cold.

"I'm sorry." I sink against the back of my chair. Suddenly, I feel deflated and small. My cheeks flush as a feeling of shame washes over me. "I shouldn't have gotten you involved. Any of you. This is..."

"Lucy..." Selima's throaty voice tries to comfort me.

What was I thinking, trying to pull off something this huge? I just ticked off the biggest demon in existence.

I leap up from my chair and race out of the room.

I failed to save Jude. Just like I failed to save Momma.

CHAPTER FORTY-NINE

– Lucy Walker –

I pull my knees tight against my chest and tilt my head back. With a sigh, I study the night sky, and wipe away stray tears from my cheeks. Who do I think I am? I was so sure I was doing the right thing. I was so sure Henry, Persephone, and Marcus were wrong, and I was right.

I jump at the squeaking grind of metal. Marcus's face appears above the ledge, followed by the rest of him. He sits beside me on the roof and pulls my hand onto his lap, tucking it between his own. We stay like that for a couple of minutes.

With a quick peek at his smooth expression, I know he's not mad at me anymore. The fact that his fingers are laced through mine is a good sign, too. "Is this where you say, I told you so?"

He gives a small shake of his head.

"You can, you know. You were right. Everyone was right," I say, abashed. "What was I thinking? I was about to unleash the greatest evil of all on Chicago."

"But you didn't."

Only because it didn't work.

He squeezes my hand. "Can I offer an alternative?"

I nod.

"I'm going to meet with Camille."

"After that night at the condo? Garret may try to hurt you again."

Marcus presses his fingers to my lips. "I'm meeting with her. Just her. No Garret."

My frown deepens. "I don't trust her."

Marcus raises an eyebrow. "You don't trust her, but you were going to trust Lucifer?"

I open my mouth to protest then close it again.

"I want to talk to her about the clan, and I'm going to suggest a truce between Garret and Jude."

I smirk. "Good luck." Now isn't the time for sarcasm, but his plan is almost as ridiculous as mine.

"I have to try, Lucy." Marcus cups my chin and forces my eyes to meet his. "For you. For me. I have to try."

My heart sinks with the most awful realization. "She'll offer you anything to get you to leave and join the clan."

Marcus looks away. "If I can be assured of your safety, I'll consider anything."

He's already decided. Marcus is going to leave me. Anger and alarm tangle inside of me. Gram's gone. Momma's gone. From the moment she arrived, I knew Camille wanted Marcus to leave with her, but this is the first I've heard from him that he's willing to go. Where will that leave me?

After my epic failure tonight, I can't bear it. Can't bear to hear Marcus's plan to leave me. I pull my hand from his and climb to my feet.

"Lucy..." He reaches for me again.

Without a word, I quickly cross the roof to the back steps. Tears sting my eyes as I leave him sitting there.

Trusting Lucifer suddenly doesn't seem so silly after all.

CHAPTER FIFTY

So many herbs—agrimony, aconite, citron, foxglove, poke, sweet grass, and toadflax. Not a single one of them will help me. I add the book to the discard pile and grab another. I turn page after page. Another protection spell, a binding spell, a seeking spell, and a spell to remove a curse.

An enchantment spell? That'll come in handy now that Marcus's mother plans to take him away. I mark the page with an orange Post-it note. I flip through more pages. My foot *tap, tap, taps* under my desk as I scan more text.

How dare you, Halfling.

I really thought Lucifer was the answer. So much for my gut. There has to be something I can do to save Jude from Garret and his army, and get rid of Camille before she takes Marcus away to the clan. Maybe if I trusted her, I would feel differently. The opportunity for Marcus to be with other protectors would be good for him. The problem is I don't believe that Camille is good for him.

Ice cubes clank against glass as I take a sip of my lemonade. I bury myself back into Gram's books.

Two-thirds of my way through the stack, I pause. My breath

bounces like a hiccup in my throat. *A vanquishing spell.* Could that be the answer? If I could send Jude someplace for a little while, at least until Garret and his team move on, then he'll be safe. I would only have to worry about Marcus and myself.

Vanquish this demon from time and space. Would the spell send him to another dimension?

What does that say in the margin? Gram's handwriting is scrunched and small. I lean over the book and squint, lowering the head of my desk lamp closer to the page.

Effective in killing demons. Don't use, unless that is the intention.

Hiccup.

I close the book with a heavy thump and add it to the discard pile. Killing Jude is not the goal. Banish? One of the books wrote about banishing a demon.

With a sigh, I hug the books I've already combed through and slide them back toward me. Time to start over. The table of contents of the first book offers nothing useful. Same with the second and third. I run my finger down page after page in book four, my eyes skimming.

Bingo! I find references to banishing.

My heartbeat flutters. Could this be the answer? Will I find a way to save Jude?

Banish you from this place forever more.

Forever more? I scour through more pages. Isn't there a temporary banishing spell? Where exactly would he go?

I check the remaining books. There's no better news about vanquishing or banishing demons. Cross those options off the list.

What about Seamus? Without Jude, who will help fight the crazed demon when he shows up again?

I lower my head and rest it on the open book. *Seamus. Garret. Camille. Jude. Marcus.* It's too much. I want carefree.

What would you know about that? The voice in my head scolds. *Carefree is something you've never had.*

A darkness seeps through me like dense fog, paralyzing me. I'm back in Lexington in my closet-sized bedroom, listening through the paper-thin walls as Momma fights with her latest boyfriend, drunk and high. She doesn't care that we're under the threat of having our electricity shut off *again* or that I'm hungry— so hungry—all because she blew her disability check on drugs. *Again.*

Lucy.

A ghostly whisper. My spider senses tingle.

Lifting my head from the book, I glance furtively around my bedroom. A shiver passes over my skin. Then another. I catch sight of my own exhale as my teeth start to chatter. The condensation on my glass of lemonade has dried in the arctic chill.

Suddenly, I hear a noise, an eerily familiar high-pitched squeak. It's out of place in my bedroom. It takes a moment before I recognize it. It's the sound I hear every Sunday morning when I squeegee the shower doors while cleaning the bathrooms. The creak of my desk chair is deafening as I spin around. That's when I see the message on my dresser mirror.

You are not alone.

My breath freezes in my throat. My chest feels tight. I can't breathe. I can't move.

The words fade like steam on a mirror after a shower.

Seamus?

My phone buzzes on the desk behind me. I sit frozen. A moment later, it buzzes again. I push off my chair and take a closer look at the mirror. No smudges. No sign of any words.

Distracted, I grab my cell off the desk. Persephone.

Henry and I think it's a good idea for you to stay at Jude's while your uncles are away.

The temperature in the room feels normal again.

I look back at the mirror.

Did I imagine it?

I text Persephone.

Not a terrible idea.

CHAPTER FIFTY-ONE

– Lucy Walker –

I grab the photo of Momma and me from my dresser and bury it in my suitcase between my jeans and tops. Marcus's feather is tucked safely into the zippered pocket. I lug it to the living room, grunting under the weight of Gram's witchcraft books.

There's a knock at the door.

"Persephone, I'm ready—"

Marcus stands in the foyer. He's the last person I expected to see after I left him on the roof.

"Don't go," he says, backing me into the apartment. His arm circles my waist and his lips meet mine. "I'll do...whatever it takes...to convince you...not to go," he murmurs between kisses. He's not mad at me at all.

My fingers slip around his neck. I pull my lips from his and bury my face against his throat. I inhale the powerful scent of his cologne. How am I going to live without our nightly visits to the roof? His kisses?

"It's ten days." I do my best to sound nonchalant. "We'll figure out a way to see each other. You can pick me up, and we'll go to the movies. I'll meet you at the street so you don't have to pass through Jude's gate."

He pulls away. "You're kidding yourself. Once Jude has you, he's going to want you all to himself."

"You're wrong about that," I protest. "He's going to get sick of me pretty quick. He may love me, being my father and all, but deep down I don't think he likes me much." I pause on that thought for a moment. "Actually, I think it's more accurate to say he doesn't understand me."

The frown on Marcus's face deepens. "You're missing the point. All he has to do is threaten to harm those you care about, and you'll fall in line."

"If you're saying he's going to prevent me from seeing you, I disagree. We have an agreement." Jude may be a lot of things, but he hasn't shown himself to be a liar.

What about the day he gave you the car? The little voice inside my head asks.

That was the day Jude added my uncles to the list of people he could use to blackmail me into behaving.

"He promised never to hurt you," I remind Marcus and the annoying voice in my head.

Marcus gives a tight shake of his head. "I'm not talking about me. This could go one of two ways. Either he's going to shower you with gifts or..."

I stagger backward as if slapped. "You think Jude can buy me?"

"The homecoming dress. The fully loaded Lexus. Don't you see? Those things were just the beginning."

I chuckle bitterly. "Here we go. Poor little girl from the trailer park."

A knock at the door interrupts us.

"Persephone," Marcus says as he opens the door. He turns to me and presses his lips to my forehead. Not quite the kind of kiss I wanted before leaving for Jude's, but Marcus seems to be on a mission to irritate and offend me today.

He leaves just then and I suspect he might feel the same way about me.

"Text me," I call after him.

He nods without turning around and trudges up the stairs.

Does this mean I'll get the silent treatment the entire time I'm at Jude's?

"None of us are happy about this," Persephone says as she grabs my suitcase. "But it's the safest place for you."

I nod absently. It's my chance to watch over Jude, to help protect him since all I achieved with Lucifer was angering him.

I had never ridden with Persephone before, and I can say with absolute certainty that I never want to again. My hands grip the dashboard and the handle over the door of her white minivan for most of the drive as she speeds and lane jumps her way to Lake Forest. She sings along to an old song on the radio, her head bobbing and her fingers tapping the steering wheel. I would laugh at her tone-deaf rendition of the tune, but my heart is lodged in my throat as she nearly clips another car.

We arrive at Jude's house in record time. My knees quake as I step out of the car. I pull my suitcase from the back of the vehicle, pausing to check out the Ziploc bags filled with what appear to be roots, herbs, and...a chicken foot? I slam the hatch closed, unwilling to take a closer look.

If I'm still alive by the time Sheldon and Bernard get home, I will sign up for behind-the-wheel classes. It's time to get my license. I'm tired of depending on other people for rides, especially ones that drive like they're competing in the Indy Five Hundred.

"Let me get that."

I jump as my father tugs the suitcase from my hands.

"Jude." Persephone nods. She glances at his monstrosity of a house, her lips pursed. "You've improved security?"

"It's safe," he says without explanation.

Jude doesn't invite Persephone inside, so I walk around the minivan and give her a hug.

"Call me if you need anything or if this arrangement isn't working out." Persephone doesn't bother to lower her voice.

"Okay." It would work out better if Marcus and I weren't mad at each other.

I follow Jude inside as Persephone pulls away. It's the first time I've been here by myself in a long time.

Jude slams the front door behind us, and we stand in the echoey foyer.

My father smiles. Happiness suits him. I wish he would wear it more often. It makes him look less scary.

"Your room is ready, and I've stocked the fridge and cabinets with all of your favorites," he says. "Cable has been installed, and I ordered a video streaming service, so you—*we*—can watch movies. There's a good bookstore downtown. I've got a full itinerary scheduled for the next ten days. A copy is on your dresser."

An itinerary? Seriously? I force a cough into my hand to hide my smile. Poor Jude. Demons really aren't good at this parenting thing. I'll have to teach him. Momma wasn't any good at being a mom, but maybe there's hope for Jude.

A loud rap at the front door jolts me. Jude's expression darkens before he turns away to open it.

Marcus?

"I heard you and Lucy were having an extended slumber party. Mind if I crash?"

Dylan.

Jude opens the door wide, and Dylan walks in with a large gray duffel bag slung over his shoulder.

Jude claps him on the back. "You're always welcome, Dylan."

I raise my eyebrows at Dylan questioningly. He winks at me.

Is it possible the old Dylan is making a comeback? I was expecting to struggle through my time here. Turns out it might actually be fun.

"I'll show you to your rooms," Jude says, leading us up the winding staircase.

Jude hasn't changed anything with the place. Heavy drapes still cover the windows. There are too many shadows. As we climb the stairs, I imagine the sunlight reflecting off the teardrop crystals of the huge chandelier dangling in the foyer. Would it throw rainbows on the walls?

One thing is for sure. I will sleep better now that Dylan is nearby.

"Lucy, you're already familiar with your room," Jude says as he pushes open my door.

He crosses the hall and opens the door to another bedroom. "Dylan, you can stay in here."

Jude pauses a moment, looking from Dylan to me, his eyebrows pulled low. He takes a long look at Dylan.

Dylan yelps and rubs his arm. "What was that?"

"A warning." Jude turns and walks away.

I stifle a laugh. Is Jude having a hard time coping with fatherly emotions?

After debating whether to unpack—I don't—I bound across the hall to Dylan's room and hop on his bed. I've never had sleepovers until I met Katie. Now I'm having one with my other best friend. I keep my fingers crossed that crabby Dylan doesn't resurface. He turns away from the window, and the heavy curtains fall back into place.

I lay on my stomach, ankles crossed. "Seriously, what are you doing here?"

Dylan slides a sideways glance my way. "You're not going to believe me."

I roll my eyes. "Try me."

"Lover boy called and asked me to stay here and keep an eye on you. I guess he trusts me now, which is more than I can say for Jude." Dylan plunks down on the bed beside me. "Did you see his look? And he zapped me. Doesn't he get that the whole attraction thing is over?"

"Marcus sent you?" I sputter. "You're right. I don't believe it."

"With the caveat that if I lay a finger on you, he'll kill me. He mentioned that part twice." Dylan smirks. "Funny thing is he didn't say a word about what would happen if you lay a finger on me."

I extend an index finger and poke his rock-hard abs.

Dylan grins. "That's such a Brandi move." He flips me over and starts to tickle me. "Noogie Monster attack!" He tries to wrap his arm around my neck and give me noogies. I shriek and slip from his grasp.

"Ow! What the...?" Dylan yells.

We both whip around to see Jude glowering in the doorway.

"We're just playing around," I tell him.

Jude looks unamused. "You." He points a finger at Dylan, then at the overstuffed chair across the room. "Sit there."

Dylan crosses the room and slumps into the chair.

Jude's gaze bounces between the two of us. Then he turns on his heel and leaves.

Dylan and I make eye contact and burst out laughing. It's just like old times. *Sort of.*

When our laughter dies down, Dylan scoots his chair a little closer, but not too close. He glances toward the door for a moment before speaking. "What are we going to do about Garret?"

The lighthearted mood is gone in an instant. "My last plan kind of fell through, so I'm coming up with a new one."

"Clue me in."

"We need to protect Jude, and we want to keep Garret away from St. Aquinas, so I'm thinking we should lure him and his team into the woods. We can use me as bait."

Dylan jumps out of the chair. "Of all the harebrained ideas, this one takes the cake. Use Jude as bait, but not you." He narrows his eyes at me. "Jude and Marcus won't go for this."

I raise my chin and glare back at him. "I have powers now. I can take care of myself."

"Yeah, right." Dylan crosses his arms over his chest. "What do you think Jude is going to do to me if he finds out I let you get yourself killed?"

❋ ❋ ❋ ❋

"Problem is you've never played sports," Dylan points out. "That's where I come in. I understand strategy and tactical maneuvering. Let's come up with a better plan."

We wander around Forever 21, checking out the clothes on the various racks. Jude wasn't keen on me leaving his house so soon after I arrived, but I told him about a shirt I absolutely had to have. I gushed on and on until his eyes bulged out of his head and his face turned red. Living with Jude may not be so hard after all.

"Here." Jude shoved a wad of cash at me.

"But I don't..."

He pointed toward his office door. "Go."

"I'll take her to the mall before she drives us both crazy," Dylan volunteered, a look of mock annoyance on his face.

"You have three hours," Jude said, tapping his watch. I caught the telltale pulse throbbing in his forehead. After the attack by the protectors, Jude has become hypervigilant. If not for Dylan, there's no way he'd let me out of the house.

Three hours is enough time to meet with Selima and buy a shirt to cover my alibi.

"What do you think about this?" I hold up a white crochet cami from the sales rack.

Dylan shakes his head. "You can afford to buy from the full

371

price racks, Lucy. How much did Jude give you? Five hundred?"

I swallow my panic. "I told him I was buying one shirt. This is a nice shirt."

Dylan hooks his arm through mine and steers me across the aisle.

"Now we're talking," he says in a girly falsetto voice as he holds a dotted tulip-sleeve blouse up for me to see. "And there's this." He presents a cap-sleeved white satin top, followed by a boxy baby-blue chambray tank top, then a black keyhole tank, and an ombré cap-sleeved T-shirt. "We have some time before we have to meet Selima. Let's make the most of it."

I giggle. I've heard Ella and Caroline talk about retail therapy. This is more fun than I had expected it would be. "I guess a couple more shirts would be okay. Besides, you have good taste."

"You could buy a lot more..."

Over Dylan's shoulder, I spot my father standing near the entrance of the store. He's not even trying to hide.

"You've got to be kidding me."

"What?" Dylan cranes his neck to see what I'm looking at.

I thrust my shirts into Dylan's arms and march over to Jude. "What are you doing here?"

"Making sure you're at the mall."

"But I told you—"

Jude studies me a moment. He glances behind me presumably at Dylan. "Be home on time." He turns and leaves the store.

I return to Dylan and take my shirts back. "He's spying on me now? Unbelievable!"

"I don't think you can pull much over Jude." Dylan scratches his chin. "What were you saying earlier about using yourself as bait to lure Garret into the woods?"

"Shut up," I snap.

Twenty minutes later we're in the food court, a shopping bag at my feet. My excitement over the new shirts is long gone.

"Don't you two look like a happy couple," Selima says as she soundlessly drops into the chair between Dylan and me.

"What are you talking about?" Dylan and I ask in unison. The look of shock on his face mirrors my own.

Selima winks. "Two girls at six o'clock—my six o'clock—clutching overpriced mocha coffees. One of them is glaring this way. Members of the Dylan fan club?"

Across the crowded room Ella and Caroline are talking with a couple of guys I don't recognize. I'm guessing they don't attend St. Aquinas. Then again, with twelve hundred students attending my high school, there's no way I'm familiar with everyone. Ella's eyes are fixed on me.

"Great," I groan. "I really don't need this."

"A protector's work is never done." Selima sighs. "You owe me. Big time." She slides her chair closer to Dylan and reaches up to stroke his cheek. Then she unleashes the most dazzling smile just for him.

Dylan's breath hitches.

She raises her face until their lips touch. It's only a peck, but the moment is so intimate that I feel like an intruder. Selima tucks her arm through his and returns her attention reluctantly back to me.

Dylan—cheeks flushed—can't take his eyes off of her.

"There," she says softly. "That should get Miss Witch off your back."

"Thanks, Selima." If Marcus was sitting beside me, that would help, too. Plus, I wouldn't feel like a third wheel. I texted him on the way to the mall, but he hasn't responded. Is he with Camille? Is she convincing him to join the clan? Has he already agreed to go with her?

"Happy to help," Selima responds. After she and Dylan exchange another cheesy smile, she grows serious. "I did some digging around."

I lean in and Dylan follows suit, tucking Selima's arm a little tighter in his.

"The attack on Jude wasn't sanctioned by Garret."

"But he was there that night. You saw his aura in Jude's house. Max saw him," I say.

"He admits to being in Jude's house," Selima says.

"Your dad cops to breaking and entering, hacking into Jude's computer and stealing information, but not to trying to kill Jude?" I say, giving her a dubious look.

"I'm not buying it, either," Dylan says. Selima frowns at him, but he shrugs.

Selima pulls her gaze from Dylan and continues. "Garret believes one of two things happened that night."

Dylan shifts uncomfortably and looks off in the opposite direction. Talking about the night he almost died can't be easy on him. I want to reach across the table and squeeze his hand, but I don't dare since he's still tucked against Selima. A moment later Dylan's expression calms. I notice Selima has both of her hands pressed against Dylan's upper arm. She is working her protector magic on him.

"First, there's been talk about some kind of power struggle within the clan," Selima says.

"You mean there's anti-Garret sentiment among some of the clan members?" Dylan asks, his voice low.

Selima nods. "Apparently, there's been unrest within the clan over the past year. Maybe longer. Since I don't live with the clan—and Garret doesn't feel his precious daughter should worry about things like clan politics—I had no idea." She rolls her eyes. "Garret suspects the battle at Jude's was intended to set him up. With the deaths of clan members on his hands, his leadership would be called into question."

"This other group, what's their beef with Garret?" I ask. "Is he too aggressive for them?"

"Not aggressive enough," Selima says.

"You said Garret suspected one of two things happened that night," I say. "What's his other theory?"

Selima struggles to look me in the eye. "That the other night wasn't an attack on Jude at all. That Jude provoked the protectors once Garret was gone, then proceeded to slaughter them."

"That's a load of crap!" Dylan's fist connects with the table.

People at the surrounding tables look our way.

"Don't make a scene," Selima scolds softly.

A moment later, conversations at the neighboring tables resume.

"What I'm saying is that someone or several someones are trying to cause trouble. Big trouble," Selima says. "Rumors are going around that Jude's got some grand plan to eliminate the clan."

"Not true!" I say. "I bet Garret's the one spreading those rumors."

"Listen to me," Selima hisses. "There's talk of removing Garret from power, putting someone else in his place. Someone more effective who will act swiftly on the slaughter that took place at Jude's house. I overheard Garret on the phone at the condo defending himself."

"To who?" Dylan asks.

Selima shakes her head. "I don't know."

Will Garret double his efforts to kill Jude? The food court suddenly feels too hot.

"Have you considered that this is all a ruse? That Garret simply doesn't want you to know the truth of what he's up to?" Dylan asks.

A frown creases Selima's brow. "I know my father's no saint. I have to consider everything."

For the umpteenth time, I check my cell. Still no message from my boyfriend. "Sorry to change the subject." Really, I'm not sorry at all. I'm not learning anything useful from Selima. The workings of the inner politics of the clan won't help me figure out a way to keep my father and me alive. "Marcus is with Camille tonight, isn't he?"

"They're out to dinner," Selima confirms.

Marcus told me he was going to meet with her. He just didn't say when. I can't help the surge of suspicion over his secrecy. Sure, I stormed away the other night when we met on the roof, but he could've told me before I left for Jude's that he was meeting Camille tonight.

It's bad enough I screwed everything up with Lucifer. Who was I to think I could summon a demon so powerful? Now, Garret and his cabinet are claiming Jude is slaughtering protectors, and Marcus is hanging out with his mother probably discussing his plan to join the clan. Is it possible that Camille wants Marcus—the person best able to help protect me next to my father—out of the way while Garret comes after Jude and me?

"Lucy? What's wrong? You're flushed." Dylan's hand twitches on the table as if he's about to reach over and take hold of mine.

I wish he would. I could use the comfort of my friend right now. My gaze travels across the food court to where Ella and Caroline stand. As if on cue, Ella throws her head back and laughs. She touches the arm of the blond guy standing beside her. Anger swells inside of me. It's not just Ella and her pettiness or the fact she and Caroline lead these super carefree lives. It's everyone else here, too.

Dozens of happy, oblivious faces. These people go about their daily lives, to school or to work, eating, sleeping, flirting, gossiping, and judging. They're not in danger.

A huge ball of energy throbs inside of me. The sound of blood rushes in my ears. I focus on the walls, the ceiling, the tables, anywhere but at the people around us. I can't risk hurting anyone. The energy...the anger...I need to release it, but I don't know where to send it.

I spot a series of three large garbage cans near the hallway leading to the restrooms. I let it go—all of it—and it's blissful as the painful knots in my stomach ease and the tension in all of my limbs releases.

Shrieks ring out as people run away from the erupting garbage cans. The contents splatter all over the walls, the ceiling, and the floor.

"Lucy!" Dylan whispers harshly. He and Selima take hold of my hands. The swirling chaos in my mind flutters, ratchets down, and finally quiets. A sudden calm washes over me.

The only person who's ever been able to ease my turmoil is Marcus. Selima meets my eyes. For just a moment, I push aside my distrust. I survey the damage I caused across the room, disappointed that I lost control. I turn back to Selima and squeeze her hands. "I'm sorry. Thank you."

She returns a small smile.

"Why don't we take this outside?" she suggests. "I have more to tell you."

We file out of the food court as four security guards question spectators about the exploding garbage cans.

CHAPTER FIFTY-TWO

– Lucy Walker –

Once we reach Dylan's car in the mall parking lot, I hop in the backseat so Dylan and Selima can sit next to each other. Dylan can barely keep his eyes off of her since that kiss. Given my experience dating a protector, I understand how captivating they can be.

"You said you had more to tell us," I prompt her.

Selima surveys Dylan and me. Her hesitation causes my heart to skip a beat. More bad news? "The protectors that died at Jude's house—the ones that weren't burned to a crisp—were drained of all their blood."

"That's not possible." I didn't see anyone draining them. "Could they have bled out from their injuries?"

Selima shakes her head. "You don't understand..."

Dylan groans and buries his face in his hands.

"What is it?" My attention bounces between the two of them like a Ping-Pong ball. "What am I missing?"

"The healing properties of the blood," Dylan whispers.

Selima nods. "Garret believes Jude drained them."

"We have Garret's mutant army who consume demon blood and now someone's stealing protector blood?" Dylan asks.

A vision of Dylan suckling at Marcus's wrist replays in my mind. How had I been so naïve to think Marcus saved me simply by wrapping me in his embrace the night of homecoming? I drank Marcus's blood, too. I cover my mouth against the bile rising up my throat. "God, I feel so stupid."

Dylan's eyes grow wide. He reaches between the seats to touch my knee. "I'm sorry. I wanted to tell you..."

"But you didn't," I choke.

"He made me promise," Dylan says, his voice desperate. "And I was afraid you would freak out."

"I am freaked out, but now I'm also mad you didn't tell me," I snap. "I told you everything that happened to you at Jude's house the other night."

"I know and I'm sorry." Dylan doesn't sound sorry at all.

"I want to know." I glare at him. "Tell me what happened that night. Don't you dare keep anything from me."

Selima touches my leg. "Lucy..."

I shake her off. "Tell me, Dylan."

Dylan exhales a heavy sigh. "I shouldn't have to be the one to tell you, but fine. *Thanks, Marcus.*"

"What happened that night?" I push.

Dylan blinks and swallows, before returning his attention to the windshield. Selima rests her hand on his thigh, and Dylan exhales heavily. Is she working her protector magic on him again?

"Persephone, Henry, and Jude did everything they could for you. The ravens, too. Everyone fought so hard." Dylan sounds sad. I feel bad making him remember, but it's his own fault. "Persephone and Henry convinced Jude to change Marcus back, so he could help you. Jude resisted at first, but Henry flat out told him you could die. You had a head wound, broken bones...had lost a lot of blood."

I close my eyes as it comes back to me. I'm overcome with the sensation of falling, feel the branches grab and tear at my skin, feel the impact of my fall. Nausea, black and thick, swells inside of me. I swallow a hiccup and press my arms tight around my stomach to ward it off.

"It was the most surreal thing I'd ever seen." Dylan's voice catches. "Marcus was disoriented. Persephone whispered to him what needed to be done. The next thing I knew, these massive wings exploded from his back. There was blood."

Blood?

Dylan shakes his head, struggles to continue. "Marcus held you and wrapped his wings around you. The thing is..." His voice dips and he clears his throat.

Selima clutches his hand. She nods, urging him on.

"The thing is his wings didn't close tightly around you. I saw what he was doing. He held his bleeding wrist against your mouth, forcing it open. He kept begging you to drink." Dylan's voice falls to a whisper. "There was so much blood. All over your face, your body, the table...on Marcus and Jude."

Did I drink?

Dylan twitches. He's shivering. Selima presses her hand flat against his leg, and within seconds the shivering stops. "You wouldn't drink until Jude commanded you to."

Just like Dylan the other night. "How...how much?" I don't know why it matters, but I want to know.

"So much that Marcus passed out."

Selima gasps, she turns to meet my eyes, her expression alarmed.

Dylan levels his gaze at me. "Jude commanded you to. Even after Marcus fell to the floor with you still wrapped in his arms. Henry and Persephone shouted at Jude to stop; told him he was going to kill Marcus."

Silence fills the car.

"What happened next?" My throat is so tight, it burns. My demon father did what any parent would do in a crisis situation. He fought to save me. But it almost cost me Marcus.

"Aiden decked Jude." A small smile pulls at Dylan's mouth then slips away. "It broke Jude's focus on you, long enough for you to stop drinking. While everyone was distracted, Aiden got Marcus out of there."

"With that much protector blood in your system—on top of all the other magic—you would heal quickly. And painlessly," Selima says stiffly.

Which was exactly what happened. Within twenty-four hours, I was healed, though I thought it was the magic of the witches and my father, not Marcus. The heightened sense of smell, the brighter, richer colors in everyday things like raindrops, flowers, and butterfly wings—and the feeling of euphoria—all of it means something different to me now. Protector blood is like a drug. I never want it again.

Selima looks thoughtful for a moment. "Lucy, do you think

Jude could be stockpiling blood in case you ever get injured again?"

Suddenly, Garret's accusations don't seem so far-fetched. Seamus is going to come after me again. He will try to kill me. If Jude is draining protectors, then I'm caught between two evils. Can I blame Garret for wanting to kill Jude and wipe me out of existence?

CHAPTER FIFTY-THREE

– Lucy Walker –

"I should've told you the truth about that night," Dylan says as he turns the corner onto Jude's street.

It still surprises me how long and dark the streets are in this part of Lake Forest. You would think a rich community would want their yards and roads well lit. They would if they knew a demon lived among them.

I squint out the windshield and notice a familiar car parked outside of Jude's gate. "What's Marcus doing here?"

Dylan swerves to the side of the road and parks behind Marcus. I slam my door at the same time Marcus climbs out of his car.

Marcus and Dylan nod at each other in greeting.

"How did dinner go with Camille?" I want him to know that I know about his secretive dinner with Camille, the woman who may be conspiring with Garret to harm Jude and me.

"She's trying to convince me that Garret's not a bad guy," he says.

Is he delusional?

Dylan leans against Marcus's car and crosses his arms over his chest. "She knows about Garret's plan?"

"She knows and she supports it," I say, smirking at Marcus. "It's great Camille is trying to convince you to make up with Garret while he's planning to kill my father and me."

Marcus's frown is immediate. "Camille passed along a warning. She said that Garret's basically gone off the reservation. He believes Jude is draining protectors, and he's hell-bent on revenge. Camille seemed afraid of him."

Camille never seemed afraid of anyone. "What about the protectors who are dosing themselves with demon blood? Did you ask her about that?"

Marcus nods. "She said she doesn't know anything about that."

How can he be so stupid?

"Don't look at me like that," Marcus says, defensively. "I believe her." He reaches for me, and I back away. He's choosing his mother—who supports the man who came to Chicago to kill Jude—over me. The pain of his betrayal layers on top of all the bad news Selima shared tonight and Dylan's revelation of Marcus's healing the night of homecoming.

Marcus rubs the back of his neck. "After I left Camille, Aiden and I paid a visit to St. Aquinas. They've been there. Garret's men. Their auras are all over the place."

My mouth goes dry. My heart beats way too fast. Fireballs, fangs, and claws could cause a lot of damage to a lot of kids at St. Aquinas. I shudder.

"Listen to me, Marcus. We have to move this away from St.

Aquinas," I say. "Let's arrange a meeting in the woods with your father."

Dylan pushes off of Marcus's car. "I hate to say this, but we need to talk to Jude," he says. "If we have any hope of setting up a meeting with Garret, we need to get Jude on board with it first."

With a trembling hand, I pull my hair over my shoulder and twist it nervously. "Let's get it over with."

Marcus's gaze flickers uneasily at Jude's mansion.

"You don't have to fight the change once you're inside. No one will see you." My voice is flat. I'm not trying to comfort him, just being practical.

"Fine." Marcus reaches for my hand, but I pull away. I'm still feeling stung. Marcus is a fool to swallow Camille's lies. He exhales heavily. "Let's go."

I expect Jude, with his super sense of Marcus, to meet us at the front door, but he doesn't.

"He's probably working," I say once we're inside. I knock twice on the double doors of his office, but there's no answer. When we enter the room, I'm surprised to see Jude's desk chair is empty.

"His car wasn't out front," Dylan says. "I assumed he had parked in the garage."

How did I miss that? A quick glance at Marcus and I see he isn't struggling.

Dylan glances at Jude's brand-new desk. "Do you think you can access his files on you?"

"Good question," I say. Jude's desk holds a laptop and a phone, both also new. The side table that normally holds the security monitors is empty. "Otherwise, we're in the dark about what the protectors know."

Jude's chair creaks as I take a seat. Being on this side of the desk is scarier than I thought it would be. Jude's a nut about privacy. What would he do if he walked in and found me nosing around?

Marcus glances at the door nervously. "You don't have to do this."

"Yes, she does," Dylan says sharply. "She's the only one in this room Jude won't exterminate for snooping through his stuff."

I nibble my bottom lip. I love Marcus for his concern, but Dylan's right. I need to do this.

Expecting a piercing alarm or poisonous darts to shoot at me from some secret compartment in the desk, I gingerly lift the lid on the laptop. Nothing happens. I sigh with relief. Then the screen comes to life.

"Crap. It's password protected," I say.

Marcus and Dylan come around the desk to stand behind me.

"It could be anything," I say.

"What if it's not?" Dylan says. "One of my dad's biggest gripes about his investment clients is that they don't take security serious enough. They complain about the complex password requirements of his company's system. They would prefer to use super basic passwords." He sits on the edge of the desk. "Most people don't use an elaborate combination of letters, numbers, and symbols on their home systems like they should."

Jude mentioned during the night of the gargoyle attack that he has heavy security on his financial accounts. Based on the theft of the files about me, I'm guessing those weren't so secure.

"What do most people prefer to use?" I ask.

"The names of their kids or some combination of all the names of the family," Dylan says.

Marcus arches an eyebrow. "You think it could be that easy?"

"It's worth a try." Dylan nods at the computer.

I pull in a deep breath as I plug the letters L-U-C-Y into the box on the screen. My heart pounds as I hit enter. An immediate response appears telling me the password is invalid.

"So much for your theory," I say, deflated.

"Not so fast," Marcus says thoughtfully. "Jude had more than one child."

"Zack." I glance at him over my shoulder. "Good call."

"Your uncle...I mean your brother..." Dylan teases.

"Marcus, punch Dylan for me." Like I need a reminder that Jude had relationships with both Gram and Momma.

"I'll bank that request for another time," Marcus says. I can feel him smiling behind me.

I type Z-A-C-K. My finger hovers over the send button. "What if the password is Zackary? How many more attempts do you think I have?"

"How did Jude refer to him?" Marcus asks.

I think back to my conversations with Jude about Zack and shake my head in frustration. "I only remember Jude referring to him as his son."

"Then you have to pick one," Dylan says.

I rub my palms on my jeans. Zack or Zackary? Gram only ever referred to him as Zack. Same with Momma. That's what I will use. I hit enter.

Invalid password.

"Forget it. We're done." I push away from the desk, my stomach clenched in a fiery stress ball, and climb out of Jude's chair.

"You probably have one more attempt. Let's give it another shot," Dylan says.

"No way." It suddenly feels like a hundred degrees in Jude's office.

"What's the worst that can happen?" Dylan asks.

"I'll put in yet another incorrect password, and the computer will lock us out. Jude will come home and know we've been messing with it."

Dylan shakes his head in frustration. "You think Jude's the one you have to fear? What about the gargoyles who are out to kill you and Jude?" He jabs his finger toward the computer. "They've already gone to St. Aquinas once. They will go back and the next time won't be a spec mission."

Reluctantly, I slide back into Jude's chair.

"Don't hate on all protectors. There are still plenty of us—the non-psychotic kind—out there," Marcus says to Dylan as he wheels the chair and me to the desk.

"Understood, but your kind tried to kill me the other night. And they're out to kill Lucy. I don't take it lightly when someone comes after me and my family."

Family. I smile to myself.

"Dylan, you said that some of your dad's clients combine all the names in the family. Can you give me an example?" I ask.

"It's mostly the first couple letters of each name."

Jude's family: Jude, Zack, and Lucy. *Wait.* There's Gram—

Vera. Would Momma be part of this? No, I'm sure Jude wouldn't have included her. I roll my shoulders out, trying to ease the tension. My fingers hover over the home row on the keyboard. With my eyes glued to the screen, I type: J-U-V-E-Z-A-L-U. My finger trembles over the enter button.

Dylan sighs. "Just do it already."

I whack the button much harder than necessary and hold my breath waiting for the reject message to appear. It doesn't. Instead, Jude's monitor populates with all of his software icons.

"We're in. Great job, Lucy." Marcus kisses the top of my head.

At the same time, Dylan groans a loud sigh of relief and pats my shoulder.

We search through his files and find one aptly called *Lucy.*

Dylan thrusts a USB drive into my hand, and I copy the file.

"We got what we came for," Dylan says. "Shut it down."

"Just a second," I tell him.

If Jude has a file on me, maybe he's got one on Marcus, too. I return to the search window and type in GARGOYLE.

Three files pop up. I copy them all.

Marcus yanks my chair away from the desk. "Jude's home," he hisses. "Shut it down now!"

I close everything down, shut the lid, then slide the USB drive into the pocket of my jeans.

We make it to the front door just as Jude enters. A flicker of annoyance registers on his face. "You go to the mall for a shirt and return with a gargoyle?"

I hold up my shopping bag. "Several shirts," I say, struggling to breathe normally.

Jude isn't amused. He glares at Marcus. "What's he doing here?"

"He saved Dylan's life the other night. Or have you already forgotten?"

"He came to warn us that Garret's men are scoping out St. Aquinas," Dylan says.

Jude's gaze narrows.

"Aiden and I picked up their auras tonight. They know Lucy's class schedule."

Jude slams the door behind him. "That's it. I'm pulling you out of school."

"Or we could arrange a meeting," I suggest. "You could reach out to Garret. Try to settle this."

Jude squeezes the bridge of his nose with his thumb and forefinger. I would laugh at the uncharacteristic gesture, if it weren't for the anger rolling off of him.

"It won't do any good," he says. "Their new secret regime is determined to exterminate me."

Of course he knows—he's frickin' Jude.

"But why?" I ask. Aside from the phony accusations, I want to know what intel my father has.

He gives a small shake of his head. "I need to make some calls. You," he thrusts his finger at me, "are not going to school tomorrow."

"What if the protectors show up looking for me? What if they attack other students?" My voice is nearly a shriek.

"Gargoyles," Dylan mumbles.

"Don't argue with me," Jude says.

Marcus twitches and jerks beside me.

I continue, determined. "I'm not putting the entire student body at risk. They want me. Set up a meeting in the woods."

If only I hadn't ticked off Lucifer. We could really use his help.

I roll my eyes skyward.

Oops. I shift my attention to the floor. *If I'm going to protect the student body and Jude, I'm going to need your help.*

"Lucy..." Marcus lays a hand on my arm. A tremor passes from him to me. He needs to get out of here.

Jude narrows his eyes. He looks at Marcus expectantly and jerks his head toward the door.

"Uh, yeah. I'll see you later," Marcus murmurs. He presses his twitchy lips to my forehead then heads for the exit. "Later, Dylan. Jude."

Jude seems to relish locking the door behind Marcus. Then he turns to me. "No school." He points to Dylan. "Keep her in the house."

As he strides down the hall toward his office, I get a quick burn across my wrist. Dylan jumps and grabs his arm and I know Jude stung him too. Stupid demon discipline.

Will he know we were in his office? My mouth goes dry as I replay everything we did from the time we got back from the mall.

That's when it hits me.

"Oh, no!" I hiss. "The laptop is in the wrong spot. I slid it closer to me while sitting in his chair, and I never moved it back." How could I have been so stupid? "He's going to know."

Dylan mulls that over. "Maybe he won't notice," he says, although the doubt in his voice fails to instill much confidence in me.

CHAPTER FIFTY-FOUR

– Lucy Walker –

"This is creepy," Dylan says as he scrolls through the photos we stole from Jude's computer. We sit on the bed in my room. The comforter, carpet, curtains are bright white. Too white.

I'm not sure—and my mind isn't capable of counting at the moment—but there has to be thirty pictures. How did Jude get these? Sure, Aiden passed information from Gram along to Jude, but this much?

There's the photo when I was six and Gram had taken me to get a haircut, my eyes looking large and soulful under heavy bangs. Then there's the photo when I was ten, a year I would prefer to forget entirely. The haunted expression in my eyes had everything to do with Momma and her first overdose. I swallow past the lump in my throat.

Dylan snorts. "This one's great, although I think you nearly strangled Sheldon."

I scoot closer to him on the bed and study the photo. Sure enough, there I sit on Sheldon's lap, roughly eight years old. My arms are wrapped so tight around his neck his eyes bulge.

"Can we skip the photos and move on to more important information?" I didn't mean for that to come out as harshly as it did, but how can I explain to Dylan the pain these old photos stir up? It's not possible for him—the super-rich, popular, star of the football team—to understand where I came from.

After a moment, I add, "I think it makes the most sense to focus on the information about the gargoyles."

Dylan sighs impatiently. "Make up your mind." He selects another file and hits enter then whistles low.

The screen populates with photo after photo of protectors. I recognize a few faces: Garret, Ronan, Flynn, and Marcus. Below each photo is a name.

I gasp when I see the word *Eliminated* typed next to several names.

"Dylan?" My voice sounds hollow. "Do you think Jude killed them?"

"I don't know, but this doesn't look good."

My eyes start to burn after staring at the photos for so long. I force myself to blink a few times.

Protectors killing and draining demons. Demons—possibly Jude—killing and draining protectors. It has to stop. Garret wants Jude. He wants me almost as much. I'm left with no choice.

"If Jude isn't going to arrange a meeting with Garret, then I will."

He jumps off the bed. "No. Let Jude do it."

I tuck my legs beneath me on the bed. "If this goes down at St. Aquinas, a lot of students will get caught in the middle. Garret's making a point of coming after me just to hurt Jude. I'll go to him, instead."

"What do you think you're going to accomplish by having a confrontation with Garret and his team? Without Jude? That's suicide."

"Listen, I need you on board, Dylan. You're incredibly strong and tactical. I can't do this without you." He puffs out his chest just a little, and I know I said the right thing.

"We'll need to ambush Garret." I pause for only a moment, nervous how he's going to react to my next statement. "We can win if you're willing to enhance my powers, like you did when we torched Jude's tree."

Dylan's expression darkens, his eyes narrow slits. "He'll kill you!"

"Not with you by my side." I've thought through many different scenarios. This is the one I keep coming back to—the only one that keeps Jude and Marcus alive.

Dylan heaves a long, slow sigh and plunks down beside me on the bed. "Tell me the plan. The *whole* plan. Don't you dare leave anything out."

My favorite Florence and the Machine song blares from the cell phone in my pocket. I hold a finger up to Dylan. "Hey, Selima, what's up?"

"Lucy, you've got to get here, to your school, now. I mean right now."

The panic in her voice makes my blood run cold. Selima is the calmest person I know.

I clutch the phone. "What's going on?"

"Just get over here." The line goes dead.

"Lucy...?" Dylan looks from my phone to me, his face a mask of worry.

"Something's wrong," I say, alarmed. I slide my half-asleep legs from under me and climb off the tall bed. Dylan is right beside me, gripping my arm as I teeter. "We need to meet Selima at St. Aquinas. We have to leave now."

"What's she doing there?"

I slip my shoes on and grab my purse. "Long story short? I gave her a tour. Now she breaks in and hangs out."

"Weird." Dylan grunts.

I glance at the bedroom door. "There's no way Jude's going to let us leave this late."

Dylan looks toward the window. "It's not that hard to get out of here, Luce."

I frown. "What do you have in mind? I doubt tying sheets together will work, especially this high up."

"You're kidding me, right? Weren't you the one jumping off Jude's roof last year?"

I raise my eyebrows at him, eager to get moving. "That was me. What about you?"

Dylan smirks. "I think I can manage."

We throw open the windows, and I climb out. Dylan follows right behind. Jumping off the roof was scary, but somehow this is scarier. Maybe because it's dark and I have no sense of depth perception or perhaps because if Jude finds out, he'll probably chain me up in the basement to keep me inside.

I grab Dylan's hand and we stand side by side on the slanted shingles. I recall Selima's frantic voice over the phone. This can only mean one thing. Garret's team is at my school. We need to get them out before morning.

Dylan squeezes my hand as we stand on the second story ledge. "Let's do this."

I nod, resolved. "Land soft. Don't lock your knees."

On three, we both leap. Before I can register fear or anything else, we're on the ground. On our feet, a rush of adrenaline passes through my body.

"Let's get out of here," Dylan says.

CHAPTER FIFTY-FIVE

– Lucy Walker –

"What does Selima do all night at St. Aquinas?" Dylan asks during our drive to our school.

"She's obsessed with the books in the old library. She takes them and sits by the floor-to-ceiling arched windows in the gym and reads by moonlight some evenings."

Or maybe she's helping the protectors in their plan to kill me, the little voice in my head whispers. Could this be a trap?

Dylan slides a sideways glance my way. "That sounds lonely. I should probably check on her sometime."

What if we don't live past tonight? that voice says.

Selima meets us at the back door of the school and lets us in. The three of us meet Marcus in the gymnasium. The giant room looks nothing like a gym with its glossy floors and windows unlike any I have ever seen. Two walls are lined with massive arched windows that, during the daytime, look out at manicured lawns and the basswood, sycamore, beech, and sweetgum trees. The sassafras trees with their leaves that turn scarlet purple in the fall are my favorites.

Marcus doesn't kiss or hug me when I walk in. Tension pours off of him.

"What's going on?" I direct the question at Marcus.

He crosses his arms over his chest and nods at Selima. "Tell them."

"I overheard a conversation between Garret, Ronan, and Flynn tonight at the condo. They're coming here. They plan to nab you in the morning then contact Jude to let him know they have you," Selima says.

"What are we going to do?" Dylan asks tightly. I flinch as his heartbeat pounds in my ears. The demon in him wants to fight. This is the first sign I've had that our connection is restored. I will have to think more about that later.

Marcus faces me, his expression determined and grim. "I won't let them touch you."

"Garret's crazed," Selima says. I notice dark circles beneath her eyes. Did she skip her time under the moon last night? "The way he was talking today...the way he's been acting. I've never seen him so focused on revenge, on killing." She paces. "I don't know their plan. Not exactly."

That gets Dylan's attention. "What do you mean by *not exactly*?"

Selima looks at each of us nervously. "Garret said he wants Lucy *taken care of*." She uses air quotes to make her point.

Dylan's anger ramps up instantly. I feel the dark energy ripple through me. "Does that mean something different in gargoyle-speak?" he asks.

"Allow me to clarify," a voice booms from across the echoey room.

We whirl around as Garret strides into the room. He looks very different than he did the night at the condo, wearing a navy T-shirt and designer blue jeans. These are clothes he can fight in.

I refuse to acknowledge my fear. We have to end this tonight.

"I came to Chicago," Garret says, as he studies the room, "one of my favorites cities, for two reasons." He ticks off one finger. "First, to kill an offending demon who has given me a lifetime of headaches."

"But what you accuse him of...you have no proof!" I say.

Even in the dimly lit room, there's no missing the menace on Garret's face. Marcus takes hold of my hand and tugs me to his side.

"Second," he ticks off another finger, "to appease my wife, we came to reconcile with her—*our*—son."

Marcus snorts.

First Jude and now Garret. Why can't anyone call Marcus by name?

"Imagine my disgrace when I discover our son has taken up with the offending demon's offspring." Garret stands still as stone as his gaze lands on me again. "My rogue son consorting with the enemy is an insult to what we are, what we stand for. I won't tolerate it."

Marcus drops my hand and takes a step forward. "What's your problem? No one's getting hurt."

"There aren't any rules against it." Selima smiles sweetly at her father. "I checked."

"Now you turn my beloved daughter against me." Garret's

piercing gaze never leaves my face. "You are a wicked, wicked thing. I'm going to kill you."

All the air whooshes from my lungs. *No!* All this time I thought I had accepted the idea of death, so long as I could save the people I loved. But I want to live. I survived life in the trailer park with Momma. I survived three—*three*—near-death experiences last year. I survived demon training with Jude.

I raise my right hand and a fireball appears. I bounce it on my palm for effect. "Not if I kill you first."

Marcus and Dylan stand ready on each side of me.

"A puny, inexperienced demon." Garret snickers. "I will squash you like a bug."

Puny?

"Enough, Father." Selima moves to stand in front of me. She wraps her slender fingers around my forearm. My anger fades and the fireball snuffs out.

"Why did you do that?" I tug my arm free. "He's here to kill me. Are you going to help him?"

"Don't be ridiculous!" Selima turns to Garret and squares her shoulders. "I know about the blood drinkers in the clan."

Garret shifts uneasily. "It's merely an experiment."

"You plan to kill Jude for allegedly draining protectors, while members of our own kind are doing the same thing to demons?"

"We needed to know the effects," Garret says, a hard edge in his voice. If it was anyone other than his favorite child confronting him, he would not tolerate it.

"When you saw what the blood did, turning protectors into those monsters, why didn't you stop?" Selima asks.

Just then Garret takes a step toward his daughter. "It's not for you to question me—"

"Because he got hooked," I say.

Garret flashes a cocky smile. "You should have kept your mouth shut, demon." He takes a step back and cups his hands around his mouth. "Team one!"

Six of the floor-to-ceiling windows shatter.

Marcus throws me to the floor and flings his body over mine. I catch a glimpse of blue jean clad legs and boots stomping toward us, the hardwood bouncing under their weight.

"Selima, get Lucy out of here." Marcus jerks me up by my arm to a sitting position. I yelp as he nearly dislocates my shoulder from its socket. "Dylan and I will stay and fight these goons."

Across the room, Dylan grabs a protector in a headlock. With a swift jerk of his neck, the protector slides to the floor dead. My stomach flips with a sickening twist as I realize he learned how to kill from Jude.

Marcus throws his shirt to the floor then hunches as wings spring from his back. He spins around and drives his fist into the face of an oncoming gargoyle. Blood splatters in multiple directions.

I'm not going anywhere. This is my fight. I glance over my shoulder to tell Selima as much at the same time I am about to leap to my feet, when I come face-to-face with Flynn. He grabs me by my hair and yanks me to my knees, his claws cutting against my skin. He's taller than he was the night of Caroline's party, on account of the demon blood he's ingested and the morphing process. His shoulder-length brown hair flutters as he expands his slate gray webbed wings.

"It's good to see you again, darling," he says in his pompous English accent. The lethal-looking fangs cause him to lisp. "Tonight is not your lucky night."

Heat blasts down my arms, and energy vibrates throughout my body. I'm unable to turn my head due to his grip. I hurl a fireball behind me.

Flynn yanks my hair as he lunges to the left. I cry out as he stands on my calves. He wrenches my arms behind my back and restrains my wrists with a plastic zip tie. I attempt to tug and twist against it, but it's too tight.

"Let's watch lover boy get pummeled," he says close to my ear.

Two of Garret's soldiers grab hold of Marcus while a third lunges at him, claws swiping. *Three against one. Bad odds.* Marcus sinks an elbow into the gut of one of the gargoyles holding him, then swings around to strike the other in the face.

Free, Marcus wrenches the attacking gargoyle's wrist. Bones snap. The two fallen beasts jump up and go at him.

"Marcus!" I struggle anew against my restraints, wincing as the hard plastic cuts into my skin. How do I get these things off? *Melt them?* I envision a fireball.

Bad idea!

Startled, I look over at Dylan. *What are you doing in my head?*

He frowns at me. *Your skin will melt, genius.*

A spell then? I suggest as I continue to pull and twist against the binding.

Better idea. Make it fast. We need your fireballs.

I close my eyes and focus on the makeshift handcuffs.

Undo these restraints
Allow me to escape
Grant me freedom
Before we are beaten

Nothing. I tug harder at the bindings, fisting my hands while I pull and turn my wrists. I wince against the pain. A trickle of wetness trails down the palm of my hand. Blood?

Doubling my focus and my physical effort, I repeat the spell and struggle against the binding. *Still nothing.*

It's nearly impossible to focus with Marcus and Dylan fighting my battle.

Visualize, I remind myself. *Imagine the zip ties snapping apart. Crumbling.*

Deep breath in then out. My lips move fast, my words silent. I sink deeper into focus as I repeat the words. As soon as I finish the spell, I start it again.

Crack! The pressure of the restraints loosens. Flooded with relief, I remind myself to keep my hands together. I don't want to alert Flynn, whose weight on my legs causes charley horse-like pain in my calves.

Selima joins Marcus as he fends off two attackers. She jumps backward to avoid an oncoming strike, spins and horse-kicks the guy in the solar plexus. Garret nods at a female gargoyle, whose pale gray bat-like wings bounce as she grabs Selima from behind.

"Get off me!" Selima whips her head around to Garret. "What's wrong with you? Why are you doing this?"

"All for the good of the clan," Garret replies.

Dylan sprints after the female gargoyle, but Ronan clotheslines him. Dylan drops to the floor, clutching his throat.

"No!" Selima and I both shriek as Ronan stomps on Dylan's chest. Dylan grabs Ronan's boot-clad foot and yanks him off balance, rolling out of the way as the gargoyle crashes to the floor.

Selima bites and kicks her captor, but the monster-fied woman braces her tightly.

"You're a traitor, Selima. You need to be punished." Garret nods at the woman again. The gargoyle drags Selima, bucking and flailing, from the room.

No way I'm going to let one of Garret's freaks hurt Selima. I focus on the female gargoyle.

Release Selima as if her skin burns to the touch
You nearly faint from the pain, it's too much
Don't bite or scratch
Because you know you're mismatched

I repeat the spell, but nothing happens. Selima and the woman are gone.

Marcus drives his fist into the face of an oncoming gargoyle, slamming him against the bleachers. The gargoyle rises unsteadily to his feet. Marcus smashes his elbow into the side of the gargoyle's skull, the soft spot high on the temple. The gargoyle falls to the ground. Marcus leaps toward Flynn and me. "Hurt her and I'll kill you," he says to Flynn. Then he turns to Garret. "This is between us. Release Lucy."

"Between *us*?" Garret snorts. "*You* were never part of anything. You weren't wanted. Not by me and, in the beginning, not by your mother."

Heat roars inside of me, settles in my hands.

"Liar!" I witnessed Camille's regret and guilt during the meeting in Marcus's apartment. "Camille always wanted Marcus. Is that why you hate him so much?"

Garret arches his body, his angry roar bouncing off the walls. Wings, black as coal, unfold before me. Garret's shirt lands in a torn heap. His barrel-sized chest heaves. He smiles, revealing dagger-sharp fangs.

Garret smacks his lips. "Time for you to go."

I hurl a fireball at Garret and instantly have a second one ready. Flynn, swearing in surprise at my unbound hands, snags my arm, swinging me around. His fist collides with my fireball. He yelps, slapping his burned hand.

"I can't trust you to eliminate one little nuisance!" Garret barks at Flynn, charging toward me.

At the same time, Marcus lunges for him.

"Back off," Garret growls. He shoves Marcus, sending him stumbling and tripping over a large netted bag of basketballs.

Flynn reaches for me with his good hand. I spin away. I crunch over broken glass, pivot, and nail Marcus's father with two successive fireballs. Garret dodges the first one. The second? Bullseye. Nailed him in the chest. He flails backward. All the while I keep moving, putting distance between Flynn and me.

Across the room, Dylan scrunches his face against the smell of singed flesh as he smashes his elbow into Ronan's face. Ronan's nose crunches and blood spurts free. The blond spiky-haired protector stumbles to the floor, blinded by his own blood.

Dylan rushes to my side. "You okay?" He frowns at my bloody wrist.

I wipe the blood on my pants. "No biggie."

"Do you think Selima can handle herself?" Dylan asks.

Ronan huddles in the corner, his hands covering his nose. He jerks it sharply to the right, coughs twice, then spits a mouthful of blood and mucus onto the floor.

Now Flynn and Ronan stalk toward Dylan and me. They both look extremely ticked off.

"I'll create a diversion," I whisper to Dylan. "Then Flynn's mine."

"Got it."

"Selima, no!" I stare at the door in mock horror.

Garret, Ronan, and Flynn all look in the same direction, ready to pounce or run. With a wave of my hand, Flynn's legs fly out from beneath him. There is a series of tinkling and scraping sounds and a heavy thump as he crashes onto a pile of glass. Blood starts to run from various gashes on his arms and torso.

Flynn struggles to his feet and comes at me. *These guys are unstoppable!* I lob a fireball at him. He bats it away and continues toward me.

I launch two fireballs at him, followed by two more. He dips and bobs, but isn't fast enough to avoid shots three and four.

Flynn's wings catch fire and he screams. Flames spread to his jeans, lick up his arms and chest then consume him. Tears cloud my vision. I press my hands to my ears. It doesn't help. His painful shrieks are unbearable. I choke back my sob, teetering on the edge of hysteria. *There has to be another way. Freak or not, I can't burn another creature alive.*

Lucy, hold it together! Dylan's voice commands in my head. *We need you right now!*

Ronan fists his hands as his friend, now silent, continues to burn. "Why can't you both just die?" He springs at Dylan, swinging hard. He rakes his claws across Dylan's face then slams his fist against Dylan's jaw. Dylan teeters backward. Ronan bares his fangs. As he angles for Dylan's throat, Dylan grabs his head with both hands. The force of the headbutt rings out with a dull crack and sends Ronan reeling. Dylan moves swiftly, jerking the gargoyle's head sharply to the left. Ronan drops to the floor.

The collision of a body crashing into wood makes Dylan and me whirl around. The force of Marcus's landing splits the floorboards beneath him. Garret's raised fist is frozen. As Marcus struggles to regain his breath, two of Garret's men stomp toward him. Their boots connect with his face, chest, and arms.

"Leave him alone!" I shriek. I heave a series of fireballs at the gargoyles as I rush at them. Half of my shots hit their mark, but it doesn't stop them. One of the gargoyles aims his thick work boot at Marcus's stomach. "Don't touch him!" *Too late.*

Marcus curls into a ball, coughing. Blood splatters on the floor in front of his face.

"Roast 'em, Lucy!" Dylan yells as he jumps over Ronan's dead body and runs toward Marcus.

Rage takes over as Garret commands the morphed protectors to continue their attack on Marcus. My entire body twitches and my earlier remorse over Flynn is gone. My entire body is slick with sweat at the energy I expend. I lob more fireballs, closing the distance between me and the monsters. One of the attackers screams as he's engulfed in flames; another leaps around, smacking out flames on his arms.

It's too late when I realize that Garret is no longer standing near his team of thugs. Suddenly, a massive arm hooks me, snatching me off the ground. Garret grips my throat with his clawed hand. As Dylan is about to capture one of Marcus's attackers in a chokehold, another gargoyle approaches from behind and kicks Dylan's legs out from under him. He falls to the ground. The beast drops onto Dylan's chest, anchoring Dylan's arms to the floor with his knees. Dylan bucks against the thug, trying to kick the gargoyle's back and head.

"Enjoy the show, demon!" Garret roars in my ear.

"No!" I grab Garret's fingers, trying to pry them from my throat. His grip tightens. I choke and gasp as his claws dig in further. *He's going to kill me!* Heat races down my arms. A fireball tumbles off my hand and lands on his foot. Garret kicks it away. My feet dangle as he raises me off the floor.

Every time Marcus tries to get up, the gargoyles beat him down.

"He's your son," I rasp. Garret squeezes harder. Stars dance across my vision.

I kick at Garret with both feet as his men pummel Marcus and Dylan. It's like kicking a tree. My shallow, intermittent inhales pick up a sweet floral smell. Marcus's blood. I would recognize it anywhere. My thoughts grow fuzzy.

"Stop!" a female voice cries out.

All commotion in the room halts. Everyone turns to Camille,

who stands just inside the gymnasium entrance, her face a mask of fury. She strides across the room and stops beside Garret. "How dare you attack my son?"

CHAPTER FIFTY-SIX

– Lucy Walker –

"Your loyalties are divided. They won't be, once he's dead." Garret's voice is steel-edged. His grip on my throat loosens just a little while he focuses on Camille.

"Don't you dare threaten my son," she says harshly. Spotting Marcus on the floor, Camille rushes to him.

"Hgggg..." I thrash against Garret's clawed hand.

Garret jerks his attention back to me briefly before he turns to watch Camille. "Shut up!"

Fast as a bullet, I punch his windpipe with my fist.

Garret drops me, doubling over, gasping for breath. "You're... going...to...pay...*demon*."

Beyond Garret, Dylan stabs his fingers into his captor's eyes. The gargoyle screams as he clutches his face and tumbles off of Dylan. Another gargoyle swipes at Dylan. Dylan jams his fingers, so they're laced with his opponent's then snaps the gargoyle's wrist. The Franken-freak rears up in alarm and rage. Dylan kicks him in the groin, and the beast drops to his knees. Dylan hobbles off, but in the wrong direction. Is he looking for Selima?

No! I need him to amplify my powers.

Garret stirs behind me. I gulp air, wheezing. *Need to get away from him.* Lightheaded, I scramble on all fours over to Marcus. There's so much blood. My stomach flip-flops from the overwhelming musky, sweet, floral smell—which I had always assumed was Marcus's cologne. It is the smell of his blood. Marcus groans, uncurling his body.

I stroke his hair. Using the bottom of my shirt, I wipe blood from his cheeks. "I'm here. Camille is, too," I croak.

Garret almost killed me. I shudder. Heat races down my arms to my hands. I yank them away from Marcus, for fear I may accidentally shoot off a fireball.

Marcus's two attackers stand behind him, hanging their heads. Neither will meet Camille's gaze. Why do they cower in her presence?

"They...need...to...be...punished," I rasp at Camille, who kneels on Marcus's other side. Every word I speak burns like hot chards of glass in my throat.

"I will see to that later. Now," Camille orders the gargoyles, "you both will heal my son."

"But the demon blood—" My hoarse voice cuts off with a violent coughing fit.

"It will be fine."

Both gargoyles slide to their knees without so much as a glance at Garret. Why so obedient? Has Camille been leading the clan alongside Garret? The two beasts bite at the skin on their wrists. The dark-haired gargoyle applies blood to the wounds on Marcus's back and wings. The blond presses his wrist to Marcus's mouth. Marcus, who is only semi-conscious, pulls away.

Saliva pools in my mouth as I imagine drinking Marcus's blood on the night of homecoming. My stomach heaves.

"Don't fight it, Marcus," Camille says. "You can't protect anyone in the state you're in, most of all Lucy. You must drink."

I frown. Since when has Camille cared about my safety?

Marcus winces as he reaches for me. Based on his swollen, misshapen fingers, I'm guessing the monsters broke them. I would roast them both if they weren't helping him now.

The blond brute attends to Marcus's face and hands.

"Don't stop until I tell you to," Camille orders the gargoyles. She rises and marches over to her husband.

Rage mixes with desperation in Garret's voice. "All these years...the longing on your face. It's always been him."

"If you ever harm my son again, be prepared to sacrifice Selima." Camille stands as still as her husband. She mimics the clawed curve of his hands, the hunch of his shoulders, though she has no claws and doesn't bear the weight of wings.

Shock and horror register immediately on Garret's face. "She's like a daughter to you."

"If you doubt me, you are a fool."

Garret narrows his eyes, bares his fangs. He grabs Camille roughly, spins her around and pins her arms behind her back.

"Release me, Garret."

She shows no sign of pain or alarm. Instead, she studies the room. Is she taking stock of everyone who came to help kill Marcus? Problem is now that Camille's disabled, she's not going to be much help.

Garret glances at Ronan's dead body and the crispy corpse of Flynn several feet away. He shakes his head in disgust. He looks toward the window and shouts, "Team two!" Then he calls over his shoulder. "Qui! How long does it take to restrain my daughter? Get back in here!"

Dylan squats beside me. He does a double take, his eyes narrowing when he sees my neck.

"Garret did that to you? I'm going to—"

I touch his arm to silence him. *Did you find Selima?* I ask mentally. It hurt too much to speak.

"I did," he says aloud. His lips twitch. "She doesn't need any help."

What do you mean? I ask.

Dylan shakes his head.

Three new gargoyles appear in the glassless windows.

"Uh, Lucy? How many more Franken-fiends do you think are standing by out there?" Dylan asks.

"Don't know." I feel as if my head is spinning. My legs feel wooden. The pain in my throat is agony. Tears fill my eyes. *I can't do this much longer.*

You're no quitter, Lucy. Marcus needs you. Dylan's voice fills my head. He grasps my hand and a surge of energy floods my limbs.

Garret nods his head toward Marcus. The three new gargoyles, baring fangs and claws, spread their wings and fly across the room toward my boyfriend.

"No!" Camille screams.

"Let's take out the newbies," I tell Dylan, pulling my hand

from his. Our brief connection was enough to fuel me. Heat races down my arms, settling in my palms.

He and I both rise. The sound of his heartbeat thunders in my ears. Does he hear mine?

Team two maneuvers around us.

"Bad idea, guys," I say, showing off the fiery beauties cradled in my palms. I draw my hands together and merge the fireballs into one big one. One gargoyle focuses on me while the other two edge toward Marcus.

"Hey, freak!" Dylan says. He steals my earlier move and sucker punches one gargoyle in the windpipe. The creep collapses with a heavy thud, clutching his throat while he gasps and chokes on the floor.

Gargoyle number two lunges to the right, faking me out, and kicks at the gargoyle healing Marcus's hands. I launch a fireball at the attacker. At close range, he's hit square in the chest. He jumps back, slapping his skin, tripping over the gargoyle tending to Marcus's back. I catch the glint of metal and gasp as slippery Franken-freak number three holds a knife over Marcus's prone body.

"A trophy, Sandor!" Garret cheers with sickening glee. "Bring me a trophy!"

Marcus's eyes flutter open. "Save...my...mother. Get out of here!" He coughs, spewing more blood onto the floor. "Leave Garret to me."

Dylan and I eyeball each other. Marcus is too weak and broken to fight his psycho father. We both know that.

A pounding fills my ears and my vision clouds over. I'm going to have to kill Marcus's father. First things first: *I've got Sandor. You take the other one.* I tell Dylan.

He nods.

Sandor spreads one of Marcus's wings, revealing row after row of bent, broken, and bloodied feathers. The gargoyle positions his knife at the base of Marcus's once beautiful appendage. He is going to hack it off.

"Think twice before you harm my son, Sandor," Camille warns.

Sandor hesitates, swallowing.

I close my eyes, allowing the heat, the energy, to course through me. All of Jude's training is paying off—either that or I'm just plain pissed off—and I'm ready for battle in seconds.

"Lucy..." Marcus says softly. "Save yourself."

"That won't be necessary." Selima glides into the room, her white wings tucked against her back. As she steps out of shadow she swipes at the blood dripping from her mouth. I gasp as she proceeds to lick her clawed fingers clean. *Eww...she drank Qui's blood?*

"Told you," Dylan says beside me.

"Selima, what have you done?" Garret bellows, his eyes bulging.

Selima crosses the room so fast she's nearly a blur. She stands before her father, taller than she was just an hour ago. I watch her profile. "What I had to do. I'm not going to let you kill my brother and my friends."

I can't see her fangs, but her lisp gives her away.

"On the count of three, we take out these goons," I whisper to Dylan.

416

Camille cranes her neck to study Garret. "How does it feel, knowing your precious daughter has turned into a monster, like you?"

"Shut up." Garret's murmur turns into a shout as he shakes her. "Shut up! Shut up! Shut up!"

The gargoyles glance from Garret and Camille back to Marcus, uncertain.

"Sandor, Demetrius, if you touch a hair on my son's head, you'll both die," Camille says. Her ruthless tone sends a shudder down my spine.

Marcus narrows his eyes and tilts his head toward Sandor ever so slightly. The knife. I give Marcus a small nod.

"Whose idea was it to start drinking the blood of your own kind, mixing it with demon blood?" Selima asks.

Garret and Camille both stand mute.

So that's what took Selima so long. She was interrogating Qui in the back room?

"You had everyone believing it was Jude—the big baddie— slaughtering protectors and draining them. But it wasn't." She stops pacing, bouncing slightly on her balls of her feet. "All this time I've been spending with Lucy, getting to know her as Camille asked—"

I gasp. Selima was acting as a double agent? *I knew it.*

"Sorry, Lucy." Selima shrugs. "Camille needed to know if you were a threat."

"She's a demon!" Garret hisses. "What more evidence do you need?"

"While I was getting to know Lucy, I spied on Garret and Camille.

Want to know what I discovered?" Selima grins her bloody grin.

Dylan leans close to me. "Damn. The girl I've got the hots for is bat-crap-crazy like her dad."

I grimace. "I hope not. I don't want to have to take her out."

Selima peers over her shoulder at Sandor and Demetrius. "Quiz question, fellas. Twenty points if you get this right. What's the telltale sign that someone's consuming a mix of protector and demon blood?" She raises her eyebrows and scans the room, waiting for someone to speak up. "Sorry, fellas, times up." She thrusts her hands toward Garret and Camille as if they are the grand prize. "You lose your mind!"

Sandor falls from his crouch, his knife clattering to the floor. His laser beam gaze slides from Garret to Camille. "You told us it was safe. That it made us better warriors."

Garret's attempt to stare down Sandor fails.

"And you..." Selima whispers to Camille. "How long have you—a human—been drinking protector blood? Why did you start? Did a sip here and there make you feel less guilty about abandoning Marcus?"

Camille narrows her eyes, but says nothing.

"That's enough, Selima," Garret warns.

Selima swipes at the droplets of blood below her mouth. The red smear gives her a ghoulish appearance. "This new regime sucks. I side with Marcus and Lucy."

Garret's face flushes crimson. He turns to the window. "Team three!"

More monster-fied gargoyles leap through the glassless windows.

Garret points to me. "Kill her!"

I struggle to think of the maneuvers Jude and Henry taught me. The harder I try to think the less I remember. I'm tired and sore in every way possible. But none of that matters because five oversized, angry-faced monsters are coming our way.

Marcus pushes himself up on all fours, gritting his teeth. Dylan and I thrust ourselves in front of him.

Take them out, the voice in my head whispers. *To hell with remorse.* I conjure two fireballs and with leaden arms lob them at the approaching gargoyles. I struggle to produce two more and hurl them, throwing my whole body into the movement. My aim sucks and the gargoyles are almost upon us.

"Lucy, Dylan, duck!"

Dylan and I lunge as five fireballs fly past us in quick succession. Jude barrels across the room, his face flushed and teeth bared. The gargoyles bob and duck the flames, but it stops their pursuit of me. I sigh in relief. My father is here to help.

"Lucy!" Dylan reaches for me, a look of terror on his face, as someone grabs me from behind, dragging me away from him.

Sharp claws clutch my throat, pulling me tight against a hard-bodied gargoyle. Across the room, Garret grins at my capture.

Lower your chin to your chest, now! Dylan yells in my head. *If he crushes your windpipe, you're toast!*

"Touch my daughter and you'll die," Jude warns from twenty feet away. "And trust me, it will hurt."

CHAPTER FIFTY-SEVEN

"Take out the demon leader. I've got the girl," Garret commands as he shoves Camille at a tall, bald gargoyle. "Take her."

Camille thrusts her knee into the gargoyle's groin.

"Oooof!" he doubles over. Before she can run off, the gargoyle grabs her around the knees and hoists her over his shoulder. Camille pounds on his back with little effect.

Garret comes after me while the remaining newcomers circle Jude.

"Dylan, no!" I yell as he thrusts himself between Garret and me.

Garret throws a punch so hard Dylan's cheek crunches. Dylan stumbles, hands over his face. Demetrius tackles Dylan from behind. I whip my hands through the air and Demetrius's legs fly out from beneath him. He crashes to the ground, pulling Dylan with him. The gargoyle howls, clutching his leg, which twists at a sickening angle under the impact of Dylan's weight.

Garret yanks me away from my captor, who joins his team against Jude. I punch Garret's hands away, anything to keep those claws from my throat. He slams me against a wall at the same time he sinks his claws into the flesh between my collarbone and shoulders. A ringing sound fills my ears. My throat burns as I attempt to inhale. Garret shakes me like a rag doll. I twist and shove, but he digs his claws in deeper. I buck up ready to punch the fangy grin off his face when suddenly, my arms dangle limp at my sides, paralyzed.

Can't move!

The world falls away, drained of all color but Garret, standing before me.

He's going to kill me!

I thrash with my hips, attempting to kick him. *Too heavy.* I whimper and collapse against the wall.

"Watch the destruction, little demon." Garret says, puffing his chest out. "Protectors will be victorious tonight."

These killers are not protectors. I want to tell him so, but I don't have the energy.

Over Garret's shoulder, Jude fights seven gargoyles. *Are they multiplying?* A black-haired female lashes out, drawing blood on his cheek. A quick snap of her neck and she's down.

"No!" The bald gargoyle holding Camille drops her on the floor and races to the dead woman.

Camille steals away to Marcus. Dylan climbs to his feet, his face sunken and drooping on one side. Demetrius attempts to follow, but his leg is dead weight and he falls back to the floor.

Dylan arrives at my side. "Let her go!" He delivers a sharp right hook to Garret's face then pummels his torso. Garret digs his claws deeper into my flesh. I cry out.

"I'm coming, Lucy!" Jude hollers. He hurls fireballs in quick succession at the closest gargoyles, with no regard for his own safety. He produces and throws fire so fast; two gargoyles spin away screaming. Another gargoyle bats several fireballs back at Jude.

"Jude!" I cry out as flames lick across his shirt. He lunges backward and rips the shirt from his body. The fiery fabric drifts to the floor.

"Over here. Now!" Garret calls to the bald gargoyle bent over the dead woman on the floor.

The gargoyle jumps to his feet, clenching and unclenching his fists. "Time to waste a demon!" He tackles Dylan, the two of them slamming against the wall beside me. Dylan shakes his head, dazed. The gargoyle glances at the dead woman on the floor. He twitches as her body gets trampled. Dylan shoves baldy and quickly delivers a hammer-fist blow to his jaw right below his ear. The gargoyle crumples to the floor. Dylan returns his attention to me.

Hold my hand, I tell Dylan, trying to hide my alarm at his disfigured face.

Dylan nods tightly, wincing at the movement. His fingers intertwine with mine. The rush is immediate. Energy flows between us.

Garret pulls me close, his teeth brushing my throat. "I've never tasted the blood of a witch."

I bite my lip and fight the urge to close my eyes. No telling what could happen in that second or two. I inhale a shallow breath then quickly struggle for another.

Must raise my hands. Need a fireball.

Even with Dylan feeding my power, my hands are useless. If only I could remove Garret's claws from my flesh.

Instead, I envision my hand clasping Garret's heart. Anything to get his pointy teeth away from my neck.

Squeezing. Squeezing. Squeezing.

Garret freezes. His lips twitch as he grunts.

Dylan grips my hand tighter, and another surge of energy courses through me. My body trembles with the flood of power.

Squeeze. I grit my teeth with the effort. I have never focused this hard before.

Garret's eyes widen in surprise. "*How...dare...you!*" He frantically tugs his hands, but is unable to pull his claws free.

My ears clog and pop, as the pressure in the gym increases. Several people groan. *Did we do that?*

Garret's mouth slackens. He blinks rapidly.

All of a sudden, the remaining windows explode. Shouts and screams fill the room as glass rains down on us.

Focus, Lucy.

"*Puny...demon...witch!*" Garret gasps, spittle hitting my face.

His body trembles with the effort to remain standing. His attempts to pull his hands free are feeble. Lucky for me.

Squeeze.

Garret slumps against me, his eyes wide, frantic. He heaves desperately. Once...twice...then nothing.

With Garret's weight against me, I can't breathe. My knees threaten to give out and I whimper as Dylan pries Garret's claws from my shoulders. The clan leader collapses to the ground.

Biting my lip against the pain radiating through my limbs, I roll my shoulders, flex my arms and hands. They work again. I nudge the clan leader with my foot. He doesn't move. Could he be faking? With a nervous glance at Dylan, I kneel beside Garret, groaning aloud from the pain, and check for a pulse.

"He's dead," I confirm.

I'm alive. Garret's dead and I'm alive. The words replay in my head as I watch Jude battle every gargoyle in the room, except Demetrius and the one treating Marcus under Camille's watchful eye.

"Your wounds look bad." Dylan kneels beside Garret's body, pulling his keys from his pocket. He gouges the dead gargoyle's wrist. "You need gargoyle blood."

"Not his!" But even as I say the words, I know Dylan's right. If I'm going to continue to fight tonight, function at all, I need to heal fast.

A blood-curdling scream rings out. Then another. And another.

A gargoyle freezes mid punch then—*poof!*—turns to dust and rains on the floor.

What the...?

The room goes dark.

"Lucy!" Jude calls out.

"Over here," I respond, not yet able to push myself off the floor.

"Dylan with you?" he calls back.

"I'm with her," Dylan responds.

"Marcus!" I yell into the darkness.

"I've got him," Camille calls back. "Can you fix the lights?"

What's going on? I had assumed another round of gargoyles had joined the battle while I was focused on Garret, but I don't hear the clomping of boots storming along the wooden floors or the other sounds of attack.

The lights return, but someone is messing with the electricity. A strobe light effect bursts into the inky blackness. Images of gargoyles, stiff and waxen, appear in spastic clips around us. Their expressions range from anger, pain, to fear.

I close my eyes. *Need this nightmare to end.*

"Stay with me," Dylan says.

"That hurts!" I open my eyes wide and gasp as Dylan applies protector blood to my wounds. Garret's blood doesn't smell as sweet as Marcus's. The pain lessens just a little.

I grab hold of Dylan's arm and tug, trying very hard not to freak out over the strobing lights and the periodic screams that echo through the gymnasium. "I don't understand what's happening. You have to help me get to Marcus." Tears burn my eyes as I stumble beside him.

Through the blinking lights, Jude makes his way toward the windows. A loud pop rings out and a gargoyle near him turns to dust. My father brushes gargoyle residue from his shoulder in flashes.

"Jude! Did you do that?" I ask once Dylan and I reach Marcus.

"No," he says. "But I know who did."

Pop!

Ronan's body abruptly turns to dust. Someone's killing off all the morphed protectors. "Jude! Make this stop. Marcus was treated with their blood. Please!"

"Go find Selima," I tell Dylan as I crouch beside Marcus.

Pop! Pop!

Two more gargoyles sprinkle the floor.

Camille kneels beside Marcus, guarding him. "No...no...no!"

Another petrified gargoyle goes poof and rains on the floor.

"Make it stop!" Camille cries out. "He didn't do anything wrong! Don't let them take my son!"

"What are you doing here?" Jude roars.

That's when I notice *him.*

A white-haired man in black clothes stands in the frame of a smashed-out window. He flicks and twitches his fingers and one of the gargoyles near Jude herky-jerks in midair like a crazy breakdancing marionette. The man snaps his fingers. A loud pop rings out and the gargoyle turns to dust.

"That takes care of him," the man says. His speech is crisp, refined. He steps from the window, landing on the gym floor. "This is chaos. You should've killed their leader long ago. Instead he nearly killed my namesake who, by the way, did your job for you."

"I had everything under control until you showed up." Jude waves his hands through the air and the strobe light effect stops. He snaps his fingers and half the lights—those that aren't smashed—turn on. "How dare you show up here unbeckoned?"

"How dare I?" the man asks, his voice razor sharp. "You would do well to remember your place, Jude."

After a pause, Jude kneels, bowing his head. "Please forgive me. I am here to serve you."

My entire body trembles as the white-haired man walks past Jude and approaches me. *Will he kill Marcus? Me?*

Mimicking Camille, I lay my hands on Marcus protectively. Marcus peers up at the man through swollen lids.

"I will spare him for you," he says to me.

"Selima and Camille, too. Please," I say. Garret's blood is not only helping to heal my wounds, my injured throat feels less inflamed.

"Very well." His eyes appear blacker than Jude's.

"Are you—?

The man nods.

"I'm sorry for summoning you. I was trying to save my father...Sir." There's so much I want to ask, but I'm too tired and I hurt and it's impossible to put my thoughts together in any cohesive manner. "Please don't hurt Jude."

He nods again. Lucifer studies me for a long moment before he returns to Jude. My father rises. I return my attention to Marcus.

My stomach heaves at the sight of Marcus's right wing, broken and charred in parts. The skin on his back and shoulder is covered in raw, open wounds.

He eyeballs my face, my shoulders, and my neck. "Did Garret hurt you?"

"I'll be fine," I rasp. I do my best to keep the shock at his wounds off my face.

Selima appears beside us and drops to her knees, about to gash her wrist for Marcus to drink. Then she hesitates, looking from me to Camille. "I drank Qui's blood. I don't know what that will do to Marcus."

Selima peers around the room, taking an inventory. Her eyes fill with tears when they land on Garret.

I reach for her. "I'm sorry. He tried to kill me."

She buries her face in her hands. "I can't believe he turned into such a monster," she sobs.

"Use Demetrius," Camille tugs the limping gargoyle behind her. "He's always been loyal to me."

"But..." Demetrius cranes his neck and stares uneasily at the body of his fallen chief.

"Marcus is Garret's son. He's next in line to run the clan." Camille's posture is erect, her head held high as she kneels beside Marcus. "Heal him."

"As Garret's *oldest* child, I'm ordering you," Selima says to Demetrius.

Camille arches one eyebrow. She clearly has more to say, but holds back for now. Camille helped Garret run the clan. That much is obvious. Is she—a human—allowed to rule now that he's gone? Would she be stealing a position that rightfully belongs to Selima or Marcus?

Demetrius rips the skin at his wrist and dribbles blood over the wounds on Marcus's back. Marcus flinches, but doesn't complain.

"We need to get him out of here," Dylan announces. "The sun's going to rise soon. The janitors get here early."

"Take Marcus to the condo." Camille tosses her keys to Dylan. "I'll see you there soon," she says, touching Marcus's cheek before leaving us for Garret. She sits beside her dead husband, resting his head on her lap.

"Camille, we have to go. All of us," I tell her gently.

"Leave us," she orders.

Dylan whistles low. Selima stares open-mouthed around the gym, tears trailing down her cheeks. That's when I notice the room. All twelve windows have been restored. The piles of dust are gone. The wooden floors look like new. No more dead bodies, except for Garret's.

"Jude?" I search the room, blinking in shock as I take it all in. "Where did they go?" I ask Dylan.

"Don't know." Dylan shrugs.

Selima climbs to her feet, wiping her cheeks. "Let's get out of here."

I have a feeling Selima won't be spending her nights reading books at St. Aquinas anymore.

I touch Marcus's cheek. "We're going to move you now. I'm sorry, but this is going to hurt."

"Let me get him." Dylan gently shoves me aside and flips Marcus over his shoulders in a fireman's carry. Marcus sucks air sharply between his teeth and swears.

"Camille," Selima calls out.

"Let us be," Camille responds without turning around.

I lead the way out of St. Aquinas. Will Camille be gone by the time the janitors show up? She's not strong enough to carry Garret's body out of here by herself. Are there other protectors in the area who can help her?

Aiden meets us in the parking lot.

"How'd you know we were here?" I ask.

Aiden looks around. "Did he arrive?"

"He? Who?" As soon as the words are out of my mouth, I know who he's referring to. My exhausted brain is operating at a slower than normal speed. "How did you know?"

Aiden's dark gaze looks past me to Marcus. "Put Marcus in my SUV. Are we taking him to Jude's?"

"Garret and Camille's condo," Selima says. "You and Lucy can follow Dylan and me."

Aiden strokes Marcus's hair, his eyes taking in Marcus's many wounds. "You're going to be okay, little brother. I promise."

Chapter Fifty-Eight

– Camille –

I stroke Garret's face. My fingers linger along his brow, trace his broad cheekbone, then trail his powerful jaw. I have loved this man forever. This beautiful, strong, confident man.

"We were supposed to do this together," I whisper. My legs prickle with sleep, so I readjust, careful not to jostle him. "We were going to create a new race of protectors. We were going to be invincible."

Garret's body temperature grows cool. *He's gone.*

"Marcus would've come around. I'm his mother. In time, he will do what I say. And we finally found Grayson's heir." I still can't believe my good luck. "I told you patience was the answer."

I glare at the dead man in my lap. "Why did you have to go and screw this up?"

Hurried steps disrupt my grief.

"We need to go. People are going to show up soon. What do you want to do about his blood?"

"We're certainly not going to waste it. Do you have your tools?"

Max nods. He slides the backpack from his shoulder and kneels beside me. He rolls out a towel and lines up a series of tubes and needles.

"Who was that gray-haired man?" I ask.

Max focuses on the needles and tubes. "Lucifer. Maybe he came at Jude's request?"

"Jude didn't look happy to see him."

"Dunno."

Could Lucy have called upon the leader of the underworld? Am I underestimating her powers? "He seems fond of Lucy." *I need to get rid of her if I have any hope of convincing Marcus to join the clan.* "If she were in peril, do you think Lucifer would take her back with him?"

Max glances at me uneasily. "I would be careful if I were you."

I grip his jaw and force him to look at me. "I pay you a lot of money, demon, so listen closely. Lucy's life is in danger. And you," I dig my nails into his skin, "will be the voice in Lucifer's ear, convincing him to take the girl away."

Max's eyes widen. "Why would he listen to me?"

"If you can't then you will be charged with killing her." I smile at the lowly demon and am rewarded by the flicker of fear in his eyes. "If you fail me, I will personally see that Lucifer, Jude, Marcus, Aiden...*everyone* knows how you've double-crossed them."

I release Max and with a grunt, I roll Garret onto his stomach. While the front of his body is sickly pale in death, his backside is splotched with deep purple bruises.

I carefully pull a large shard of glass from my husband's back.

The wound is horrific and lovely. Max can wait a few minutes to drain Garret. I draw my hair back in a makeshift ponytail with one hand, lean over, and claim what is mine. The taste is familiar and sweet, like cotton candy and peonies after first bloom. My ears fill with the sound of fast-moving rapids. I lap the blood slowly, tenaciously, then faster, needing more. My hair falls in a veil around my face as I grab hold of Garret with both hands.

My great love is gone, but I have the clan. Always the clan. Need to tie up one loose end. Make that two.

CHAPTER FIFTY-NINE

– Lucy Walker –

"I'm not going to drink," Marcus moans. His cheek is pressed against the tabletop in Camille and Garret's kitchen. The open wounds on Marcus's back make me teeter.

"Please, Marcus." Selima rips open the flesh of her wrist and offers her blood to Marcus. He shoves her away weakly. Dylan and Demetrius brace Marcus by the head and shoulders, forcing him to remain still.

"Marcus." Aiden squats beside the table to make eye contact. "You're one of the three people left in the world who knows my secret."

He touches Marcus's hair gently. It's the second gesture of tenderness I've seen from Aiden, and both of them have been for Marcus. "The burns on your back are serious. We can't take you to a hospital. Between the wounds and your damaged wings, it's not possible to retract them. The cuts could scar, get infected. Leave you maimed. Let them heal you, please."

"No," Marcus says.

Aiden yanks his shirt over his head. He turns around, but not

434

before I see the web of angry scars decorating his back. Dylan and I exchange a look of shock and horror. What happened to him?

"Do you want to wind up like me? An amputee?" The pain in Aiden's voice causes my throat to close. Aiden the demon is also Aiden the protector? Or ex-protector?

"I don't want to go crazy like them," Marcus says roughly.

"Garret and Camille have been using for a long time." Selima presses her hand over the wound in her wrist, so she won't waste her blood. The dark circles under her eyes make me question whether she should be donating her blood.

"Garret much more so than Camille," Demetrius admits, hanging his head.

"The ritual of drinking the blood of a protector is for situations like this, for dire injuries. It wasn't meant to be used like a street drug," Selima says bitterly. "Demon blood...that's a whole other issue."

Demetrius stares at the floor.

I approach the head of the table. Aiden removes his hand and steps back to make room for me. "Let her heal you, Marcus, please," I say.

"She drank Qui's blood," Marcus hisses.

"I love you," I say as I gently stroke his undamaged cheek. "I need you. Let someone else take away your pain for a change."

Marcus sighs. He lifts his head an inch. "Dylan?"

"Right here." Dylan kneels down so he and Marcus are at eye level.

"Promise me," Marcus says.

"Anything," Dylan says.

"If I turn into one of those monsters or a junkie—the first sign of it—take me out."

I gasp. "Marcus, you don't know—"

Aiden grips my arm. I swallow the rest of my protest.

"Promise me!"

"I promise. Happily," Dylan says grimly.

Every muscle in Marcus's body visibly relaxes. "I'll drink, but only Selima's."

Selima releases her hand from the gash, which has already begun to heal. She tears the skin again and immediately places her wrist against Marcus's mouth. She sways just a little.

I touch her arm. "You've given enough."

Selima stares me down until I back away. "Now." She nods at Demetrius to begin round two. He gashes his other wrist and applies more blood to Marcus's wounds.

I bite my cheek until I taste copper, holding back my revulsion for Marcus's sake. The sweet smell of the blood makes my stomach recoil. Selima and Demetrius's blood smells similar to Marcus's. Similar but not the same.

I startle, pain radiating up my arm. I glance at the red welt forming, where Dylan just pinched me. Hard.

"Hold it together," he whispers. "Do it for him."

CHAPTER SIXTY

– Lucy Walker –

I press my face to Marcus's chest, my arms wrapped around him. Our legs are intertwined as we lay on my bed in the near darkness. The glow of a street light filters in through my windows. It's been three days since the battle at St. Aquinas, and Marcus is finally able to lie on his back. I have my soul mate all to myself. I feel as happy as a cat as he strokes my hair.

"He's really gone?" Marcus asks.

My feelings of bliss are immediately squashed by guilt. *Jude.*

"Dylan and I searched his house. Aiden, too. Jude's car is in the driveway, but he's nowhere to be found. He's not answering his cell, either."

My father *always* answered my calls. "Garret's dead. Lucifer shouldn't have taken Jude."

Marcus's body tenses. I'm about to ask him if he's in pain, but restrain myself. I don't want to get the stink eye from him again.

"Do you think Jude hates me, wherever he is?" I ask. "For conjuring Lucifer?"

"Garret's team of junkie protectors were going to kill him."

437

Marcus tucks a lock of hair behind my ear. "You saved him. And as far as what's-his-face, let's not address him by name."

I chuckle uneasily. "Why not?"

Marcus clears his throat. "We assume he's in hell with Jude, but we have no way of knowing. Just in case, I don't want him to think you're beckoning him."

"I can't believe Aiden performed a second conjuring with Max and Warrick."

"They were only trying to help," Marcus says.

"I know." I peek up at him. "What happens now with Camille?"

He sighs. "She has to answer to a higher authority. She can't rule the clan as a human, and they know about the blood drinking. Laws were broken."

I prop myself up on my elbow. "I spoke with Selima yesterday. She said Camille's in custody."

Marcus hesitates then nods; his expression pinched.

"What is it?" I ask, touching his arm.

He shrugs. "I can't help but wonder what life would've been like if Garret hadn't been driven crazy by his habit, if Camille hadn't been an addict." He glances at me then away. "Maybe I would've joined the clan—been part of something. Or maybe not."

I killed Garret. He left out that part. Would life with the clan been better for Marcus? He could've surrounded himself with people who understand and accept him. He could've finally dispelled his belief that he's a freak. He could've had a family.

I can't bear his pained expression any longer. "It's not like you're barred from the clan. Selima's talking to other protectors, trying to get a sense of things." I snuggle against his chest to hide my worry.

Marcus sighs as he slides out from beneath me. "I have to go."

It would be so easy to spend the night together, with my uncles out of town. But my boyfriend needs his time on the roof. Now more than ever.

After Marcus leaves, I slide under the covers and curl up in a ball. My brave face sags. For the past three days, my thoughts have been filled with snapshots of Garret's face as I squeezed the life out of him. Flynn's screams still haunt my dreams. And Jude is being held somewhere against his will. I'm responsible for all of it.

CHAPTER SIXTY-ONE

– Lucy Walker –

"Was it the right thing to do?" I ask, my voice barely more than a whisper. I run my fingers over the rough texture of Marcus's wing as the moonlight casts shadows over his stone form. We sit on the roof of the apartment building.

"Lucifer saved Jude. And you." Aiden's voice is equally quiet. "According to Selima, there were two dozen more gargoyles outside the school, ready to fight."

I shudder as I consider what might have been, and I wrap my hoodie tight around my body. The buzzing chorus of cicadas fills the night air. I scoot closer to Marcus and feel the cool of his stone form seep into me.

"Demetrius called today," Aiden says. "The counsel wants to meet with Marcus."

It's happening.

Aiden raises his gaze to mine. "Marcus has good instincts. He's got good people like Persephone and Henry to help advise him."

Marcus is going to leave me.

"And you," I tell him, averting my gaze as my heart threatens to break.

"Selima will be with him, if he decides to go."

It's Marcus's chance to be among others like him, to learn the ways of protectors. "He needs to go." I force the words from my burning throat.

Aiden nods. "He needs to hear that from you."

What will my life be like without Marcus? The thought is too painful, so I push it away. I have to do what's right for Marcus.

A breeze passes over us, raising goose bumps on my skin. Aiden's brow furrows, his eyes darting as if he's searching for someone.

"Is there something you're not telling me?"

"I don't think he's gone."

This isn't about Marcus. I lean forward. "But you said..."

"Jude would never leave you. Ever," Aiden says. "The only way Lucifer was going to get him below ground was to personally escort him. But..."

"But what?"

"Everything's felt different since he arrived that night."

"It still feels different?" I ask.

Slowly, Aiden nods.

I really don't like the look of apprehension on his face. "Is Marcus in danger now that Lucifer's here? Am I?"

"Lucifer won't harm you," Aiden says. "You're his namesake, which is the equivalent of his being your godfather, but on steroids. Demons take it very seriously."

What about my uncles? My friends? Marcus?

"Lucifer is known to be possessive." Aiden pauses, deep lines creasing his forehead. "Jude wasn't keen on sharing you, but this will be worse."

What does that mean for the people I love? Will they be in danger?

I tuck my trembling hands into my sweatshirt pockets. "When we conjured him, you said we had to leave the door to the other dimension open in order to send him back. Let's send him back. Now."

Aiden gives a small shake of his head. "He tricked us. Lucifer knew the timeline, and he intentionally blew it." His lips pull into a humorless smile. "It's been a long time since he's tasted freedom. Now he's got you. He has a successor with Jude—albeit an unwilling one. There's no way he's going back."

The longer Aiden goes on, the more I worry. We just overcame a massive battle. Thanks to Lucifer, we survived. What will that victory cost? "You know a lot about him."

It takes a long time for Aiden to respond. When he does, his expression and his shoulders sag. "I should. He's my grandfather."

CHAPTER SIXTY-TWO

– Lucy Walker –

"Welcome home!" We all cry in unison as my uncles walk through the front door.

I throw my arms around Sheldon and Bernard, laughing at their surprised expressions.

"We've missed you, Luce," Bernard says, planting a kiss on my cheek.

"Wait 'til you see the souvenirs we brought for you," Sheldon adds excitedly.

"She definitely deserves them after helping Persephone," Henry says with a smile. His eyes are void of their normal twinkle.

"Why don't you boys unload the limo," Persephone instructs Marcus and Dylan while she delivers glasses of wine to my uncles.

"No problems while we were gone?" Sheldon asks, surveying the living room. *Does he think I threw a party?*

"Everything's fine." Persephone waves him off. "Lucy gets an A plus for her hard work while you were gone. My projects are caught up, she stayed on top of her homework, *and* her job with the Douglas kids."

And I killed Marcus's father. Not only did I lose Jude in the process, but I might lose my boyfriend, too.

Henry's eyes land on me and narrow. I force a big smile and he relaxes. I'll have to be more careful with my thoughts, since apparently I wear them on my face.

Sheldon wraps his arm around my shoulder and squeezes. "I'm proud of you. You truly are like your Gram."

"Not that we doubted you," Bernard adds with a wink.

My smile falters. How would they react if they knew what really went down in their absence?

Henry holds the door for Aiden who's carrying three large, delicious-smelling pizzas.

My stomach growls.

"What did we miss?" Bernard asks as Marcus and Dylan deliver their luggage and shopping bags next to the couch.

I take a deep breath and force another smile. "Marcus has a sister. She couldn't be here today, but you'll meet her soon. She's great."

Sheldon nods at Marcus. "If she's anything like your mother, I'm sure she's delightful."

"Camille is her stepmother," Marcus clarifies stiffly.

Dylan flashes his pearly whites. "Selima's pretty awesome."

"Hmmm," Sheldon elbows Bernard, his eyebrows bouncing. "Seems we missed plenty."

"Pizza's getting cold," Aiden calls from the kitchen.

As I dole out pizza and napkins and refill wine glasses, Marcus smirks. "You can't help mothering people."

"I don't mind," Dylan says with a mouthful. "Especially if she gets me a Coke."

I deliver sodas to Dylan and Marcus, popping one open for myself. Doesn't Marcus understand? Growing up I had to mother Momma. Now it's what I do with the people I love. Plus, the busier I stay, the less my mind can dwell on the horrors that occurred at St. Aquinas.

My uncles entertain us with stories of sunbathing iguanas, Capuchin monkeys, visits to volcanoes, white-sand beaches, and their quest to spot as many different birds as possible.

Aiden glances at Marcus at least every five minutes. Seems I'm not the only mother hen in the group.

Dylan pulls his phone from his pocket when he thinks no one is looking.

"She'll call you when she gets home," Marcus tells him for the third time.

Dylan puts his phone away. "I wanted to help move her from the dorm."

Selima turned out to be good after all.

"Seems we're both cursed with stubborn, independent girls," Marcus tells him.

A wave of jealousy washes over me. Will Dylan hang out with Selima and forget about me? Is this the end of our friendship?

Marcus lifts my chin until our eyes meet. Setting his plate on the table, he takes hold of my hand and tugs me close. "I love you. Everything's going to be okay."

His touch calms me, and for the moment, I almost believe him. "I love you, too."

"I'd like to make a toast," Bernard announces, dabbing at his eyes. "You're all very special to Sheldon and me. You're more than neighbors. More than friends even. We're grateful that you helped take care of Lucy and the three-flat while we were gone."

"Doesn't sound like much of a toast to me," Aiden teases.

"What he's trying to say is...you're more like family," Sheldon says.

"Here! Here!" the group cheers in unison as we clank glasses and pop cans.

My heart swells so big it actually hurts. When I was nursing Momma with a hangover in the trailer park, feeling alone and unhappy, I would never have guessed I could feel so loved. Now that I have everything I want, who's going to come and try to take it away?

You know who, the little voice in my head says. Garret's gone, but Seamus is still out there. And what about Marcus? Will he stay or will he go? I shiver, my body breaking out in a cold sweat. I close my eyes, feeling lightheaded, and teeter against Marcus.

"What's wrong? You're pale," he murmurs in my ear.

I grasp his hand. "Nothing. Don't let go."

He brushes his lips against my hair. "I've got you. Always."

– THE END –

To All My Reader Friends

I hope you enjoyed reading *The Girl and the Gargoyle*. I received so many comments from readers of *The Girl and the Raven*, asking what's next for Lucy, Marcus, and Dylan. I'm so excited to give you the second installment in the series.

Do you want to share the love? The best way to help other readers find this book is to leave a review. Please consider leaving your feedback at the place you purchased the book as well as at Goodreads.com and BookLikes.com.

I love to hear from readers. Visit me through my website: paulinegruber.com, where you can connect with me through Facebook, Twitter, Instagram, Pinterest, and Tumblr.

Thank you for reading *The Girl and the Gargoyle*.

Want to know the latest?

About book releases, book signings, contests, and general updates? Sign up for my author newsletter here: http://bit.ly/1mNbrJe

Book One: The Girl and the Raven

Haven't read *The Girl and the Raven*? Available now in print and digital editions from your favorite online retailers.

Book Three: The Girl and the Demon

Lucy, Marcus, and Dylan's story continues. Available now in print and digital editions from your favorite online retailers.

ACKNOWLEDGMENTS

My sincere gratitude to the following:

Dennis – For your unwavering support and for being my rock.

Dale – The greatest sister ever. Thank you for always being there for me and loving Lucy, Marcus, and Dylan as much as I do.

Lynn Johnston – In addition to being a fantastic development and content editor, you're a profound mentor and human being. Thank you.

Andrea Dickinson – Thank you for being a great copy editor. It's such a pleasure to work with you.

Kayle Allen – I couldn't ask for a better critique partner. You understand the voices and personalities of my characters, and you know just the right amount of trouble to heap on them. Thank you.

Chuck, Phil, Royelle, and the rest of my Katten family for your support.

To my incredible team of beta readers: Royelle Kashiwahara, Marissa Gracia Friese, Lisa Whalen, Bonnie Gill, and Nicole Floress—thank you from the bottom of my heart. You are amazing!!!

A special thank you to the winners of the Facebook Character Naming Contest:

I'm very excited to list the winners of the Facebook name contest. Originally, I was looking for help naming two new supernatural male characters for the sequel to *The Girl and the Raven*. However, there were so many fantastic suggestions that I took FIVE names for *The Girl and the Gargoyle*. Thank you so much to everyone who participated. The winning names are as follows:

- **Flynn**, a gargoyle (suggested by Gerald Kelel)
- **Grayson**, ex-clan leader of the protectors/gargoyles (deceased) (suggested by Mary Miller-Rademaker, Pam Noles, and Peggy Burt)
- **Ronan**, a gargoyle (suggested by Angela Neff)
- **Warrick**, a demon (suggested by Nick Parrish)
- **Zeke**, a demon (suggested by both Colette Cocokios and Amanda Lynn Matheson) ***During final revisions, Zeke's name was changed to Max. A couple of my beta readers found the similarity between Zeke and Uncle Zack confusing. I still love the name and hope it use "Zeke" in a future series.

Enjoy an excerpt from Book Three

THE GIRL
AND THE
DEMON

PAULINE GRUBER

DRAGONFLY INK, LTD.

CHAPTER ONE

– Lucy Walker –

I stop abruptly once inside St. Aquinas High School's cafeteria. It's so different. The makeover had nothing to do with fireballs or gargoyles. The huge space had been repainted over the summer. One wall features a large mural depicting teenagers of every race. Missing from the group are gargoyles, demons, and witches. Another wall features a massive Wildcat, the school mascot, with daggerlike teeth and razor-sharp claws. So much like Marcus's father, Garret, after he morphed that night he tried to kill me.

"Hi junior," Katie Stevens teases as she grabs my arm. Her smile immediately fades. "Hey, what's wrong? You look like you're going to puke."

I swallow the lump of fear in my throat. *Garret is dead. He can't hurt me now.*

"First day jitters." I suppress a shiver and pull my best friend into a tight hug.

Katie's tan skin glows against the white button-down shirt of her uniform after two months in Fort Myers, Florida. Her white-blond hair looks nearly radioactive from days of sunning on the beach.

In a student body of approximately one thousand four hundred students, we arrive for the second of four lunch periods. Throngs of students shove past us, their conversations so loud that I have to yell for Katie to hear me.

"I don't care that we texted and talked all the time, I missed you like crazy," I say, squeezing closer to her to avoid sharp elbows and pushing bodies.

"I missed *you* like crazy," Katie says. "There's no way I'm going to let my dad keep me until the day before school starts next summer."

I feign grumpiness. "I *told* you—"

"I know you did!" Katie exclaims, her deep ocean blue eyes wide. "But—"

"You were too busy spending those couple of weeks after school ended—"

"With Trevor," Katie says with a grin.

"With Trevor," I say at the exact same moment.

My best friend's expression turns serious. "Things seemed pretty intense between you and Marcus. I really didn't think you noticed."

That's an understatement for what happened when Marcus's father showed up in Chicago. Violent chaos is a more accurate description of what went down in St. Aquinas's gymnasium before sophomore year ended. I killed Marcus's father after he tried to kill me, my father, and Marcus. His thugs tried to take out Dylan. When school ended, Marcus, Dylan, and I were still

454

reeling from it all. But Katie is not part of that world. She has no powers. I can't ever tell her monsters are real. For her own safety I need to keep her as far away from my supernatural life as possible.

"Drama with Marcus's family," I say with a heavy sigh. "Were your dad and stepmom sad when you left?"

"For the first time...yes." Katie laughs. "If I knew getting a part-time job during my stay would make them miss me so much, I would've done it last year. They were actually teary-eyed at the airport. That hasn't happened since I was twelve."

"Katie Stevens, an official member of the workforce? It's about time, slacker," Suzy Rodriguez announces, squeezing out of a horde of students entering the lunchroom. "Thanks for waiting for me." She raises her face and takes an exaggerated sniff at the air. "Sweet, tangy barbeque... I bet they're serving pulled pork sandwiches. One of my favorites. Cloe's too."

Katie and I both hug Suzy.

"Not all of us are lucky enough to have a family that owns a chain of super popular resale clothing stores. Talk about guaranteed employment," Katie playfully complains, tugging on Suzy's long dark brown hair.

Suzy's mom and two of her aunts opened their first store ten years ago and the family is in the process of opening a third location before Christmas. Suzy has promised to put in a good word if one of us wants a job, but I love the kids I nanny too much to leave them.

"Between the stores, creating my art, and running my music blog, I've been working for years," Suzy says with an air of authority. "I'm a pro with art and business. You, on the other hand, are an amateur."

Katie laughs. "I'll have a job for the rest of my life. So what if I wanted one more year of freedom?"

"We're seventeen," Suzy says to Katie and me with a glimmer in her eyes, "and upperclassman." She surveys the lunchroom. Tables are filling up fast as more students bustle around us. Lunch trays clatter onto tables. The buzz of conversation is nearly deafening. "Have you seen anyone else yet?"

"No. We just got here," I tell her.

"Ella and Caroline are there, in the upperclassman section. You can't miss Ella's hair. It's like a burst of flames in the sea of people," Suzy says.

I follow the point of her finger, but don't see them through the crowd. Honestly, I don't try too hard. While I have adjusted to the massive size of St. Aquinas College Prep and the overabundance of homework, my stomach hurts at the notion of having to see Ella every day. "Should we place bets on how long it will take before Ella makes fun of my accent?" I ask bitterly.

Since I moved from Lexington, Tennessee to Chicago and joined Katie's circle of friends the summer before our sophomore year, Ella has taken cruel pleasure in trying to tear me down and make sure I understand the hierarchy of our group. According to her, I sit at the lowest rung.

Katie grimaces. "She's just jealous. Look on the bright side. It's a new year and she had a fun summer. I bet she will be nicer to you."

"You're far cooler than she is. Have you seen her music

collection?" Suzy asks, mimicking a gag. She squints across the room. "Cloe's there now, too."

Katie nudges me. "Let's go get food. I'm starving."

One of the reasons Katie and I hit it off so well is our mutual love of food. We're both always hungry. Her mom jokes that we each have a tapeworm.

"When are you going to come over so we can make lasagna and enchiladas for my mom and Jerry?" Katie says as we join the line with lunch trays in hand. "It was your idea to start cooking for them. Now they keep asking."

I am determined to learn how to cook two of the dishes my father used to make for me. Once he returns home, I plan to surprise him by cooking for him.

"Weekday evenings. We can knock out homework first. Or maybe Saturday nights after I get home from nannying for Mr. and Mrs. Douglas."

"Why not Sundays?" Katie asks. "I thought that would be the best day since you're off of work."

Katie has no idea about my witch lessons and demon training.

"My dad hasn't come home yet. I'm still checking on his place on Sundays." My voice falters on that last part. I know what's coming next.

"When are you going to invite me to go with you? I've always wanted to see your dad's mansion," Katie asks as she hands her student ID card to the woman at the register to scan and pay for her lunch.

Sure, come over. Don't mind the demon that may or may not be hanging around, eager to kill me. Pass.

"My dad has strict rules about no friends at his house," I tell her.

"Does that rule apply to Marcus, too?" Katie asks with mock innocence.

The truth is that both Marcus and Dylan Douglas join me at Jude's. Dylan for our joint demon training. Marcus for company and protection while I check to see if Jude has returned or if Seamus McAllister, the aforementioned demon who wants to kill me, is lurking.

At the upperclassman table, I sit beside Katie and as far away from Ella as I can get. I'd rather deal with Katie's sulk over the no invite to my dad's house than Ella.

"It's time to schedule our first social event of the year. Who's up for a séance?" Ella asks, less a question and more of a command to us, her less significant underlings. Leave it to Ella to come up with something dangerous on our first day of school.

Caroline Appleberg grins, revealing her perfect, toothpaste commercial worthy teeth. "The night of your slumber party? Sounds spooky and fun!"

"Maybe we can call on Jim Morrison or Kurt Cobain," Ella says to Suzy. She winks one reptilian blue-green eye.

"Cool!" Suzy and Katie say in unison.

"How about modern-day rock stars?" Caroline mocks playfully, smoothing her silky blond hair with her hand.

Cloe Gardner fixes her deep brown eyes on Ella, her fingers still typing away on whatever game she plays on her phone. "My grandmother says messing with spirits is not a good idea. Something about bad juju."

"Old people have no sense of adventure," Ella scoffs. "I've been reading up on it. I know exactly what to do."

Since when did Miss Makeover become a séance expert? More likely she will manage just enough to cause trouble. Losing my father to a summoned demon last year makes me wonder what kind of unfriendly spirits Ella could accidentally conjure up.

I realize too late that I groaned aloud.

Ella narrows her eyes at me. "Wait... Are you *afraid*, Lucy?"

Such a witch!

I meet her gaze head on. "Nope. Cloe's grandmother happens to be right. It's a bad idea."

Katie's gaze moves from Ella to me, her brows scrunched nervously.

Ella grins, narrows her eyes at me. "So, don't come. The rest of us are going to have a great time."

"It's reckless, Ella. Have a sleepover. Watch movies. Have a dance party or group pedicures. Crank call the football team. But skip the séance. *Please*," I say.

Ella arches a sharp eyebrow at me. "I did a lot to prepare for this. My plans are set. When did you turn into a nervous old woman?"

She and Caroline chuckle.

"Her hillbilly accent is as annoying as ever," Ella whispers to Caroline, not trying all that hard to keep her voice down.

At least Caroline doesn't laugh this time.

"Give it a rest, Ella," Katie snaps.

Caroline claps her hands together, grinning like an over-energized cheerleader. "How was everyone's summer? Come on, we've barely seen each other since sophomore year let out. It's time to catch up."

"I spent most of the summer at the beach," Ella says, an edge to her voice. Is she feeling stung that Katie stood up to her for one of the first times ever?

Everyone else takes turns sharing the highlights of their break. Caroline is sort of dating Dylan's football teammate, Chad. Cloe worked as a counselor at a science camp for kids and is still dating Darick. Suzy juggled her job, her art, her music blog, and time with her boyfriend, Shawn. Katie shared the highlights of her summer in Fort Myers.

"What about you, Lucy?" Cloe asks, pulling her eyes from the screen of her phone.

"Worked, mostly, and hung out with Marcus," I say, focusing on my lunch, *and coping with the emotional fallout of murdering his father.*

CHAPTER TWO

– Lucy Walker –

As the final bell rings on my first day of school, I zigzag my way through the halls, rushing as much as I am able to through the packed crowd. My breath catches at the sight of him. Marcus stands a head taller than most of the students at St. Aquinas, not that he attends my school. Marcus is a senior at St. Patrick's, an all-male college preparatory Catholic high school. He has already changed into blue jeans, a white T-shirt, and a gray and green button-down shirt, which is untucked. His messy chestnut-colored hair begs for my fingers to sink into its thick mass. Our eyes lock and my pulse quickens in response. The smile that spreads across my face is immediate. My day just got a whole lot better.

"Hey," he says as I reach my locker. It would be impossible for anyone without proper school identification to get through St. Aquinas's security, but friendship and favors gained Marcus a permanent guest pass. Marcus pulls me to him and our lips meet. We've both gotten over our aversion to PDA.

As Marcus's fingers wind through my long, black hair and his calming protector touch soothes me, I no longer care about Ella's crazy slumber party plans or facing another year of her biting criticism.

"You're the best," I say, breathless, as I pull away.

"Ready for our date?"

A date. It sounds romantic. Touring my father's house to see if he's made it home is the exact opposite. We keep looking for Jude, but his car remains untouched in the garage, his computer sits in the exact spot on the desk in his office, and his refrigerator—which Marcus and I cleaned after the last of the food rotted—is only stocked with cans of soda, juice, and some snacks that Marcus and I brought over. Sure, Lucifer helped us with the battle in the school's gymnasium against the gargoyles, but afterward he took my father. Originally, I wanted Lucifer to take Jude, but with Garret out of the picture there was no need for my father to be taken to the underworld for his protection and mine. When will Lucifer release Jude so he can come home? Will the ruler of hell use this as a way to control me?

"Any chance you'll let me drive today?" I ask Marcus as we exit the school building. I don't know why I bothered to get my license. Arnold, the long-time driver for the Douglas family, still picks me up and drops me off from my nanny job caring for Dylan's younger brother and sister. It's apparently for liability purposes. That doesn't bother me since I'm not a huge fan of driving in the city. What does bother me is that I have finally grown to love my car and my boyfriend refuses to sit in it.

Marcus slings my backpack over his shoulder, squinting into the sunlight. "It's as if Jude possesses it. Sorry, but I'm miserable every time I climb into that thing."

Protectors and demons have been enemies since the beginning of time. Whenever Jude was near, it would trigger Marcus to release his wings. The problem was that most of the time Marcus wasn't in any place private and had to fight to suppress the change. It's painful for him to endure.

I take his hand in mine. "Maybe it's psychosomatic."

Marcus twists his mouth thoughtfully. "You think so?"

I give him a wide-eyed look that screams *Duh!* Since the day my demon father gave me the Lexus as a belated sixteenth birthday gift, Marcus has been a giant grump about it. He doesn't understand that if I had refused a gift from Jude, someone in my life would have paid the price. That's how Daddy Demon works.

"You don't have to come with me," I say, hesitantly. "I can move his car and water his plants without you."

"Don't even think about canceling our date," he says. "Besides, it's too risky for you to go alone."

I spot his black Toyota Camry near the end of the aisle, but he steers me toward the side lot where I'm parked.

"Let's take your car," he suggests. "I want to test your theory."

"Seriously?" I ask, shocked. "Who are you and what have you done with my boyfriend?"

Marcus slides inside my dark blue ES 350 with a deep breath and clicks in his seatbelt. "Let's do this," he says with a nod and a shudder.

As we maneuver out of the lot, static blasts from my stereo speakers. I pound the dashboard twice as Marcus switches through all of my radio station presets. The static persists.

"Must be a loose wire or something," he says through gritted teeth as he switches from the radio to a CD. "I'll take a look at it when we're at Jude's."

"Thanks." I steal a glance at him. The reason for our get-together this afternoon is twofold. In addition to checking on Jude's house, he is going to give me an update on his mother. "Any word from Selima?"

Marcus nods stiffly. It's hard to tell if his grim expression is due to the subject of his mother, the suddenly sucky stereo, or being in my car. Maybe all three.

"The council is taking a hard position with my mother." He rakes his fingers through his hair. "They believe she and Garret were equally responsible. They want somebody's head. Since Garret's dead, they are going after her."

A few months ago Marcus's mother, Camille Bergmann, showed up in Chicago—and in his life—for the first time since he was four years old, bringing along the biological father Marcus never knew, Garret Bergmann. Garret was the leader of the protector clan and on a mission to destroy the powerful demon they believed was killing their kind. That powerful demon was, yep, my father. Let's just say I bet you will never have a more awkward first meeting with your boyfriend's parents.

"But your father was under orders, wasn't he? Or at least he wasn't working alone." I shake my head in disgust. "I hated Garret—given that he was trying to kill you and me and my father—"

"Don't forget Dylan," Marcus adds dryly.

"And Dylan—but how convenient that suddenly everyone is surprised and appalled that Garret was creating a team of psycho soldiers. This was several years in the making. Isn't that what Selima and her mother believe?"

"Exactly. While Camille isn't innocent, she shouldn't be the only one held responsible," Marcus says darkly. "There were others involved. Others who are high up in the clan."

Marcus's defense of his mother is passionate. I struggle to sound invested on her behalf. Since Camille's arrival in Chicago, I never got a warm and fuzzy vibe from her. In fact, she struck me as cold and calculating. What kind of woman abandons her young son?

"I would still like to know where they got all the demon blood to dope the protectors," I say once I merge onto highway I-90. I force all judgment and condemnation out of my voice and strive for curiosity. I don't want my boyfriend mad at me for picking on his mother.

Marcus doesn't answer right away. I risk a quick glance at him and find him busy working through something mentally, his brows pulled low as he quirks his lips back and forth. "Me too. Aiden talked to Max, asked him to look into it," Marcus finally says.

Aiden is not a fan of Max which is weird because I think they used to be friends. I don't know what the beef is between Marcus's brother and the red-haired demon. While Max has always struck me as sneaky, he proved helpful both times I needed him. However, my gut tells me there is more on Marcus's mind than demon blood and Max.

"How long will the clan council hold your mother in custody?" I ask, eager to keep him talking. "Selima said it's only house arrest during the investigation, right?"

"Until they finish their *due diligence*," Marcus mocks, his voice sullen. "They haven't disclosed a timeline."

While we sit idle in traffic before exiting onto I-94, I reach over to squeeze his hand. Camille will never win Mother of the Year, but neither would my own mother. Marcus just got Camille back. It's got to be tough on him to lose her again. What happens if she's found guilty? Is there such a thing as protector prison? Silence stretches between us. I glance at Marcus as he clenches and unclenches his jaw. His eyes fix on the passing landscape once we are moving again and I wonder if he registers anything he sees or if he's focused on thoughts about his mother. That's when I notice his free hand curled into a fist on his lap.

"Since we're testing a theory, tell me how you're doing in my car. Any demon vibe?" I ask, trying to lighten the mood.

Marcus continues to focus out the window. "It's okay."

I give it a couple more minutes. He continues to brood. "Is there something you're not telling me?"

At the same time the words leave my lips, a sick feeling settles like lead in my stomach. The feeling that started when Camille and Garret first showed up in Chicago, the one that told me they would convince Marcus to leave with them. After Garret's death and Camille had been ordered back to the protector clan—wherever that top-secret location happens to be—for interrogation, all the external drama from the battle faded away. Things settled down. That's when the internal drama—the gut-wrenching guilt—took over. I never thought I could kill a person. *It was him or us,* the voice in my head reminds me for the hundredth time.

For months I have been haunted by nightmares of the battle, confronted by the vision of Garret's face, watching the life leave his eyes. I can't sleep an entire night without feeling the throbbing pulse of his heart in my hand as I squeezed the life out of him with my magic. I swore I would never, ever execute that kind of magic again. While Garret's death sticks with me like a thick, dark cloud, my fear of Marcus leaving had been quieted.

That ended two weeks ago. Marcus's mother was placed on house arrest with twenty-four-hour security while the council initiated an investigation. Selima left Chicago to return to the clan to talk to her own mother and their friends. The grim look on Marcus's face clues me in that things are not going well.

He narrows his big brown eyes, scrunches his brows fiercely. "I have to go. Soon. The council is questioning everyone who has knowledge about the army, anyone who was at the battle. Those who survived." He mumbles that last part.

My breath sticks in my throat. I can't pull it in and I can't push it out. Marcus will go to Camille, to the protector clan. He has never been around other protectors—*gargoyles* as my father would say. Will he come back after being around his own kind? After he tastes what it's like to feel *normal*? What about Garret's death? Will that become part of the council's inquiry? Will Marcus be blamed for what I did? Could all of this be a ploy by Camille to take him from me? From everyone else who loves him? My lungs burn.

"Accelerate, Lucy!"

Cars honk behind me. A dark red SUV speeds around us, the driver flipping me the bird as he passes.

My lungs fill and the daze clears. I grasp the steering wheel firmly with both hands and press my foot on the gas pedal. My car responds immediately and lunges forward.

"I have knowledge about what happened," I say, an edge of panic in my voice. "Will the council want to speak with me? I should go with you."

Marcus shakes his head. He rests his hand on my thigh. Within seconds the panic diminishes. "So far questioning is limited to protectors. Selima is coming back to Chicago. She and I will go to the clan together once they call for me."

"You don't know when that will be?" I ask. The calm in my voice surprises me.

"Maybe two weeks. I'm really not sure. Selima will fill us in once she gets here," Marcus says. He studies my profile. "Camille needs me. I have to try to help her."

Once Camille has him, she won't want to let him go.

"I know," I say, determined to keep my eyes on the road. The panic is gone, but sadness takes its place. If I can focus hard enough, maybe the tears won't fall.

CHAPTER THREE

– Lucy Walker –

"We've been at this for two Sundays in a row. It doesn't work!" I drop the shoelace-sized leather string and the crystal attached to it on the stack of maps covering Persephone's kitchen table. The gemstone lands with a heavy thud as I scrape my chair back. With the heels of my hands, I rub my dry, tired eyes. Persephone's head turns in my direction, her black, wiry curls bouncing with the movement. She and Gram, together with Henry Klein, were best friends. They also happened to be witches. While the gene skipped Momma, I was the lucky one who inherited Gram's magic.

The tiny yellow and orange wildflowers that decorate the wallpaper past Persephone's shoulder grow fuzzy in my vision.

"You're destined to be a great witch, Lucy. Your grandmother was powerful, more than Henry, more than me. Once you inherit her powers, we will teach you how to use them."

I still don't believe Persephone. The demon powers I inherited from my father continue to develop. My witchy powers, despite everyone's efforts, have not.

"Be patient, Lucy," Persephone says from across the table where she and Henry study the *Book of Shadows.* "Scrying is the most difficult divination skill to master." She eyes the golf ball-sized crystal, her forehead creased. "You need to relax, open your mind. Some visions are the tiniest of glimpses. Pay close attention."

I shake my head at the same time I pull my hair over my shoulder and twist it roughly around my fingers. A gentle late afternoon breeze moves across my skin, thanks to the open window above the sink. "According to Aiden, we can't locate my father through scrying if he's in another dimension."

Henry uses his finger to mark his spot in the spell book as he peers at me through his wire-rimmed glasses. The deep sea-foam green of his Polo shirt highlights the green of his eyes. "We can't be sure Lucifer took him...home."

I roll my eyes. "Home for demons is hell, Henry, which is absolutely another dimension."

Henry gives me a wink and nods at the crystal, encouraging me to get back to work. "Which herbs did you use to supplement your divination powers?"

"Broom and cherry," I say.

Persephone stiffens, her expression alarmed. "Good grief and goddesses almighty. You didn't make tea with the leaves of the broom plant, did you? It's poisonous."

I shake my head. Standing, I pull a small fabric bag with fancy drawstrings from my pocket and present it to them. "I made a sachet. Dried broom leaves plus cherry pits. Nothing ingested." I stuff the bag back into my pocket and sit down.

"Excellent choices. Those dried leaves are also great for protection," Henry commends.

Persephone utters a sigh of relief and sips her tea.

"Since you mention protection and the only being I currently need protection from is Seamus McAllister, could you provide clarification about demons and immortality," I say as I palm the crystal, absently wondering once again if I will pick up energy from the magical object.

Persephone and Henry both nod, urging me to continue.

"Jude—and demons generally—are immortal. That part I get. But how does one die, get destroyed...or whatever? If I'm going to try to slay Seamus, I need to know. I mean, I get it that my fireballs can disable him, but I want to know how to get rid of him...permanently."

"You never told her?" Henry asks Persephone, surprised. He turns back to me quickly. "Not that you should ever confront him on your own."

I nod. "Of course."

Persephone's mouth puckers in consternation. "I had assumed Jude and Aiden covered that. She would use her demon powers to destroy him, since they are currently more powerful—and more in line with what's needed to get the job done."

Henry pushes his glasses up his nose and eyeballs me gravely. "Beheading and fire."

I wince. *Beheading?* Almost immediately I register the second thing Henry said. *Fire.* The very thing some demons are gifted with—the ability to create and throw fire—can destroy them? Suddenly I recall the night of the homecoming dance when Jude killed Seamus's daughter, Daphne, in a blaze. My shock turns to revulsion as I remember the smell.

"When Jude killed Daphne, he didn't decapitate her," I point out.

Henry frowns as he considers this. "He would've had to separate her ashes, then buried them in different locations."

"No way around that rule," Persephone confirms.

I nod stupidly, unable to shake the memory of Daphne's screams—no matter how brief—and that horrible smell.

I will the nausea down. "Decapitation and fire...why separate the ashes?"

"Because skipping that last step makes the first two pointless," Persephone admonishes me. She huffs mightily as she pushes herself out of her chair. She winces.

"Persephone." I jump out of my chair to help her.

Henry reaches for her at the same time.

Persephone waves us both away. Once standing, she takes several breaths. Her face is red from the effort. "My hip. It's determined to make my life hell on earth." She moves to the stove to fix another cup of tea. "If a demon is burned to ash, he or she can regenerate. It's only if the ashes are separated and kept apart that a demon is truly destroyed," she says on her way back to the table.

What was Garret's plan the night of the battle at St. Aquinas? Was he and his ginormous team going to decapitate the demons that night? Did he have a flame thrower waiting outside the gymnasium with the rest of his morphed soldiers?

"This is the only way to end Seamus. If you and whomever else is helping you don't dispose of his ashes properly, he will come back," Henry says, eyeing me so intently it's like he's trying to burn this information into my brain through my eyeballs.

When Seamus McAllister returns to Chicago—and we all know it's only a matter of time—will I have the opportunity and the skill to destroy him before he kills me? Could I finally have a chance to live my life without someone trying to slaughter me?

Persephone clears her throat. "Time to get back to your lesson." She points to the decorative bowl three-quarters full with rainwater sitting on the counter. "Maybe water scrying is more for you. Put the crystal aside and give it a try. Did you read the book I gave you last week?"

I nod halfheartedly. "There's no point," I mutter to myself as I slump onto the chair and pick up the leather strap. Jude's in hell with Lucifer, against his will. Now that Garret is dead and no longer trying to kill my father, I should be honing some other magical skills to help get Jude back instead of wasting my time with magical GPS. If Jude and I took on Seamus together, we could win. After we separated Seamus's ashes, my father would know the best places to hide them.

During my training session with Aiden earlier today, I once again asked for his help to bring my father home. Of course, he said my suggestion to summon Lucifer was pointless. The door between our worlds never closed after I brought him to Chicago to help save my father and me from Garret and his army. He can go between dimensions any time he wants to.

"He's been aboveground having a grand time while Jude's stuck managing things in the underworld in his absence," Aiden had said.

473

"Lucifer's here?" I had asked, a squeak in my voice as my heartbeat thudded in terror.

Aiden shook his head, impatiently tossing one of several massive haystacks he had set up around Jude's backyard in order to train me to hurl them using spells and hand gestures. "Not *here* in Chicago, but aboveground, so to speak. It's been a long time since he's been away from his own dimension. No doubt he's traveling the world, living it up like a king. But..."

I had raised my eyebrows at Aiden's tight expression. "But?"

"You're his namesake..."

His words left me unsettled. "I know... I know...a much bigger deal than being a goddaughter."

Aiden's glare was immediate. "Lucifer will be back for you."

Every muscle in my body clenched. His words struck me as a threat. Or a warning. Maybe both. "That's what you keep saying."

"He's not going to tolerate your snotty attitude or your defiance. Jude's a pussycat in comparison."

While Jude is all demon-dad like—short tempered, violent, and absolutely clueless when it comes to parenting, *especially* a teenage girl—he had developed another side. He cooked delicious meals for me—*vegetarian* meals. He rented movies and took the time to watch them with me, sitting in his fancy rose-colored chair while I lounged on the adjacent emerald green couch. He wore a sort of bored or tolerant expression the whole time. When I studied his face, though, I noticed his eyes soaked in every little detail on the TV screen.

My father was also protective in a ruthless sort of way, training me so I could take care of myself against Seamus and

Garret and all the other enemies who hate Jude and, by extension, me. Jude is fatherly in a dad-on-steroids kind of way, but he does love me. It's all his good traits that help me to try to move past the bad parts.

My cell vibrates on the table next to the map, pulling me back to the present. My witch mentors glance at me, their gazes heavy with expectation. Marcus and I are supposed to meet up tonight and I still have to figure out what excuse to make to Henry and Persephone. I read my boyfriend's text message.

Any luck scrying?

No. I want 2 bail, but H and P might skin me alive.

I palm the crystal absently. What if Persephone and Henry have been wrong all along? Maybe I'm not destined to be a great witch like Gram. Even with Lola, the family raven and Gram's familiar, passing Gram's powers to me nothing much has happened. The witch powers seem unresponsive. I don't know what to do. What if my great and powerful destiny leans more in the direction of my demon genes?

My phone buzzes again.

I prefer u w-skin intact. Working late at St. Pat's w-Father Bill. Let's meet 2morrow night instead. It's time 2 go flying.

My heart sinks. No Marcus tonight. I raise my gaze to meet Persephone's.

"You're not planning to cut your lesson short are you?" she asks, eyebrows raised.

"I'm not going anywhere," I tell her, feeling deflated.

"We heard about Marcus's plans to attempt to help his mother," Henry says. "How are you holding up?"

475

Just the mention of Marcus leaving causes a lump to form in my throat. Of course they know. Did Marcus tell them? Or had Aiden filled them in? "Okay." I turn away from their watchful eyes and move to the counter. The delicate cream-colored lace curtains that decorate the window above the sink shift as another breeze blows through, providing relief from the late August heat. Persephone's apartment takes up the third floor of my uncles' three-flat apartment building. They inherited it from Gram after she died. My uncles and I have the largest apartment on the first floor while Marcus and Aiden live on the second floor.

As I pause at the counter I allow myself a moment away from the scrutiny of my witch mentors. Marcus appeared unaffected when he informed me that he would be leaving soon. How is it so easy for him to go? How could he postpone our night together? Suddenly we have so little time left.

That fear of Marcus leaving is nothing new. There is an expiration date on our relationship. The countdown started the day we met and never stopped. I hadn't been sure what would take him from me until the day his mother showed up in Chicago. The fact that she's with the protector clan, under investigation for her part in Marcus's father's crimes should've put me at ease. If she is found guilty and incarcerated, she will go to prison, right? Then she can't manipulate Marcus into leaving with her. Who knows what will happen with the investigation? Meanwhile, the timer keeps counting down. That blasted *tick-tock, tick-tock, tick-tock* echoes around my brain like a cruel joke, threatening to drive me crazy.

What happens when the timer runs out and Marcus leaves?

Will the pain of missing him destroy me? I had watched Momma fall apart every time one of her relationships ended. Marcus is a million times better than any of the deadbeats Momma dated. Plus, I am nothing like her. The fact remains that Marcus is going to leave to try to help his mother and he will be around a whole bunch of other protectors for the first time in his life. Marcus will no longer be the freak he considers himself to be. How liberating that will be for him. Why would he want to come back to Chicago?

Darkness fills my mind as my gaze falls to the bowl of rainwater on the counter next to me. With a sigh I hold my hand over the bowl, absently moving my fingers as if to play the keys of a piano. A deep need takes over, a need for relief from the heaviness inside me. If I were in the massive backyard of Jude's Lake Forest house, I could hurl fireballs. That always releases the darkness, the heavy sadness. Inside Persephone's kitchen that isn't an option. Gently, words slip into my thoughts like a poem. The phrases appear in my mind, random at first. I repeat them quietly. The sounds are nothing more than whispered sorrow as they pass through my lips.

Bring on the rain
Allow it to wash away my pain
His leaving preordained
Loss of a loved one, again

Even my dreams know my time with my boyfriend is coming to an end. Two nights in a row I felt the crushing weight as we said goodbye on the roof, a black suitcase at his feet which was covered with decals featuring some of his favorite bands, while his hands cupped my face. His eyes burned as the words he has only ever uttered in my dreams passed through his lips: "if only you hadn't killed my father."

Bring on the rain
Allow it to wash away my pain
His leaving preordained
Loss of a loved one again

My fingers continue tap, tap, tapping the air above the beautiful pale blue glass bowl. All of a sudden drops of rain the size of tears drip from my fingers into the bowl. Startled, I nearly cease the movement of my fingers. I force myself to continue. As I repeat the words the rain continues to fall from my drumming-on-air fingers. A surge bolts through me. *I am performing a spell. This is witchcraft!*

A loud gasp to my left gives me a start. Persephone. Henry flanks my right side, his eyes wide.

How had I slipped so deeply into the spell that I didn't hear Persephone and Henry's chairs scrape as they pushed away from the table? The creaky old floorboards should have given them away as they approached the counter, especially Persephone with her bad hip that makes every other step land more heavily than Henry's.

"When did you learn to do this?" Persephone asks, her voice full of awe as she studies the water droplets.

As I slow the tinkling motion, Henry urges me to continue,

fascination in his voice. I continue to make it rain in the bowl and hope neither of them notice the tears brimming in my eyes.

Persephone and Henry are like family to me. I love them both, but there's no way I can share my feelings with them. Even now as they witness my magic—magic caused by fear and heartache— it feels wrong to be in their company. I should be alone right now.

The oppressive weight of my emotions lingers, the sound: *tick-tock, tick-tock, tick-tock*, continues to repeat in my mind.

"Can you shift the spell like we talked about during our last session?" Persephone asks. Her voice is eager, encouraging.

I release the spell and the raindrops cease. With a flick of my wrist, I change the movement of my fingers to a twirl, slow at first and gradually picking up speed. I focus on swirling water.

If only you hadn't killed my father. Marcus's voice from my dream accuses.

A breeze hovers over the bowl, then dives into the water. The liquid laps and waves, animated with the power of the miniature wind, splashing onto the countertop. That's when it hits me. This absorption into the magic...into the spell work...is something I usually feel when performing dark magic. It's a new feeling when executing white magic. A glimmer of optimism and hope edges into my mood.

I move my hand in a gentle, slow rhythm, encouraging the water to sway, back and forth, back and forth. I find the motion of the rainwater hypnotic, soothing.

"Tell me your thought process, from start to finish," Henry urges.

His request causes me to mentally scramble. There is no way I am going to share my emotional turmoil over Marcus, or the never-ending guilt over murdering his father during the battle. Never mind that it was done in self-defense.

As much as possible I erase the emotion from my face, from my voice. I respond as Lucy the student, not the girl who will soon lose the one guy who has ever made her feel special and worthy of love.

"I focused on making it rain," I say.

Henry grabs his notebook from the table and logs my intention together with his own observations. Only after he and Persephone have experimented with a spell and perfected it will they put it in the *Book of Shadows*, the spell book they—and Gram—have kept since the beginning.

"Don't you see?" Henry whispers, his voice filled with excitement.

"See what?" I ask weakly, not sure if he was talking to Persephone or me, but suddenly feeling wrung out. The whole point of today's lesson was to locate Jude. "None of this is going to help bring my father back."

Henry's bright expression falls. Persephone touches my arm.

"I don't know when—or if—Jude will come back. Now Marcus is going to leave." So much for keeping my emotions to myself. There's no stopping the stupid tears. My willpower is gone. I swipe at my cheeks. I gesture to the rainwater, where I had magic-made tears. "I can't get excited about this. Not when it hurts so much."

"I'm sorry, Lucy," Persephone says. She doesn't try to hug me. That's not who she is and I'm grateful.

"Can I go home now?" I ask glumly.

Henry nods. He doesn't hide his disappointment.

About the Author

Pauline Gruber is a self-professed music junkie, cat wrangler, and travel nut. She went to Paris in the 90's where she discovered a love of three things: croissants, old cathedrals, and gargoyles. Deciding that the paranormal world could use a new kind of hero, Pauline translated her fascination with the protective gargoyle into a suspenseful love story. She is the author of the series: *The Girl and the Raven, The Girl and the Gargoyle,* and the forthcoming novel, *The Girl and the Demon.* By day, Pauline is a legal assistant for a Chicago law firm where she borrows identities and incorporates them into her books. If you tell anyone, she'll deny, deny, deny.

Pauline lives outside of Chicago with her precocious black cats.

Made in the USA
Middletown, DE
29 April 2022

64990359R00291